WWW.BEWAREOFMONSTERS.COM

PRAISE FOR SEAN ELLIS

"What follows in *Savage* is much more than a political thriller. Robinson and Ellis have combined technology, archeology, and even a little microbiology with the question they ask better than any other authors today: what if?"
—Suspense Magazine

"Sean Ellis is an author to watch closely."
—David L. Golemon, NY Times bestselling author of *The Mountain*

"Sean Ellis has mixed a perfect cocktail of adventure and intrigue, and [*Into the Black*] is definitely shaken and not stirred."
—Graham Brown, NY Times bestselling author of *Nighthawk*

"Some books are just plain unbridled fun; others are edge of the seat gripping entertainment. Some make you think; a few open your eyes. Sean Ellis is a magician, doing it all with a deftness that pulls you in and draws you along from page one breathlessly to the end of the book, offering mysteries galore, bad guys with the blackest hearts and a good old fashioned hero to kick their evil arses. I had a blast."
—Steven Savile, international bestselling author of *Silver*

"Sean Ellis writes action scenes that rival those of Clive Cussler and James Rollins."
—James Reasoner, NY Times bestselling author of *Texas Rangers*

"Sean Ellis delivers another high-octane romp [with *Magic Mirror*], exploring mythical lost civilizations and alternative histories, with the unrelenting pace of your favorite summer blockbuster."
—Stel Pavlou, bestselling author of *Gene*

"I'll admit it. I am totally exhausted after finishing *Oracle*, the latest Jade Ihara page-turner by David Wood and Sean Ellis. What an adventure! I kept asking myself how the co-authors came up with all this fantastic stuff. This is a great read that provides lots of action, and thoughtful insight as well, into strange realms that are sometimes best left unexplored."
—Paul Kemprecos, NY Times bestselling author of *Medusa*

"[*Dodge Dalton* is] high flying adventure at its best. Cleverly conceived, original, and multi-layered, the action literally jumps off the page and takes the reader through unexpected twists and turns."
—Rob MacGregor, NY Times bestselling author of *Indiana Jones and the Last Crusade*

ALSO BY JEREMY ROBINSON

ALSO BY SEAN ELLIS

Jack Sigler/Chess Team
Callsign: King
Callsign: King – Underworld
Callsign: King – Blackout
Prime
Savage
Cannibal
Empire

Mira Raiden Novels
Ascendant
Descendent

The Adventures of Dodge Dalton
In the Shadow of Falcon's Wings
At the Outpost of Fate
On the High Road to Oblivion
Against the Fall of Eternal Night

Cerberus Group Novels
Herculean
Helios

Secret Agent X
The Sea Wraiths
The Scar
Masterpiece of Vengeance

Novels
Magic Mirror
The Sorcerer's Ghost
The Prisoner
Wargod
(with Steven Savile)
Flood Rising
(with Jeremy Robinson)
Camp Zero

The Nick Kismet Adventures
The Shroud of Heaven
Into the Black
The Devil You Know
Fortune Favors

Novels with David Wood
Hell Ship
Oracle
Destiny
Changeling
Mystic
Outpost
Arcanum

HELIOS

A Cerberus Group Novel

JEREMY ROBINSON
AND SEAN ELLIS

BREAKNECK MEDIA

Visit Jeremy Robinson on the World Wide Web at:
www.bewareofmonsters.com

Visit Sean Ellis on the World Wide Web at:
www.seanellisauthor.com

Sean and Jeremy dedicate Helios *to all the readers...*
Thanks for taking the journey with us!

HELIOS

ODYSSEY

PROLOGUE

A distant land, long ago…

"**First the Sea** God curses us. Now the Sun God laughs at our misfortune."

"Gods," the king said and spat on the sand. "I have had my fill of the gods and their cruel jokes."

The mariner raised his fearful eyes. "Your blasphemies are what have brought us to this place. You mock the gods at our peril."

The man's insolence was yet another reminder of the king's abasement. How long had it been since he had seen the fields of his kingdom? How long since he had felt his wife's embrace? Would he ever find his way home? And if he did, would he find anything left of his former life? These men were all that remained of the fleet he had set out with, so many years ago. Somewhere along the way, he had ceased to be their king, commanding their respect and obedience. Now, without even a ship to call his own, he was nothing to them.

He touched a finger to the pouch that hung around his neck, feeling the outline of the object concealed within, the orb in which the blind seer had shown him his future.

Another joke from the gods.

"Enough about the gods. We are men. We live or die by our own choices." He turned away, contemplating those choices.

Gods or not, his shipmate was not wrong.

The sea was calm now, after the upheaval that had wrecked their ship—the last of his original fleet. The storm had killed more than half the crew, casting the survivors upon this unfamiliar shore. Even if he could compel the sailors to dare the Sea God's wrath once more, they had no ship. There were not even enough timbers remaining from their vessel to build a raft, much less a vessel large enough to carry them home.

And if we had a ship, would we be able to find our way?

The Sea God had cursed them, sending a storm to blow their ship to the far edge of the world. It had taken them years just to find familiar waters, and then, with their destination so close....this.

A sea of a different kind began at the water's edge. Sand stretched out to the east as far as his eyes could see. It baked under the scorching gaze of the Sun God, vanishing into a silvery mirage that looked like water, but was only pure heat. There were no trees to hew for timbers. No plants to provide food or shade. No fresh water to drink.

If they remained here, they would perish.

Is it my fault? Did my hubris bring this curse upon us? He shook his head. *Gods and curses. Empty superstitions.*

"We will move inland," he said. "This desert cannot go on forever. We will find water and food. We will survive—not by the whim of the gods but by our own wits."

The sailors looked at one another, refusing to meet his gaze.

He uttered a short, harsh laugh. "Very well. *I* will go inland. And I will survive by *my* wits. Join me and live, or trust the gods. I care not."

Without waiting to see who among them, if any, would choose to follow, he turned his back to the sea and began walking. He could not fault them for their slavish devotion to superstitious beliefs. They were simple men. Uneducated and fooled by the trickery of the priests, misled into believing that natural forces were manifestations of divine power. He found it strange that they were comforted by the idea that the pain and suffering was all part of some mad game played by the gods. Belief meant their lives, as short and miserable as they were, had some greater purpose.

It was a seductive notion, to which even he was not immune.

The catastrophe that had brought them here was almost enough to make a believer of him. The sailors had imagined themselves caught between two terrible monsters: a gyre, like a serpent with teeth the size of mountains, and a whirlpool that swallowed ships whole. Monsters or no, it had been an event unlike anything he had ever witnessed.

The attack had come without warning, in the middle of the night. There had been a sound, louder than any thunderclap, and then the sea had vanished beneath them so abruptly that, for a few seconds, they had all floated in the air like birds. Then the first monster took the ship in its jaws, breaking the vessel in two, flinging men overboard and dashing them upon rocks that had never before seen the sun's light. Even as the survivors clung to what remained of the ship, the sea returned to devour them. How long they churned in the vortex, he could not say, but at last they were vomited onto this strange shore.

It was almost enough to make him believe in the gods again, as was the fact that any of them had come through it alive. Whether the gods existed or not, he would never again beg them for favor or mercy.

The shimmering mirage retreated, always just out of reach, but in time, he glimpsed mountains rising up like islands. They seemed real enough, but one of the peaks was hidden behind a dense black cloud.

An omen? His men would surely think so, but all of them had chosen to remain behind.

As the mountains drew closer, the receding mirage revealed other signs. Columns of white smoke rising up from the desert floor—not manifestations of divine power, but simple cook fires.

Fires meant people, perhaps a settlement, as well as food and water, but he was immediately on guard. Strangers could be even more fickle than the gods, especially in these unknown lands. Would they meet him with hospitality or violence? The possibility of the latter was not enough to convince him to turn aside, but he stayed wary as he closed the distance.

He could soon discern tents, stretching in either direction as far as he could see, and closer still, the people themselves, tending small flocks and herds.

Nomads.

He had an instinctive dislike for those who chose such a life, calling no land their own, taking what they pleased from the earth and then moving on when there was nothing left, but he knew from experience that exile was not always a willing choice.

His approach did not go unnoticed. The shepherds and drovers scurried away, and other men—harder-looking men—came out to meet him.

They were a ragged lot, dark and sinewy from years of toil under the harsh sun. He supposed he appeared much the same way to them. Unlike him, they were armed with bronze swords.

He raised his hands to show that he posed no threat. One of the men strode forward and barked out a command, or perhaps it was a question, in a language he did not recognize.

"My ship was wrecked," he said, waving his hands up and down in an attempt to pantomime what he was saying. He finished by crashing one fist into the other in hopes of simulating the wreck.

The men shared a look and a few incomprehensible words, then their apparent leader motioned for him to join them. He followed without hesitation. That they had not shown any aggression thus far was a positive sign, and he had no intention of insulting them with undue caution. If it was their intent to harm him, he was already as good as dead.

They led him into their strangely deserted camp. The faces of women and children stared out from tents, watching him. Did they know where he was being taken, and what fate awaited him there?

He thought that they would take him into one of the tents, but they passed through the camp without slowing, and kept going, toward the smoking mountain.

Beyond the far edge of the camp, the terrain began to rise, sloping all the way to the foot of the mountain. Large creatures moved about on the slopes—too large to be sheep or goats... Cattle perhaps? But there appeared to be no plants upon which to graze. The man leading the group followed a route that kept the creatures at a healthy distance.

The sun lowered into the western sky and the camp vanished into the heat haze behind them, and still they walked onward, drawing closer to the mountain. It had not looked very imposing from a distance, but as they approached, the immense weight of the place reminded him that men also worshipped mountains as gods. Perhaps these men did. Perhaps they were going to take him before their Mountain God for judgment.

Or sacrifice.

The party moved into a dry river bed, following it into a draw that carved down the slope. They encountered a bearded man stationed as a guard at the head of the trail leading up onto the mountain. Words were exchanged, and the bearded man gave him an appraising look before turning and heading up the trail.

The other men sat down on the ground. He sat down as well. It was hardly the strangest thing that had happened to him in the course of his travels.

Afternoon became evening, and then dusk was upon them. One of the group coaxed the coals of the watchman's fire to life, and that seemed unusual. Where had they found wood to burn as fuel? He had not seen a single tree since being thrown up onto the shore of this strange land.

The men spoke to one another in their shared tongue, their voices not louder than a murmur, but he could sense their anxiety. They were nervous, scared even, but of what he could not say. Certainly not of him; he was in their power.

It's the mountain, he thought. The setting sun revealed the fire behind the cloud of smoke that shrouded its summit. Lightning danced across its face, and peals of thunder rolled down the slope in an unceasing assault on the senses.

One of the men jumped up, the rest doing the same in the space of time measured by a heartbeat. He got up as well, and saw two men moving down the trail in their direction—the watchman and... Someone? Something?

It was a man, or at least it walked upright like one, but his face was hidden behind a strange mask or veil. A faint glow emanated from the fabric, but it was surely a trick of the light.

In his earliest memories, the castaway king had heard stories of how the gods disguised themselves to walk among men. His pulse quickened.

The newcomer strode forward until they were almost face-to-veil.

"My ship wrecked," he told the mysterious figure, repeating the pantomime he had used earlier.

"You are Grecian?" The voice, muffled by the heavy fabric, was weak and halting. An old man's voice. The words however were in the king's own language.

"I am," he replied, and he thought better of saying more. If the old man spoke his language, then perhaps he also knew of his reputation, and that might not be such a good thing. "You know the language of the Greeks?"

There was a grunt from behind the veil. "You should go. It is not safe for you here."

"I would gladly take my leave, but alas, I have no ship. I humbly beg your hospitality for myself and my men while we build another."

"We have nothing to spare. Return to your men. Lead them elsewhere."

The king frowned. "We are lost. This land is unknown to us. Without food and water, we will perish."

The veiled figure sighed. "That is something we share, Grecian. If it is God's will, we will survive until tomorrow. I do not believe he brought us here to perish."

"Which god?"

"There is only one."

The cryptic answer was no more frustrating than anything else the man had said, and the king sensed that further supplications would prove futile. At least these people were not openly hostile. Still, he could not return to his men empty handed.

"The herd that I saw." He gestured to the dark hillside where he had seen the creatures. "Are they your animals, or wild beasts that we may hunt for meat?"

"Stay away from them," the veiled man said, his voice not quite as weak as it had been a moment before. "Those are holy creatures. It is death to approach them."

"'Holy creatures,'" the king muttered. "Another god laughs at my misfortune."

Despite the brusque reception from their leader, the men escorting him offered him a few sips of water and a mat to lie on, though the incessant thunder prevented him from sleeping. The next morning, they led him back to the seaward edge of the camp and bade him goodbye in their strange language. He took it as a hopeful sign. Perhaps the old man would reconsider.

He arrived at the shore to find the survivors gathering bits of flotsam from the sea. They had managed to catch a few fish, which were drying in the sun, but fresh water remained elusive, as did any source of wood.

The sailors seemed almost disappointed by his return, as if they believed the gods might deign to show them favor once he was gone. They greeted the news of the nearby encampment more enthusiastically, and began plotting to raid the nomads.

"It seems I did not make myself clear," the king told them. "This is not a mere tribe of tent dwellers. They are a nation. They would come down upon us like the sea."

"What of these sacred cattle?" one of the sailors asked. "You say they roam wild outside the camp, with no herdsman to tend them."

"Their god tends the herd," the king reminded them.

"Their god," the sailor spat back. "Not ours. We will go at night, under the cover of darkness. Surely their god can spare one cow."

"If you slaughter their sacred animals, they will never help us."

"We do not need to kill it," another man said. "We can return it in exchange for water and food."

The men were desperate beyond reason, and the king knew that opposing them would be as fruitless as his appeals to the leader of the nomads.

They set out after noon, traveling northeast across the scorching sand, giving the nomad camp a wide berth. Some of the men carried clubs and crude spears fashioned from timbers and other detritus, and knives of knapped stone. The king trailed along behind them, quietly protesting their rash course of action, but ready to cast his lot in with them if the need arose. They were his men after all, his subjects, even if they rejected his counsel.

By late afternoon, they passed the northernmost limit of the nomad camp, and continued toward the smoking mountain. It was not long before they caught sight of the strange cattle roaming the foothills.

Up close, he was less certain of his original impression of the beasts. There was no question that they were living creatures, but instead of fur, their hides looked as rough as the stony soil upon which they stood. They were big, too—bigger even, than the legendary Minoan bull. They were not behaving like cattle or any other kind of grazing animal, though. They were not grazing at all, but moving back and forth, slowly, ominously, never stopping.

What are those things?

"This is a mistake," he said.

The men paid no heed. One of them, carrying a length of rope that had been left behind by the tide, approached the nearest animal. It gave no indication that it noticed his approach or was even aware of his existence. Emboldened, the man ran up alongside the animal—its shoulders towered above him—and he threw the loop of rope around the beast's head.

The creature continued moving, dragging the hapless man along. Undeterred, he got his feet under him and tried to pull himself up onto the animal's back, with the intent of mounting it like a horse. But as soon as he touched it, there was a loud crack, like the sound of a ship's mast snapping in half during a gale. The man was flung away, crashing to the ground in a smoking heap just a few steps away from where the king stood, a distance of fifty paces. For a moment, the air was filled with a sharp smell—the smell of lightning—but it was just as quickly replaced by the odor of burning flesh.

It is death to approach them, the old man had said. Now the king understood what he had meant by that.

The other men stared in disbelief at their fallen comrade. Then, almost in unison, they raised their weapons and charged the creature.

"No!"

The king's warning fell on deaf ears. The men closed to within a few paces of the creature and attacked. As the first blow was struck, the world vanished in a flash of light, and he saw no more.

TREMOR

ONE

Chelyabinsk Oblast, Russia—Present Day

"This is not what I expected."

George Pierce glanced over his shoulder at the young woman seated in the rear of the rented SUV. Fiona Sigler stared out the window at the landscape passing them by, a featureless grassy steppe stretching out to the horizon. "What were you expecting?"

Fiona turned to meet his gaze and shrugged. "Well, you know... Russia. I thought it would be more..." Another shrug. "Russian."

"You do realize," Pierce said, "that Russia is the largest country on Earth, geographically speaking, with many diverse ecoregions? It's not all Doctor Zhivago and frozen tundra. I hope they taught you that at that expensive private academy your father sent you to."

"Yes, Uncle George," Fiona said, with more than a little exasperation. "I just didn't expect it to look so much like Kansas."

Pierce smiled. Fiona was not wrong. He knew on an intellectual level that Russia—all six-and-a-half-million square miles of it, fully one-eighth of the Earth's habitable land—was comprised of a variety of climates and topographical zones. But the world outside the windows of their rented SUV bore little resemblance to his preconceived notion of what they would encounter during their excursion to Chelyabinsk

Oblast. In truth, he had not known what to expect, but not anything so dull.

"Too many hills," Erik Lazarus murmured from behind the steering wheel. "Kansas is a lot flatter than this."

Fiona's eyes widened in disbelief. "Is that even possible?"

"Aside from the fact that the road signs are all in Cyrillic," Lazarus said, "it looks a lot like where I grew up."

Pierce hid a smile. He sometimes forgot that the brooding Lazarus, a physically imposing man of few words, had grown up in the US Midwest. Iranian by birth, Lazarus had been adopted as an infant by an American couple—Derek and Ruth Somers—and spent his early years in rural Illinois, though it was his subsequent life experience as a Special Forces operator that seemed to define him.

Lazarus was right about the terrain, though calling the gentle undulations 'hills' was a bit of a stretch. Still, as a trained archaeologist, Pierce knew that even minor variations in the landscape could hide discoveries of monumental importance—especially here.

The archaeological significance of this particular parcel of Russian real estate had only been recently established. In 1987, Soviet surveyors preparing to flood the area to create a reservoir, to support the local iron mining industry, had discovered ruins thought to be associated with the Sintashta culture. The Bronze Age proto-Indian people had occupied the steppe to the east of the Ural Mountains, possibly as early as 2000 BCE. The site, named Arkaim—the word translated imprecisely to 'arch'—had been called Russia's Stonehenge, owing to its circular layout and possible significance as an ancient astronomical observatory. Like Stonehenge, Arkaim had become both a tourist destination, albeit a regional one, and a Mecca for believers in UFOs and other paranormal phenomena.

As an archaeologist specializing in the Classical Era, Pierce had only a passing familiarity with the Sintashta culture. In his new role as the Director of the Cerberus Group—the public face of the very secret

Herculean Society, an ancient organization dedicated to preserving and protecting the legacy of the man whose life had inspired the legend of immortal Hercules—Pierce had been compelled to take a closer look at Arkaim.

During the course of a highly classified mission just a few months earlier, an American military special operations unit had discovered the remains of a megalithic city—predating even four thousand-year-old Arkaim—in the Ural Mountains, just a few hundred miles to the north. Contained within that nearly pristine site, was evidence of a prehistoric race of giants known as 'the Originators.' Their advanced—and possibly alien—technology had influenced the rise of human civilization, and in the wrong hands, it could just as easily end it.

The architectural similarity and close proximity of Arkaim suggested that it might also hide Originator artifacts, and that possibility obligated Pierce to take pre-emptive action. If there were Originator artifacts at Arkaim, or even clues hinting at the existence of that ancient and possibly otherworldly race, it was imperative that they not fall into the wrong hands. When technology with the potential to enslave or exterminate the human race was concerned, pretty much any hands were the wrong hands. It was the mission of the Cerberus Group to keep those things secret.

In his youth, Pierce had dreamed of being Indiana Jones, a dream that had directly fueled his interest in archaeology. But in his role as Director of the Cerberus Group, he was more like the workman from the final scene of *Raiders of the Lost Ark*, hiding the prize away in a secret warehouse at Area 51, never to be seen again. He hated it, but he also knew that there was a very good reason for it. The upside was that sometimes, like today, he got to be Indiana Jones before he turned into Area 51 guy.

"The turn-off is coming up," a disembodied female voice said. "Five hundred yards."

"I see it," Lazarus said, easing off the gas pedal. "Thanks, Cintia."

Pierce glanced down at his satellite-enabled smartphone, which rested in a bracket mounted to the dashboard of the vehicle. The screen displayed a real-time GPS map, with their route and destination outlined in blue. But the voice that had issued from the speaker did not belong to an automated system, at least, not in the literal sense. Cintia Dourado was the Director of Technology for the Cerberus Group. She was probably more comfortable interacting with computer networks than she was with actual living humans. However, under her outlandish appearance of dyed hair, tattoos, and facial piercings, along with fashion choices that could only be described as eclectic, the Brazilian-born computer expert was still very human.

Partly because her job required her to stay close to the computer, but also because she was moderately agoraphobic, Cintia preferred to work from Cerberus Headquarters, beneath Castel Sant'Angelo in Rome. That was by no means a limitation, though. If the worldwide computer and satellite network was like an orchestra, then Cintia was the conductor, and together they made beautiful music.

"No problem," Cintia replied. "I'm going to get the babelfish online, but if you get lost, you know where to find me."

Lazarus turned the vehicle onto a rutted but serviceable dirt road and continued forward at a slower pace.

"And this is where we leave Kansas behind and head over the rainbow to Oz," remarked the woman sitting beside Fiona in the back seat. Augustina Gallo was not only a professor of Classical History at the University of Athens—on an indefinite sabbatical to work with the Cerberus Group—but she was also Pierce's girlfriend. Despite her name and her obvious Mediterranean ethnic heritage, Gallo was as American as a Georgia peach.

"Flying monkeys, I can deal with," Pierce said. "Russian bureaucrats, on the other hand, may prove a little more daunting."

"That's easy," Fiona chimed in. "Just have Erik drop a house on them."

Pierce thought he saw a hint of a smile touch Lazarus's lips.

Although his acquaintance with Pierce went back more than half a decade, Lazarus, along with his girlfriend, geneticist Felice Carter, had only recently joined forces with Pierce to create the Cerberus Group. Lazarus's official title was Director of Operations, but in practical terms, he was their protector. Pierce could not imagine anyone better suited to the job. In addition to more than a decade of military service, Lazarus was rhinoceros-strong, focused, and owing to an experimental serum that promoted rapid cellular regeneration, he was damn near indestructible.

Carter had her own unique...attributes.

Several years before, during a research trip to the Great Rift Valley, she had been exposed to a retrovirus containing genetic material from one of humanity's oldest shared ancestors. Stranger still, through a process known as *quantum entanglement*, Carter had become a living evolutionary kill-switch. The science of it boggled his mind, but the short version was that her mind and body had become entangled with every other human being on the planet. A hive mother to the human race.

When faced with an extreme threat, Carter could—without consciously intending to do so—psychically overpower anyone in the immediate area, transforming them into a sort of zombie protector driven to mindlessly defend her. Unfortunately, the effect was permanent. Fortunately, thus far the only people to suffer the effect were the aggressors who had intended her harm, but there was no guarantee that innocent bystanders or even her close friends would be spared if the circumstances were dire enough. And no one knew what would happen if Carter ever suffered a mortal injury. Because distance wasn't a factor, the effect might be universal.

It was a dangerous ability, but Carter had dedicated herself to mastering mental discipline techniques, and she was confident of her ability to keep it under control. Still, keeping her out of harm's way seemed prudent. Since their current mission did not call for her particular skill set, Cerberus's Chief Scientific Adviser had elected to stay behind so she could continue an ongoing research project of special interest to Pierce.

The role of Fiona Sigler—she was not literally Pierce's niece, but might as well have been—in the Cerberus Group was not as well defined as the others. She had an intuitive understanding of language mechanics and was well on her way to completing an undergraduate degree in linguistics with a second major in archaeology. That by itself made her a valuable addition to the team, but it was only the tip of the iceberg where Fiona was concerned. A Native American from a nearly extinct tribe in the Siletz Confederation of the Pacific Northwest, Fiona was the last surviving speaker of a language that was believed to be a direct offshoot of the 'Mother Tongue,' an ancient and mysterious form of expression that transcended mere communication.

It was nothing less than the language of creation.

In the Kabbalist tradition of Judaism, people like Fiona were called *Baalei Shem*—Masters of the Word—capable of using this secret, possibly divine language for miraculous purposes. If the stories from the Bible were true, it had been done many times throughout history. There were other possible explanations for the effect, ranging from metaphysics to quantum physics, but the bottom line was that a master of the Mother Tongue could literally change the world with a word.

Five years earlier, Pierce would have scoffed at the idea, but he had seen far stranger things.

The Siletz tribal language was not the Mother Tongue, but it was similar enough to give Fiona a foundation upon which to begin reconstructing the lost language. Her grasp of the Mother Tongue and how to use it was improving, but as she was often quick to point out, there was more to it than saying 'Abracadabra' or whatever the Mother Tongue equivalent was. There was an intentional aspect to it as well, mind over matter. Thus far, her 'fluency' was limited to the creation of golems—crude automata made from earthen materials like loose rock or clay—and to a lesser degree, the ability to change the density of solid rock. She, and anyone in close proximity, could walk through walls. The latter would be a handy trick for investigating subterranean chambers, if she was ever able to perfect the skill.

If Pierce's suspicions about Arkaim were correct, she would soon have an opportunity to test herself. Although the site had not been fully explored, it was believed that an elaborate system of tunnels were hidden beneath the partly excavated ruins. Any Originator artifacts that might be on site would be found there.

A short drive on the dirt road brought them to a grassy meadow with rows of parked vehicles. Just beyond the cars, vans, and mini-buses, were a slew of colored tents. A couple dozen people, who looked like a motley representation of Russian society, moved between the parking area and the tent city. Some wore the casual attire of vacationing tourists, but others wore blousy red and saffron robes that made them look more like day-trippers from a Yogic ashram or a Buddhist monastery.

"Is this an archaeological reserve or a Dead concert?" Gallo asked.

"Arkaim has a certain counter-culture appeal," Pierce said. "Think of it as Russia's Sedona."

The comparison was apt. Like Sedona, Arizona, Arkaim was believed—at least by those inclined to believe—to be an anomaly zone, with frequent reports of UFOs and other unexplained phenomena. People from all over the region visited the site in hopes of having just such an encounter.

The odds favored a rational explanation—mass hysteria influenced by the power of suggestion—but there was a remote chance that something else was going on at Arkaim.

"Best to avoid making eye-contact," Lazarus said, as he shouldered an over-sized backpack containing their survey gear, along with a couple of items Pierce hoped they wouldn't need.

"Cintia, is the babelfish up and running?"

"I hate that you call it that," Fiona muttered. "I'm sure it's like copyright infringement or something."

If she overheard the comment, Dourado gave no indication. "Just say the words."

The babelfish, named for a fictional creature from a science-fiction novel, was Dourado's sophisticated instantaneous translation system, instantaneous of course being a relative term. Rather than relying on computer-generated translations, which were awkward and often unreliable, the babelfish employed real human translators, recruited from the vast new labor pool of the modern 'gig economy' and networked together by a computer-based voice communication platform.

While it was not a revolutionary idea, what made the babelfish unique was its security. By employing multiple translators simultaneously and feeding most of them randomly generated alternative phrases, no one translator would ever hear an entire conversation. The person hearing the foreign language and supplying an English interpretation for the field user—Pierce in this case—would not be the same person to translate the reply. Such extreme measures were unnecessary for simple interactions, but intelligence services could extrapolate broad conclusions from irrelevant and fragmentary data supplied by informants and electronic eavesdropping programs. Given the secretive and sometimes dangerous nature of Cerberus Group operations, there was no such thing as too careful.

Pierce fitted a custom-made Bluetooth device to his ear and recited a test phrase as he got out of the vehicle. "The quick brown fox jumped over the lazy dog."

There was a momentary pause, and then an electronic approximation of his own voice repeating the phrase, but in Russian, issued from the speaker on his phone. Satisfied with the test, Pierce led the group across the field toward the Arkaim preserve's entrance.

The site was intended as an open air museum, where visitors could move about freely. There were a handful of modern structures—trailers and cottages for the archaeologists and other workers—and a small building that housed some of the artifacts discovered at the site that doubled as the administrative center. Pierce headed there first and approached one of the guides, a young man wearing a red T-shirt emblazoned with Cyrillic characters.

The babelfish also had a visual component for translating text, and a quick glance at the phone's display informed Pierce that the image on the shirt was the logo of 'The Museum of Man and Nature.'

Pierce introduced himself. "My associates and I are representatives of the World Heritage Committee. We're here to begin the preliminary evaluation of the nomination."

It was a cover story, but only partially untrue. Pierce was still a credentialed agent for UNESCO's World Heritage Committee, the international body dedicated to preserving ancient cultures and combating the illegal trade of antiquities. Arkaim had not been nominated for World Heritage preservation status, but it was a plausible fiction, and more than enough to afford them unrestricted access to the site.

The young man's look of confusion only deepened when the babelfish device began uttering words in his own language, but as the awkwardness passed he began nodding.

"Follow me," Pierce heard, as the young man led them from the building.

So far, so good.

The young man led them out across the site, past groups of visitors and toward two structures that resembled Mongolian yurts made out of mud bricks. Although the buildings looked like dwellings preserved from antiquity, they were the most recent additions to the site—replicas of Sintashta houses—and the first step toward a proposed full-scale reproduction of ancient Arkaim. Nearby, a group of young men and women, a few wearing the same T-shirt as their guide, were removing dirt from a shallow trench with garden trowels. Pierce, recalling his own time as an undergrad digging in the dirt, felt a twinge of nostalgia, but his musings were interrupted when a middle-aged man climbed out of the excavation to meet them.

Pierce repeated the introduction he had used with the young guide but before the translation could be supplied, the man spoke in halting English. "World Heritage Committee? United Nations? I did not know we had been nominated."

The man's expression was guarded, but it was evident that he considered the nomination of Arkaim a great professional honor. He smiled. "Forgive. I am Sergei Zdanovich. I am... How do you say? The boss, here."

So much for technology, Pierce thought, tapping a button on the babelfish to mute the feed. He extended his hand. "A pleasure to meet you, Dr. Zdanovich. We're in the early stages of the nomination. Nothing formal yet. That's why we're here."

"Excellent. Yes. I will give you tour."

Pierce smiled. "That's not necessary. In fact, if it's all the same to you, we'd prefer to just wander around for a while. Take a few pictures. Nothing intrusive, of course."

Zdanovich registered mild irritation at the suggestion, but then spread his hands in a gesture of accommodation. "Of course."

"Thank you." Pierce started to turn away, but then stopped himself as if remembering something. "Oh, I heard that you discovered the entrance to a series of subterranean passages. Could you point me in the right direction?"

The Russian's frown deepened. "What is name again?"

Pierce sensed the cracks appearing in his cover story, but he answered truthfully. "Professor George Pierce. University of Athens."

Zdanovich gave a little nod and turned to the young man who had led them to the excavation. He mumbled something in Russian, prompting Pierce to reactivate the babelfish a little too late, then added, "Gennaidy will show you."

The young man in the red shirt gestured for them to follow and struck out across the site. After a few steps, Pierce glanced back and saw Zdanovich heading toward the administrative center.

"Is that going to be a problem?" Lazarus asked in a low voice.

"Maybe," Pierce admitted. "Depends on how hard he shakes it."

"We should have just snuck in after dark," Fiona whispered.

Although it had been his decision to make the initial survey in the open, Pierce wondered if his young protégé wasn't right about that. He had considered but rejected a clandestine approach, for the simple reason that the potential risk outweighed the potential reward. They didn't even know what they were looking for, or if there was anything to be found at all. What they needed more than anything else was time. Unfortunately, Zdanovich was turning out to be Pierce's worst nightmare come true: a Russian bureaucrat, protecting his little fiefdom.

He tapped the Bluetooth device again to open a direct line to Dourado. "Cintia, can you monitor the site for outgoing phone calls?"

"Piece of cake," Dourado promised.

"We stick to the plan," he told the others. "If we find something, we can always try Fiona's plan."

Gennaidy, ignorant of his superior's suspicions, led them across the site, which consisted of bare earth, pock-marked with exploratory trenches. Pierce's practiced eye spotted the curving foundation of the old city. It wasn't hard to imagine moving through the city as it had once been, a massive walled citadel rising from the steppe, with streets and channels to supply fresh water. At the outer edge of the circle, on the western side, near what had once been the main entrance, a rope barrier had been erected around a sheet of plywood lying flat on the ground. Gennaidy held the ropes down for them and then pointed to the plywood.

Under there.

Pierce thanked the young man and dismissed him. "We can take it from here."

Gennaidy appeared confused and uncertain about what to do next, so Lazarus placed a hand on his shoulder and made a gesture that, while not threatening, conveyed the message: *Get lost.*

As the young man slunk away, Dourado's voice chirped in Pierce's ear. "You were right. Zdanovich is calling it in."

Pierce grimaced. "Keep me posted." He turned to the others. "The clock is ticking. Let's get to work."

TWO

Beneath the plywood, they found a square vertical shaft cut into the stone. The bottom, glistening with seepage, was eight feet down, but there was an opening and a wooden ladder on the east wall of the pit that looked promising. Lazarus opened his backpack and took out four small LED headlamps, which he distributed to the others. He also produced and began snapping together the disassembled pieces of what looked like a metal detector. The device—a Nitek Groundshark—was a portable, ground-penetrating radar unit.

Unlike a metal detector, which could, with varying degrees of success, locate metallic objects buried a foot or so below the surface, the Groundshark's GPR could detect non-metallic objects, density changes, and void spaces. Any of those might indicate sealed chambers and passages, and the Groundshark could detect them through several feet of solid ground. While ground penetrating radar could not plumb all the secrets of Arkaim, a quick sweep of the site could point the way to those secrets, or confirm that there were none to be found. Once the GPR unit was assembled, they descended the ladder and headed into the passage.

As they moved forward, Pierce moved the Groundshark back and forth, not only across the floor, but also up and down the walls. Although the uniform dimensions of the tunnel bore witness to the labor of the ancient artisans, the meandering course of the tunnel suggested that the workers had enlarged naturally occurring fissures in the limestone, which the GPR revealed to be solid.

After fifty feet, the tunnel opened into a large chamber, with three more passages radiating away in different directions like the spokes of a wheel.

"I'll sweep this room," Pierce said. "You guys scout the passages. Be careful. We can't afford to lose anyone in here."

"Yes, dad," Gallo said.

Fiona giggled for a moment, but then seemed to grow more serious. As she studied the passages, contemplating the choices, Pierce saw her lips moving ever so slightly. He exchanged a glance with Gallo, who just nodded, confirming his suspicions.

Fiona was using the Mother Tongue, asking the earth to tell her which way to go. Or trying to, anyway. After a few seconds of this, she started down the middle passage, but whether it was because the ground had spoken to her, or just a lucky guess, there was no telling.

"You think she knows something?" he whispered.

Gallo shrugged. "I wouldn't bet against her."

Pierce checked the display on his phone and saw a circle-slash where the signal bars should have been. Zdanovich had likely already discovered that they weren't there in any official capacity, and might even have contacted the authorities. Pierce didn't think their deception would warrant an arrest, but they could be kicked off the site and deported.

Gambling on whether or not Fiona had sensed something during her communion with the stone was exactly what he was going to have to do, and time was the currency at stake.

"All in," he said, heading after the young woman. Gallo and Lazarus fell in behind him.

The passage sloped downward, the gradient slight but constant. The wall curved as they continued onward, spiraling down. It wasn't perfect evidence of Originator influence, but it was very suggestive.

He quickened his pace, catching up with Fiona, but they were forced to stop. Although the passage continued at least as far as their flashlights could reveal, it was flooded.

"Must be a cave-in further down," Pierce said. He glanced over at Fiona. "Is there something important down there?"

Fiona shook her head, uncertain. "I'm not... I don't know what this is. It's like this whole place is talking to me." She turned, a guilty look on her face. "Not literally, if that's what you're thinking."

"I'm not thinking anything, Fi." Pierce studied the flooded passage, wondering if he should try wading out into it with the GPR unit.

And if I find something, he thought, *then what?*

"If we could shift whatever's blocking the passage," Lazarus said, "it might drain out. A small shaped charge might do the trick."

"Or it might bring the roof down on our heads," Pierce countered, shaking his head. "Let's keep that plan in reserve. Fi, I hate to ask, but do you think you could..." He left the question unfinished, dangling in the air between them.

"Use the Force? That's why you brought me along, isn't it?"

Pierce forced a smile. "Can you do it?"

"I can try." She turned to the flooded passage again, took a deep breath and closed her eyes. A minute passed with no visible effect, then two. Pierce was just about to call the attempt a failure when ripples began to distort the mirror-like surface of the water. Then the flood disappeared, revealing damp stone. Further down the passage, where the water was deeper, the process was more gradual, but the water line dropped. Somewhere further down the tunnel, the dam had broken.

It's working, Pierce thought. He turned to Fiona, ready to congratulate her when she left off her efforts. He was surprised to find her staring back at him, wide-eyed and horrified.

"It wasn't me."

"Not—"

A deep boom, like the inside of a thunderclap, interrupted. The sound was so loud, so intense, that Pierce was knocked off his feet. He lay on the cave floor, stunned, lying beside the others. He struggled to rise, but the disorientation lingered. The ground shook beneath him.

Cracks appeared in the limestone walls, radiating out like tongues of lightning. The air grew thick with grit and dust.

"Fi!" Gallo shouted. "Whatever you're doing—"

"I'm not doing anything!"

Lazarus's voice roared above the din. "It's an earthquake! We need to move!"

The big man reached out from the gloom, pulling Pierce to his feet, but the ground was still lurching back and forth like the deck of a storm-tossed ship. Pierce reached out to Fiona, but another shift threw him against the wall. Lazarus succeeded where he had failed, scooping Fiona up in his arms. "Go!"

Pierce found Gallo leaning against the opposite wall. He took her hand, but before they could start back up the passage, another thunderous detonation wrenched their world sideways. The dust cloud, illuminated by the diffused light of their headlamps, began swirling. A blast of air, like the wind ahead of an approaching subway train, raced down the passage. There could only be one explanation.

"It's collapsing," Pierce shouted.

Large pieces of rubble began raining down on them.

"What do we do?" Gallo said.

Pierce turned, whipping her around to face the other direction. "Run!" And then a second later, Pierce yelled again, "Down!"

THREE

Cerberus Headquarters, Rome, Italy

Although she had lived most of her life in the stable—geologically speaking—Seattle area, Felice Carter knew an earthquake when she felt one. The floor lurched beneath her, the jolt strong enough to bounce the lab table and everything on it into the air. The heavier pieces of equipment began vibrating across the tabletop. Lighter items—mostly glassware—went flying, shattering on impact with the floor or the walls.

Carter's first thought was outrage at the hours, days even, worth of research that had just been destroyed. None of the genetic samples or chemical agents were dangerous, but replacing them would be time-consuming and expensive.

Her second thought was that she needed to get to safety.

The floor was still moving, though not with the same violence as the initial bump, and she was able to stay upright. The question was, where to go? She recalled hearing that the safest place to be in an earthquake was a doorway—something about load-bearing walls and the shape of the door frame.

Was that still true when the doorway in question was in a subterranean laboratory, a hundred feet below the foundation of a thousand-plus-year-old tower?

Absent any better options, she decided she should give it a try.

As she reached the open door, hugging the upright frame to stay on her feet, the scientist in her wondered about the epicenter and the magnitude of the temblor. Her field was biology—specifically bio-chemistry and genetic engineering. Seismology was a different branch of the science tree, but thinking in terms of data and numbers—the universal language of all the sciences—made it seem a little less frightening.

She remembered a few things from her general science courses. Earthquakes occurred when there was movement along fault lines, cracks in the Earth's crust that were sometimes pushed together or pulled apart by geological forces. The initial jolt at the beginning, when the stored energy in the opposing land masses was released, was the moment of greatest violence—like a stone cast into a lake, disrupting the surface with a chaotic splash. The subsequent shaking was the ripple effect, the shockwave spreading out from the epicenter. That was not to say that the gentler shaking wasn't dangerous. As long as the earth was moving, there was risk, but

Carter took comfort in the fact that the worst had passed. Aside from a few broken test tubes, the damage appeared to be minimal.

Then the lights went out.

The desolate blackness lasted only a fraction of a second before battery-powered emergency lights flashed on, illuminating the path to safety. But they left most of her world shrouded in funereal shadows. She stayed where she was, praying to gods she didn't even believe in for the ground to stop moving.

One of them must have been listening. Although Carter thought she could still feel the world rocking beneath her, the shattered fragments of glass on the floor laid still. The quake appeared to be over.

She pushed away from the doorframe and hurried down the hall. There would be aftershocks, and she didn't want to be underground when things started moving again. But getting out of the subterranean complex was not her first priority.

"Cintia?"

"Dr. Carter?" A quiet voice reached out to her from the gloom. "Are you okay?"

Carter felt a surge of relief. "I'm coming."

A few more steps brought her to Dourado's office. The room was in disarray, but the strangest part was the absence of light emanating from the multiple LED screens that lined the room. Dourado, her face and fuchsia hair coated with plaster dust, sat in her ergonomic chair surrounded by the lifeless monitors, looking bereft, like someone struck deaf, dumb, and blind.

"Cintia, come on," Carter urged. "We need to get out of here."

The computer expert looked up at her and blinked. "The generators should kick on soon."

"That doesn't matter. We can't stay down here."

"But Dr. Pierce... The team... They need us."

Carter glanced at the black screens. Dourado's computers weren't just magic windows through which she could escape reality. They were her connection to the rest of the team at the Russian archaeological site.

More importantly, the computers were the team's connection to her, their lifeline if something went wrong.

The hardware in the room wouldn't be of much use to the team or anyone else if the ceiling crashed down on them, though. Carter was about to tell Dourado as much when the screens began lighting up, displaying a welcome message, as the central operating system booted up. The overhead lights flickered to life as well.

Dourado breathed a sigh of relief. "See?"

Carter pursed her lips. "Can't you do this from your tablet?"

Dourado shook her head. "There are too many systems running. Too much data to manage."

Carter sank into an empty chair. Dourado was not going to budge, that much was clear. Maybe Pierce would be able to talk sense into her. "How long until you can re-establish contact with them?"

"That's the other problem. They went underground. We'll have to wait until they come out. And they don't even know what's happening."

"The earthquake?"

Dourado shook her head. "The Russians. They didn't buy Dr. Pierce's cover story. They're sending FSB officers to detain them."

Carter forgot all about aftershocks. "And you don't have any way to contact them?"

"Not until they come up for air." She frowned at the screens. The welcome message was gone, but now another notification was being displayed:

Unable to connect to network.

"And not if I can't get online." Dourado grabbed a wireless keyboard off the nearest desk and began typing.

Carter tried to follow what she was doing, but the dialogue boxes and command prompts were popping up and disappearing too quickly for her to make sense out of any of it. "Maybe the quake knocked out the Internet."

"It did," Dourado confirmed. "Local lines are down. But we have a satellite back-up. No way the quake touched that."

A few seconds later, a new message appeared:

Connection established.

Dourado pumped the air with her fist and then resumed typing. A new page opened on one of the screens, a blank white square, just waiting to be filled up with information. After about thirty seconds, more words appeared:

Connection timed out.

Dourado spat out an oath in her native Portuguese, and started over, but the results were the same.

"Is the satellite out, too?" Carter asked.

"No. I mean, I don't know."

"Maybe the lines are jammed," Carter suggested. "Too many people trying to use it at the same time. That's a thing, right?"

"For cellular and land-lines, yes." Dourado's expression twisted in disdain. "This is something else. Let me try something."

The woman's fingers flew over the keys and then she pumped her fist in success. "Yes! I'm on a restricted military satellite. Let's see how bad this earthquake was."

She entered a new command, and the white window was replaced with the logo of the United States Geological Survey. A moment later, it was replaced by a map of the world, with the continents rendered in white and the oceans in gray. Both land and sea were marked with dots of varying size.

The dots, Carter realized, were individual earthquakes recorded by USGS instruments over the course of a week, and the sizes of the dots were a measure of the respective intensity of each quake. According to the legend at the bottom of the map, yellow dots indicated quakes older than twenty-four hours, tan meant quakes less than a day old, and red was reserved for quakes less than an hour old.

All the dots on the map were red.

"That's not..." She glanced at Dourado. "Is that right? All those quakes happened at the same time?"

The other woman didn't reply, but continued to stare at the map, eyes wide in horrified disbelief.

Carter gave the map a second look. There were several red dots, many of them overlapping, up and down the Italian peninsula. They ranged from small to moderate in size, which Carter supposed was a good thing. There were a few very large red dots scattered around the globe, mostly along the Pacific Rim, but by far the largest concentration of quakes was in an area comprising Saharan Africa, the Middle East, and all of Europe, as far east as the Urals.

Carter let out a gasp as the significance of that hit her. Now she understood Dourado's concern. A medium-sized red dot covered the border region of Russia and Kazakhstan—the area where the Cerberus team was operating.

Underground.

"I'm sure they're alright." The platitude sounded hollow in her own ears. She swallowed, feeling helpless, and turned back to the map. "Did all these earthquakes really happen at the same time?"

Dourado tapped a few keys, opening a sidebar next to the map. There was a list of quakes, with detailed information about the location, depth, magnitude, and time of occurrence, and while the screen only showed the first ten or so quakes, one commonality was apparent.

Every single quake had occurred at almost the same time: 1000 hours UTC.

As if reading Carter's mind, Dourado brought up several different news feeds from all over the world on different screens. The BBC newsroom was in chaotic disarray, the anchors apologizing for the lack of information and admitting that they were unsure if their broadcast was even hitting the airwaves. The American 24-hour news networks seemed to have a better handle on the situation, with bold graphics and screen crawls repeating what little they knew. Reports were still coming in. Most of the quakes, including the one that had rocked Rome, were minor—5.1 magnitude or less. Enough to break a few windows and crack the sidewalks, but not enough to cause major structural damage. Less developed areas in North Africa and the Middle East, where building codes were lax if they existed at all, had not fared as well. Some places had suffered extensive damage. The number of casualties was unknown, but estimates ran to seven figures. The one clear message they were sending out confirmed what Carter had surmised from the USGS map. The quakes, hundreds of them, had occurred simultaneously, and that was indeed remarkable.

A bleach-blonde anchor on CNN asked her guest, a seismologist, about it.

"It is unusual, Ashley," the man replied. "Large earthquakes can be felt around the world. The magnitude nine Indian Ocean earthquake in 2004 caused the whole planet to vibrate."

"But that was just one quake," Blonde Ashley said.

"Right. We're breaking new ground with this one...if you'll pardon the pun. This wasn't a domino effect, with one quake triggering others. These were simultaneous earthquakes, and that's something we can't explain."

Carter had heard enough. She turned to Dourado and made a cutting gesture, a signal to mute the audio. "We need to look into this."

The other woman returned a blank look. "Our people might be in trouble. That's the only thing that matters right now."

"And what are we supposed to do to help them?" Carter shot back.

"What are we supposed to do about that?" Dourado asked, pointing at the screens. "It's terrible, but natural disasters aren't our job." She winced, as if regretting the comment. "I suppose we could coordinate with the Red Cross, but—"

"Is it?" Carter asked. "A natural disaster, I mean?"

Dourado's expression changed to reflect confusion. "What else could it be? You don't think..." She trailed off as if unable to even speculate about Carter's thought process.

"You heard what he said. Simultaneous earthquakes don't happen. Not naturally. This is something else."

"What?"

"A new weapon. Some kind of earthquake machine. Runaway fracking. I don't know. But we need to find out."

Dourado gasped and whispered something to herself. She swung her attention back to the screens and began entering information. After a few seconds, a list of search results for 'earthquake machine' appeared on one of the screens. One particular term stood out to Carter. "HAARP?"

"It stands for High Frequency Active Auroral Research Program. It's a U.S. military research facility in Alaska, supposedly built to study the ionosphere for the purpose of improving radio communications."

"Supposedly," Carter echoed. "What was the real purpose?"

"Well, if you believe the conspiracy theorists, they were trying to build a weapon that could create extreme weather, control people's minds, set the atmosphere on fire, or..." She allowed a dramatic pause. "Cause earthquakes."

Carter chose her next question carefully. "Is that what you think it is?"

"I believe that powerful people would like to be able to do those things, and that the U.S. government could probably do some of it if they wanted to."

Carter couldn't disagree with the latter sentiment, but that didn't mean she was ready to get fitted for a tin-foil top hat. "I'll take a look at it. Can you send these to my tablet?"

Her tablet was back in her lab, which was still trashed. She wondered again at the overall wisdom of staying underground, but then decided that Dourado was right. Cerberus HQ was the place they needed to be.

"On second thought, I'll just work on it here, if that's okay with you."

The other woman appeared somewhat discomfited at the prospect of sharing a workspace, so Carter added, "If there are any aftershocks, we may need to evacuate. Probably best that we stay together. And I want to be here if...when...you make contact with the team."

Dourado gave an unenthusiastic shrug. "I guess you're right." Her gaze flickered to a news broadcast and then her eyes went wide. Carter turned and saw a message displayed in bold graphics: 'Sun Stands Still?'

Dourado restored the audio.

"...unconfirmed reports from observers that the sunrise on the East Coast was late." The anchor drew out the last word for emphasis. "By at least a full minute. John, is that even possible?"

The guest commentator shook his head. "Ashley, sunrise and sunset times vary from place to place because of the Earth's curvature, so it's not unusual for there to be disagreement between the time when the Internet says the sun should rise in a given place, and when you actually see it happen."

"But John, these reports are coming from observatories up and down the East Coast. They're saying that the sunrise was late. Now, we all know that it's the Earth that moves, not the sun—"

"Most of us," the seismologist said with a nervous laugh. "There are still a few Flat-Earthers out there."

Ashley pressed on undaunted. "People are asking, is there some connection to these earthquakes? Did the Earth stop moving?"

John shook his head. "No, Ashley. That's just not possible. Look, people are freaked out right now. I get it. This is nothing more than a misinterpretation of the data. I promise you, there's a rational, perfectly boring explanation for this."

Carter wasn't so sure. She turned back to Dourado. "Something's going on. Something big, and we need to figure out what it is before it happens again."

FOUR

Arkaim, Russia

Lazarus hunched his shoulders forward, sheltering Fiona from the debris raining down, and hurried down the passage, trying to outrun the collapse. Fist-sized chunks pelted him with increasing frequency. Each impact felt like a sledgehammer pounding his body. He took no comfort in the fact of his own invincibility. If a larger chunk came down on them, putting himself between it and Fiona would make little difference to her.

"Look out!"

Lazarus glanced back in response to Fiona's shout. Through the haze of headlamp-lit swirling dust, he could see the ceiling coming down like a gigantic flyswatter.

He turned his eyes forward again and realized that the collapsing section stretched out ahead of them, well past Pierce and Gallo, who were a few steps ahead of them.

He ground his teeth together and braced himself.

Maybe it wasn't as heavy as it looked.

Maybe he could buy Fiona the fraction of a second needed to get out in front of the cave in.

Probably not.

More chunks of stone rumbled to the ground all around them, bouncing like rubber balls...

No, not bouncing. Rising.

It was as if the world had turned upside down. The cascade of debris reversed direction, falling up instead of down, coming together, coalescing into...

He looked down at the girl in his arms. Fiona's lips were moving, speaking ancient and powerful words.

A tall figure, like an enormous statue, materialized from the gloom, hands raised to catch the falling slab. Lazarus ran past without slowing, but out of the corner of his eye, he saw the golem compressed like a gigantic spring under the weight of the collapsing ceiling.

A loud grinding noise chased after them, then the boom of an explosion. Another blast of wind buffeted him, pelting him with stones and filling the passage with choking dust, but the thing he dreaded most did not occur.

Fiona's golem had saved them.

Blinded by the debris cloud, Lazarus skidded to a complete stop. The ground was no longer shaking underfoot, and the cave-in appeared to have stopped, leaving the passage quiet.

"I think it's over," Fiona whispered.

Lazarus nodded. "Good job back there."

She started to say something then broke into a coughing fit.

"Cover your mouth," he advised. "Don't breathe this shit in." He peered into the haze and saw a faint glow ahead. "Pierce! Sound off!"

Pierce's voice, faint and broken by spasms of coughing, reached out to him. "We're okay."

Lazarus set Fiona on her feet and then guided her forward through the settling dust until they reached Pierce and Gallo.

"It wasn't me," Fiona croaked. "I didn't cause this."

"I know, Fi." Pierce gave her shoulder a pat, but Lazarus detected a note of uncertainty in his tone. Something had caused the cave-in, and the timing of it was an uncomfortable coincidence. "All the same," he added, "Let's...ah, watch what we say down here."

Fiona frowned but nodded her assent.

"How far down do you think we are?" Gallo asked.

"I'd say we only moved about fifty yards..." Pierce glanced at Lazarus for confirmation.

"Fifty max," Lazarus said. "Maybe less."

"Given the slope of the passage, I'd say we're thirty feet down."

"Doesn't sound so bad when you say it like that," Gallo remarked. "I suppose we're going to have to burrow our way out like gophers."

"If we have to," Pierce said. He surveyed the area. The dust was settling, revealing a rubble-strewn passage that continued deeper into the earth. "Since we're here, we might as well take a look around. Maybe there's a back door."

Gallo raised a dubious eyebrow. "You ever heard the saying: 'If you find yourself in a hole, stop digging'?"

"Will Rogers." Pierce managed a grin. "But I'm an archaeologist, Gus. 'Dig deeper' is always the right answer."

Gallo rolled her eyes, then turned to Fiona. "Fi, honey, you said this passage spoke to you. What did you mean?"

"It was like a...gut feeling. I don't know how to describe it."

"How about now?"

"It's still down there."

"Dig deeper," Pierce said. "This is what we came for."

Whatever the cause, the effects of the cave-in seemed less pronounced the deeper they went, but there were still sections of the passage so choked with rubble that they had to crawl on hands and knees, single file, to get through. At each obstacle, Pierce shot Fiona a questioning look, and the answer was always the same.

Down.

As the young woman's certainty about what lay below them increased, so did Lazarus's apprehension. The safety of the team was his responsibility, and the deeper underground they went, the harder it would be to do his job.

The curvature of the passage was gradual but constant. They were in a descending spiral, orbiting the center of the old city above. The air was musty, the walls still damp from being submerged. Then some two hundred yards from the site of the cave-in, the passage turned inward and opened into another open chamber, more than a hundred feet in diameter.

"If my mental GPS is still working," Pierce said, shining his light up at the vaulted ceiling. Despite being riddled with cracks, it was mostly intact. "We're right under the center of Arkaim."

Gallo was more interested in the walls, specifically, a uniform line ringing the chamber, about eight feet above the floor. Below that line, the walls were still wet. "Where did all the water go?"

Lazarus looked around for the answer to that question. The room had been flooded with enough water to fill a short course swimming pool. For that much fluid to drain out so quickly would require a sizable opening, maybe another tunnel leading to a more extensive cave network, which in turn might mean a path back to the surface. But there did not appear to be any other exits from the chamber.

Fiona said nothing, but walked out into the middle of the vast hall, as if drawn to an invisible beacon in the exact center of the room. "Here," she called out, kneeling and gesturing with palms down. "It's here. I'm going to try something."

"Fi, are you sure that's wise?" Pierce said. "After what happened earlier—"

"I told you. That wasn't me."

"Let her try, George," Gallo said. "It's not like our situation can get much worse."

Pierce's frown indicated that he disagreed, but he took a step back and nodded to Fiona.

She turned slowly, as if trying to find a precise position, then her lips began moving. At first, Lazarus couldn't hear what she was saying, but after a moment, he began to feel a deep hum, like the notes of a bass violin reverberating out from her chest cavity, building in intensity.

Then the floor began to move.

He shifted his stance, spreading his feet apart, as if he was standing on the deck of a storm tossed ship. Pierce and Gallo did the same, but after the initial lurch, the motion smoothed out.

The stone floor began rotating and descending at the same time, like a bolt slowly screwing itself deeper into the Earth's crust. After a full turn, the movement ceased. The passage through which they had entered was now about ten feet above the floor, but several more openings were revealed, spaced out evenly around the edge of the chamber.

Fiona was grinning. "Told you."

"Well done." Pierce stepped forward and gave her a nod. "Sorry I doubted you." He turned, probing the enlarged chamber with his lamp. "I think we can safely say this architecture is not consistent with the Sintashta culture."

"Just as we suspected," Gallo said. "Arkaim was built atop the ruins of a much older civilization."

"The Originators," Pierce confirmed. "The Sintashta must have known about it. It would explain Arkaim's circular design. But I doubt anyone has been here in thousands of years. That earthquake probably shook things up, activated this elevator mechanism and drained the passage."

Fiona shone her light down one of the passages. "That's the one."

There was nothing different about the opening, but she had not led them astray yet. "We need to hurry, though. I think this place has an automatic reset."

As if on cue, the floor shuddered and started to move again, rising this time, as it rotated in a counter-clockwise direction.

"Go!" Lazarus shouted. He scooped Fiona up in his arms and sprinted across the turning surface. Pierce and Gallo were right behind him, following his lead as he adjusted course every few steps to keep the correct passage in view, even as the rising floor began to eclipse the opening.

He reached the entrance with plenty of time to spare, but in the brief moment it took him to set Fiona down, the opening moved sideways several feet and closed another six inches. Fiona dropped flat and scrambled forward, plunging head first into the passage.

The floor kept moving beneath him and Lazarus had to keep walking forward just to stay in front of the opening, which appeared to be sinking as the ground rose beneath him. The top of the passage was like a slow motion guillotine, a rough stone blade that would slice through anything caught between it and the floor of the chamber.

Gallo arrived next.

"Dive for it," he shouted, guiding her headfirst into the passage.

The opening was just three feet high, the gap shrinking by inches with each passing second. He took another step forward, reached back for Pierce and propelled him through. The moving floor caught Pierce's shirt in a scissor pinch, but Lazarus gave him a hard push that ripped him free of the trapped fabric, and Pierce vanished into the passage.

Two feet now.

Pierce's face appeared in the shrinking gap, his headlamp shining into Lazarus's face. "Hurry."

But Lazarus knew the chance to slip through had already passed. He shrugged off his backpack and shoved it into the opening. Twelve inches. Not enough.

He dropped flat and kicked the pack. The contents shifted, and the heavy duty nylon scraped through. He snatched his foot back as six inches became five...four.

"Erik!" Pierce cried out.

"Don't worry about me. I'll find anoth—"

His shout bounced off the blank stone wall as the gap vanished, leaving him alone and cut off.

FIVE

Cerberus Headquarters, Rome, Italy

It did not take long at all for Carter to recognize that she was out of her depth. She was able to muddle through the wealth of information, particularly the official documentation that included very precise data she could verify for herself, but her unfamiliarity with the subject left her feeling underequipped. Distinguishing fact from fiction, where the more extravagant claims of the conspiracy theorists were concerned, was not her forte.

The stated goal of the HAARP project, Carter learned, was to use radio waves to excite plasma in the ionosphere—a five-hundred-mile-thick region of the Earth's atmosphere, which began almost fifty miles above the surface—and then observe the results. In layman's terms, the HAARP scientists were using a thirty-three-acre microwave oven to set the upper atmosphere on fire, just to see what would happen.

It was easy to see how people could be alarmed by that prospect. A single match was all it took to start a raging forest fire.

The idea had originated in the 1980s from an unlikely source, a physicist working for a petroleum company who was looking for an alternative means of transporting Alaska's energy bounty out of the remote wilderness, to the port city of Valdez, hundreds of miles away. The proposed idea was to use that energy on site to power a microwave beam which would excite plasma in the ionosphere. How the energy would be recovered was not apparent, but the idea of heating the ionosphere opened the door to other intriguing possibilities of interest to the Cold War era military.

With precisely aimed radio waves, it might be possible to nudge tropical cyclones on the other side of the world, or see through solid ground to detect hidden enemy bunkers and missile silos. The potential was significant enough to prompt the construction of the quarter-billion dollar antenna array, but whether it had delivered on any of those extravagant aims remained uncertain. The scientists denied that such lines of research were being pursued, and the conspiracy theorists and critics made claims that defied the limits of reason.

According to official sources, HAARP was an enormous antenna array—one hundred and eighty antennas, lined up in a thirty-three acre rectangle—capable of both receiving and transmitting high frequency radio waves between 2.7 and 10 megahertz. By contrast, commercial FM radio stations operated between 88 and 100 megahertz, and military-grade radar frequencies reached into the gigahertz range, as did most microwave ovens. Even if the official specs were understating the output potential of the HAARP array, there were limits that could not be exceeded. HAARP was a powerful antenna broadcasting a weak signal, into a region of space that was bombarded by broad spectrum electro-magnetic radiation. Every second of every day in its 4.6 billion years of existence, the sun showered the Earth with 170 billion megawatts of EM radiation. It collided with gas molecules in the upper atmosphere, stripping away electrons and creating bands of ionized plasma visible to the naked eye. The effect was known as the Aurora Borealis in the north, and the less well-known Aurora Australis in the south. By contrast, HAARP's maximum output was 3.6 megawatts.

HAARP could be compared to a struck match, but the ionosphere wasn't a dry forest—it was already on fire. One more little flame wouldn't make much difference.

But there were claims that Carter could not ignore. A Russian military journal had warned that heating the atmosphere might result in an electron cascade capable of destabilizing or flipping the Earth's magnetic poles, which would wreak havoc with electronic communications and even leave the planet's surface vulnerable to deadly cosmic radiation. Another claim, which under any other circumstances would have seemed ludicrous, was that HAARP could be used to transform the upper atmosphere into a lens to redirect solar radiation, amplifying or refracting sunlight in a way similar to what had been reported on the East Coast of the United States.

Had someone, using the HAARP array in Alaska or something like it on an even bigger scale, triggered the global explosion of earthquakes and the unusual solar event? Based on her understanding of the science, it was unlikely but not unthinkable.

"I need a consult," she said after ten minutes of reading. "With an expert."

Dourado, who had spent the time immersed in the alternate reality of cyberspace, glanced over. "What kind of expert?"

"Physics," Carter decided.

"You'll need to narrow it down a bit," Dourado said.

The question flummoxed Carter for a moment. What sort of expertise did she need? "I need someone to help me make sense of HAARP, but who can also tell me a little about the earthquakes and the solar event."

"So an expert but not a specialist." Dourado scanned through several pages of virtual information. "Most fields of physics deal with theoretical applications, so we'll focus on applied physics. I'll cross-reference with people who worked on HAARP or similar projects."

A list of names appeared on the screen, along with a brief curriculum vitae detailing academic affiliations, areas of research, notable papers written, and significant awards won. There was an additional notation at the end of each listing, the words 'Recruitment code', followed by a three digit number.

"Recruitment code? What's that?"

"This is the database of scientists who might be valuable to the Herculean Society. That's how Dr. Pierce found you."

Carter had not been aware of it, but it seemed like a logical arrangement. "What do the numbers mean?"

"There's an algorithm... It's kind of complicated, but the short answer is that the computer looks at a variety of factors."

"What kind of factors?"

"Like I said, it's complicated. Some geniuses are easier to work with than others. And there are a few I wouldn't trust with the key to the washroom. If someone scores above a certain number, we make sure that they receive funding or employment with one of our subsidiaries. All very discreet of course. It takes more than a high score to get admitted to the inner circle."

Carter wondered what her recruitment score had been, but thought better of asking.

"I'm not looking to hire anyone. I just need to ask a few questions."

Dourado gestured to the screen. "Take your pick."

"Can you organize it by proximity? I think this is going to take more than a phone call."

The page refreshed, displaying candidates from across Europe. One name stood out to her, a Japanese scientist—Ishiro Tanaka—working in Geneva, Switzerland. Although his CV was extensive, including eighteen months at HAARP, his recruitment score was conspicuously lower than the others.

"Tanaka's in Geneva," Carter murmured. "CERN is in Geneva."

CERN—the European Organization for Nuclear Research—was one of the world's leading scientific institutions. It was also the location of the Large Hadron Collider, a particle accelerator ring twenty miles around, where physicists tried to, among other things, recreate the Big Bang and produce miniature black holes.

"It is," Dourado confirmed, "But Tanaka works for Marcus Fallon at Tomorrowland."

"Fallon? I feel like I should know that name."

"He's like Mark Zuckerberg, Elon Musk, and Bill Gates all rolled into one."

Carter, a native of Seattle, recognized the last name, but the other two were no more familiar than Fallon's. "I guess I'm a little behind the times. How long would it take me to get there?"

Dourado began checking travel information. "It looks like the earthquakes have everything screwed up right now. The trains are all on hold until the track repairs and inspections are complete. Flights are backed up. No word on how long that will last."

"What about the roads? Can I drive it?"

Dourado brought up a map with the most direct route from Rome to Geneva marked in blue. On the map, it looked like a short distance; Switzerland and Italy were neighbors, but the two cities were separated by more than five hundred miles. "No major road closures being reported, but it's a good nine hours."

"I can always listen to an audiobook."

"Maybe I can pull a few strings. Geneva is also where the International Red Cross and Doctors Without Borders are headquartered. Maybe I can get you on a relief flight."

Carter kept staring at the map. "Cintia, can you put the earthquake map up again?"

Dourado did so with a keystroke. Carter moved closer, staring at the clusters of dots.

There it is. Why didn't I see this before?

"Does it look to you like Geneva could be the center of the earthquake activity?"

"I...guess?"

"The quakes all happened at about 1000 UTC. What's the time difference for Switzerland?"

"Same as here. Plus two hours during the summer."

"So the quakes happened at noon. When the sun was directly overhead, more or less." One of the problems with working in an underground laboratory was that it was easy to lose track of the time. "What's the time difference between Switzerland and New York?"

"Six hours," Dourado said, without having to think about it.

"So the quakes were hitting the East Coast at about six a.m. Shortly before sunrise. Which according to multiple reports, was more than a minute late."

"You think there's a connection?"

Carter continued to stare at the map. "Tell me about this man Tanaka works for."

"Marcus Fallon. Easy. He's kind of a hero of mine. The ultimate tech guy. He invented The Stork."

Carter shook her head to signal her ignorance.

"'He brings bundles of joy!'" Dourado seemed to be mimicking an announcer's voice. "No? The Stork is a robotic aerial parcel delivery system...a package drone. It's revolutionized online retail." Dourado shrugged then went on. "Fallon is on the forefront of robotics research and AI. They use his software in self-driving cars. But his real passion is space colonization. His facility in Geneva, Tomorrowland, is a test laboratory focusing on robotic systems for building space stations and terraforming other planets."

"So he would have use for someone like Tanaka. Does he have any military contracts?"

"I don't know, but he's an American living in Switzerland, so I'd say probably not." Dourado narrowed her eyes. "As much as I don't want to believe it, if anyone was capable of building a bigger version of HAARP, it would be Marcus Fallon. He's got the genius and the money to do it."

"I'm not accusing him, Cintia. I just want to ask a few questions."

"That's not what I mean. If he *is* responsible for what happened today, he's not going to put out the welcome mat for you. Maybe you should wait until..." She left the sentence unfinished, but it was easy enough to figure out what she had left unsaid.

"I'm sure we'll hear from them soon." Carter gave her a patient but reassuring smile. "Look, it's probably nothing. I'll ask Tanaka my questions, and that will probably be the end of it. But if something more is going on, every second might count. Saving the world is what we do, right?"

SIX

Arkaim, Russia

The four-foot drop to the passage's limestone floor knocked the wind out of Fiona. Before she could recover, Gallo landed on top of her, slamming her down a second time. She lay there stunned for several seconds, aware of the chaos behind her but unable to do anything to help. The wall blocking the end of the passage continued to move for a few more seconds as the chamber floor finished its rotation, then all was still. As Pierce turned and sagged against the wall, Fiona realized that Lazarus was no longer with them.

Without any hesitation, she began speaking the words—the same words that had come to her almost unbidden in the chamber above.

In her efforts to unlock the Mother Tongue, Fiona had operated from the assumption that the Siletz tribal language, which her grandmother had taught her, contained echoes of the original master language, much the same way that Romance languages—Spanish, Italian, French, and others—were connected to Latin roots. Drawing out those traces was a process of trial and error, but she had achieved some success by chanting old tribal songs and prayers, while focusing on a specific task. It was like trying to figure out the solution to a combination lock by turning the dial and listening for the clicks of the internal mechanism.

The correct words were only part of the solution. There was also a mental component to it. The phrase that brought golems to life was simple, but the shape and size of the stone automatons was variable, a function of her focused intent.

As she spoke, using every word and phrase she could remember from her tribal language that had anything at all to do with opening doors or making stones move, she closed her eyes and tried to visualize the passage as it had been only a few moments before. She imagined the rock floor transforming into something as insubstantial as smoke, and Lazarus stepping through to rejoin them.

Nothing happened.

Nothing was going to happen.

"It's not working."

It wasn't me.

"Try again." Pierce said. "You made it work before."

She shook her head.

"Erik is trapped up there," Pierce insisted. "We can't leave him."

"I know." Her voice was sharper than she intended. She took a deep breath, trying to quell her rising panic.

George put a hand on her shoulder and asked, "What's different now?"

"I'm too far away."

"You were standing in the center," Gallo said. "That's important?"

"I think so."

"You also knew where to go. And which passage to take." Gallo looked down the new passageway. "How about now?"

Fiona realized that her concern for Lazarus had blinded her to the subtle sensation that had guided her earlier. She took another calming breath, closed her eyes, and reached out for it again. She had been exaggerating a little when she had said that the place was speaking to her. It wasn't anything quite so overt. The feeling was more akin to an urge, like irresistible curiosity. And as she pushed down her concern for Lazarus, the feeling returned.

She turned and faced down the passage. "We need to keep going."

Gallo glanced over at Pierce. "I hate to say it, but I think you were right, George. We need to keep digging."

George looked back at the sealed passage behind them, and then nodded. "If anyone can take care of himself, it's Erik."

"I think when we find what we're looking for, we'll be able to get him out of there."

He hefted the scuffed backpack onto his shoulder and gestured for her to lead the way. "I believe you."

As before, the passage followed a gradual but constant curve, spiraling down, auguring deeper and deeper into the limestone karst beneath the ruins of Arkaim. The further they traveled, the more convinced Fiona was that they were on the right track. She was worried about Lazarus, but she also believed that the only way to help him was to find whatever the ancient Originators had concealed deep underground. She just wished there was a way to let him know that he had not been forgotten.

After what felt like fifteen minutes of walking, the passage open-ed up, as if the spiraling borehole had intersected an enormous underground void. The passage was still there, only now it was more of a balcony cut into the wall of a circular chamber, curling around it like the threads on a screw. Stalactites and flowstone cascades hung down from the ceiling like extrusions of cooling candle wax, but otherwise, the walls and ceiling were artificially smooth.

Fiona approached the edge and shone her light into the darkness below. Something glinted up at her, like a single star twinkling in the night sky. Pierce and Gallo joined her, and two more stars appeared— their headlamps reflecting from the still surface of a pool.

"That's where we have to go," she told them. "It's down there."

"What's down there?" Pierce pressed, but she had no answer for him.

The balcony—more of a ramp—corkscrewed around three more times before disappearing beneath the surface of the pool. Pierce stopped at the water's edge, gazing into it, but the mirror-like surface revealed nothing of what lay beneath. He turned away and shone his light on the wall to their left. "It looks like the water level fluctuates quite a bit. Probably with the seasons. Could have been the city's water reservoir."

"No." Fiona shook her head. "I mean, it might have been that, but it's something else, too." She turned so that she was facing the center of the pool. "That's where I have to be. This whole place revolves around it like an axis."

"Looks pretty deep," Gallo said. She nodded to Pierce. "I don't suppose there's an inflatable raft in that pack."

"We'll have to put that on the list for next time." George gave a nod to Fiona. "But we don't need one."

Fiona smiled and lifted a victorious finger. "Now *this* I can handle." Then she focused on the water and whispered, "*Emet.*"

It was the Hebrew word for 'truth,' but like many other words in that language, it had deep roots in the Mother Tongue. *Emet* was part of the longer phrase *versatu elid vas re'eish clom, emet*, which, when combined with a focused intention, could bring golems to life, though *emet* was usually enough to do the trick, if her head was clear.

The perfect mirror-like surface of the pool was shattered by dozens of ripples, which intensified into a churning froth. Pierce took a step back as water splashed onto the walkway. "You'd think I would get used to this, but every time I see it, I'm impressed all over again."

Fiona smiled, but tried to ignore him as she held the Golem's image in her mind's eye. Pieces of rock—some as big as monster truck tires, some mere grains of sand—came together to animate the inanimate.

A colossal man-shape erupted from the water, soaking the three figures on the walkway. Most of the golem was submerged, everything below the middle of its massive chest. The top of its head was more than twenty feet above the surface, suggesting the pool itself was at least twice as deep. An arm rose out of the water, a massive hand made of irregular stones cemented together with thick sediment. It reached out for Fiona.

She didn't flinch. It wouldn't hurt her; it couldn't hurt her. Despite its monstrous proportions, the hand, along with the rest of the golem, was an extension of her own consciousness.

The hand came down in front of her, palm up, as if extending an invitation. She stepped onto it, then turned to Pierce and Gallo. "Coming?"

The two exchanged a look, a silent dare perhaps, then joined her on the golem's open palm. Fiona barely had to think it, and the golem was moving, twisting its body and bearing them out to the center of the chamber, right where Fiona knew they needed to be.

"What the hell is that?" Pierce whispered.

A metallic sphere the size of a softball hovered just a few inches above the surface. Despite the disturbance caused by the golem's emergence from the pool, there was no trace of moisture on the object.

"I think it's what we came here for," Fiona said, reaching out for it.

Pierce caught her wrist. "Slow down. We don't know what that thing is."

"It's safe." She couldn't explain how she knew it, she just did. "Trust me."

"You know I do." Pierce let go. "I also know your father will throttle me if I let anything happen to you."

"That's probably true," she said with a grin. As she started to reach for it again, something broke the surface beside the object. It was brown and shiny, segmented like a serving platter-sized cockroach. Pierce pulled her hand back, and this time, she didn't protest. The creature disappeared with a faint splash.

"Okay. Gross. What was that?" Fiona pointed where the creature had submerged.

"Some kind of subterranean crayfish," Pierce said. "Probably harmless, but let's not tempt fate." He reached out for the orb. "I'll just grab the thing and you can—"

Behind them, Gallo let out a yelp. Fiona glanced back just in time to see her punt a large arthropod, which had climbed out of the pool and onto the golem's hand. The kick sent it flying, but even as it sailed away, Fiona spotted three more of them crawling up the stone colossus's forearm.

They were much bigger than she'd first thought, with three-foot-long segmented bodies connected to the eighteen inch-wide carapaces. Dozens of six-inch long legs protruded from the bodies—they reminded Fiona of Freddy Krueger's knife-blade glove both in appearance and the way they moved. The creatures looked like a cross between a pre-Cambrian trilobite and a giant centipede.

Only bigger. Much bigger.

Two more of the creatures appeared on the golem's fingertips.

"Fi," George said. "Can the big guy lend us an assist?"

Fiona nodded and a simple thought command, practically a reflex, caused the golem to raise its other hand out of the water. It began sweeping the creatures off itself the way she might brush lint from a sweater. Unfortunately, the crawling things were on that arm as well, and dozens more of them swarmed across the golem's shoulders.

"Crap," she muttered. "I thought that would work."

"Fi!" Pierce kicked at another of the creatures racing toward her, but after sliding just a few inches, the thing dug its claws in the golem and held on.

Fiona sent another mental command to the golem, shifting the hand on which they stood closer to the hovering orb, so close that the hand bumped against it.

The sphere didn't move. Despite the fact that there was nothing visibly supporting the strange metal ball, it was as immovable as Fort Knox. She tried again, willing the golem's hand to slide underneath the object, but instead of moving the sphere, the hand was forced under the surface. Cold water sloshed over her feet, and with it came several more of the giant arthropods. She commanded the golem to raise its hand, but as soon as it encountered the sphere, it was stopped cold.

"This could be a problem." She knelt down and put her hands on the sphere—it wasn't solid, more like a woven wire mesh—and even though she knew it would be futile, she tried to lift it.

Nope. The sphere was as unyielding as a mountain.

The answer hit her like a slap. This was the center. The axis.

As Gallo and George kicked the creatures back, she recited the same chant she had used to open the passage above.

For a fleeting instant, she felt the orb change, becoming light and pliable. Her fingers dimpled the surface, crushing it, as if it was no more substantial than a paper lantern.

Then darkness rushed up out of it and swallowed her whole.

SEVEN

For a long time after the floor stopped moving, Lazarus remained still. There was a chance that his team would find the means to activate the mechanism controlling the ancient elevator. In fact, he knew they would exhaust every effort to do so, and if and when they succeeded, he knew he would have to be ready to move. After five silent minutes, however, he began considering his options.

The single passage back to the surface beckoned him. While it was true that tons of earth and rock now filled that tunnel, he could not ignore the most obvious route back to the surface. It might take days for him to dig through, weeks even, most of it spent in total darkness since the battery on his headlamp would only last a few hours at best, but time was something of which he had plenty. Such was the nature of his curse. He was a regen, virtually indestructible.

His fingers would crack and bleed from tearing and digging, but then they would heal and he would keep going. He would suffer dehydration and starvation. His body would begin breaking down fat reserves and muscle tissue, and then when there was nothing left, his organs would fail and he would die, but then he would wake up, and begin again. To say that it would be unpleasant was the worst kind of understatement, but there were worse ways to die over and over again. He had once spent four days at the bottom of a lake in Africa, drowning, then coming back to life only to drown again. That experience, in part, had prompted him to change his last name from Somers to Lazarus, after the Biblical personage who had died and spent four days in a tomb before being brought back.

He wondered how many days he would spend in this tomb?

The regen serum he had been exposed to, many years before, promoted rapid cellular growth—healing—but it was not a pain-free process. Every single test subject who received the serum had experienced total mental breakdown from the unimaginable pain associated with recovery from mortal wounds. He had flirted with that rabid madness once or twice himself in the early days. But he had returned from that dark abyss through intense mental discipline cultivated since early childhood.

Rage was something he knew how to master.

Even so, being buried alive would test his discipline, and push the limits of what he knew he could endure.

But what other choice did he have?

He wondered what the others were doing, whether they were still trying to find a way to reverse what had happened, or if they had resumed exploring the ancient city. Would they find another exit? If not, their situation might prove much more dire than his.

He decided to have another look around the chamber. Perhaps they had missed something in their initial hasty survey. Unless they had misread the signs, the earthquake had caused the ancient elevator to cycle the first time. Maybe there was another way to trigger it again, something simpler than an incantation in the Mother Tongue.

He moved around the circumference of the chamber, scrutinizing the smooth walls and brushing away pieces of rubble to see if a fulcrum release trigger or some other mechanism lay concealed beneath. When his search proved fruitless, he returned to the center and began searching the place where Fiona had stood.

Nothing.

"Looks like I'm going to have to dig," he muttered.

Despite being barely louder than a whisper, the sound of his voice echoed back at him, disrupting the unearthly silence that he hadn't even been aware of. Then, the floor began moving again.

Lazarus felt a surge of hope. *Was that it?* Was the mechanism activated by sounds—any sound, not just the Mother Tongue— emanating from the exact center of the chamber?

The question of how it operated seemed less important than the bigger question of whether he ought to go through. As the floor rumbled through its downward cycle, he wondered if he ought to remain where he was so he could open the passage for the others when the time came to leave. But if he was wrong about the trigger, this would be his only chance to rejoin them, and for better or worse, staying with the group was the best way to protect them.

The floor shuddered to a stop and he was confronted with a different problem.

Which of the passages lining the outer wall was the correct one?

He closed his eyes, trying to remember what the room had looked like earlier, and where the elevated opening back to the surface had been located relative to the passage Fiona had indicated. His memory told him one thing, but his gut wasn't so sure.

How long did he have? Fifteen seconds?

The floor started moving again, forcing him to decide. He sprinted across the floor, angling toward the passage he hoped was the correct one. If it wasn't...well, it had to lead somewhere.

He reached the opening with plenty of time to spare, and dove through headfirst. The landing wasn't as graceful as he might have hoped for, a little like stepping off a high-speed treadmill, but he scrambled back to his feet and took off running.

"Pierce!"

No answer.

He kept going, sprinting down the curving passage, nagged by the fear that he was moving further away from the others. Then he heard shouting, faint but urgent, and a different set of concerns took over.

The passage opened up, giving him a glimpse of what was happening far below. He couldn't make out all the details, but he could see that the others were in trouble, stranded on some kind of enormous statue in the middle of a subterranean lake, under attack by... He couldn't say what the things were, but there were a lot of them.

Pierce was swinging the backpack like a club, knocking the creatures back into the pool. Gallo was back to back with him, kicking at the squirming things and covering his blind side. Another figure lay between them, not moving at all.

Fiona!

Lazarus felt a fist close around his heart. He threw himself forward, leaping off the balcony and out into open space above the pool. He had no idea how deep the water was, or how many of the creatures might be lurking beneath the surface. Ultimately, it didn't matter. Whatever happened, he would survive it, and then he would help the others.

But was it too late to help Fiona?

He hit the water feet first, throwing his arms out wide to put on the brakes. The pool's depth, or lack thereof, wasn't a problem. The bottom remained out of reach. The cold was a shock, but one he was ready for. Before his downward plunge was finished, he started pulling himself through the water, kicking furiously to reach the surface. After a few seconds, he began to feel the familiar burn of carbon dioxide building up in his lungs. He needed to breathe, but the surface remained out of reach.

A memory of drowning arose unbidden, blindsiding him. He doubled his efforts, frantic now to reach the surface before necessity forced him to take that lethal liquid breath. Fiona needed him. Pierce and Gallo needed him. If he drowned, his death would only be temporary, but theirs would be forever.

"No!" he raged, the shout turning into a storm of gas bubbles that swept across his face.

He was not going to die this way.

Not again.

He swam harder, reaching up and pulling the water down with frantic strokes. He kicked his legs back and forth, as fast as he could.

His right foot snagged on something. He kept kicking, trying to dislodge it, but the thing held on tight.

No, not now.

Another one of them landed on his thigh, sinking in claws that felt like thorns dipped in acid. Then they were all over him, immobilizing his arms and legs, tearing into his flesh, bearing him down once more into the depths.

EIGHT

The darkness is absolute, like the inside of a coffin buried under a hundred feet of earth. She cannot see the plants that no longer grow, or the nearby river, frozen into ice harder than diamonds. She cannot see anything.

The ground beneath her feet is impossibly dry, the moisture long since leached away by the bitter cold, and no matter how carefully she walks, every time her foot comes down, it makes a sound like bones breaking.

"Where has the light gone?"

She turns toward the voice. It is Raven. In the darkness, his bright plumage is as black as everything else, but she can hear the faint sound of his feet as he hops from foot to foot, unable to bear the touch of the frozen ground.

"My father took the sun and the moon from the sky," she says, feeling both sadness and guilt at his selfishness. "So that he will not have to share their light with anyone."

"There is enough light for all. Why would he want it all for himself?"

She does not know the answer.

"You are his daughter," Raven says. "Surely, if you asked him, he would restore the light to the sky for you."

"He will not do it for me."

"Perhaps there is something we can give him in exchange for just one day of light."

She knows it is a futile endeavor. "What could we give him that is better than the sun and the moon?"

"I know of a light that is even brighter and more beautiful."

"Then you have no need of the lights in the sky."

"This is a different kind of light," Raven says. "A light that can melt a frozen heart."

"My father's longhouse is far from here. I cannot find it in the darkness."

"I can help you find it, if you will let me ride upon your shoulder so that I do not have to walk on the cold earth."

Although she does not believe anything can melt her father's frozen heart, the possibility of finding her way out of the darkness is not something she can ignore. "I know that my father's house is on the shore of a lake that feeds the river, but the water is frozen as hard as the ground. I cannot tell where the land ends and the river begins. And I cannot tell which way is upriver."

Raven hops up onto her shoulder and whispers in her ear. "If you sing to the river, it will wake up and sing with you."

Sing? Sing what?

She realizes it doesn't matter, so she begins singing whatever comes into her mind, and as she does, the ice—all of it—melts, and the river joins in the song. She moves toward the sound, and soon there is a splash as she steps into the rushing water. She turns until she knows she is facing upstream. Now she knows which direction to go.

She hears another splash and realizes that Raven has leapt off her shoulder and into the water.

"Raven!"

She listens, but there is no reply. The only sound now is of the river, rushing all around her.

Raven is gone.

She wonders what to do now. She can find her way to her father's house now, but without the light Raven promised, she will never be able to convince him to return the sun and the moon to the sky. At least in her father's house, she may hope to catch some glimpse of the sun, and feel its warmth again.

The longhouse is not far away, but as she draws close to the sturdy structure of logs and earth, she hears her father's voice. Shouting. Yet, there is something different about the sound. Curious, she goes nearer and sees radiant light shining from within.

"Higher!" shouts a new voice, child-like and full of innocence, and very, very familiar.

"I cannot throw it any higher, grandson," booms her father.

Grandson? How can this be?

She is her father's only child, and she herself has no husband. Her father guards her as jealously as he guards his other treasures.

She goes closer, and pushes past the heavy blanket that covers the door. Her father is there, and so is her son. They are playing, throwing the sun and moon about the room, as if the shining lights are nothing more than pine cones. As she looks at the boy, she remembers bringing him into the world, suckling him, nurturing him, and yet she also knows that none of it is true. It is a fiction, spun of spider silk and dreams, but it is a fiction her father believes.

Now she understands what Raven meant when he promised a light brighter than the sun. The light of a grandfather's joy.

"Let's go outside, grandfather" the boy cries, but it is not a boy, and not her son. It is Raven, wearing the skin of a beautiful human child. "I can throw it higher than you can. I'll show you."

Her father, blinded by the light of joy, does not see how Raven is tricking him. "Oh, you think so, little one? Here, take the sun. I will take the moon. We will throw them together, and you will see who can throw higher."

The two of them—the angry old man who is, for the moment, not quite so angry, and the boy who is not a boy—rush past her, outside into the open. Without a moment's hesitation, the boy draws back and throws the sun with all his might.

Or so he makes it seem. The golden light barely rises above the roof of the longhouse before falling back into the boy's hands.

"Oh, ho!" cries the old man. "Impatient, are we? Now it's my turn. Watch this."

He bends his knees, reaching down as if to gather strength from the earth itself, and then hurls the moon up, up, up into the inky blackness.

Suddenly, with a rustling, Raven bursts out of his human skin, spreading his wings and lofting into the sky. One talon clutches the sun, the other grasps at the velvet darkness, tearing tiny holes in the firmament as he claws higher and higher, chasing the still rising moon.

The old man cries out in dismay, but whether he mourns the loss of his prize or the loss of his joy, she cannot say. His cry becomes a shout, then a peal of thunder, chasing after Raven. He howls again and again, beating the Earth in frustration, and the Earth shakes with such ferocity that the longhouse falls apart, but nothing he does can bring Raven back. And while he rages, the moon sails past the horizon and slips behind the firmament.

The sun, knowing that it is almost free, begins to burn brighter, too bright to look at. Raven cries out in agony as his feathers blacken, burnt by the sun's touch, but he does not let go. His talons tear still more holes in the sky, but as the sun rises higher, its light pushes back the darkness, transforming night into day, restoring life, filling the world with light...

Fiona came to with a start, legs jerking, feet reaching for the ground that was no longer under her. She threw her hands out, as much to catch herself as to grab hold of this new reality in which she found herself.

There was something in her fist, a crumpled piece of shiny fabric. *Where did that come from?*

"Fi!" Gallo shouted. "Thank God."

"Aunt Gus...?"

"Get up, Fi. We're in trouble."

She sat up, the memories flooding back in, but her recollection of the darkness, of Raven stealing back the sun and the moon, did not slip away as dreams usually did.

The giant trilobite-centipede creatures were everywhere now, swarming toward them. They were so close that she could see their black eyes, tipping long stalks that protruded from the segmented carapaces, and chattering mandibles.

"Did you see that?" Pierce pointed out across the water. "That was Erik!"

"Erik?" Fiona hadn't seen anything. She looked around but there was no sign of him. "Where is he?"

"In the water." Pierce swung the backpack again, knocking another of the attacking creatures out across the pool. He looked her in the eyes, entrusting her the same way she'd seen her father do with his teammates. "You're my heavy hitter, Fi. You can help him."

She scrambled to her feet and started kicking at the creatures. They were a lot more solid than she expected, like striking a bucket full of water, but her first kick launched one of the trilo-pedes into the air. The second one however, caught the sole of her hiking boot in its mandibles. She gave a yelp that was part frustration, part fear.

Pierce stepped in and brought the backpack down like a hammer, crushing the arthropod's shell, releasing an explosion of rust-brown guts.

She shook her foot, but succeeded only in separating the pincer-like jaws—which were embedded in the rubber sole of her boot—from the crushed body. *Focus,* she told herself.

The golem's hand rose, lifting them high above the surface of the pool, and it moved toward the spiraling walkway where they had first arrived. Even before it stopped moving, Fiona leapt onto the path and scrambled several feet until she was well clear of the water-line.

As soon as Gallo and Pierce were clear, she commanded the golem to move away, but as it did, half-a-dozen of the trilo-pedes dropped off the stone hand and began scurrying up the walkway toward them.

Fiona ignored the creatures and focused her intentions on the golem.

Find Erik.

The stone automaton plunged its head and shoulders under the water with a splash, sending out a wave that crashed against the wall below where Fiona and the others were standing, soaking them with spray.

A few seconds later, the golem emerged again, one of its massive fists curled around a motionless human form. The hand opened to deposit Lazarus at their feet, and Fiona saw that he was covered in trilo-pedes. Rivulets of diluted blood streamed down the walkway, as the squirming creatures continued tearing into Lazarus's flesh.

Pierce started forward, probably intending to attack the menacing creatures with his bare hands, but Fiona beat him to it.

Prompted by another silent command, the golem's hand detached at the wrist, splitting into five human-sized golems that landed on the walkway with a rapid series of earth-shaking thumps. They were rougher-looking than the giant; the large pieces of stone comprising them did not allow for fine details, but what they lacked in aesthetic appeal, they more than made up for in sheer power.

Two of them bent over Lazarus and began smashing trilo-pede carapaces between their bowling ball-sized fists. The other three began stomping the advancing creatures with reckless abandon, splattering the walkway with green-brown goo. In a matter of seconds, Lazarus was bug-free, and the area around them clear of the creatures.

Pierce and Gallo rushed over to the unmoving Lazarus and took hold of his arms, dragging him further up the walkway, even though the threat was held at bay. A moment later, the big man convulsed, breaking free of their grasp. He curled into a fetal ball and gave a great racking cough, spewing water from his mouth and nose, and then he howled as if he was being burned alive.

His agony was palpable, and for a fleeting instant Fiona felt like she might pass out again. Pierce and Gallo recoiled as well, but the moment passed. Lazarus mastered the primal fury-beast his resurrection had almost unleashed. He blinked several times, his head jerking as he took in his surroundings. His clothes were riddled with little gashes, each no more than an inch long, and through them, Fiona could see bright pink skin—new skin—growing back at an accelerated rate to replace the chunks torn away by the trilo-pedes. Beyond him, the golems continued stomping the creatures, each stone footfall sounding—and feeling—like a blow from a sledgehammer.

"I'm okay," Lazarus rasped, his face still contorted as he endured the unimaginable pain of rapid healing. He rose to a kneeling position. "Looks like you guys didn't need me after all."

"We're just glad you made it," Gallo said, but despite her welcoming and relieved tone, her body language told a different story. She was afraid of him, afraid that he might lose control of the fury-beast and kill them all.

Fiona knew better, but her attention was divided between controlling the golems and grappling with the mystery of her strange... dream? Vision?

She squeezed her fists tighter and realized she was still holding on to the bunched up piece of shiny fabric.

"Can you walk?" Pierce said.

Lazarus nodded. "If I have to, I can run."

"I don't think we'll need to do that, as long as Fi can keep our retreat covered."

"What are those things?" Gallo asked.

"Some kind of pre-historic crawdad," Pierce said. "There could be an entire isolated eco-system down here. Fortunately, we've got what we came for, so I think we can forego further exploration."

Fiona realized he was staring at the thing in her hand. "This?"

She held it up, opening her hand, and as she did, the fabric expanded with a pop. Instead of an amorphous crumpled mass, a perfect sphere, the size of a softball, now rested on her palm.

She remembered it now, remembered trying to pick it up and how unmovable it had been.

And then I passed out. That can't be a coincidence.

It was feather-light now, like holding on to a soap bubble. She applied gentle pressure with her fingertips, distorting the precise symmetry, but it popped back into shape as soon as she relented.

"Okay, that's a neat trick," Pierce said, bending down to take a closer look at the orb. "Looks like it's woven from some kind of memory metal wire. Definitely not from the Sintashta period."

He straightened and glanced over his shoulder at the waterline. Trilo-pedes were still emerging from the pool, crawling up onto the walkway, only to be obliterated by Fiona's golems.

"But that's a discussion for another time," he went on. "Fi, you brought us this far."

"She needs a minute," Gallo said, moving closer to Fiona. "You passed out back there. Are you okay? Did something happen to your insulin pump?"

While she could bend earth and rocks to her will, Fiona's own body was not always as cooperative. Diagnosed with Type 1 insulin-dependent diabetes, she managed her blood sugar with a sophisticated computer-controlled insulin pump, tucked in an inside pocket at her hip, but in stressful situations—being trapped underground and menaced by giant bugs, for example—her body chemistry got too far out of whack, and she crashed.

She knew what that felt like, and this wasn't it.

"The pump's fine," she said. "I'm fine. How long was I out?"

"Just a few seconds." Gallo's forehead creased with concern. "Are you sure you're okay? Was it that thing?" She pointed to the orb.

"Maybe. I'm not sure. I had a...vision. Maybe it was just a dream. My subconscious trying to tell me something."

"What did you see?" George asked with sincere interest.

"It was something from an old story my grandmother taught me: Raven Steals the Light." She saw the others exchange a concerned glance. The vision...dream...memory...whatever, was still vivid in her memory, but the relevance of the underlying message was not so clear.

If you sing to the river...

"The river," she blurted. "I think this pool is connected to an underground river. If we can find it, we can follow it to the surface."

The same intuitive certainty that had brought her down to the lowest reaches of the ancient city was now telling her that she had everything she needed to get them back out.

If you sing to the river, it will wake up and sing with you.

But she did not need the river to wake up. She needed it to sleep again.

She didn't even attempt trying to explain it. She wasn't sure there were even words for it. Instead, she put both hands on the sphere, lightly, so as not to crush it, and she began to sing, chanting the same tribal song she had sung in the vision of Raven.

And just as in the vision, the water listened.

NINE

Geneva, Switzerland

Carter felt only a little guilty about the deception that had secured her a seat aboard an Italian military transport bound for Geneva. Although she wasn't a medical doctor, she *had* done international relief work in Africa. She felt a certain kinship with the men and women who were willing to set aside their lives and rush headlong into the jaws of a crisis to help the helpless.

In her own way, she was doing the same, which was why she was able to hold her head up high as she filed off the plane with all the other volunteers. Then she slipped away from the queue to pursue her own mission of mercy. If she was right about the earthquakes having an other-than-natural cause, then her actions might save thousands of lives.

Although there were ongoing widespread power outages across Europe, the television news networks were already back up and running, chronicling the disaster for the few who possessed the means to watch. Carter did not have access to a television, but as she got off the plane and turned on her satellite-enabled smartphone, she received a flurry of messages from Dourado, most of which contained links to various news agencies. She skimmed the articles and briefs, and was pleased to learn that most of the quakes had caused little more than cosmetic damage, with minimal loss of life.

There were a few exceptions, though. An 8.1 magnitude temblor off the coast of Portugal had done extensive damage to Lisbon and the surrounding areas. The subsequent 30-foot tsunami had done even more damage all along the coasts of Portugal, Spain, and Morocco. Though the number of confirmed dead was still low relative to the population in those areas, estimated casualties were in the tens of thousands. A 7.5 quake had been reported in the Hindu Kush mountains, affecting parts of Afghanistan and Pakistan, and while few details had emerged from that remote region, similar events through-out history suggested the death toll would be in the thousands. What made the situation even more tragic was the fact that the minor damage and disruptions in cities across Europe would further delay relief efforts.

Carter read the articles quickly, gulping them down so that the scope of the tragedy wouldn't overwhelm her. The most bitter news was contained in the last message, just three short words:

Still no word.

George Pierce carried a satellite phone just like hers, capable of sending and receiving from almost anywhere in the world. Unfortunately, the phone relied on line-of-sight. It didn't work underground, and underground was where Pierce and his team had gone before the quakes had begun. That Pierce still hadn't checked in, two hours later, could only mean one thing.

They were still underground.

Not thinking the worst was impossible. Lazarus and the others might already be dead, or worse: buried alive and dying, unable to reach the surface. And there wasn't a thing Carter could do to help them.

Her response, which wasn't a response at all, was even briefer:

Arrived.

She put the phone away and headed outside. She was traveling light, as was her custom. No luggage, not even a carry-on. It was not her intention to spend the night, but if she had to, she could buy whatever she needed.

A skycap directed her to a waiting taxi, and the dutiful driver opened the rear door for her. As she slid inside, her attention was drawn to an LED touch screen—about the same size as her tablet computer—mounted to the back of the driver's seat. On the screen were two rows of virtual buttons, each one marked with a language choice. Assuming that it was some kind of onboard entertainment system—and most likely not a complementary amenity—she ignored it, waiting for the driver to take his place and inquire about her destination.

A moment later, a disembodied female voice began speaking. The first utterance was in French, a language that she spoke, though not fluently. The same voice carried on in German—at least Carter thought it was German—and then in Italian, another language she was picking up. Regardless of the language, the statement was the same.

"Please select your language from the menu," the voice said in English.

With a sigh, she tapped the button marked 'English.'

"Welcome," the voice said. "Please state your destination."

Carter raised an eyebrow. "Welcome to the twenty-first century," she murmured.

"I'm not sure I understood," the voice replied. The screen went blank for a moment, then a virtual keyboard appeared. "Please say or enter your destination."

Carter cleared her throat and enunciated her answer. "Tomorrowland."

"Searching." The screen refreshed again, displaying several choices: An electronic music festival in Belgium, a revival cinema showing the 2015 Disney film of the same name, and a nightclub called *No Tomorrow*.

"Do you see your destination here?"

Carter shook her head, then she remembered she was talking to a machine. "No."

"Please state your destination."

Carter kicked herself for not having done her homework, and wondered if she would have better luck just talking to the driver. "I'm trying to find Marcus Fallon. Or Ishiro Tanaka."

"Searching." The screen blinked again and the list changed. There were a few personal listings, though none of them contained the exact combination of first and last names. But one item on the list stood out to her. "Space Tomorrow," she said. "That's the one."

The screen changed to show a full business listing for Space Tomorrow, which included location, phone number, and the name of the founder, Marcus Fallon. "Is this where you want to go?"

"Yes," Carter said, starting to feel a little exasperated by the process.

The fare for the trip appeared on the screen along with a menu of buttons. "Please choose your payment option."

As Carter made her selection and swiped her credit card, she recalled an article she had read about something called *shadow work*, which was the name economists used to describe the shift to self-service and automated systems. Shadow work was everywhere, from self-service checkout lines at grocery stores to automated ordering systems at restaurants. It was widely preached that automated customer service systems were preferred by consumers, especially the younger, hipper, Millennial crowd, who enjoyed the freedom of taking charge. In fact, it was the businesses that benefited, because instead of paying employees to interact with customers, the customer became an unpaid laborer—grocery clerk, waiter, travel agent—without any meaningful savings in the exchange.

Like it or not, this was the future.

At least they hadn't replaced the taxi driver yet.

As the cab pulled away from the curb, she realized she was wrong about that, too. The man sitting in the driver's seat was looking at his smartphone—one hand holding it, the other swiping right—and he was paying no attention to the road ahead. But the wheel turned and the car accelerated, pulling into the flow of traffic.

The car was automated, too.

Carter's panic was immediate but short-lived. The computer brain controlling the car was probably more attentive than the human driver on his best day, and with 360 degrees of constant observation through integrated video and radar surveillance systems, it was certainly more aware than any human driver ever could be. The human operator, though he probably didn't realize it, was only there to facilitate the transition to a completely automated system. In five years, nobody would think twice about sliding into the back seat of a fully automated taxi.

She settled back and tried to enjoy the ride, but everywhere she looked, she saw reminders of the recent upheaval—downed trees and power lines, cracked concrete, boarded-up windows, and broken glass. There had been several small quakes in the area, all occurring simultaneously, multiplying the destructive intensity of the seismic waves. Fortunately, no lives had been lost.

Fallon's corporate complex was situated a few miles to the north of the airport, on the shores of Lake Geneva. The ride was short and uneventful. As the taxi pulled to a stop at the gated entrance to the walled compound, the LED screen flashed to life with the message:

You have arrived.

The voice of the computer echoed the message, and then asked if she wanted the taxi to wait for her.

"No, thank you," she said, feeling a little awkward speaking with the machine, and ignoring the real flesh-and-blood human sitting in the front seat. The driver—or rather the driver's-seat filler—did come to life long enough to let her out. Then without a word, he got back in, and the car drove off.

At least he didn't act like he expected a tip.

The gate was unmanned—what a surprise—so she put herself in full view of the security camera and waited to see what would happen. She expected to hear another disembodied voice from an intercom, but instead the gate rolled back. As she stepped through, an electric golf cart rolled up and stopped beside her. Unlike the taxi, this vehicle did not have even a token human operator.

"Welcome to Tomorrowland, Dr. Carter."

The male voice—smoother than the automated system in the taxi, but no less artificial—did not surprise her. The fact that she had been recognized did. "I...ah...thought this place was called 'Space Tomorrow,'" she said, trying to hide her dismay.

"Space Tomorrow is the name of Mr. Fallon's company. Tomorrowland is our unofficial nickname for this facility."

Our? Maybe the voice did belong to a real person.

"Please, get in. I'll take you to Mr. Fallon."

"Actually, I'm here to see..." She stopped herself. "Were you expecting me?"

"Not exactly, but I will let Mr. Fallon explain."

She hesitated a moment, looking around at the manicured green lawn and sculpted topiary. In the distance, she could see buildings, but there was not a living soul anywhere to be seen. She settled onto the cart's cushioned bench seat. "I guess I'll talk to Mr. Fallon, then."

The electric vehicle executed a smooth, precise turn and headed down the paved drive, while behind her, the gate rolled back into place, sealing her in.

Over the low hum of the electric motor, she heard the noise of activity. The high-pitched whine of saws tearing through wood, the grinding of concrete mixers, the rapid-fire report of nail guns... She hoped they were just nail guns. Tomorrowland had not come through the earthquakes unscathed, but the repair crews were already busy fixing the damage. But as the first of the buildings came into view, she realized that one of her conclusions was mistaken. There were no repair crews, at least not human ones. The work was being done by robots.

They were utilitarian, more upsized WALL-E than C-3P0, though even that was an imperfect comparison. Their bulldozer-sized tracked bodies sprouted numerous appendages, articulated with hoses and telescoping chrome hydraulic actuators, some tipped with pincer-like clamps, and others with the power tools she had heard from afar. The robots moved with abrupt efficiency, performing a complex but beautiful synchronized ballet. Damaged sections of wall were cut down and removed, and just as quickly replaced with studs and sheets of plywood, cut to size and fastened in place in a seamless and unending progression. There were no mistakes, no 'measure twice, cut once' redundancies of effort, and no rest breaks. Carter recalled that Dourado had described Tomorrowland as a facility for testing robotic systems for space stations, but the reality was far more impressive than her wildest sci-fi fueled expectations.

The cart pulled up to one of the buildings and stopped. Carter noted a conspicuous lack of signage to differentiate the buildings, which seemed odd. The disembodied voice spoke again. "Mr. Fallon is in the Operations Center. A guide will show you the way."

"Thank you," she said, feeling the same strangeness about the interaction as she had earlier. It occurred to her that she had not experienced a meaningful interaction with an actual human being since leaving the airport.

Her guide turned out to be another robot, albeit much simpler in design than the builder-bots. As she stepped through the door, something that resembled a scaled-down Segway scooter with a round yellow disk where the handlebars should have been, rolled toward her. "Hello, Dr. Carter," The voice was female and pleasant, and Carter detected a faint accent. Some kind of personality subroutine, no doubt. "Please, follow me."

The guide-bot spun around, facing down the carpeted hallway, but did not move until Carter started walking. Once she did, it managed to stay just a couple of steps ahead of her. As they went along, Carter noted the plain décor. Evidently, there was no room in the budget for interior design or creature comforts. Stranger still, none of the doors had doorknobs. This mystery was explained when the guide turned toward one of the doors and it swung out into the hallway without any direct contact.

Automatic, Carter mused. *Naturally.*

The door led into a large open room—it reminded her of a budget hotel conference room—and she was relieved to see two actual living people seated in folding plastic chairs around a folding plastic table, which was lined with laptop computers and other electronic devices. On the back wall of the room hung three large plasma screens, each one depicting rows of mathematical formulae. The men at the table turned to look at her, and one of them—he had pale, freckled skin and wiry red hair, and he looked far too young to have any sort of authority—began walking toward her, a tablet computer still gripped in one hand.

Carter tried for a winning smile. "Mr. Fallon, I presume?"

"Who are you?" he said, with more than a trace of suspicion.

She wondered at his ignorance. Hadn't her identity already been well-established? She decided to roll with it. "I'm Dr. Felice Carter."

The guide-bot spoke up. "You selected Dr. Carter for Proteus Team, Mr. Fallon."

This explanation surprised Carter, but seemed to resolve the confusion for Fallon. "Ah, I see. My apologies, Dr. Carter. You've come at a rather bad time for me."

"I...ah, actually, I didn't..." She stopped and forced a smile. "I'm sorry, but what is Proteus Team? And how do you even know who I am?"

Fallon glanced back at the table for a moment as if trying to decide whether she was worth his time. "From time to time, I need to bring in freelancers to consult on some of my projects, so to save time, I pre-screen potential candidates and assign them to project teams. If you were selected for Proteus Team, then your field must be biology, correct?" He looked down at his tablet. "Display Carter."

"Micro and genetics," she replied. "So you just drafted me onto this Proteus Team?" *Just like the Herculean Society and their recruitment codes.*

Fallon continued looking at the tablet as he spoke. "As I said, it's a prescreening measure to save time. There are twenty-three teams, each with at least a hundred candidates. Rather than issuing ident cards and credentials on a case-by-case basis, we streamlined the process by entering the likenesses into the facial recognition database. In the event that your expertise was called for, a proper invitation would have been made, along with suitable compensation for your time."

He looked up and met her eyes again. "I'm afraid the protocols I put in place to welcome you didn't anticipate the possibility that you might drop in of your own volition. I'm sorry I can't give you a proper welcome. Proteus is part of our terraforming initiative, and we're still in the conceptual phase with that. I would love to talk to you about the possibility of introducing genetically modified extremophiles into the Venutian environment, but as I said, this is kind of a bad time. Again, I apologize for wasting your time. I'll have some information sent to you, and maybe we can see about reimbursing you for your time and expenses."

"Actually, Mr. Fallon, I'm here on an unrelated matter. I'm looking for Dr. Ishiro Tanaka."

Fallon was nonplussed, but Carter saw the other man react. She recognized the Japanese man from the photograph that accompanied his CV. He was clean-shaven with a modest business-like haircut, but ten years older than Fallon. Without waiting for Fallon's reply, she started toward the table. "Dr. Tanaka, I just wanted to ask you a few questions."

Fallon hastened to intercept her. "Dr. Carter, you can't just barge in here and start interrogating people."

She ignored him and continued to focus on Tanaka. "I understand that you're an expert on microwave heating of plasma in the ionosphere. I was hoping to get your professional opinion on whether these earthquakes could be manmade, specifically the result of something like the HAARP array."

She expected him to scoff, dismissing the very notion as baseless conspiracy theory, not worth the trouble of a detailed debunking.

But Tanaka did not scoff. Instead, he swallowed nervously.

He wasn't the only one.

Fallon stepped in front of her. "Dr. Carter, I don't know what you're doing here, but I'm going to have to ask you to leave."

"You know something," she persisted. "Dr. Tanaka, were the earthquakes man-made? Did someone use HAARP or something like it to trigger the earthquakes?"

Fallon's forehead creased in thought. He looked at Tanaka for a moment, then back at Carter. "Perhaps you can be of some help to us."

"She's a biologist," Tanaka said. Despite his obvious ethnicity, there was no hint of an accent in his speech. "What would she know about this?"

Fallon ignored the comment. "Dr. Carter, to answer your question, HAARP had nothing to do with what happened today, but you are correct about one thing. The earthquakes were man-made."

"How can you be sure?"

"I thought that was obvious. I made them."

TEN

Arkaim, Russia

A silence hung over the group as they made their way out of the ice tunnel into a natural cavern system. Pierce couldn't tell if his companions had been left speechless by the enormity of what Fiona had accomplished, or if, after everything else they had witnessed, they were taking this latest miracle in stride. He decided it was probably both, a not inappropriate oscillation between two opposing reactions that set up an interference pattern to cancel out everything else.

Miracle. As a scientist, he was uncomfortable with the word. It felt like a cop-out. Every phenomenon had an explanation consistent with the Laws of Physics. Period. Admittedly, sometimes the explanation was beyond the comprehension of even the best theoretical minds, or as science fiction writer Arthur C. Clarke had asserted, 'Any sufficiently advanced tech-nology is indistinguishable from magic.' Falling back on words like 'miracle' or 'magic' was just plain lazy.

Then again, he was an archaeologist, not a physicist or an engineer. He didn't need to understand how Fiona had—using the Mother Tongue, or that weird ball of memory metal, or some combination of the two—turned the pool in the subterranean chamber into a skating-rink. At the same time, she had opened a tunnel through the ice that spiraled even deeper beneath the surface. It was enough for him to believe that an explanation did exist.

The strangest part was that it wasn't even that cold. The ice was freezing to the touch, but the surrounding air was tolerable. It was as if the heat energy had been stolen away from the liquid water through some kind of endothermic reaction, rather than a more conventional exchange of heat with the surrounding environment.

Instant freezing by means unknown. Not a miracle, not magic, just a technology none of them could explain. Pierce might have said the same about his smartphone.

Bottom line, they were moving again, hopefully in the right direction.

The ice tunnel brought them to an outflow pipe—like a culvert deep beneath the surface of the pool—where the water drained out of the ancient city and joined an underground river. The passage rose, like the trap assembly in a flush toilet, then dropped in a frozen waterfall that splashed down the limestone wall. That was where the ice ended. Below them, the river was a glistening black void, a good twenty feet across, flowing through a deep canyon-like groove that cut through the uneven floor of the cavern.

Fiona offered no explanation for it, but said, "We should go upriver."

"That will take us to the surface?" Pierce asked.

Fiona nodded.

"You saw that in your vision?" Gallo asked.

"Sort of. I think the vision was just my brain's way of making sense of it all."

"I'd still like to hear more about it," Gallo said. "You mentioned the Raven?"

Fiona shrugged. "Just Raven...no 'the.' He's a trickster figure in the mythology of the Pacific Northwest tribes, but his tricks usually worked out for good in the end."

"And you saw Raven in your vision?"

"Sort of. It's like I was inside the story. How Raven stole the sun and moon. My grandmother taught it to me. Well, a version of it. Every tribe tells it a little differently."

"Not an uncommon thing in oral traditions," Pierce observed.

"Tell us," Gallo pressed.

"We should keep moving," Lazarus said in a low, grave voice. Despite the fact that his clothes were now bloody tatters hanging from his large frame, he seemed to have made a full recovery from the wounds inflicted by the trilo-pede swarm, but Pierce knew how demanding, physically and mentally, the regeneration process was.

As they made their way into the cavern, following the course of the underground river, Fiona related what she had seen in her dream of Raven.

"And is that the way your grandmother taught it to you?" Gallo asked when she reached the end of the story.

"There were a few differences. In the original version, Raven waits until Girl stops to take a drink of water from the river, and changes himself into a tiny little fish, which she swallows without realizing it. Later on, she gives birth to the baby boy—Raven in a new disguise. I guess the idea of swallowing a fish and getting pregnant always seemed kind of silly to me. Maybe that's why the dream was different."

"Interesting variation on immaculate conception," Gallo remarked. "Were there any other differences?"

"In the story, Raven first meets the girl outside her father's house. She isn't lost like I was in the vision. She doesn't have to follow the river, and she doesn't have to thaw it out with her song. I figured that part was my subconscious telling me how to get out of here."

Pierce nodded. "You blacked out when you touched that thing." He pointed at the orb Fiona still held in her hand. "Maybe it was telling you what to do, but your subconscious used the story to put it into a context you could understand."

"Why that particular story?" Gallo asked. "Have you been thinking about it recently?"

Fiona shook her head.

"Do you think it means something?" Pierce asked.

Gallo shrugged. "Hard to say. I'm a historian, not a psychologist. But it's an interesting story."

"Seems like your basic turning of the year myth," George said. "The sun vanishes as the solstice approaches. A deity—in this case the raven, a winter bird—transforms into a human to bring it back."

"Well that's one way to interpret it," Gallo countered. "But if, as you suggest, that orb is trying to tell us something, maybe we need to open our minds to other possibilities."

Pierce gave a noncommittal grunt. "Are you getting anything from it now, Fi?"

"I don't think so. But it feels like we're still going the right way."

Thousands of years of water flowing through the surrounding karst, eroding the limestone as it followed the path of least resistance, had created a cave system that was easy to navigate. Lazarus, however, seemed to grow anxious as he brought up the rear.

Pierce dropped back. "Should we be worried?" he whispered.

"Always." Lazarus gave him a tight smile. "Those things back there—"

"The trilo-pedes?" Fiona asked, looking back at them.

"Private conversation," Pierce said with a tight smile. He forgot how well-trained her ears were at detecting language, even when the words were whispered. And he had to admit, her name for the enormous arthropods was appropriate.

"There were a lot of them in that pool," Lazarus went on. "And it looked to me like they were drawn to us. Or to that thing Fiona is carrying."

"You think there might be more of them here, in the cave?" Pierce found himself wishing that Fiona had brought along one or two of her golems. Before venturing into the ice tunnel, Fiona had uttered a short command, '*Tesioh fesh met*,' one of the very few phrases in the Mother Tongue she had mastered, to disassemble the golems, just to avoid confusion if the buried city was ever discovered again. With the threat from the trilo-pedes neutralized by the ice, there was little reason to keep the golems, and besides, she could always make more if the need arose.

"I think there are probably a lot more of them here," Lazarus said. "This is their primary habitat, not that pool. They'll have the advantage here, even over Fiona's golems. I'll feel a lot better when we're back under the sun. Until then, all we can do is keep moving."

"George," Gallo called out. "Look at this."

Pierce jogged forward to join her and found her examining a wall adorned with streaks and splotches of black and red. It didn't take too much imagination to see animal shapes, and human figures.

"Looks like we're not the first people to discover this cave," she said.

"That's a good sign, right?" Fiona said. "It means there's a way out."

"No," Pierce countered. "It just means there *was* a way out twenty thousand years ago. A lot could have changed since then."

Before Pierce could amend his pessimistic assessment, there was a splash behind them, followed by a scrabbling sound. Pierce turned his headlamp toward the sound, just as something emerged from the river channel, heading right for them.

It was a trilo-pede, but bigger, with an armored thorax as broad as a queen-sized mattress, tapering into another six-feet of segmented tail.

It also wasn't alone.

"Just once," Pierce grumbled, "it would be nice to have a few minutes to look around."

ELEVEN

Geneva, Switzerland

I made them.

Carter felt a mild surge of panic at Fallon's revelation. He would not have made the admission if he had any intention of allowing her to walk out the front door.

She wasn't afraid of him, though. Not by a long shot. Her panic arose from the possibility of what might happen if the man was stupid enough to threaten her.

Yet, there had been no threat, not even an implicit one. Fallon did not come across as a mad scientist or a maniacal Bond villain, crowing about having the power of life and death in his hands. Rather, he seemed almost embarrassed.

Not 'I just caused a global catastrophe that killed thousands of people' embarrassed, Carter thought. *More like 'Whoopsie, I just backed over your cat' embarrassed.*

"We haven't established a connection yet," Tanaka snapped. He *was* afraid of what she might do with the knowledge. "This was purely an optical test. The earthquakes couldn't have been caused by anything we did."

"Come on, Ishiro," Fallon countered. "Coincidences like that just don't happen." He looked at Carter again. "Let's get you up to speed."

"She's a biologist—"

"She's a scientist, led here, and to *you*, by impressive deductions. Let's read her in. Maybe she'll give us a different slant on this."

Carter's anxiety ebbed a few degrees. Whatever else these men were, they weren't madmen bent on destroying the world.

Fallon returned to his seat at the head of the table and began entering commands into a laptop. One of the wall screens began changing. Without looking away from what he was doing, Fallon said, "I'm going to assume that you're familiar with what it is we're trying to do here."

Carter advanced and took a seat at the table. As she sat down, she took out her phone and laid it on her thigh. "By here, you mean Tomorrowland...or is it Space Tomorrow?"

Fallon gave a mirthless laugh. "I wanted to call the company Tomorrowland, but Disney sicced their lawyers on me."

"Lawyers." Carter smiled. She also tapped the icon on her phone screen to open a voice-chat application that would stream every word uttered in the room to Dourado in Rome. "As I understand it, you're trying to develop robotic systems to advance space exploration."

"Exploration. Colonization. We were supposed to have moon bases and space stations by the dawn of the twenty-first century. What happened? A loss of vision, that's what. Well, that and the fact that space is exceptionally hostile to organic life. Science fiction did us all a huge disservice by making it look easy."

He gave a dismissive snort, then seemed to realize that he was straying from the point. "Colonizing space...building space stations and livable habitats *is* possible. You probably saw my robots when you came in. To borrow a phrase from an old TV show, 'We have the technology.' With just the robots I have here at Tomorrowland, I could build a self-sufficient lunar base in six months, using raw materials from the moon itself. But the real goal...the Holy Grail...is terraforming. Making the other planets in the solar system habitable." He paused a beat. "You're familiar, I assume, with the concept of the Goldilocks Zone?"

Carter nodded. "It's the hypothesis that life can only exist in a very specific range of temperatures. Earth is just the right distance from the sun. Venus is too close, and therefore, too hot. Mars is too far away, too cold for liquid water to exist on the surface."

"Actually, Mars lies within the habitable zone, and Venus is marginal, but yes that's the gist of it. Temperature is the variable. If we could modulate the amount of solar energy reaching those planets—send more sunlight to Mars or the moons of Jupiter, offer Venus some shade—then terraforming moves from science fiction pipe dream to plausible reality. We would also be able to shut down global warming here, and make the Earth a little more habitable again."

Carter felt a glimmer of understanding. "Manipulating sunlight. Smoke and mirrors on a planetary scale. That's what you were trying to do."

"Not trying," Fallon said, with more than a little pride. "We did it. We stopped the sun for ninety seconds."

"How?"

"Like you said. Smoke and mirrors. More mirrors than smoke, actually."

She nodded at Tanaka. "You said it was an optical test. You used microwaves to heat the ionosphere and create a plasma lens, right?"

"The ionosphere? That's nothing." Fallon returned his attention to the computer for a moment, entering a final command. "Do you know what a Dyson Swarm is?"

"Is it anything like a Dyson Sphere?"

Fallon nodded. "The Dyson Swarm is a variation on Freeman Dyson's theoretical proposition that a sufficiently advanced species would, out of necessity, need to utilize all the available energy from its home star. One way to do this is the Dyson Sphere, a shell built around the star, collecting all the radiant energy. As engineering projects go, that would be pretty ambitious. You would need several planets worth of raw materials to create something like that. The Dyson Swarm proposes using free orbiting solar collector satellites rather than a solid structure. Obviously, that would greatly reduce the amount of energy that could be collected, but the yield would be tremendous. Enough energy to colonize the entire solar system. Maybe even fuel interstellar near-light-speed spacecraft. Last year, astronomers observed unusual fluctuations in the light coming from a star 1,400 light years away. The most plausible explanation for these dimming periods is a Dyson Swarm, built by an intelligent alien civilization."

"I've heard about that. I've also heard that they probably aren't alien structures at all, but comet fragments."

Fallon smiled. "They aren't comet fragments. And they aren't alien megastructures, either. When Dyson first proposed his idea in 1960, he couldn't conceive of any other way to harness a star's energy, but today we know that light can be focused and refracted with strong magnetic fields. With the technology that we have today, it's possible to utilize a considerable portion of the sun's energy without building a physical shell or a swarm of collection satellites. All we need, is a few of those."

He pointed at the wall screen, which now displayed an image of what appeared to be the Earth, viewed from space. Just visible in the faint blue band where the Earth's atmosphere meets the vacuum of space, was a jagged black shape.

"Its unofficial name is 'the Black Knight Satellite.' It's an electromagnetic anomaly orbiting the Earth, first detected in 1899 by Nikola Tesla, while he was conducting radio experiments. But he had no idea what it was. It wasn't until the 1950s, when the idea of sending man-made satellites into orbit became a reality that anyone considered the possibility that the signals Tesla picked up might be coming from an object already in orbit. Over the next two decades, there were several sightings from reputable sources—U.S. Air Force pilots, naval tracking stations, astronauts. The government moved quickly to cover them up, dismissing interest in the phenomenon as UFO hysteria. In 1973, a Scottish astronomer published his hypothesis that the object was an alien space probe that had been in orbit for thousands of years. Somewhere along the line, the name 'Black Knight' stuck."

"Aliens?" Carter made no effort to hide her smile.

Fallon seemed not to have heard her. "NASA says it's a thermal blanket from the International Space Station."

Carter took another look at the object on the screen. It did sort of look like a crumpled-up blanket floating in zero-G. "You're sure it's not?"

"Could a blanket do this?"

As if on cue, the misshapen object on the screen began to expand and swell, like a bag of popcorn in a microwave oven. In a matter of seconds, it transformed into a perfectly symmetrical sphere, glowing brighter and brighter until the screen was filled with radiance.

Fallon turned away, looked at Carter. "That's our mirror. The footage you're seeing is from a satellite I sent up six months ago to keep an eye on it. From a discreet distance, of course. This is from three hours ago. The test."

Three hours ago, Carter thought. *When the earthquakes hit.*

A full minute passed before the brilliance receded to a pinpoint, and as the afterglow faded, Carter saw that the object had returned to its original irregular shape. She turned back to Fallon. "What is it?"

"It's a meta-material. Carbon nanotubes spiraling around an alloy core of copper, with tungsten and molybdenum. At least we think so."

"You *think?*"

"The experimental results are consistent with that identification," Fallon said. "Our hypothesis is that the satellite was originally part of a larger structure that almost collided with the Earth. The main body fell into a near-polar orbit, while smaller pieces fell to Earth as meteorites. Fragments of the same material have been recovered at various meteor impact sites around the planet, which is how we were able to confirm the age of the satellite. It's 13,000 years old.

"The U.S. government took an interest in it after World War II. We know that because civilians investigating the Roswell crash in 1947 reported finding a piece of metal that was as pliable as fabric, but always returned to its original shape."

"Roswell? Aliens again?"

Fallon shook his head. "What crashed at Roswell was an experimental military aircraft utilizing a piece of the meta-material recovered from one of the Black Knight meteorites. An early attempt at a stealth plane. The so-called 'alien bodies' recovered from the site were ordinary human test pilots who experienced a physical alteration after exposure to the meta-material. It's safe to handle under everyday conditions, but when stimulated it can have...unpredictable results."

Carter wanted to hear more about *unpredictable results* but Fallon didn't give her a chance to ask.

"Roswell was a rare failure. Almost every significant technological breakthrough in the last fifty years came out of the effort to reverse engineer that meta-material. Just the effort, mind you. No one has been able to duplicate it."

"*Is* it alien?"

"The Black Knight *is* extraterrestrial in origin, as was the meta-material used in the Roswell aircraft. By extraterrestrial, I mean that it didn't originate on Earth. That doesn't mean that it's the product of an extraterrestrial intelligence, though."

Carter got the distinct impression Fallon believed that to be the case, even if he wasn't willing to go on record with it. "How did you activate it?"

"I managed to acquire the Roswell meta-material fragment—a case of being in the right place at the right time with the right offer. By incorporating it into our antenna array, we were able to generate a focused beam of microwave radiation at the precise frequency of the satellite, which produced a sympathetic electromagnetic field around it. EM fields can refract or magnify light just as effectively as a glass lens. More effectively, since the photons don't have to interact with a solid medium. The sun produces a staggering amount of energy, of which only an infinitesimal fraction reaches Earth. The trick is producing and maintaining a field big enough to manipulate that fraction."

Or turn it into a weapon, Carter thought, imagining Fallon as a little boy, using a magnifying glass that looked like the Black Knight satellite to incinerate an anthill. Even if he wasn't malicious, Fallon was reckless. "And it never occurred to you that something like that might be dangerous?"

Tanaka spoke up, his tone defensive. "There's not a shred of proof linking these earthquakes to our test."

"I'm not here looking to assign blame. I just want to make sure this doesn't happen again. Ever. Off the record, is it possible that there's a connection between your experiment and the earthquakes?"

Tanaka glowered but said nothing. Fallon spread his hands. "I'm afraid it's more than just possible. It happened.

"Earthquakes are caused by the sudden release of energy stored in the Earth's crust, usually from the movement of tectonic plates." He pressed his fingertips together to simulate the oppositional forces. "The energy builds up over long periods of time—thousands of years—and then it's released in a sudden sharp movement that sends out seismic waves. Something we did today must have caused all that stored energy, in faults all over the world, to be released simultaneously." He allowed his fingers to slip past each other with an audible snap.

"Could disrupting the Earth's magnetic field do it?" Carter asked. "A lot of people were worried that HAARP might trigger a pole reversal."

"Magnetic pole reversals have occurred many times in the past. On average, every million years or so. There's no evidence that those pole shifts were accompanied by seismic disturbances, though, and in any case, there's no evidence of severe electromagnetic disturbance. No, I think the culprit is gravity, specifically, tidal forces.

"You probably know about ocean tides. As the Earth rotates, the sun and moon exert a constant gravitational pull on the oceans. But the tides also affect the Earth itself, not just the crust, but the whole globe, creating a measurable bulge that moves as the Earth turns. We don't notice it because it's happening on a global scale. Over the last few billion years, the planet has reached a sort of equilibrium—seismically speaking—with these forces, much the same way a spinning top will straighten up after an initial wobble. But imagine what would happen if that equilibrium were to be disturbed by some external force. It would be like bumping the top."

Carter nodded. "So the Black Knight didn't just bend sunlight. It bent the sun's gravity waves, too?"

"That's my working hypothesis."

"But it's over now, right? The top is spinning normally again?"

"I see no reason why it shouldn't. The sun's tidal force is less than half that of the moon. I know it may not seem like it, but the bump was slight. These earthquakes would eventually have happened anyway. Some of them might have been much worse, so in a way, this is a good thing. I don't think we'll see the same level of seismic activity moving forward."

It took Carter a moment to digest what Fallon was saying. "Moving forward? Are you serious?"

"Progress only moves one way. And if the data support this hypothesis, we might be a step closer to cracking the problem of artificial gravity."

Carter narrowed her gaze at him. "What would have happened if the 'bump' had been a little bit harder? What would have happened if you had kept it turned on for two minutes? Or five? Or an hour?"

Fallon looked away, unable to endure her scrutiny. "That's not going to happen."

"You need to shut this down. Put the genie back in the bottle." The exhortation was as much for her own benefit—and hopefully for Dourado's eavesdropping ears—as for Fallon's. His cooperation was unlikely at best, and even if he agreed to suspend his research, that was no guarantee that he or someone else wouldn't pick it up again at some future point—uncorking the bottle and letting the genie out once more. "You said you needed the Roswell fragment of meta-material to activate the Black Knight. That's the only way to do it, right?"

"Technically any piece of it would work, but that's the only fragment I'm aware of."

"So we get rid of that and problem solved."

Fallon bristled. "I'm not going to just throw it away."

"That's exactly what you're going to do." Carter took a deep breath, squaring her shoulders like a lioness preparing to pounce. While her unique...*condition*...was not something she could exercise with surgical precision, the mere fact of its existence, of the fury she could unleash, allowed her to project strength, menace even, and that was a force almost as powerful. "Right now, the governments of every civilized nation on Earth are asking themselves if someone has invented an earthquake weapon. I figured it out. They will, too. They probably already have. They'll be coming for it and for you, and unlike me, they won't ask nicely."

When Fallon did not reply, she pressed her attack. "This is how you save the world, Fallon. Bury it deep before someone uses it to start the next arms race. Because if you don't, you'll be responsible for whatever happens next. Today was an accident. Tomorrow will be mass murder."

Fallon sagged a little under the verbal assault, which did not escape Tanaka's notice. "You can't be considering this."

Fallon was silent for a few seconds. When he spoke, his manner was subdued. Defeated. "If Einstein had known, at the beginning, what his research would lead to..." He leaned back in his chair, leaving the thought unfinished. "Maybe we did move a little too fast with this."

Carter forced herself to relax. It wasn't the decisive victory she might have hoped for, but it was a huge step in the right direction. *Now I just need to figure out how to get that meta-material away from him.*

Tanaka, who had been glowering at his employer, looked down at his computer screen, his face registering consternation, then alarm. "This isn't right."

"What is it, Ishiro?" Fallon asked.

Tanaka tapped a few keys and the picture on the wall screen updated with a flicker. It still showed the Black Knight with the curve of the Earth behind it, but from a different angle, which altered the satellite's appearance. A moment later, Carter realized it was more than just a change of perspective. The Black Knight was expanding again.

The transformation was more gradual than before, like the slow movement of a clock's hour hand, where before it had been as quick as the sweep-second hand.

"What's happening, Ishiro?"

"I don't know. It may be responding to Earth's magnetic field or background radiation."

Fallon's anxiety was palpable, as was Tanaka's helplessness. Carter shared both emotions. "What will happen when it finishes changing? Another bump?"

"It depends on the timing," Tanaka said. "If full deployment happens on the nightside, probably nothing, provided it cycles down again. If it deploys on the dayside or stays that way when its orbit brings it back around..." He shrugged. "A really big bump."

"You turned it on," she said. "Can't you turn it off again?"

Fallon passed the question to his scientist. "Can we?"

"Another pulse perhaps." Tanaka seemed to be thinking aloud. "An attenuating frequency."

"Do it."

Tanaka nodded and started tapping keys on his computer, but after a moment he slammed his fists down on the table. "I'm locked out."

"Locked out?" Fallon and Carter asked the question simultaneously.

"We're being hacked. Someone is overriding our system." Tanaka looked up. "That must be why the satellite went active."

Fallon bent over another of the computers and for several seconds, the only sound in the room was the faint clicking of plastic keys. The tension multiplied with each passing second until Carter couldn't take it anymore. "If we pull the meta-material—the Roswell fragment—out of the antenna array, would that shut it down?"

Fallon looked up at her, then at Tanaka. The Japanese scientist shook his head. "The satellite is out of our control. Removing the meta-material might make things worse."

"Or better," Fallon countered, jumping to his feet. "We'll try it."

"Marcus!"

But Fallon was already heading for the door. "Have a cart waiting for me out front," he said, as he passed the waiting guide robot. "We're going to the array."

The robot slid forward, putting itself between him and the exit.

Fallon barely managed to stop short of crashing into it. "What are you doing? Get out of the way."

"Your presence is not authorized," the electronic voice said. "Please remain where you are. Security has been notified."

TWELVE

Arkaim, Russia

A third mattress-sized trilo-pede squirmed up out of the river channel to join the other two. Their enormous shells bristled with spiny horn-like extensions, but it was the clacking mandibles that projected real menace. The four humans who had blundered into their subterranean domain were good for just one thing: food.

Lazarus started toward them, pausing long enough to shout back over his shoulder. "Get out of here. I'll try to slow them down."

Pierce turned away, arms wide in a herding gesture, though Fiona and Gallo needed no coaxing. They ran to the extent that the topography would allow it, but in the ambient glow from their head-lamps, Pierce saw another of the creatures rising out of the river channel ahead of them. But something else came out of the river with it, a man-sized golem formed of smooth, fist-sized rocks and mud. It leapt onto the back of the nearest trilo-pede, slamming its underbelly down against the cavern floor.

Way to go, Fi! Pierce thought, intending to shout the words, but before he could follow through, the trilo-pede began thrashing, flinging pieces of the golem away like drops of water until nothing was left. Instead, Pierce said, "Bigger!"

"I don't have anything to work with," Fiona complained.

The ill-fated golem had bought them a few seconds, just enough time to slip past the creature. Pierce looked back, trying to gauge its speed, and saw Lazarus come up behind the monster and scramble onto its back.

The creature tried to throw him off, but Lazarus was not as easy to dislodge as a rough, hastily constructed golem. He reached down and seized one of the protruding spikes in each hand, but holding on wasn't his intention. He flexed his legs, and then, with a howl of primal rage, he pulled. There was a sickening, sucking sound as the segments tore loose from the creature's body in a spray of dark fluid, trailing long ropes of tissue.

The trilo-pede's thrashing intensified, and with his handhold no longer connected to the thing's body, Lazarus was hurled clear. He landed on his side, but somehow managed to turn the crash into a roll. Then he was back on his feet in an instant, brandishing a piece of trilo-pede exoskeleton the size of a car's bumper. As the wounded creature struck at him, he thrust the end of the shell between the chattering mandibles, and with his full weight behind it, he rammed it deep into the trilo-pede's body.

"George!"

Pierce turned his gaze forward again and saw the reason for Gallo's shout. To his left, the river channel widened and flattened out, disappearing as the river spilled out onto the cavern floor, forming one enormous puddle that stretched from wall to wall. Water dripped and trickled from the walls, raining down from the stalactite-studded ceiling fifty feet overhead. The walls were riddled with gaps and holes where the flow had eroded the limestone, but none were big enough to accommodate a person. There were no other passages. This was the source of the underground river.

They had run out of cavern. He looked back again, and saw Lazarus running with two of the giant trilo-pedes close on his heels.

"Fi, please tell me you've been holding back."

The young woman did not answer, but her eyes closed and her lips began moving. Pierce wasn't sure what she was attempting, or if she even knew herself.

Fiona was adept at creating golems, but the shortage-of-raw-materials problem had not gone away. The cavern was mostly solid. The river had long ago carried away or dissolved most of the rocks that might have been suitable for that purpose. Golems—the term had come from Jewish folklore—were an attempt to reproduce the Biblical miracle of Adam's creation by breathing life into a body made of clay or loose soil. The *emet* incantation could animate a human or animal simulacrum, and to some extent, define its shape, but it couldn't transform solid rock into something more pliable or cause a fully formed rock giant to step out of the limestone walls.

Which was not to say that could *not* be done. The Mother Tongue was the language of creation, the very words God had used to bring the universe into existence. In the past, Fiona had created Golems out of solid stone. A mountainside, in fact. But she had not memorized the phrases, and by the end of her ordeal, she had forgotten much of the Mother Tongue that had been revealed to her. She was relearning what she'd lost, but she was not there yet. Pierce had also seen Fiona change solid stone into something as ephemeral as smoke. Surely there was something she could do, something she could *say*.

"What about the sphere?" Gallo shouted, pointing to the ball of memory metal Fiona was still carrying. "Is there a way to use it?"

Fiona didn't acknowledge the question, but a sudden chill rising up from the flooded floor of the cavern suggested that she was already working that angle. With a faint, almost musical crackling sound, the water underfoot crystallized. The ice crept up the walls like a time-lapse video of a spring thaw running backward. The walls froze. The steady dripping ceased as icicles formed on the stalactites.

Lazarus, the only one of them still moving, lost his footing. His legs shot out from beneath him and he landed flat on his back, sliding across the ice-slicked surface, out of control. The trilo-pedes pursuing him hesitated at the ice margin, probing it with their steak knife-sized leg tips, then they started forward again.

"Fi, I don't think—"

A noise, like a series of explosions deep within the surrounding karst, cut Pierce off. The cracks and holes in the walls began spreading, opening wider like yawning mouths, as the water deep inside the rock froze and expanded. Huge chunks of limestone broke loose, spilling onto the floor all around them. The upheaval shattered the scrim of ice on the floor, and for several seconds, it was all Pierce could do to stay on his feet.

The tumult was too much for the trilo-pedes. The squirming giants twisted around and vanished back into the darkness. That was little consolation to their former prey, for at that moment the ceiling started crumbling as well.

Pierce threw up a hand in a hopeless attempt to shield himself as icicles and chunks of stone, some bigger than he was, started breaking loose and crashing down all around him.

"Get to cover," he shouted, reaching for Fiona, intending to drag her out of harm's way, but the cave-in was happening all around them. There was no outrunning it and no shelter.

Then something else broke through the canopy overhead.

Daylight.

We almost made it, Pierce thought, as a sliver of light grew and the ceiling above him started to fall.

But instead of dropping straight down and crushing Pierce and Fiona to oblivion, the rock shifted sideways, as if rebounding off an invisible force field. In the corner of his eye, Pierce saw more stones moving in defiance of gravity, coming together like building blocks. They formed a squat, blockish man-shaped golem. It spread its arms out, catching the last few pieces of falling rubble, but as it did, the friction of dry stone grinding together began to overwhelm the tenuous connections holding the construct together. Fiona threw a hand out, delaying the creation's collapse long enough for it to take one lurching step toward the nearest wall, where it slumped in a mini-avalanche.

Lazarus was the first to grasp what Fiona had just done. He pointed to the newly created rock pile. "There's our exit."

They scrambled up the loose and uneven stone staircase, climbing the last few feet to reach the edge of the hole. The late afternoon sky was visible through it. Pierce helped boost Fiona and Gallo, then he took his turn, and Lazarus brought up the rear.

As Pierce's head cleared the opening, the first thing he saw was a jumble of brightly colored fabric strewn out on the ground before them. The subterranean journey had taken them in a circle around the site of old Arkaim, and had brought them up near the banks of a small creek at the edge of the campground—or what remained of it anyway. Between the earthquake and the sinkhole collapse Fiona had triggered by freezing the groundwater, only a few of the tents were still standing. There was no sign of the campers and New Age tourists who had occupied them.

Pierce took a minute to get his bearings, then turned in the direction of the nearby parking lot. Despite everything that had happened, the expedition to Arkaim had been a success. The memory-metal sphere Fiona had recovered was the sort of artifact the Cerberus Group had been created to keep under wraps, even if they had no idea where it had come from or what its purpose was.

Time to boogie.

He was just about to reach for his phone to call Dourado and let her know that they were all still alive when he heard someone shouting. The words were in Russian, but sounded officious, which wasn't surprising since the man shouting at them from the other side of the hole was wearing a dark military-style uniform. He was also holding a rifle, which was pointed at them.

Pierce had stashed the babelfish hardware in the backpack. Trying to take it out probably would have been the wrong thing to do, but he had a pretty good idea what the man was saying. Something along the lines of 'You're under arrest,' or 'Hands up,' or maybe even 'Go ahead, punk. Make my day.'

Crap.

As he skirted along the edge of the hole, the man unclipped a walkie-talkie from his belt and uttered a few harsh-sounding words into it.

Probably calling for reinforcements, Pierce thought. *Double crap.*

Dourado had warned him that the archaeologist in charge of the site—what was his name? Z-something—had reported Pierce to the cultural authorities. Pierce didn't know if the man heading their direction was a policeman sent to deal with them or a soldier securing the site in the aftermath of the earthquake, but either way, it would be almost impossible to slip away with the memory-metal sphere.

"Fi, you got any more tricks up your sleeve?"

The Russian shouted again, probably ordering him to stop talking. Pierce waggled his hands in the air in a show of surrender. The man reached the edge of the sinkhole, glanced down into it just for a second before bringing his gaze back to Pierce. Then he stopped and looked down again, eyes wide in disbelief. He breathed a Russian curse as he brought the barrel of his rifle down and took aim at whatever it was he saw below.

Even though he knew it was coming, Pierce jumped a little when the first shot was fired. Lazarus however, seized the initiative. "Now. Run for it."

Fiona and Gallo took off running, but Pierce hesitated, half-expecting the Russian to start shooting at them. The man never looked away from his target in the sinkhole, though.

That must be some golem, Pierce thought, glancing down.

It wasn't a golem.

"Go," Lazarus urged. "Get to the car."

Pierce jolted into motion just as the Russian's smoking rifle went silent, its ammunition supply exhausted. Pierce caught a glimpse of the man trying to replace the spent magazine, then the man simply wasn't there anymore. Something had seized hold of him and dragged him down into the pit.

"Go!" Lazarus urged again.

A trilo-pede body came out of the sinkhole, then another and another, like the tentacles of a giant octopus, probing the unfamiliar daylight world—testing it, tasting it.

Pierce ran.

Fiona and Gallo had already reached the rented vehicle, and Pierce was nearly there as well when he spied two more uniformed men running across the parking area on an intercept course. Lazarus poured on a burst of speed and managed to reach the driver's side door before the Russians could close half the distance.

Not that they were paying attention to the fleeing humans anymore. Both men were staring in astonishment at the creatures undulating across the grass, heading in their direction. The Russians opened fire, but the bullets didn't seem to have any effect on the advancing creatures.

Pierce climbed into the passenger seat and Lazarus started the engine. The tires threw up clods of turf as the vehicle shot forward. Pierce looked over his shoulder, curious to see what would happen next, but Lazarus turned out of the parking lot and he lost sight of the battle. "You think the Russians will be able to handle those things?"

Lazarus shrugged. "They're not so hard to kill."

Pierce grinned. "Easy for you to say."

"The longer the Russians spend dealing with them, the better our chances of making it across the border and into Kazakhstan, so maybe it's better for us if they do have to work for it a little."

Pierce knew Lazarus was right, but he still felt a little guilty for unleashing the monsters on Arkaim.

He allowed himself a long overdue sigh of relief. The world was safe again. Mission *finally* accomplished.

He dug out his phone to call Dourado and tell her the good news.

THIRTEEN

Geneva, Switzerland

Fallon stared at the robot with an expression somewhere between amusement and irritation, like a long-suffering parent dealing with a defiant toddler. "Run voice and facial recognition again. Verify authorization, and then do as instructed."

"Your presence is not authorized," the robot said again. It scooted six inches closer to Fallon, tilting its sensor disk toward him, exuding menace. "Please remain where you are. Security has been notified."

Fallon glanced over at Carter and grinned weakly. "It happens."

Carter saw nothing funny about the situation. She was about to tell him as much when she felt her phone vibrate. She glanced down at it and saw Dourado's face displayed above the words 'incoming call.' The voice-chat app was still running. Dourado wanted to keep their conversation discreet. Carter tapped the screen to receive the call and turned away, lowering her voice to a discrete stage whisper. "I'm here."

"I heard everything," Dourado said. "This is very bad."

"You're telling me."

"Whoever is hacking Fallon's computer network is also controlling that robot."

"I kind of figured that. Somebody doesn't want us shutting the antenna array down." The full significance of that sank in. The earthquakes and the solar event had been an accident, an unforeseen consequence of Fallon's recklessness, but what was happening now was intentional. "Cintia, someone's using the Black Knight as a weapon."

"Then they're playing Russian Roulette," Dourado replied. "That thing could destroy the whole planet if it gets out of control. Who would take that chance?"

"I don't know. We'll figure it out once we shut it down. Any ideas on how to get past this robot? Does it have an off switch?"

"Probably not where you'll be able to get to it," Dourado said. "But it sounds like a pretty simple machine. You should be able to outmaneuver it."

Outmaneuver? Carter turned around and took another look at the robot. Dourado was right about its design being simple. Two large wheels mounted on a rectangular base, which probably contained both its CPU and a self-balancing mechanism to keep it from tipping over. "Okay, hang on a sec. I've got an idea."

She shoved the phone into her pocket and started toward the door. The robot shifted to meet her approach. "Your presence is not authorized."

When she did not stop, it started rolling toward her, projecting menace as its calm artificial voice finished the canned warning. "Please remain where you are..."

Carter side-stepped and took a quick step forward. The robot shifted to block her, reacting faster than any human, but the one thing its sensors and programming could not do was anticipate what she would do next. She cut back in the other direction, and then sprang forward, launching herself onto the robot's base. As soon as her feet touched down on the molded plastic housing, she wrapped her arms around the upraised sensor disk and threw her weight sideways. The robot tilted up on one wheel and toppled over. As it passed the point of no return, Carter hopped clear.

The robot's wheels spun helplessly, which caused the mast with the sensor disk to whip around in a circle, forcing Carter and Fallon to scramble out of the way, but after a second or two, some internal safety switch was tripped and it went still.

Fallon was livid. "What are you doing? That's not a toy."

"No, it isn't," Carter said. "It was a problem. I dealt with it. Maybe this hasn't sunk in yet, but you aren't in control of this place any more. Now, can you get us to the antenna array?"

"Fine," he growled through clenched teeth.

He took a step toward the door then stopped again.

"Well?" Carter asked.

"It's not opening."

"Oh, for the love of..." She reached out to open the door, but there was nothing to grab ahold of. "Who thinks doors without doorknobs are a good idea? Are we trapped in here?"

Fallon's mouth worked but he had no answer.

Carter studied the door, looking for some vulnerability in the electrically-powered computer-controlled system. There were no hinges, which meant the door opened outward into the hall, and that gave her an idea.

"We need to drag that table over here." Without waiting for Fallon or Tanaka to join her, she crossed the room and grabbed one end of the table. It was a lightweight folding rectangle, made of plastic or some similar composite material, durable enough for everyday use, but nowhere near as heavy or solid as a wood or metal table would have been.

It'll have to do.

She tipped it over on its side. The edge banged against the carpeted floor, the noise causing both Fallon and Tanaka to wince. Neither of them had made a move to help her.

She folded the legs up and maneuvered the upended table around the toppled robot, lining it up perpendicular to the door, leaving a gap of a couple feet. "Never mind," she muttered. "I'll do it."

She lowered her shoulder to the back edge of the table and then, like a sprinter bursting forward at the sound of the starter's pistol, rammed it into the door. The lightweight table was a far from ideal battering ram, flexing in the middle with the impact, but enough of her momentum was focused into the leading edge to burst the internal latch free of the bolt hole. The powerful electric hinges kept the door from flying open and started trying to close it again, but the blow created a narrow opening between the door and the frame. Carter shoved the table forward again, forcing it through the gap to ensure that the door didn't close again, then used it like a pry-bar to force the opening wider.

"Little help?"

Fallon shook off his stupor and moved up to assist her. "Would you please stop breaking my things?"

"News flash," she grunted, as she squirmed half her body through the gap. "Your things are already broken."

She stuck her head out into the hallway and saw two more of the upright wheeled robots scooting toward her. They were identical to the one that had guided her in—and then turned on them—except that instead of a bright yellow, their sensor disks were glowing fire engine red. A stentorian male voice, amplified as if by a bullhorn, barked out, "Halt. You are being detained."

"I guess security really has been notified," Carter muttered. With a heave, she scraped through, spilling out onto the carpeted floor.

"Halt," the robot voice repeated. "Do not move, or you will be forcibly subdued."

Despite the warning, Carter started to rise, but then she spotted bright red pinpoints of light shining from something mounted under the robots' sensor disks. The lights reminded her of lasers—not the kind in science fiction movies, but the kind used in supermarket scanners and CD players.

And close-range gun sights.

She glanced down, saw two star-bright red dots on her chest, and threw herself flat again.

A loud pop, like a balloon bursting, signaled the discharge of some kind of compressed air weapon. Something flashed above her and embedded itself in the wooden door behind her with a faint *thunk*. She looked up and saw two long, twisted wires extending from the robot to the door. The rapid clicking sound of a pulsed electrical discharge confirmed her suspicions that the robots were armed with Tasers.

She took little comfort in the knowledge that the machines were only trying to stun and not kill her. If she couldn't get Fallon to the antenna array, and soon, the distinction would cease to matter. But she was encouraged by one thing. Unlike bullets, Taser electrodes weren't designed to penetrate flesh. Or anything else.

She rolled over, reasoning that a moving target was harder to hit than a stationary one, and grabbed ahold of the folding table that still protruded from the doorway. A single sharp pull brought it the rest of the way out into the hall and in the same motion whipped it around so it was between her and the robots. There was another pop and she felt a faint thump reverberate through the tabletop, as a second Taser shot hit, with no more effect than the first.

Carter peeked over the top of her shield. The security robots were only about ten feet away. Their advance had stalled but they were still blocking her path to the exit. She looked back at the door and saw Fallon wriggling through.

About damn time, she thought. "Do these robocops of yours have anything more powerful than Tasers?"

Fallon stared at her for a moment as if flummoxed by the question, but then shook his head. "No. I don't want to hurt anyone."

"Of course not."

Tanaka came through after Fallon, which both surprised and pleased Carter, as she had expected the Japanese scientist to stay behind. If removing the meta-material from the array didn't shut the Black Knight down, his expertise would be critical to figuring out what to do next.

When both men were crouched down beside her, she raised the table a few inches off the ground and said, "Follow me."

Without further explanation, she started forward, as fast as her crouched stance would allow. The robots barked another warning, but they stood their ground. Carter didn't slow. Instead, she raised the shield a little more, just high enough to clear the twelve-inch diameter wheels on which the machines rolled. As the tabletop collided with the robots' sensor disks, the impact tipped the robots over backward. Carter let the table fall flat, pinning the machines to the ground beneath it, and then clambered over and sprinted down the hallway toward the exit.

Another automatic door—this one made of half-inch-thick glass—blocked the exit, and as expected, it remained closed as she approached. She pushed on it and tried shouldering it open, but it didn't budge. Desperate, she looked around for something—a chair or some other solid object—to smash through the glass, but Fallon had designed his building with robots in mind. There was no reception desk or visitor lobby, no creature comforts at all. Just the door and the hallway leading into the building.

A strident blast of sound ripped through the relative quiet, causing her to wince in real pain. She whirled around, wondering if this was some new sonic weapon being employed against them, and she saw a grinning Fallon with one hand on a small red fire alarm button mounted to the wall.

"Try it now!" he shouted.

Carter pushed on the glass, and the door swung open. *Some kind of safety override feature*, she thought. *That would have been nice to know about a few minutes ago.*

She headed through the door and waited for Fallon and Tanaka to catch up. There was no electric cart waiting to bear them to the antenna array. "How far away is it?"

"Not far," Fallon said, taking the lead. "Half a mile."

It would take seven or eight minutes to walk half a mile—four or five to run it—and that was assuming they didn't run into any more security robots. How long did they have before the Black Knight finished deploying and started either scorching the Earth with prolonged solar radiation or ripping it apart with tidal forces?

Not far? It might as well have been in another country, but what choice was there?

Fallon took off at a jog, running deeper into the complex of buildings. Carter followed, looking for a large parabolic satellite dish, or something that resembled the pictures she had seen of the HAARP array in Alaska—which in pictures looked like two dozen old-fashioned TV antennas lined up in military formation—but

Fallon's destination turned out to be something else: a one-story windowless parking garage.

"We're driving?" Carter asked, as they headed through the doorless opening leading into the structure.

Fallon glanced back. "You didn't think we were going to walk?"

He stopped just inside and stared out at the arrayed vehicles. Carter was surprised to see how many of the parking spaces were filled. There were more than a dozen different vehicles. She wouldn't have guessed there were so many human employees at Tomorrow-land. Fallon was evidently a generous employer, too. There were no minivans or soccer-mobiles in the lot, just luxury sedans and sports cars.

"Which one's yours?" she asked.

"They're all mine. Just trying to decide which one." He threw her a defensive look. "What? I like cars."

She shook her head and muttered. "First world problems."

Fallon angled toward the closest vehicle, a blue Tesla Model 3. He tried the door handle but it didn't budge. "What the hell?"

"Don't you have the key?"

"There are no keys. It's biometric." He held his fingertips against the handle for a few seconds before trying again, but the result was the same. "It's not recognizing me."

"There's a lot of that going around. Somebody doesn't want you shutting that antenna down." Carter scanned the other cars. "You got anything low-tech in here?"

Her eyes roamed the line of sleek modern vehicles and settled on a classic 1960's, silver sports car with elegant spoked wheels. It looked like something from an old James Bond movie. "What about that one?"

"Perfect," Fallon flashed a mischievous grin, and ran to the vehicle, which was unlocked. Fallon went to the right side, which confused Carter for a moment—*does he want me to drive?*—until she realized that the car was configured for right-side driving. Without complaint or protest, she squeezed into the cramped back seat, allowing Tanaka to have the front passenger seat, while Fallon started the vehicle.

Driving the silver car seemed to energize Fallon. He slammed the gear-shift lever into reverse and the car jolted violently as he let out the clutch, backing out of the parking space with a screech of rubber. He shifted again, and the car shot forward, whining in protest as he maxed first gear before reaching the garage door.

Despite the cramped seating arrangement and Fallon's over-excited driving, Carter was relieved to finally be moving in the right direction, and even more relieved when, after less than a minute of tearing down the paved road, Fallon brought the sport's car to a skidding stop in front of a small cinder block structure at the end of the drive. Just visible behind it was an elaborate structure of wires and metal rods that looked a little like an electrical transformer hub.

"See?" Fallon said, throwing the door open. "Not far."

"This is dangerous, Marcus," Tanaka said, breaking his self-imposed silence. He waved his tablet, and Carter saw that it was still displaying the real time feed from the Space Tomorrow satellite trailing the Black Knight. Evidently, the hacker had only locked them out of control function, allowing Fallon to keep his eyes in the sky. "We don't know what will happen if we interrupt the signal."

Fallon waved a dismissive hand. "It's not going to make things worse. Until we can get control of the transmitter back, this is the right thing to do."

Carter withheld comment and followed the two men at a distance. Tanaka's wariness concerned her—*What if he's right?*—but she had no expertise to inform her opinion, and in any case, she was more inclined to agree with Fallon's approach.

Fallon opened a utilitarian metal door—a regular door with a door knob and no fancy electronic gizmos—and went inside, with Tanaka close on his heels. Carter remained outside, but she could feel heat radiating from the interior, which was dominated by an enormous machine enclosed in a non-descript metal housing from which sprouted a pair of thick insulated cables. A loud electrical hum emanated from the device. Fallon opened a small access door on its side, revealing a nest of wires and processors, and then reached inside. The loud hum stopped.

He reached in a little further and rooted around for almost a full minute before emerging. Something that looked like a scorched, crumpled piece of tightly woven window screen, about the size of a washcloth, protruded from his closed fist.

"That's it?" Carter asked.

It looked too ordinary to be so dangerous.

Fallon cocked his head sideways and smirked. "Doesn't look like much, but it's probably the rarest material in the world." He turned to Tanaka. "Any change?"

Tanaka looked down at the tablet for several seconds, then shook his head. "As I feared, it's not responding. We should restore the transmitter. Maybe whoever did this knows how to shut it down."

"No." Fallon was emphatic. "I'm not going to take that chance. The transmitter stays offline until we can get control of our systems again. Speaking of which..." He nodded to the waiting car. "It's time to take back Tomorrow—"

The declaration faltered and died as Fallon's stare fixed on something in the distance beyond. Carter followed his gaze and saw why he had been rendered speechless.

One of the bulldozer-sized construction robots Carter had passed on the way in rolled into view from behind one of the main buildings. Another one came after it, and then several more. Six of them altogether, moved single-file, like floats in a Christmas parade. When the last of them was clear, the formation broke apart and reshuffled until the machines were lined up side-by-side, like a cavalry charge, sweeping toward them.

FOURTEEN

Carter grabbed the end of the memory metal fragment and tore it from Fallon's grasp. It felt strange in her hand, cool to the touch, with a texture like a handful of little springs. Fearing that it might ooze out of her grip, she shoved it into her pocket and darted for the right side of the car. She slid behind the steering wheel, clutched, and turned the key. As the engine roared to life, Fallon stuck his head in through the passenger side door.

"What are you doing?"

"Leaving," she said, putting the car in gear.

Fallon's jaw worked but she cut him off before he could articulate his protest. "Get in. If you want to fix this, we have to go now."

"Ishiro, let's go," Fallon said without looking away, and then as an afterthought, he muttered, "Shotgun."

As they climbed in, Carter checked on the advancing robot wave's progress. They were still about a hundred yards away, and while not built for speed, they were moving faster than a human could run. Two of them blocked the road, while pairs on either side rolled across the landscaped greenspace, crushing topiary shrubs and throwing up huge clods of dirt with their metal treads. Getting around them was going to require more than fancy footwork and a plastic table.

As soon as the two men were inside, Carter let out the clutch. The car shot forward, and she hauled the steering wheel around, requiring almost a full-body effort since the car didn't have power steering. She carved a tight U-turn that brought them back around onto the road, facing the construction-bots. "Is there another way out of here?"

"That's the only road."

Carter surveyed the off-road possibilities. The pavement was bordered by hedges, which the second and fifth robots were obliterating with complete indifference. Beyond the hedgerow, there was a grassy expanse about twenty yards wide. It ended at Lake Geneva's shore on one side and a stand of trees on the other. But most of the open space was dominated by the robots at the ends of the formation. "Do those things have any weaknesses?"

Fallon blinked as if he found the question insulting, but then shrugged. "They're built for heavy labor...construction. They aren't war machines."

"Could have fooled me." She considered the statement a moment longer. "What does that mean exactly?"

"It means they don't see us as an enemy. You can't just splice in a line of code and turn a construction machine into the Terminator."

"So you're saying they're here to... fix us?" Try as she might, Carter couldn't see how the distinction mattered.

"I'm saying they don't think strategically." Then he added, "And they can't turn worth a damn."

"Why didn't you say that in the first place?" Carter accelerated again. She pushed the gas pedal, let out the clutch, and the car shot forward like a robot-seeking missile.

"What the hell are you doing?" Fallon cried out, flailing his arms as if trying to stop himself from falling.

When the wall of robots was just fifty feet away, she slammed on the brakes and cranked the steering wheel, sliding into another U-turn, now only a few feet ahead of the advancing machines. In the rear-view mirror, she could see hydraulic manipulator arms unfolding above the tracked chassis like the legs of some gigantic praying mantis reaching out to crush them in its pincers.

Carter floored the gas pedal again, and the car shot forward as one manipulator arm, tipped with an over-sized circular saw, came down. There was a shower of sparks as the blade struck the pavement, mere inches from the rear bumper. She cut the steering wheel to the right and the robot made another grab for her, but as it did, it veered into the path of the neighboring machine just as it also tried to attack.

The air behind them was filled with an ear-splitting shriek and the crunch of metal being torn apart, as the two machines tried to occupy the same space. Chunks of debris began raining down all around, pelting the back of the sports car, even as Carter cut back the other direction.

The two robots were hopelessly entangled, and after only a few seconds of struggling, they gave up the fight. As the advancing line moved past the wreckage, the others closed ranks, making sure that the road was blocked. And they kept coming.

Carter made a wide sweeping turn, leaving the road surface, crashing through the hedges on the roadside, and carving twin furrows in the lawn like a teenager on a joyride. The tires slipped on the soft ground, spraying out loose dirt as they dug down, looking for something solid to grab onto. The car fishtailed and slid sideways as she fought to maintain control.

When the arc of the turn brought them back around, she straightened the steering wheel and gave the car a little more gas, headed toward the machine moving along on the right side of the pavement. Another human, or an artificial-intelligence capable of strategic thinking, might have realized what she was planning to do and taken steps to head her off, shifting the entire formation to block her. But the construction robots stayed on course, as if daring her to a game of chicken.

When she was still a good fifty feet away, she steered to the side, angling for the wide open gap between the machines and the trees. The robot responded, but its slow, jerky turn gave Carter all the time she needed to zip past.

She then angled the car back toward the pavement. Behind them, the machines were reversing course, but couldn't keep up with the sleek sports car once she got the tires back on the asphalt.

As they shot down the road, heading back toward the complex of buildings and away from both the array and the wayward construction robots, Carter kept accelerating, winding out each of the gears in the five-speed transmission. As she shifted into fourth, the speedometer was already tipping sixty—miles per hour, not kilometers. Evidently, this ride predated Europe's embrace of the metric system.

"You know how to drive a stick," Fallon said. "That's rare nowadays."

She shot him an annoyed look. "Are you hitting on me?"

She almost added, *My boyfriend won't like that,* but just thinking it reminded her that Erik and the others were all still missing.

"Of course not," Fallon replied, though the mischievous gleam in his eyes suggested otherwise. "Just noticing."

Her ability to drive a manual transmission had more to do with necessity than any particular love of driving. She had spent a good part of the last few years in remote parts of Africa, where older vehicles were more common and more reliable—or at least easier to maintain—than the newer, more technologically advanced models. Driving wasn't a luxury activity for her, it was a necessary thing, and often a matter of survival. Sometimes her own, or sometimes survival for a village full of people a hundred miles out in the bush, desperate for a cure to some tropical disease. That had meant being able to drive whatever was available in any conditions.

Still, Fallon's car was a pretty sweet ride. She felt kind of bad about what she was going to have to do next.

The turn-off to the garage flashed by. Ahead in the distance, she could just make out the entrance to the compound. "I don't suppose there's any way the gate is going to open for us."

"Probably not," Fallon admitted.

"Good things these old cars don't have airbags."

Fallon nodded but then realized what she was saying. "Oh, you're not going to..." Leaving the sentence unfinished, he reached down to the upholstered arm rest on the center console, and flipped it up to reveal several small switches.

"Bumper extensions," he said as he flipped a couple of them, then straightened in his seat, gripping the dashboard with both hands in anticipation of the impending crash.

Carter didn't know what he was talking about, and she was too focused on the approaching gate to care. Out of the corner of her eye, she glimpsed movement. A driverless electric cart, possibly the same one that had delivered her to Fallon's building, was rolling down a side-road on an intercept course.

She pushed the car harder, winding out fourth gear, and shot past the intersection before the cart could cut her off. There was a slight jolt as the robotic vehicle grazed the sports car's rear end, but they were going too fast for it to make any difference.

Carter kept watch for more kamikaze carts as the gate drew closer, but the hacker was out of tricks. She gripped the wheel and kept the pedal to the floor, closing the remaining distance so quickly that it came as a surprise when the front bumper slammed into the metal gate.

The barrier flipped up and spun around in mid-air, registering a glancing blow on the car's roof. Carter felt the impact shudder through the vehicle's frame and heard the engine whine in protest for a moment, but that was it. She downshifted as they reached the main highway. Traffic was light, and she barely touched the brakes as they skidded through the turn, crossing to the far lane that would take them back to Geneva. Then she accelerated again.

Beside her, Fallon let out his breath in a long relieved sigh. "Not bad. I'm glad we're on the same side. Though you are kind of hard on my toys."

"Your toys tried to kill us." She glanced over at him, wondering if they really *were* on the same side. "We need to get somewhere safe and figure out our next move."

"Our next move is taking back Tomorrowland. That hacker may have caught me with my pants down, but he's played his hand. It's my turn now, and payback's a bitch."

Despite the bravado, Carter knew he was right about their priorities. Removing the memory metal from the transmitter had not shut the Black Knight satellite down, so regaining control of the array was imperative. "I have a friend who might be able to help with that."

She was about to dig out her phone to call Dourado, but a flash of color in the rear view mirror stopped her. A familiar-looking blue car had just turned onto the highway behind them. "Is that your Tesla?"

Fallon craned his head around. "Son of a bitch," he snarled.

"I'll take that as a 'yes.' That must be our hacker."

Fallon shook his head miserably. "No. It's autonomous."

Two more cars, one a cream-colored sedan, the other a sleek black coupe emerged from the Tomorrowland gate to join the pursuit. She couldn't discern the make or model, but there was little question that they were also from Fallon's stable. "You turned your cars into robots?"

"No, they come that way. Self-driving cars are inevitable, so a lot of car makers are getting a jump on it by pre-installing the hardware in newer models. Actually, the design uses some of my patents, so I guess you could say it was me."

The significance of that was not lost on Carter. Their unknown foe could turn any autonomous car on the road against them.

The blue car was closing the distance. In terms of speed, the Tesla was more than a match for the older, classic sports car, but its real advantage was the computer brain controlling it, informed by an array of cameras, radar, and laser sensors, with reaction time measured in picoseconds and no fear whatsoever. The black car swung out from behind the Tesla and pulled up alongside it, matching its speed. Both vehicles were so close that Carter could see their distinctive hood ornaments—the stylized T with wings of Tesla motors on the blue car, and the blue and white checkered circle that identified the coupe as a Beemer.

Fallon saw them, too, and to Carter's astonishment he gave a little laugh. "Ha. Watch this."

He reached for the armrest again, and this time Carter could not help but glance down as he threw one of the switches.

A cloud of black smoke billowed out behind the car, blocking her view of the two pursuit vehicles. "A smoke screen?" she asked, incredulous. "Seriously?"

"Whoops," Fallon said. "Wrong one." He flipped a different switch.

Although the two vehicles were still partially hidden by the dense cloud, Carter could tell that something was happening. The blue car swerved into the coupe, and then both cars were spinning as if they had hit a patch of ice...

Or an oil slick.

The BMW went sideways and then flipped and started tumbling down the highway before disappearing once more in the smoke. The Tesla veered off the road and crashed into a fence.

"You made a spy car," Carter said, with more than a little disgust. "Or are you going to tell me those are standard features, too?"

"They are for this car," Fallon said with a grin. "This is the actual Aston Martin DB5 from *Goldfinger*. All the gadgets from the movie were actually built into the car. I got it at auction a few years ago."

The smoke screen petered out, but there was no sign of pursuit behind them. Or any other traffic for that matter. The opposite lane was turning into a parking lot.

"Someone sold you a car with actual working spy weapons? Oil slicks and machine guns? Missiles?"

"There aren't any missiles," Fallon replied, sounding just a little rueful. "And the machine guns were just props. I had to switch those out, but believe me, I wouldn't have paid what I did for this car unless the gadgets were functional. Never would have dreamed I'd actually get to use them."

"You just dumped oil all over a Swiss highway, and all you can think is 'dreams come true?'" Even as she said it, she remembered that she was up to her neck in this mess because of Fallon's reckless—almost sociopathic—disregard for consequences.

"You said it yourself. My toys are trying to kill us. Well, I just used one of my toys to save us. And I *am* letting you drive."

Carter had no argument for either point. "Just don't use the oil slick again if you can help it."

"Couldn't even if I wanted to. It's a one-shot deal. Smoke screen and oil slick are gone, but we still have road spikes, tire-shredder hubcaps, and of course the machine guns. Oh, and don't worry about the ejection seat. That was never functional."

"Pity," she muttered, entertaining a fantasy of pushing a button and shooting Fallon through the roof. She shook her head to clear the image. "If we can't get back into Tomorrowland, we may need to come up with some alternatives. What would it take to build a new transmitter?"

"Well, the Roswell Fragment is the critical component. Aside from that, any large radio telescope with a 10 gigahertz frequency transmitter should suffice." Fallon looked back at Tanaka, as if for confirmation. "There's at least a dozen of them in Europe. I think the closest one is in France."

"Finding the right antenna isn't the problem," Tanaka said. "It's time. We're—"

"Look out!"

Carter had been watching the road the whole time but saw nothing to warrant Fallon's cry of alarm. Unsure of where to look for the threat, she chose the only route that she knew was clear—straight ahead—and floored the gas pedal again.

The Aston Martin shot forward again. As they raced ahead, she spied movement in the mirrors—not a car, but something else. A flying something.

"It's a Stork," Fallon sputtered, anger in his tone for the first time since the nightmare began. He swore, punching the dashboard. "Bastards. They hacked the Storks."

The Storks, Carter recalled, were Fallon's robot delivery drones, the source of the fortune that had made everything else possible.

Robots, self-driving cars, and now delivery drones, she thought. *This is how the robot apocalypse begins.*

The drone—a hybrid construct of airfoils and helicopter rotors about the size of a bicycle turned on its side—appeared in the mirror, falling further and further behind with each passing second. Advanced technology or not, the Storks didn't have the power to keep up with the Aston Martin.

There was a flash of movement in front of them, and before Carter could react, another Stork slammed into the windshield. The steering wheel spun through her fingers—not a robot seizing control of the car, but simply momentum and acceleration. Then the world turned upside down.

CHARIOT

FIFTEEN

Astana, Kazakhstan

Three hours, **Pierce** thought. *I'm gone for three hours, and the whole world goes to hell.*

He was still trying to make sense of what Dourado had told him. She had been a little frantic, no doubt about that, but the things she was describing taxed his comprehension.

Global earthquakes? The sun stopped in its tracks? A 13,000 year old alien satellite? Robots? And worst of all, Felice Carter in the thick of it, all alone.

He glanced over at Lazarus, seated across the aisle of their chartered plane. The big man, now wearing a T-shirt and sweatpants purchased from a gift shop, had recovered from his wounds, but even though his face was stony and unreadable, Pierce knew he was seething inside. He was angry at a perceived failure to protect the woman he loved.

That was Lazarus's curse. He believed it was his responsibility to save everyone.

Pierce understood. He felt just as helpless and angry.

The elation and relief they had experienced after escaping from the caves under Arkaim had started to evaporate during the mad dash across the border of Kazakhstan, when Dourado failed to pick up the phone. Pierce's mood had diminished a little more with each successive attempt, but it had not occurred to him that something might be wrong in Rome, or that the source of the problem would turn out to be a threat of global proportions.

He was still having trouble wrapping his head around that.

Worse, Dourado had lost contact with Carter. At last report, Carter, along with tech billionaire Marcus Fallon and a physicist named Ishiro Tanaka, were being chased by an army of actual killer robots intent on preventing them from shutting down the errant Black Knight satellite. Pierce was less clear on the details, but that was some kind of massive electromagnetic mirror, diverting both the sun's light and heat energy, and its gravitational influence. The threat was difficult to fathom, but the greater mystery—the identity of the enemy who seemed so intent on preventing Fallon from correcting his mistake—was an even more troubling mystery.

The earthquakes had played havoc with international air traffic control. The skies were being kept clear for relief flights, though Pierce had been assured the restrictions would soon be lifted. Every second they spent stuck on the ground just made him more helpless, but that was nothing compared to what Lazarus was feeling.

Pierce stared at his phone, wondering if he should call Dourado again, to check if there was any word from Carter. He knew it would be a futile gesture, though. Dourado would call the instant she knew something. Worrying wasn't going to accomplish anything.

"I think this is all connected," Fiona said, breaking the long silence.

Pierce looked over and saw the young woman staring at the metal orb they had recovered from beneath Arkaim. "It sounds like the Black Knight and this Roswell memory metal are made from the same stuff as that sphere. But what happened had nothing to do with you finding it."

"I'm not so sure about that. But that's not what I mean."

Before Pierce could ask her to elaborate on the first statement, Gallo addressed the second. "Your vision. Raven stealing the light."

Fiona nodded. "You were wondering why I dreamed that particular story. Maybe the sphere was communicating with the other pieces of memory metal. Maybe *it* knew what was happening. Or was warning me about what might happen."

"Like a prophecy?" Pierce felt about prophecies much the same way he did about magic and miracles. Sure, they happened sometimes, but there was a rational explanation. There had to be.

"No," Gallo said, with unexpected certainty. "It was an explanation. This has happened before."

Fiona was as surprised as Pierce. "What do you mean?"

"According to Cintia, the Black Knight is at least 13,000 years old. Its arrival coincides with the dawn of civilization—"

"Well, that depends on your definition of civilization."

She ignored him. "Nearly every civilization on Earth practiced some form of Sun worship. The Sun God was almost always the most important deity to the ancients. And there's always a story like this. A god stealing the sun or losing control of it somehow. When Fiona told us about Raven, I thought of the Phaethon story."

"Phaethon, the son of Apollo?" Fiona asked.

Gallo nodded. "Technically, it was Helios, not Apollo. Phaethon begged Helios for a chance to drive the sun chariot. That's the part that reminded me of the Raven story."

"But Phaethon lost control of the sun chariot and would have burned up the Earth if Zeus hadn't killed him with a thunderbolt. That's almost the opposite of what happened with Raven."

"It is," Gallo said. "But what if the stories are describing the same event? An actual solar crisis, but from different global perspectives?"

Pierce shook his head. "All these myths came out of stories intended to explain the changing of the seasons and cosmic events, like eclipses, to primitive people who didn't understand how the universe worked."

"That's the accepted version, of course, but we both know better, George. Those ancient civilizations *did* understand. They weren't primitives. They mapped the stars. Built observatories. They knew the Earth was round, no matter what they tell kids in school. They were too sophisticated to need reassurance about the cycle of the seasons or eclipses. Those stories are referencing a universal event. Just like the flood myths."

Pierce let that dubious comparison slide. "Let's say you're right. Why does it matter?"

"Because if this has happened before, then it means there's a way to shut it down."

"Felice is already working on that."

Gallo wagged her head sideways in a gesture of polite disagreement. "This Fallon fellow is a child playing with matches. We need a fire extinguisher."

"Is that what this is?" Fiona held up the orb.

Gallo glanced at Pierce. "George, what do you think?"

Pierce rubbed his chin. "I think we can safely say that it might be part of the solution, but that sphere hasn't seen the light of day—if you'll pardon the pun—in at least five thousand years. Maybe a lot longer. Maybe not since the time of the Originators."

"What happened to them?" Fiona asked. "Who were they? Aliens?"

"Gods," Gallo murmured.

"Quite possibly the inspiration for them," Pierce admitted.

"In Greek mythology," Gallo continued, "the gods were not the embodiment of the forces they represented, but rather masters of those forces. Helios wasn't the sun personified, but the master of the sun, which took the form of a chariot he drove across the sky. The sun chariot is ubiquitous in Indo-European mythology. The Norse. The Celts. It's in the Rig Veda. There's even mention of a divine chariot in the Bible."

"I'm familiar with the stories," Pierce said. "UFO enthusiasts think those are all primitive descriptions of alien spaceships."

"What if they are? What if the sun chariot is an Originator spaceship? Maybe the Black Knight is what Fallon thinks it is, an alien device for harnessing and redirecting the sun's energy. And the sun chariot is the vehicle used for going back and forth to turn it on. That's what we need to do to fix this. Fly up to the Black Knight and shut it down."

"Fly up? In an ancient alien spacecraft?" Pierce sighed. It was outlandish, but outlandish was par for the Herculean Society's course. "Assuming it's possible, in the story, Phaethon lost control of the chariot and nearly destroyed the Earth." He looked at Fiona. "Raven was scorched by the sun. That's why his feathers are black. Approaching it could make things worse."

Gallo pointed to the orb. "It's alien technology. Has to be. And it responds to Fiona. To the Mother Tongue. There aren't a lot of other options."

George gave a nod. She was right about that. "But we'll have to find the chariot first."

"And Felice." Lazarus spoke quietly but his tone was as hard as a diamond.

Pierce nodded. "We know Fallon's experiments caused this. That's where we have to focus our efforts. But Erik, you go after Felice."

"You're sure?" Lazarus looked surprised. He'd overcome the PTSD caused by drowning hundreds of times in a row while clawing his way out of a lake. He was back to full fighting strength now, physically and mentally, and for him, the mission always came first. But even a seasoned fighter like Lazarus could be undone by worry for a loved one. For him to bring his full force to bear, he first had to find Felice, whose presence and expertise would also be beneficial.

"I'm sure," Pierce said. "Go find her, and when you're done you can *both* help us save the world."

SIXTEEN

Gallo felt a flush of guilt. "I didn't mean..."

Pierce waved her off. "Don't worry about it. We'd just be in his way." He took out his phone and tapped the screen twice, once to place the call, and once more to put the phone on speaker.

Dourado picked up on the first ring. "Still no word," she said.

"About our flight, or from Felice?"

"Take your pick."

"Doesn't matter. Change of plans. Erik is going to Geneva to help Felice. If he asks, and he probably won't, give him whatever help he needs with travel arrangements."

"Just Erik? What about the rest of you?"

Pierce looked over at Gallo. "Gus, where do we start?"

Gallo was at a loss, feeling put on the spot, but Fiona jumped in. "Cintia, we need to find the chariot of Helios, the Sun god."

"Oh. Let me Google it."

Gallo wasn't sure if Dourado was joking or not, but the brief exchange helped her organize her thoughts. "What we're looking for is a real world connection to Helios. Temples. Specific locations mentioned in the myth that correspond to real locations. I'd look it up myself..."

"I understand." There was a slight pause. "Okay, the most significant ancient site associated with the worship of Helios is the island of Rhodes, just south of Turkey."

"Of course," Gallo murmured. "The Colossus."

"The Colossus of Rhodes, one of the Seven Wonders of the Ancient World, was dedicated to Helios. There's a whole file on it in the Herculean archives."

"We can save that for another day," Pierce said.

"The Dorians brought Helios worship to Rhodes, probably from Corinth on the Greek mainland. There was a small temple to Helios there, but he was never very important to the Greeks. The only other place associated with Helios is Thrinakia."

Gallo nodded. "From the Odyssey. After escaping Scylla and Charybdis, Odysseus landed on the island of Thrinakia, where Helios's daughter Lampetia tended his sacred cattle and sheep. Odysseus was warned to avoid the island, and especially the herds, but his men were hungry and killed some of the cattle. Helios demanded retribution. He threatened to stop the sun from shining on the Earth if the mortals weren't punished, so Zeus sent a thunderbolt to destroy them. Odysseus survived but was exiled to Ogygia, the island of Calypso, for seven more years."

"Stop the sun from shining," Pierce mused. "Sounds like he was threatening to cause a solar event."

"Why does a Sun God need sacred cows?" Fiona asked, shaking her head. "And people think Native American stories are weird."

Gallo gave her a thoughtful look. "That's an excellent question."

"It is?"

"If experience has taught us anything, it's that, while there is more than a little truth in the old myths, we have to be careful about taking everything at face value."

"Right. Chariot equals spaceship." Fiona shrugged. "And sacred cows equal what?"

She meant it as a joke, but as she said it, her eyes got a faraway look. "A chariot is pulled by horses...a power source. There's a logic to the symbolism.

"Helios had cattle and sheep, right? Cattle for meat, sheep for wool. If we accept that Helios was an alien...an Originator...maybe he was the guy in charge of solar power. What would he need that would correspond to meat and..." She looked down at the orb again, squeezing the springy metal. "Wool?"

"I'll be damned," Pierce muttered. "I think you're onto something. I'll bet if we take that thing to Thrinakia, you'll be able to use it like a compass to find the chariot."

"Unfortunately," Gallo said, "like so many other locations from the Odyssey and the Heraklion, we don't know where it was, or even *if* it was. Ancient geographers thought it might have been Sicily, or Malta. But they were just guessing, and obviously they had no idea that there was a world beyond the Pillars of Hercules."

Pierce nodded. "Cintia..."

"Let me guess," Dourado said. "You need me to cross reference all locations in the Odyssey with actual known locations and create a computer simulation of the actual route Odysseus traveled. Already on it."

"Actually I... You know what, never mind. I like your idea better."

"According to Homer, Odysseus and his crew arrived at Thrinakia after passing Scylla, a six-headed sea monster, and Charybdis, a giant whirlpool that's often associated with the Strait of Messina, between Italy and Sicily. That's the main reason why Sicily is often identified as Thrinakia. Before that, they were on the island of Circe, the sorceress—also a daughter of Helios. Circe told Odysseus that there were two routes back to his home, the Kingdom of Ithaca. The route he chose took him to Thrinakia, but the other route would have taken him through the Wandering Rocks, the same rocks that almost destroyed the Argo. Traditionally, the Wandering Rocks are associated with the Bosporus Strait, the passage between the Black Sea and the Sea of Marmara. So if Odysseus had to pass through the Wandering Rocks to get back home, that would put Circe's island in the Black Sea. Nowhere near Sicily."

"Not to mention the fact that the Bosporus is the only water route out of the Black Sea," Pierce put in. "There isn't another, so Circe couldn't have offered Odysseus a choice."

Gallo shook her head. "There's no way to make the geography described in the Odyssey fit the map unless we reject all our preconceptions about where Odysseus, or the person who inspired him, actually traveled."

"Too bad Alexander's not around anymore," Pierce muttered. "He'd probably know exactly where it is."

Alexander Diotrephes, was one of many names used by the immortal explorer who had inspired the legend of the demigod Herakles, or as the Romans called him, Hercules. Alexander—Hercules—had not actually been the son of the god Zeus, but in a way, he had descended from the heavens, or more precisely, from an alternate dimension. After an extended stay on Earth—several thousand years of walking among humans—he had recently returned home. He had formed the Herculean Society to preserve his legendary legacy and to protect humankind from dangerous truths about the universe. Before leaving he had entrusted its care to Fiona's father, Jack Sigler. He had, in turn, appointed his good friend George Pierce to oversee day-to-day operations under the auspices of the Cerberus Group.

While many of the stories about Hercules were exaggerations, the product of multiple retellings over the course of the centuries, there was more than a grain of truth in all of them, a fact they had discovered a few months earlier when retracing the legendary Labors of Hercules. Gallo had been astonished by the revelation that Hercules's travels had taken him well beyond the limits of the then-known world.

Inspiration hit like a lightning bolt. "He did know!" She sat up a little straighter. "It's in the *Heracleia*. Look in the Cerberus archives, Cintia. You should find scans of it."

The *Heracleia* was an epic poem about Hercules, believed to have been written by Homer—the very same poet to whom the Odyssey was attributed. There was only one physical copy of the poem, written on leaves of papyrus, and locked away in a hermetically sealed vault at Cerberus headquarters in Rome, but there was also a virtual version Gallo had studied.

"Okay, I've got the scans," Dourado said. "But it's all in Greek."

Gallo had done a full translation of the poem and knew that her notes were somewhere at Cerberus HQ, but there was no time to send Dourado on a scavenger hunt. "Send me the files. I know what to look for."

She picked up the phone and began scrolling through the images. It was like picking up a treasured book from childhood. The more she read, the more she remembered of her initial translation.

"Here," she announced after almost twenty minutes of reading. "In this passage, Herakles is talking about an encounter with a goddess 'whom the Egyptians call Hecate.' She tried to seduce him to steal the secret of his long life, and when that didn't work, she tried to trick him into stealing one of the undying beasts who graze 'upon the slopes of the mountain where no mortal dares to go, across the sea in the land of the sun's rising.'"

Pierce nodded. "Okay, that does sound familiar. Hecate is the goddess of sorcery and witchcraft. That could be another name for Circe. Undying beasts could be the cattle of Helios and 'the land of the sun's rising' could be describing Thrinakia."

Gallo nodded. "Hecate is Greek, not Egyptian, but the Egyptians *did* worship a goddess named Heqet, a fertility goddess and a symbol of the Nile during flood season."

"Now you're losing me."

"This makes sense, George. Cows were sacred animals in Egypt long before there was any kind of civilization in the Greek isles. In Egyptian mythology, the symbol of the goddess Hathor was the horns of a cow holding the sun. Hathor was either the daughter, wife, mother, or female personification of Ra, the sun god.

"Homer was guilty of getting things mixed up, especially when it came to geography. He probably did it intentionally. But maybe he let something slip here when he mentioned the Egyptians. Maybe the land of Circe is actually somewhere along the Nile, in Egypt. Thrinakia, the land of the sun's rising, where the sacred cattle are kept, lies across the sea, to the east."

"Which is it? From Egypt, you have to go north to get to the sea, not east."

"The Mediterranean is north," Gallo said with a grin. "But the Red Sea is due east."

Pierce rubbed his chin. "The Red Sea, huh?"

"It's not as crazy as it sounds. The Egyptians dug canals connecting the Nile to the Red Sea going back as far as the nineteenth century BCE. Odysseus would have known about that route. According to the poem, after the Trojan War, Odysseus and his men raided a city called Ismaros, in the land of the Cicones. Now supposedly, that's one of the fixed geographical points, but remember that the events described in these poems took place before the Greek Dark Ages. A lot of places all around the Mediterranean took their names from locations mentioned in the stories, rather than the other way around. So the people that Homer calls Cicones could be almost anyone."

"Sort of like the way Native Americans are called Indians," Fiona said. "Because Columbus thought he had landed in India."

Gallo nodded. "Sort of like that. Some historians have speculated that the city Odysseus called Ismaros was actually Lothal, on the Indian peninsula. It was one of the richest port cities in the ancient world. Odysseus almost certainly would have known about it and he might have considered it a worthwhile prize, especially after the other kings divided up the wealth of Troy.

"After the raid on Ismaros, the poem says he was blown off course and spent the next ten years trying to find his way back home, which when you think about it, doesn't make a lot of sense, if he's in the Mediterranean or the Black Sea."

"Okay," Pierce said. "For argument's sake, let's say you're right. The land of Circe, a.k.a. Heqet, is Egypt. Where's Thrinakia?"

"It would also have to be a place with very little flora or fauna; otherwise, Odysseus's men would not have had to kill Helios's cattle. So a desert, and there's a lot of desert on the eastern shore of the Red Sea. Thrinakia is also described as a triangular island. In fact, the word translates as 'three corners.' There are some small islands in the Red Sea, but nothing with a mountain. However, a primitive sailor might not be able to distinguish a small peninsula from a large island."

"Sounds as if you've already got a place in mind."

"I do. A triangle of land, mostly desert, with a mountain that's considered sacred even today. Thrinakia is the Sinai Peninsula."

SEVENTEEN

Geneva, Switzerland

It took a few seconds for Carter to realize that the car had stopped rolling, and another few for her to recognize that she was upright.

Unhurt? That was debatable.

She looked over and saw Fallon, dazed but also uninjured.

"Hey!" she said. "Still with me?"

He mumbled something incoherent.

She tried the door, but it was jammed shut, so she wriggled through the hole where the side window had been. The Aston Martin had come to rest on a grassy patch alongside the road. A crowd of onlookers had gathered, but no one approached. Carter heard sirens in the distance, then a different noise, a high-pitched whine, growing louder.

It was another Stork drone, flying over the road, heading right for them.

She stuck her head inside the car. "Come on. We need to go."

"Go?" Tanaka asked, as he crawled from the back seat, still clutching his tablet computer. "Go where?"

"Does it matter?" She pointed to the tablet. "Leave that."

He held it closer, as if fearful that she might try to take it away from him. "I need it to access the satellite."

"The hacker is using it to track us." She glanced up at the incoming drone. It wasn't moving very fast, but it would be on them in a few seconds. "That's the only reason he didn't shut you out completely. No electronics." She tossed her phone aside. "Either leave it behind or stay here with it."

"She's right, Ishiro." Fallon had extricated himself on the opposite side and was circling around the wreck. "We'll get a clean computer. Leave it."

Tanaka scowled, but threw the tablet through the open window, into the car, without further protest.

Carter spun on her heel—a mistake, as the abrupt movement sent a throb of pain through her upper torso—and then she ran for the tree line. Fallon and Tanaka followed close behind. As expected, the drone appeared to be homing in on the car or something in it, and just before the three fleeing figures ducked into the woods, the flying robot slammed into the car behind them.

The trees marked the boundary of an urban park, with paths and trails, allowing them to slow to a more discreet walking pace. Carter recognized the place as the Conservatory and Botanical Gardens of Geneva, a repository of rare plant species from all over the world. It was the sort of place in which she might have lost herself under better circumstances, both as a biologist and as a tourist. Unfortunately, there was no time to enjoy the beautiful sur-roundings. While there was no sign of further pursuit from rogue machines, Carter knew it was only a matter of time before the local authorities started looking for the trio who had fled the accident's scene. No doubt at least a few of the witnesses had captured their likenesses on video.

"We need to keep moving," she said.

"And go where?" Fallon shot back.

"You mentioned a radio telescope in France. If we could get there, we could build a new transmitter and shut the Black Knight down, right?"

Tanaka shook his head. "We may have only a few hours before another solar event begins. I don't see how we could get there in time."

"It might as well be on the moon," Fallon added. "Tomorrowland is still our best chance. We need to regain control of the network."

Carter sighed. "All right. I might be able to help with that."

She found a pay phone outside the small restaurant at the center of the park, and placed a collect call to Cerberus Group headquarters.

A few seconds later, she heard Dourado's overjoyed voice. "Thank God, you're safe."

"I'm not sure 'safe' is the right word."

"Just hang on. Erik is on his way to meet you."

"Erik?" Carter's heart skipped a beat. "You've heard from them?"

As Dourado brought her up to date, Carter felt some of her anxiety about the situation slipping away. She wasn't alone anymore. Her friends were safe, and Lazarus was on his way to help her, while the rest of the team was headed to the Sinai Peninsula.

She wasn't sure what to make of their working theory about the sun chariot of Helios. That it sounded crazy didn't faze her. She had seen a lot of crazy things, particularly since coming to work for the Cerberus Group. As she saw it, the real problem was time. Finding the sun chariot, if it still existed at all, might take days. Weeks, even. If Tanaka was right, they might have only hours.

"Erik just left Istanbul," Dourado went on. "He should be there soon. I'll arrange a safe house and hire a car to pick you up."

"Cintia, that's great, but right now, there's not a whole lot Erik can do to help." She hated saying it, but it was true. There wasn't anyone she'd rather have by her side against a human foe, or even a mutant hybrid monster, but his physical strength wouldn't be much use against robots and hijacked computer networks.

"What do you need?"

"I'm glad you asked." Carter grimaced, feeling even worse about what she was about to say next. "How would you like to meet your hero?"

EIGHTEEN

Under normal circumstances, leaving the relative shelter of the secret Cerberus Headquarters facility beneath Castel Sant'Angelo would have been almost unthinkable for Dourado. For as long as she could remember, she hated being outdoors, exposed to a world so big that she felt like she might get sucked away into space if she stood too long under the open sky. And then there were all the people, each one a potential predator, just waiting for a chance to pounce on her—figuratively, but maybe literally, too.

People couldn't be trusted. The world was too big, and she was so small, so insignificant. That was why she preferred the digital world. In the virtual landscape of cyberspace, she was a goddess. That she was able to even think about venturing outside was a testimony to how far she had come since her panic-stricken youth in Belem, Brazil. Indeed, under normal circumstances, her value to the Cerberus Group would only have been diminished by venturing out into the open world, away from the hardware that imbued her with such god-like omniscience.

These were not normal circumstances, though, and that made the experience a little more tolerable.

Getting through the airport was miserable, but probably no more so for her than for everyone else. The terminal was crowded with people who had seen their scheduled flights delayed due to the disruption in air traffic caused by the global earthquake. But at least she was indoors. Her flamingo-pink hair and facial piercings attracted the attention of her queue-mates, some giving her judgmental frowns, but more offering nods and smiles of approval.

The short flight to Geneva wasn't as bad as she thought it would be. The plane's cramped interior made her feel safe, like a comforting hug, which helped keep her mind off the fact that she was hurtling through thin air five miles above the surface of the Earth. Yet, for all her coping skills, what made the trip endurable was the knowledge that she was on her way to meet Marcus Fallon.

She had not been exaggerating when she called him a hero of hers. If anything, she had downplayed her feelings about him. Fallon was the personification of the future she had dreamed of all her life. Like no one else in the field of robotics, he had bridged the gulf between the limitations of the physical world and the limitless possibilities of cyberspace.

What Fallon did was similar to what Fiona could do with the Mother Tongue. She could create golems out of clay and loose earth and then bring them to life with an ancient language to do her bidding. He created robots out of metal and plastic and brought them to life with binary machine language to do his. The big difference was that, while the Mother Tongue was nearly extinct, computer code was a language that anyone could learn and which Dourado already spoke fluently. And now she was on her way to use that knowledge to help the man she idolized regain control of his wayward creations. She felt like a street kid tapped to play in the World Cup final match.

As she made her way through the Swiss airport, though, she felt a little of the old familiar panic setting in. As excited as she was at the prospect of helping Fallon, she would still have to brave the world outside.

A large figure stepped in front of her and even though the rendezvous had been pre-arranged before she left Rome, Dourado nearly jumped out of her skin.

"Erik," she gasped.

That was all she could say for a few seconds, but Lazarus didn't seem to notice. "The pink hair was a good idea. Hi-vis. Easy to spot."

She wasn't sure if that was his attempt at humor. Probably not. He didn't strike her as the sort of person to crack jokes, though in truth, she did not know him very well. Their orbits rarely crossed.

Joke or not, he made no further comment as he led her outside to the stop for the shuttle that would take them to the rental car pick-up lot, and that was fine with her.

Thirty minutes later, the ordeal ended with their arrival at the safe house where Carter, Fallon, and Tanaka had gone following the escape from Tomorrowland. The initial meeting with Fallon was a blur, and she was pretty sure she had embarrassed herself by fawning over him, but a few minutes later she was back in her environment, using her laptop to remotely probe the security of the Space Tomorrow mainframe and intranet.

Carter greeted the news of her intent warily. "Won't the hacker be able to track us here?"

"He can try, but I'm spoofing our location."

With Fallon's help, she was able to establish off-site administrator privileges, after which it was a simple matter to begin searching for the Trojan horse that had allowed the unknown hacker to hijack Fallon's robots and turn them against him. But after employing every anti-virus measure and security subroutine in her arsenal, along with a few that Fallon suggested, she could find no evidence of the incursion.

"What does that mean?" Carter asked.

"It means that the hacker covered his tracks very well," Fallon said

Dourado thought that was oversimplifying it. "It's got to be someone already on the inside. Someone with full access to the network."

Fallon shook his head. "No. That's a very short list, and everyone on it is above suspicion." He glanced at Tanaka and received a nod of confirmation. "We're looking for someone who's just that good. When we find him, I may have to offer him a job."

"A job," Carter murmured, as if thinking aloud. She fixed her gaze on Dourado. "Someone with the skill to do this could pretty much have anything he wanted, right? Why do this?"

Fallon waved a dismissive hand. "He's just trying to make a statement."

"You mean like, 'I can destroy the world if I want to?' That's quite a statement."

"Hackers are ego-driven creatures, prone to delusions of godhood."

Dourado could not disagree with the sentiment. "If that's all this is, then the incursion is probably over. He's made his point. Maybe he'll try to blackmail you at some point in the future. But if it's something more, he might be waiting for us to make the next move."

"Challenge accepted." Fallon rubbed his hands together in a show of eagerness. He turned to Dourado. "What do you say? Ready to beat him at his own game? When he pops his head up again, we'll be waiting with a sledgehammer."

As excited as she was at the thought of testing her skills against the unknown enemy, Dourado also felt a twinge of apprehension. If the hacker was that good, the sledgehammer might come down on her head. Up to this point, all she had done was look in the windows, so to speak. Once she started giving remote commands to the network, the hacker would be alerted to her presence, and he wouldn't be fooled by her spoofed location. "Maybe we should be ready to move," she said. "Just in case."

Carter laid a hand on her shoulder in what seemed to be a gesture of encouragement.

Dourado accessed the robotics interface, which allowed her to interact with all the autonomous machines at Tomorrowland, and began the two-step process of learning how the system was structured, and testing the robots to see if they would respond to her commands. As before, there seemed to be almost no evidence of the cyber-attack. The robots were functioning normally, doing their job without any active oversight. Maintenance robots had already begun repairs on the two construction-bots that had been damaged.

"The storm has passed," Fallon declared. "I'll still have to figure out how he cracked my security, but it's safe to go back in."

"Safe?" Lazarus, who had, after an understated reunion with Carter, remained in the background, now broke his silence. "It's an ambush. He wants you to go back. You've got something he wants."

Carter took a swatch of metallic fabric from her pocket. "You mean this?"

Lazarus nodded. "This wasn't just a data breach. He has plans for that antenna array and the Black Knight. He needs you to get it working again. That's what he's waiting for. He'll wait until you do that to make his move."

"I'm not sure we have a choice in the matter," Tanaka countered. "Like it or not, that antenna array is the only way to eliminate the threat of another solar event."

"Not the only way," Dourado countered. "There's the sun chariot."

Fallon raised an eyebrow. "Dr. Carter told me about your friends' excursion to the Sinai. I'll admit, it's intriguing. It would go a long way toward explaining where the Black Knight came from. But we're facing a time crunch here. And I believe in cleaning up my own messes. Technology caused this problem, and technology can fix it."

Lazarus did not back down. "You aren't in control of the technology. What's to stop the hacker from turning it against you again? Self-driving cars, drones. There's a lot of stuff out there with your hardware that could be turned into weapons. If we go in there, we might make the situation a lot worse." He shook his head. "We have to let Pierce handle this."

Tanaka gestured to the computer. "May I use that for a moment?"

Dourado regarded him warily. She didn't like people using her hardware, messing with her settings, downloading God-only-knew what kind of crap off the Internet. "Why?"

"If I can access our surveillance satellite, I should be able to determine how much time we have before another event."

"I guess that's a good reason." She got up from her chair to make room for him, but stayed close, looking over his shoulder as he entered a web address into the browser. A moment later, a three-dimensional map of the Earth appeared, encircled by an orbital tracking line that ran more or less from pole to pole.

Dourado had known about the Black Knight satellite long before she overheard Fallon telling Carter about it. She knew that the authorities had dismissed it as a modern legend, cobbled together from assorted radio anomalies, questionable eyewitness reports, and erroneous scientific interpretations, but she also knew that was exactly what they *would* say to keep the truth from getting out. Just like with HAARP.

Tanaka stared at the screen for only a few seconds before making a dire announcement. "It's worse than I feared. The Black Knight will be fully deployed by 1800 UTC."

Carter shot a glance at her watch. "Eight o'clock local. Forty minutes, give or take. But at least it's after sunset."

The physicist shook his head. "No, you don't understand. The satellite is currently moving above the Western hemisphere. It's daytime there."

Dourado knew what that would mean. A solar pause above the Americas would trigger another series of tidal earthquakes along the geologically fragile Ring of Fire. California would be devastated. Tsunamis and abnormally high tides would inundate coastal areas, where most of the population was already concentrated. And if it continued longer than a few minutes... If it went on for hours or days...

"That's it, then," Fallon said with grim finality. "We can't wait for your friends to pull a rabbit out of the hat. We need to go back to Tomorrowland. Right now, if not sooner."

"Forty minutes," Carter murmured. "Cintia, can you reach George?"

"I can try." She tapped Tanaka on the shoulder, and when he had vacated the chair, she sat down in front of the computer again and initiated a call to Pierce's satellite phone. It took several seconds for her to establish a connection, but instead of Pierce's voice, the only sound to issue from the speakers was a burst of static, and then silence as the call dropped. Dourado turned to Carter. "I think it's up to you."

Carter turned to Lazarus. Dourado couldn't read the big man's impassive expression, but Carter seemed to draw strength from him. She faced Fallon. "You think you can shut it down?"

"If I can't, no one can." He grimaced, perhaps realizing it was the wrong thing to say. "Yes. We can do it."

"Cintia, you can deal with the hacker? Keep him off our backs long enough to do this?"

"I'll do my best."

"I guess that's all any of us can do," Carter said with sigh. "All right, let's load up. We're going to Tomorrowland."

NINETEEN

Mount Sinai, Egypt

Pierce stared at his phone in frustration. "Call ended?" he grumbled. "Call didn't even start."

"Was that Cintia?" Gallo asked. She had to shout to be heard over the throaty roar of the helicopter's engine. "What did she say?"

"Don't know. The call dropped."

"I hope everything's okay."

Me too, Pierce thought. Dourado had called earlier to let him know about her decision to leave Cerberus Headquarters to join Carter and Lazarus in Geneva. Her expertise would give them an edge in dealing with the situation there and perhaps unmask the enemy that now seemed intent on turning the ancient Black Knight satellite into a weapon of mass destruction. Her decision surprised Pierce—she wasn't exaggerating her agoraphobia—but he had given her the go-ahead. Dourado was a lot tougher than she believed. Now he wondered if she was regretting the decision.

"If it's important, she'll try again," he shouted. "Probably just checking up on us."

They had come a long way in just a few short hours, from Kazakh-stan to Istanbul, and then on to Sharm El-Sheikh on the tip of the Sinai Peninsula, where Pierce had used his UNESCO credentials to wrangle a military helicopter flight to Saint Catherine's Monastery—a World Heritage Site—on the slopes of Mount Sinai.

This was not Pierce's first visit to Egypt, but the world had changed since his last visit. The rising influence of the Muslim Brotherhood in Egypt and of ISIS on the world stage had not only brought the specter of terrorism to the reliably tourist-friendly Arab nation, but also a threat to the ancient monuments for which the nation was most famous. Islamic militants had called for the destruction of the pyramids and the Sphinx, which they condemned as temples to false gods. Pierce did not consider it to be an idle threat. A similar declaration made by the Taliban government in Afghanistan had resulted in the destruction of the fifteen-hundred-year-old Bamiyan Buddha statues in 2001, and more recently, ISIS fighters had destroyed ancient Roman temples in Palmyra, Syria. Pierce was a little apprehensive about traveling to Egypt, especially without Lazarus present to advise him on matters of security, but recent attacks in Paris and Brussels had demonstrated that nowhere was truly safe. And right now, the looming solar crisis trumped all other considerations.

Saint Catherine's—its official name was 'Sacred Monastery of the God-Trodden Mount Sinai'—built in the sixth century, was one of the oldest Christian monasteries in existence. It housed the world's oldest continually operating library, which contained, among its many other treasures, the Syriac Sinaiticus, a fourth century copy of the Gospels—the oldest copy in existence. Of course, the significance of Mount Sinai to all three of the world's major monotheistic faiths went back much further.

According to the Bible, Mount Sinai was the place where God had first called Moses to lead the Israelites out of Egypt, and then later presented him with the Ten Commandments. Whether this particular mountain was the same mountain recorded in the Biblical account was a matter of some debate, though. There were at least thirteen other sites believed by Biblical scholars to be the *actual* site of the divine encounter.

Pierce had been drawn to archaeology after watching the movie *Raiders of the Lost Ark* as a young boy. From the moment he walked out of the theater, he had dreamed of searching for the lost Ark of the Covenant—an artifact straight out of the Bible—just like his hero Indiana Jones. Now that he was the caretaker of the Herculean Society, he found himself crossing paths with those larger than life stories in ways that would make Indiana Jones jealous of *him*.

The helicopter landed just beyond a large garden, a few hundred yards from the monastery's fortress-like walls, which sat at the base of the mountain, as if guarding the approach. Pierce couldn't make out many details. They had seen a few scattered lights in the nearby tourist village as they made their approach, but the monastery appeared to be in a total blackout. Pierce was afraid that it might be deserted, but as the helicopter's rotor blades began to wind down, a tiny light appeared in front of the monastery gates. It began moving down the path toward them.

"Here comes the welcoming committee," Pierce said.

He threw open the side door and stepped out into the brisk night air as the light drew closer. He could now see that it was a handheld electric lantern, and the hand that held it protruded from the voluminous black sleeve of an *exorasson*—the robe worn by Orthodox monks. Pierce couldn't quite distinguish the monk's face, but the ambient glow from the lantern did reveal a prodigious beard spilling half-way down the man's chest.

Pierce stuck out his hand. "Are you Father Justin? I'm Dr. George Pierce, from the World Heritage Committee. We spoke on the phone."

"Yes." The man held the lantern higher and gave a slight bow.

Pierce sensed the monk wasn't going to accept the offered hand, so he drew it back before things got awkward. "Sorry about the late hour, but as you can imagine, we've got our work cut out for us." When the man didn't reply, Pierce added, "You know, because of the earthquakes. Lots of damage to survey."

"Please don't think us ungrateful." Father Justin's English was perfect, without any trace of an accent. But there was more than a trace of irritation. "Surely there are others whose need is greater than ours. Would not your time and resources be better spent helping those who have lost everything?"

Pierce spread his hands in a show of helplessness. "That may be true, but I'm a cultural preservation expert, not a rescue worker. This is what I do, and I take it very seriously."

"As do we. For seventeen centuries we have tended to this holy place. This is not the first time an earthquake has shaken our walls. We will repair the damage as we always have. That is what *we* do."

Pierce managed a diplomatic smile. He was receiving the message— *We don't want you here*—loud and clear, but he had no intention of slinking away. He was prepared to wave the UN flag in the monk's face all night if he had to. He was pretty sure that Father Justin wasn't going to call and check his bona fides like Zdanovich, the Russian administrator at Arkaim. Even if he did, St. Catherine's Monastery *was* a World Heritage Site, and Pierce, as an inspector-at-large, was justified in paying the place a visit, even if he wasn't being honest about his motive.

"We just need to look around for a little while, take a few pictures for our report, and then we'll be out of your hair. We'll be very discreet. You won't even know we're here."

Father Justin wasn't quite ready to throw in the towel. "It may take several hours for you to document everything. I'm afraid we can't accommodate you overnight, and I doubt that you will be able to find lodging in the village. The damage was quite extensive there as well. Perhaps it would be wiser for you to return in the morning."

"We're prepared to work through the night."

The monk gave a heavy sigh. "Very well."

"Great. Let me just grab my team."

Pierce returned to the aircraft to give Gallo and Fiona the news, and to update the pilot, a cocky young Egyptian army officer, who looked barely older than Fiona. Pierce had no idea how long the search would take. If Fiona could make the memory-metal sphere work like a dowsing rod, they might find the sun chariot in a matter of minutes. So for the moment it seemed prudent to have the aircraft standing by.

Father Justin regarded the two females with a pinched expression, but made no comment as he turned on his heel and shone the lantern toward the gates. "Follow me."

"I don't think he was expecting women," Fiona whispered.

Pierce grinned. "I don't think it's going to be a problem. Just be glad this isn't a mosque or a synagogue."

"Actually, there *is* a mosque here," Father Justin said, looking over his shoulder. "But if you knew anything of our teachings, you would know that women are greatly esteemed in the Orthodox Church."

Pierce ducked his head in embarrassment. "I didn't mean to imply—"

The monk made a sweeping gesture. "This place honors a woman, Saint Catherine of Alexandria, a child..." Here, he turned and gazed at Fiona, "About your age, I imagine, who devoted her life to studying the teachings of Christ. She condemned the Roman emperor Maxentius to his face for his cruelty, debated his wisest advisors, and won, converting many of them to Christianity, even though doing so meant instant martyrdom. Maxentius imprisoned her, tortured her, but she would not renounce her faith. More than two hundred individuals, including Valeria, the wife of Maxentius himself, came to her in prison, begging her to deny her faith. Every one of them were so moved by her words that they, too, confessed faith in Christ and were martyred. After her execution, angels brought her body here, to the Mountain of God. It is said that a healing spring flowed from the place where she was buried."

Fiona gave a wry smile. "I like her."

Justin stared back for a moment, and then nodded. "Yes. She still has that effect on people." His demeanor softened a little. "Why have you truly come here?"

Pierce exchanged a glance with Gallo, but before he could figure out his next move, Fiona took the bull by the horns. "We told you the truth. We are here because of the earthquakes."

"But not to survey the damage?"

"No. We're trying to stop any more of them from happening."

"And how do you propose to do that?" He waved again. "From here, no less?"

Fiona's smile did not falter. "With a miracle, of course."

Pierce allowed himself a tentative sigh of relief. Fiona's approach was spot-on, and despite his initial surliness, the monk seemed to be warming up to her. Pierce took a step back, nodding for her to continue.

"A miracle." Justin nodded, as if intrigued. "Are you here to pray?"

"In a manner of speaking," Fiona replied. "We know that this was a holy mountain long before the monastery was built. We're looking for something that has probably been here a lot longer."

Some of the cleric's earlier wariness returned. "You're treasure hunters."

To Pierce's dismay, Fiona did not deny the accusation. Instead, she held out her hand, displaying the sphere of memory metal she had recovered from deep under Arkaim. "We're looking for something like this."

The monk shone his light on the artifact, bending close to inspect it, then stood up straight. "I am sorry. There is nothing like that here."

Pierce sensed a curiosity in the man, a desire to know more, despite himself. He decided to take a page from Fiona's playbook. "This artifact was made by an ancient civilization called 'the Originators.' They don't appear in the historical record, but they do show up in the myths and legends of other cultures that we do know about. The ancients thought they were gods, but they didn't have any magic. Just technology."

"Gods," Justin echoed, thoughtfully.

"The Originators created a device that can harness solar energy." Pierce went on. "Unfortunately, it can also cause seismic disruptions. Earlier today, the device was used, and you have seen the results. We believe there is another device here that can stop it."

Justin spread his hands helplessly. "As I have said, there is nothing like that here."

"Please," Fiona said. "There's got to be something here. Just let us have a look around."

Justin stared at her for a few seconds, then managed a tight smile. "We are not in the habit of refusing those who come here praying for miracles."

TWENTY

Death rode to the holy mountain, not on a pale horse, but in a pair of road-weary and battle-scarred minivans. The men inside the vehicles speeding along Nuweiba Road, the highway that snaked through the lesser peaks, all the way up to the infidel church on the slopes of sacred Jabal Musa, were killers, freshly blooded after a swift surprise attack on a police checkpoint further down the mountain.

The firefight had been unavoidable. There was no hiding the fact that they were armed to the teeth. Most carried AKS-74 carbines, but their arsenal also included an RPG-7 anti-tank rocket launcher. So even though killing policemen wasn't their primary mission, it had been a necessary action. A prelude to what would soon happen when they reached the end of the road. And, from what Abdul-Ahad al-Nami could discern after listening to the subsequent conversation of his fellow passengers, their first chance to kill in the name of the Prophet.

They were all strangers, all young men like him, gathered from Egypt and all over the Arabian Peninsula, all full of zeal for the fight. At first, he was not sure that he should trust any of them. However, the more he heard, the more he knew that they were his brothers, fellow soldiers who had heard the trumpet of Israfil.

Israfil was one of the Malak—a messenger of God, an angel— who would sound the trumpet on *Yawm al-Qiyāmah*—the Day of Resurr-ection. But Israfil was also the *nom de guerre* of a senior organizer in the army of the Caliphate—the Islamic State—or at least that was how he had introduced himself to Abdul-Ahad a few months earlier, in an online forum where holy warriors gathered to indulge their passion for *jihad*. Over the ensuing weeks, Israfil had opened the young man's eyes to the urgency of the times and prompted him to be ready. The Caliphate had been restored, and soon the armies of Rome would gather on the plains of Dabiq, for the final battle. Abdul-Ahad had wanted to travel to Syria and join the fight, but Israfil had urged him to be patient, promising him a far greater role in the outworking of God's plan.

Tonight, he had made good on that promise, summoning Abdul-Ahad and the others to a coffee shop in Suez, where the minivans and the weapons were waiting, along with the mission: go to the Jabal Musa and stop the agents of *Masih ad-Dajjal*—the anti-messiah—from defiling the sacred ground where Moses spoke to God.

Israfil had explained that the outcome of the great battle between good and evil would be decided here, on the holy mountain, and Abdul-Ahad knew that it was not an exaggeration. He had heard the news reports, of the earthquakes, and the signs in heaven.

The end of all things was upon them.

He glanced down at the pictures Israfil had sent them, pho-tographs of the enemy's agents. A man, a woman, and a girl—all Westerners.

Abdul-Ahad had no reservations about killing women or children, not if they were servants of the anti-messiah.

Tonight, they would kill the enemies of God, and, he did not doubt, they would be welcomed into Paradise as martyrs.

But first, the world would burn.

TWENTY-ONE

Almost from the moment she tried to attune herself to the orb, Fiona knew they wouldn't find the sun chariot at the monastery. "It's not happening," she told Pierce. "I'm not getting anything."

"Let's try moving around a little."

She knew, with the same vague certainty that had guided her into the subterranean labyrinth beneath Arkaim, and then back out again, that it would be a futile effort. But she nodded and followed Pierce around the thirteen hundred year old religious complex anyway.

Before leaving them to conduct their search, Father Justin had played the tour guide, telling them the history of the monastery, explaining that there had indeed been a Christian presence on the mountain as far back as the fourth century. The monastery was a more recent addition, going back to the ninth century. It had been built to protect the monks from Bedouin attacks. While the rest of Christendom had suffered through the Dark Ages, with churches across the Holy Land being razed or turned into mosques by the conquering Saracens, Saint Catherine's had endured.

There were several different chapels inside the walled fortress, along with, as Justin had earlier intimated, a mosque, converted from an older Christian church during the Fatimid Caliphate between 900 and 1100 CE.

"This is a holy place to all the Abrahamic faiths," Justin explained. "Moses is revered as a prophet in the Islamic tradition, and this mountain where God spoke to him, is held as sacred. The Prophet Mohammed himself issued a covenant—the *Ashtiname* of Muhammad—sealed by his own hand, granting us protection in perpetuity. The only concession was this mosque, which we maintain to this day."

"I guess that explains why the Islamic State leaves you alone," Gallo observed.

"We rely upon God for protection," Justin said. "However, it may be that this peace that has endured for a thousand years is God's way of showing us all—Christian and Muslim alike—that co-existence is possible.

"You may go where you wish," he told them. "I would only ask that you respect the sanctity of this place, and please, remove your footwear before entering the Katholikon." He gestured to the enormous church basilica dominating the interior of the walled complex. "It is holy ground today, as it was in the days of Moses."

Wandering the monastery was like being in an M.C. Escher painting. Inside the high walls, the buildings were jumbled together, connected by stairways that led up to rooftops, and tunnels that ducked beneath old stone buildings, no two of which were the same shape or size.

The earthquake had left its mark on the monastery. Although none of the buildings had collapsed, everywhere they turned they had to pick their way through piles of rubble. Some areas were blocked off, but Fiona didn't need to visit every nook and cranny of the site to know that they weren't going to find anything.

Maybe Gallo had misinterpreted the reference in the Heracleia. Maybe there was no sun chariot at all.

No. She pushed the thought away. She had seen the vision of Raven for a reason, and this was it. There was a way to fix what was happening, and she was going to find it. *But if it's not here, where is it?*

After twenty minutes, Father Justin rejoined them in the northeast courtyard of the monastery, as they were putting their shoes back on. He did not seem at all surprised by their lack of progress. "Why did you believe that you would find what you seek here?"

"We didn't choose this place randomly," Pierce said. "In ancient texts, this place was called Thrinakia, the island of the Sun God, Helios—"

"I have read the Odyssey, Dr. Pierce. In the original language. Sinai is not Thrinakia."

"There are other stories," Gallo said. "Stories older than Egypt itself, about the Sun god's herds that roam a mountain across the sea to the east of the Nile."

"Herds? Cattle?"

"Cattle are a symbol of agriculture. Domesticating cattle made civilization possible. The Egyptians worshipped cattle, and I believe that's what Homer was alluding to when he spoke of the sacred herds of the Sun God on Thrinakia. There are universal truths hidden in those stories."

Justin considered this for a moment. "Interesting."

Fiona sensed the monk wanted to say more. "Do you know something? Have you heard about sacred cattle here?"

"I would not use the word sacred. However, when Moses led the sons of Israel out of Egypt, he brought them here. For forty days and nights, Moses spoke with God upon the mountain. Right up there." He gestured to the darkness above the monastery complex. "During his absence, the sons of Israel fell into despair. They begged Aaron, the brother of Moses, to make a god for them to worship."

"The golden calf," Pierce said, nodding. "I had forgotten that one."

"When Moses came down, carrying the Covenant, written by the very finger of God upon tablets of stone, he saw the people worshipping a calf of gold. What has always intrigued me is that, in the book of Exodus, chapter thirty-two, the sons of Israel do not tell Aaron what sort of god to make. And when Moses questioned him, he said: 'They said to me: Make us gods, that may go before us: for as to this Moses, who brought us forth out of the land of Egypt, we know not what is befallen him. And I said to them: Which of you hath any gold? and they took and brought it to me: and I cast it into the fire, and this calf came out.'"

"Wait," Fiona said. "The calf came out of the fire? On its own?"

It sounded like a golem to her.

Justin smiled. "Aaron was trying to shift the blame. The Bible is very clear that he was the craftsman of the golden calf. But it is interesting, is it not? It would seem there have been sacred cows here after all."

"What happened to it? The calf?"

"Moses pulverized the idol and mixed the powder with water, which he forced the sons of Israel to drink."

Fiona grimaced. "Harsh."

"Not as harsh as what he did next. Moses gathered his cousins, the sons of Levi, and instructed them to put the evildoers to death. Twenty-three thousand in all."

Fiona had no response to that.

Justin went on. "That is how Moses recorded the story, and I accept it as true, but I also recognize that it was written more than a generation later, to instruct the children of those who made the Exodus from Egypt. It is a cautionary tale, warning of the dangers of willfulness and apostasy. Perhaps there is more to the story that we do not know. Details that would help us grasp how the God of Moses was also the God who came to live among us and offer his life on behalf of sinners."

Pierce waited for him to finish before turning to Gallo. "Are you thinking what I'm thinking?"

Gallo nodded. "It's possible. There are similarities."

"You guys want to share?" Fiona said.

Gallo offered the explanation. "Odysseus was warned to leave the sacred herd of Helios alone, but his men disobeyed him. They took some of the sacred cattle and ate them. They also sacrificed some of them. As a punishment, Zeus killed them all. Except for Odysseus, of course."

"It's not the same," Fiona countered.

"No, but it might be referencing the same event, just like the story of Raven and the story of Phaethon are similar. It means we're on the right track."

"I choose to accept that the Bible is the revealed truth of God. That is enough for me." The monk stared off into the distance for a moment, as if contemplating a weighty decision. "There is something I want to show—"

A bright flash, like a nearby lightning strike, cut short his sentence. Before anyone could comment, there was a loud boom, followed by a shock wave that hit Fiona like a gut punch.

"What was that?" she gasped.

Pierce, looking as stunned as she felt, then managed to reply. "I think it was the helicopter."

Father Justin stared at the explosion, a horrified expression on his face. He crossed himself. "We're being attacked." He shook himself out of his stunned stupor and turned to them. "Quickly. Follow me."

TWENTY-TWO

Geneva, Switzerland

As they looked through the open gates of Tomorrowland, Dourado could not help thinking of the haunted amusement park from a Scooby Doo cartoon. It wasn't just the name, though that was part of it. Although it was still early, not even eight o'clock yet, the sprawling campus was dark. Not a single light burned in any of the windows in any of the buildings, and yet, there was a subtle energy in the air, an undercurrent of activity.

Machines lived here, clockwork ghosts haunting the shadows. Under any other circumstances, she would have found that cool, but tonight, it just felt creepy.

"Not good," she muttered.

Lazarus parked the rental car just outside the already repaired gates and they disembarked, heading through on foot. The logic behind this move was straightforward. If things went pear-shaped inside the walls of Tomorrowland, it would be far easier to outmaneuver the robots on foot, and keeping the car outside the walls would ensure a quick getaway once they made it through the gate. And, as long as things didn't go south, transportation inside the complex wouldn't be a problem. There was an automated cart waiting for them just beyond the gateposts.

The transport-bot greeted them. "Welcome, Mr. Fallon."

"We need another cart," Fallon said. "Scan my guests in and give them full access, on my authorization."

"Yes, Mr. Fallon. Another cart is on the way."

Fallon flashed a triumphant smile at Lazarus. "See? Told you."

Lazarus stared back, his expression impassive but unimpressed. He had advised shutting down all the robotic systems remotely before attempting to enter the compound, but Fallon had argued against that measure, reasoning that it would make little difference. If the hacker did attack the network again, turning the robots off wouldn't slow him down in a meaningful way, while keeping the robots operational in the meantime would facilitate their mission. Dourado agreed with Fallon, but she did not share his confidence that they had seen the last of the hacker.

The one concession Fallon had allowed was to disable the network's outside Internet connection. Once on site, they would be able to interact with the computer and the Space Tomorrow surveillance satellite shadowing the Black Knight, but no one outside the complex would be able to do so. Unless the hacker was on site, he would not be able to carry out another attack.

Of course, if the hacker was an insider, perhaps one of the very few human employees in Fallon's operation, then it was possible that he *was* there, hiding in one of those dark buildings, waiting for them to step into the trap.

The second cart arrived less than a minute later, and the five of them climbed aboard—Fallon and Tanaka rode together in the first vehicle, while the trio from the Cerberus Group rode in the second. Dourado maintained a constant vigil, monitoring the network from her laptop. There was no indication that a second incursion was in progress, but if Lazarus was correct, the enemy would not make a move until they were right where he wanted them.

They made one stop in the heart of the complex, at a building Carter identified as 'the Operations Center,' just long enough to procure a second laptop computer. Then they continued on to the array site. The plan was for Fallon and Tanaka to restore the Roswell fragment to the transmitter and begin working to regain control of the Black Knight satellite, while Dourado stood ready to repel any cyber-attack.

As they made the drive to the outlying location, Dourado noted Carter staring at the surrounding terrain. The carts' headlights revealed some of the damage caused during the latter's earlier visit. There was no sign of the construction robots that had come after them, but the pavement was scarred and stained with oil, and the landscaping to either side of the road had been obliterated.

Dr. Carter probably feels like a veteran, visiting an old battlefield, Dourado thought. For the first time since leaving, she found herself wishing she had stayed in Rome.

The carts stopped in front of the concrete building that housed the transmitter. Fallon got out and came over to Carter. "I'm going to need that piece of meta-material now."

Carter, unsurprised by the request, held out her hand. When she opened her fist, the crumpled fabric popped back to its original shape—a flat plane. Fallon took it and headed into the building, with Tanaka close on his heels. Lazarus and Carter remained outside with Dourado, sitting in the cart, watching the network status for any sign of trouble.

Carter checked her watch. "Seven forty-five," she said. "Fifteen minutes. I don't know whether that's plenty of time, or if we're cutting it close."

"It is what it is," Lazarus said. "Worrying about it isn't going to change a thing."

Dourado knew he was right, but the wait was excruciating. She checked the network status again—unchanged, as expected—and then opened the browser page Tanaka had used earlier to check the satellite's status.

The orbital map showed the satellite moving above North America. It was almost six o'clock p.m. on the East Coast, midafternoon on the Pacific. She thought about the map showing the distribution of earthquakes during the earlier incident and wondered what it would look like if they failed. How many red dots would there be? Where would the tsunamis strike?

How many people would die?

She found a link to the video feed from the surveillance satellite and clicked on it. A small player window opened in one corner of the screen, and after a few seconds, the live image appeared. She saw the curve of the Earth—brown land and gray-green sea—and the light blue band of atmosphere transitioning into the void of space. Right in the middle of it all, like a misshapen black fly sitting on the screen, was the Black Knight satellite.

It looked like the pictures Dourado had seen of it on the Internet.

"Is this right?" she said aloud.

"Is what right?" Carter looked over her shoulder at the screen. "No. That's what it looks like when it's dormant. Fully deployed, it will look like a glowing sphere. That must be an old picture."

Dourado checked the time stamp. "No. This is live."

Behind them, a loud hum began to emanate from the transmitter building.

Carter hopped out of the cart and headed for the open door. "Fallon," she called out. "Are you seeing this?"

The door slammed shut.

"What the—"

Before Carter could complete the rhetorical question, the electric cart closest to the door lurched forward, heading right toward her. She threw herself to the side, just barely getting out of the way. The cart continued forward, maneuvering as it moved, until its front end was kissing the door. The cart held it shut, blocking the entrance to the transmitter building.

Lazarus leapt from the cart, then spun around and pulled Dourado along. "It's starting."

She stumbled after him, her free hand still gripping the laptop, struggling to process what was happening.

He pulled her to the corner of the little concrete building. She couldn't see the carts or the door. "Stay here," he told her, then he ran out of her view. The concrete walls muted the hum of the transmitter, and she could hear Carter shouting Fallon's name, demanding an explanation.

It's starting, Lazarus had said.

Was he talking about the transmitter?

She glanced down at the computer screen again and saw that the image had changed. The Black Knight, still hanging in space about the Earth, was changing shape before her eyes, unfolding. Expanding. The change was rapid. She could already see the first hints of the sphere it would become.

Somehow, instead of shutting down the Black Knight, the reactivation of the transmitter had accelerated the process.

Or had it?

"Fallon!" Carter cried out, and then there was a loud, insistent banging sound as she beat her fists against the metal door.

Dourado barely heard. Her attention was fixed on the computer screen, but she wasn't watching the live feed anymore. Instead, she was navigating into the archive of footage from earlier in the day. She entered the time code for one hour earlier. Then two hours. Three.

Each picture showed a different perspective, but there was one unchanging constant. The Black Knight itself.

Dormant.

Inactive.

The Black Knight had not posed any threat at all.

Not until thirty seconds ago.

Suddenly, she understood everything. She understood how the hacker had defeated the Tomorrowland network firewall, hijacked the robots and autonomous vehicles, and then melted away, leaving no trace.

Lazarus reappeared, dragging Carter after him. "Cintia. It's starting."

"I know," she groaned. "They lied to us."

He shook his head. "I'm talking about the robots. The carts. You need to get control of them. Move them away from the door so we can get in there."

Even as he said it, she heard the rhythmic clanking sound of metal treads moving on asphalt in the distance, growing louder by the second. The construction robots had come out of hiding and were headed their way.

The hacker had made his move.

But there is no hacker, she realized. *There never was.*

She turned back to the computer, steeling herself for the life-or-death cyber-battle to come.

On the video player screen, the Black Knight began to shine with blinding, radiant solar energy, and Dourado knew that, on the far side of the world, the sun had just stopped moving.

TWENTY-THREE

Mount Sinai, Egypt

There was another explosion, so close that the flash and the bang happened almost simultaneously, and a section of the ancient wall that had stood for more than a thousand years disintegrated in an eruption of rubble. The second blast confirmed that the first one had not been an accident.

The monastery was under attack.

Beams of light pierced through the smoke and dust, probing the interior and heralding the arrival of the attackers.

"Come with me," Justin hissed. "Quickly."

They had just rounded the corner of the Katholikon basilica, when the noise of gunfire reached Pierce's ears.

Definitely an attack, he thought. *So much for enduring peace.*

Justin led them into a narrow alley behind the basilica and pointed to an enormous tree with long leafy vines growing from a raised bed. Pierce had noticed it during their earlier wanderings. It was the only one of its kind inside the walls. Even in the middle of a crisis, Justin could not forget who he was. "This is the bush from which God spoke to Moses. Behind it, there is a passage that leads out onto the mountain."

"An escape route," Pierce said. "Good thinking."

Justin shook his head. "It's the pilgrim's path. A sacred route leading to the Cave of Moses, where he hid himself when beholding the glory of God. It is not meant for you, but..." He paused and crossed himself again. "When you are outside, you will see the path. Keep to it, for if you stray, you will in all likelihood wander the mountain until you freeze to death. The path will lead you to the cave. Hide there. If I am still alive when the sun rises, I will find you."

He pointed to the tree again. "Go. May God keep you and watch over you."

As if to underscore the urgency in his voice, there was another burst of gunfire. A section of wall high above them shattered, as a dozen bullets tore into the ancient stone. Pierce shielded his eyes with one hand until the debris stopped raining down. When he lowered his hand, Father Justin was gone.

Pierce climbed up onto the elevated soil bed and drew back the branches to expose what looked like a drainage hole. "Go!"

Gallo went first, clambering up and scurrying under the foliage, disappearing into the dark hole. Fiona was next, but as she brushed past him, Pierce felt a jolt, like an electric shock, pass through the branches and into his hands. He let go with a yelp and looked around for a moment, wondering what had happened. For a moment, he thought that one of the explosions had damaged a buried electrical line, but then he remembered that the power was out in the monastery.

Weird, he thought, and then he ducked under the vines and plunged into the passage. Whatever its cause, the shock did not reoccur.

Pierce's headlamp revealed the smooth, baked-clay brick wall, Fiona's backside, and not much else, but there was enough room for him to crawl on hands and knees without scraping his back against the ceiling. There was more sporadic shooting behind them, the noise of the reports distorted by the tunnel's acoustics. Pierce tried not to think about the carnage they were fleeing, or the senseless hate that had motivated it. Maybe the terrorists would be content with vandalizing the monastery, sparing the monks' lives.

He could hope.

The tunnel sloped downward for its full length, about a hundred and fifty feet, and then deposited them onto the desert floor at the foot of the south wall, facing the mountain slope. The walls muffled the sound of the ongoing assault, but Pierce knew the fortress would not contain the violence any more than it had protected those within.

He located the path Father Justin had spoken of, a well-trampled foot trail, dotted here and there with dark stains.

Blood.

He recalled what Justin had said about holy ground and taking off their shoes inside. The pilgrims who followed this secret route probably took that admonition very seriously.

As the grade increased, their pace faltered to a walk, and soon all three of them were struggling for breath. The monastery was a mile above sea level, and the summit of the mountain was at least another half-mile higher.

With their increased elevation, Pierce could see down into the monastery. Columns of smoke rose from two or three small fires, the rest of the darkness illuminated by occasional flashes of gunfire. Then he spotted lights outside the walls, a small group of men skirting the exterior of the monastery.

"Lights off!" he ordered the others, switching his own headlamp off as well.

Had they been spotted?

"Looks like we're going to have to skip the Cave of Moses," he said, keeping his voice low, barely louder than a whisper. "We'll skirt along the base of the mountain and then double back. I doubt these guys will stick around much longer. I'm sure the Egyptian army has already heard about this, and the cavalry is on the way."

"Do you think they're here for us?" Fiona said.

"Possibly," Pierce replied. "Maybe our cover story was too convincing. ISIS couldn't pass up a chance to take UN hostages."

Gallo spoke up. "George, what if this isn't Islamic extremists? You heard what Brother Justin said about the charter of protection. No Muslim would defy the Prophet like that. What if they're here because of what we're looking for?"

"How would they even know?" Fiona asked.

It makes sense, George thought, and then he turned to Gallo. "You're right. We have to consider what Felice discovered in Geneva. Somebody caused that. Intentionally. Maybe they're trying to create a weapon, or maybe they just want to bring the apocalypse, but they have the resources to make it happen. Who's to say they don't have an army, too? If they've learned what we're looking for and why, then they would want to stop us. Or take it for themselves. The question is, how would they even know about us in the first place?"

"Maybe they hacked our phones? Cintia was worried that there might be a mole in Fallon's inner circle."

As much as he didn't want it to be true, he knew she was right. As usual.

The timing of the assault, and the fact that the attackers were moving up the hill, was all the proof he needed.

Worst of all, the sun chariot wasn't even there, or if it was, it was hidden so well that Fiona could not sense its presence.

"It doesn't change what we have to do," Pierce said. "We just need to stay alive—"

The ground heaved beneath him, knocking him flat. He slipped a few feet down the slope before catching himself, but even before he stopped sliding, he knew the sudden disturbance wasn't another explosion. The ground was still moving under him.

"Earthquake!" Fiona shouted.

Pierce stayed down in a prone position, hugging the ground to avoid being launched into an uncontrollable downhill slide, but as the frightful shaking went on, the seconds stretching into minutes, he could not help but wonder if this was the beginning of the solar event Dourado had warned about.

If it was... If the Black Knight satellite had been activated again, redirecting the sun's light and gravity, the tremor would only be the beginning.

A noise, loud like a thunderclap, split the air, and a wave of heat flashed over Pierce. His nostrils filled with a strange smell, a mixture of burning dust and freshly turned soil. There was a second report, more distant, but still very loud, and then another, the two overlapping. Pierce couldn't tell if the noises were from bombs or maybe rocket-propelled grenades exploding on the slopes around them, or something related to the quake. Regardless, there was nothing he could do to protect himself. His life or death was in the hands of fate.

Then the shaking stopped.

"George!" Gallo's cry was choked by a mouthful of dust, but at least she was alive.

"I'm okay. Are you? Fiona, are you okay?"

"I'm okay," Fiona replied, then added. "The Black Knight just woke up again."

Pierce pushed himself up to a crouch and, despite the unresolved threat from the monastery attackers, flipped his headlamp on.

The dust motes caught in the beam of light made it look like a solid thing, but amid the haze, he spotted Gallo and Fiona, both huddled just a few feet away. He crawled over to them, hugged them for a moment, and then shone his light on the mountain, scouting a route to freedom.

Below them, a hundred yards away, the line of glowing artificial lights advanced up the slope—the monastery attackers, homing in on Pierce's headlamp. As he stared down at them, Pierce saw a tiny flash, barely bigger than a spark, followed half-a-second later by the report of a rifle shot.

"Down," he called out, flipping off his light and pressing himself flat. "We can't stay here."

"We can't very well move either," Gallo said. "You saw it, didn't you?"

"Yeah," he grunted. "I saw."

As if being hunted by killers armed with guns and rocket launchers wasn't going to be challenging enough, fate had decided to increase the difficulty setting. Pierce's brief glimpse of the mountainside had revealed the quake's aftermath. The ground had split apart all around them. Long fissures, bleeding acrid smoke into the chilly night air, now crisscrossed the slope. Without the aid of artificial light, Pierce could just barely make out the ground in front of him. The jagged cracks in the terrain were a shade darker than the brown soil.

"Slow and steady," he said. "We'll crawl out on hands and knees if we have to."

"Uncle George!" Fiona's voice rose with increasing urgency, as she called out. Pierce couldn't see her face, but he could make out her silhouette. She was pointing into the nearest crack.

The fissure was glowing a dim red, but getting brighter by the second, like the coils of an electric heater warming up. Pierce's first thought was that they were witnessing volcanic activity, but as the light grew, rising through the spectrum—orange, yellow, and then bright white—he realized the cause was nothing as ordinary as a rising magma plume.

Something was alive down there, moving in the depths of the Earth, like an embryonic dragon squirming through the cracks in its eggshell, struggling to be born.

TWENTY-FOUR

Geneva, Switzerland

Felice Carter felt like throwing up. How had she not seen this coming?

Smoke and mirrors.

Deception.

Fallon had invited her into his inner circle and then distracted her with the imaginary external threat of the hacker.

Even now, confronted with the reality, she couldn't quite reconcile it with what she had experienced. Why had Fallon gone to such extremes to deceive her, particularly at the beginning, when he had complete control over the Black Knight satellite and the Roswell meta-material fragment? It made no sense.

She placed her hands flat against the concrete walls and took a deep breath. She didn't need to see them, and the wall itself posed no obstacle. All she needed to know was that there were two men inside the structure, and one or both of them were going to unleash an apocalypse if she didn't act.

A hand touched her arm, distracting her. She looked up and saw Lazarus. His face was impassive, but she could see the question in his eyes.

Are you sure you want to do that?

"I have to stop them," she said.

"Wait."

That was all he said.

She knew the reason for his apprehension. It had not been concern for the men inside the transmitter building that prompted him to intervene, but rather concern for her. If she did this, if she touched their minds and permanently stripped away their free will, it would be the same as killing them. Two more souls added to her tally.

The first few times her... ability...had become manifest, it had been something out of her control, an autonomic response to a threatening situation. Yet, knowing that did not assuage her feelings of guilt. Those incidents had prompted her subsequent quest to develop a mental discipline regime to keep the power in check, and had motivated her to spend years of her life helping fight disease in developing nations.

If she unleashed the ability now, it would be deliberate, intentional.

But no less necessary.

Behind Lazarus, one of the large construction robots trundled down the drive. She couldn't tell if there were more behind it, but this time, she didn't have a souped-up spy car in which to escape. Not that she had any intention of running.

Dourado's fingers flew over her laptop's keyboard. She muttered as she worked, letting Carter and Lazarus know that she wasn't ignorant of the threat. "I see it. It's not recognizing the admin account I set up, but I created a backdoor that he doesn't know about. If I can... I'm in."

Lazarus half-turned to look at her. "Can you shut the transmitter down?"

"I don't know that part of the system."

"The robots then?"

"Working on it."

Lazarus turned back to Carter. "Let's try it this way first."

She nodded. "Hurry."

Lazarus pulled away from her and ran back to the front of the building, where the two electric carts blocked access to the door. She followed, but only as far as the corner, observing from a discreet distance.

He walked up to the cart blocking the door, dropped to a squat and hooked his hands underneath it. With a howl of primal fury, he stood up, lifting one side of the thousand pound vehicle. There was a tearing sound—Carter hoped it was his clothes bursting at the seams, as his muscles bulged with the effort, but she knew it was probably his tendons snapping. The cart tilted up and then passed the point of no return, tipping over onto its side, clearing the way to the door. Lazarus stood there for a second, breathing heavily, face contorted in pain, then he reached for the doorknob.

Carter spied movement behind him, but before she could shout a warning, the second cart surged forward, slamming into Lazarus and pinning his legs against the door with a sickening crunch.

"Erik!"

She rushed toward him, but he held up a hand, forestalling her. Through teeth clenched against the pain, he whispered, "Cintia."

Without retreating, Carter turned back to the computer expert. "Cintia! You've got to shut them down."

"I'm trying!"

The construction machine was just fifty yards away, close enough that the noise of its metal treads on the pavement was almost deafening. Despite Lazarus's earlier warning, Carter moved forward, joining him at the door. She braced her back against the wall, pushing against the cart, trying to force it away from the door. As before, it refused to budge. Despite his injuries and the awkward position in which he had been pinned, Lazarus pushed as well.

The cart shifted a few inches, but then the wheels began spinning, pushing back. Lazarus howled again, as the vehicle slammed him into the door a second time.

The construction robot was now just twenty yards away, its spider-like manipulator arms unfolding above its tracked chassis. The large circular saw-blade tipping one arm was already spinning.

Ten yards.

"Get out of here!" Lazarus shouted.

Carter had no intention of leaving. Instead, she turned to face the wall, placed her hands against it, closed her eyes and prepared to unleash her power against the two men inside.

The noise abruptly ceased.

Carter opened her eyes and turned to look at the now motionless construction robot, which had come to a complete halt, almost touching the rear of the cart, its manipulator arms stretched out above her. The saw blade was still spinning, but hissing as friction brought it to a stop. The only other sound was the hum of the transmitter on the other side of the door.

Then she heard a shout from around the corner. "Yes!"

"Cintia? That was you? Can you back these things away?"

Dourado stepped into view, her attention still glued to the computer in her hands. "I had to do a blanket shutdown. He's fighting me hard."

Carter tried pushing the cart again. It rolled without resistance, but only for a few inches before bumping up against the motionless treads of the construction-bot. It was enough of a gap for Lazarus, his face twisted with pain, to extricate himself. But it was not enough to get into the transmitter building.

"Keep trying," Carter said. "I'll see if I can distract him."

She was relieved that circumstances had provided her an alternative to unleashing her power, but whether this was a true reprieve or a postponement remained to be seen. She pulled the door open a crack and shouted inside. "Fallon! Stop this! Now!"

The reply was a shout loud enough to be heard over the hum. "I'm afraid Mr. Fallon is indisposed."

"Tanaka?" Evidently, Marcus Fallon was guilty of recklessness and bad judgment, but not responsible for activating the Black Knight. "What did you do to him?"

"He'll live. At least a little while longer."

"Why are you doing this? You know what could happen?"

When Tanaka didn't answer, she glanced over at Dourado, who made a rolling gesture with her finger. *Keep him busy.*

"Let me guess," Carter went on. "You saw the potential to turn this into a weapon, but Fallon didn't want that."

"Ha!"

"Have I got that backward? Is Fallon the one who wants to weaponize it?"

"He's naïve," Tanaka said. "He thinks he can save the world. He's a fool."

"And you? What do you want? To destroy it?"

Silence.

"Seriously?" Carter asked. "You *want* to destroy the world?"

"I don't expect you to understand."

She glanced over at Dourado. A nod. *Almost there.* "Try me."

"The world can't be saved, Dr. Carter. Not by you. Not by Fallon. All you will do is prolong the suffering. Life is a mistake. A brutal, terrible joke that's already gone on far too long."

Carter recognized the rhetoric. Tanaka was a pessimist. Not merely a gloomy, glass-half-empty Eeyore, but he was a believer in the nihilistic philosophy that life—all life—was meaningless.

No wonder his Cerberus recruitment score was so abysmal, she thought. "Seven billion people deserve a chance to figure that out for themselves. You don't get to make that decision for every-one else."

"Seven billion," he echoed. "A hundred years from now, they will all be dead, and ten billion more will have taken their place, living short, ugly, miserable lives. Billions more after that. Suffering. Dying. I am not destroying the world. I'm putting it out of its misery. I'm sparing untold billions the horror and pain of existence.

"I thought perhaps I could use HAARP to do it, but the transmitter wasn't powerful enough. Then, when Marcus approached me about the potential of the Black Knight satellite, I knew I had been given a second chance. I'll confess, the gravitational anomaly was an unexpected bonus, but ultimately unimportant. The world will not be shaken apart. It will die entombed in ice."

"You're going to stop the sun, is that it? I'm pretty sure it's going to take more than a couple of minutes of that to have the kind of effect you're looking for."

The hum stopped.

Carter looked over to Dourado, but the latter shook her head. *Not me.*

Tanaka had shut the transmitter off. Was he surrendering?

She returned her attention to the door. "So why do it? Why go through all this?"

There was a long silence. Maybe he wasn't giving up after all. Lazarus got to his feet, his broken legs already healed. He leaned against the side of the car, gathering his strength to shove the remaining cart out of the way and end the threat. Then, Tanaka spoke again.

"Call it proof of concept."

Even before he finished speaking, Dourado let out a dismayed shout. "No! Damn it!"

Distracted by the outburst, Carter didn't see the construction-bot's manipulator arm swinging toward her, but Lazarus did. He threw his arms around her and tackled her out of the way.

The mechanical arm struck the cart, smashing through the fiber-glass housing and knocking the machine sideways. Carter caught only a glimpse of it as Lazarus scooped her up with one arm and scrambled around the corner, dragging Dourado along as well.

There was a harsh ringing sound, as the robot's circular saw began spinning again, but it was drowned out a moment later by the clank and rumble of metal treads moving against the pavement. Carter had just got her feet under her when the machine rolled into view, lowering the saw to slice them all apart.

Lazarus thrust Carter and Dourado away, well outside the reach of the mechanical arm, then spun around, ducked under the sweep of the blade, and leaped onto the base of the robot.

Carter recalled what Fallon had said, about how the construction robot wasn't programmed for combat. The same appeared true for self-defense. It lumbered forward, trying to seize hold of her and Dourado, oblivious to the stowaway.

Dourado stumbled, going down on one knee. The computer flew from her hands and skittered across the ground. Dourado let out another wail of dismay and crawled after it. Faster than Carter could draw breath to shout a warning, the robot arm with the saw blade moved into position above Dourado and then sliced straight down.

TWENTY-FIVE

With an indifference only possible for a computerized automaton, the construction robot brought its spinning saw down on Dourado, but in the instant before contact was made, the blade shifted sideways. With an eruption of dirt, the blade buried itself in the ground, just a few inches to her right.

Before she could move, almost before she realized she was still alive and intact, the manipulator arm reversed, the saw tearing free of the earth. She rolled left, scrambling on all fours to put some more distance between herself and the robot, but she knew it wouldn't be enough.

The manipulator arm shuddered, and began moving *away* from her. The saw plunged down again, burying itself deeper into the ground than the first strike. Then, with an ear-splitting shriek, a six-foot long section of the manipulator assembly broke loose from the hydraulic joint. Lazarus, his arms still wrapped around the other end of the disarticulated appendage, leapt from the base of the machine.

The damage seemed to have no real effect on the robot. Its other arms came forward, clamps and manipulator claws opening wide to grasp him, treads moving as it lurched ahead.

Instead of retreating, the big man wrenched the saw blade out of the ground, spun around like an Olympic hammer thrower building up momentum, and then brought the blade down hard on the treads.

The air rang with the impact. The severed appendage twisted out of Lazarus's grasp and he half-staggered backward, scrambling to avoid being run down. The blow, however, had done what he intended.

The robot's left track came apart, one end flinging about like a decapitated snake, and then the left side stopped moving. The massive machine spun around, its one remaining track causing it to pirouette, and it slammed into the transmitter building, smashing an enormous hole in the concrete wall.

Dourado, still in full-flight-mode, retreated several more steps before realizing that the battle—man versus machine—was over. What she had failed to do with technology, Lazarus had accomplished with brute force.

She stopped running and leaned over, resting her hands on her knees until her breath returned and the urge to throw up passed. Carter hastened over and embraced her, but the moment of triumph lasted exactly that long.

"Heads up!" Lazarus shouted. "We've got incoming!"

Three more of the construction-bots rolled into view and turned toward them. Lazarus bent to retrieve the makeshift axe that he had used to take down the first machine, but Dourado knew the odds of defeating all three were not good.

She looked around for her computer and found it.

Both pieces of it.

Lazarus had spared her from the first swipe of the saw blade, but in so doing, he had diverted the blade down onto the laptop, slicing it in two.

"So much for that idea."

Lazarus hefted the broken saw-arm and stood his ground. "Get to cover," he shouted. "I'll deal with them."

Carter grabbed Dourado's arm and pulled her toward the wrecked robot. With her free hand, she pointed to the hole in the building. "In there!"

Of course! Dourado thought. *We'll force Tanaka to shut the robots down.*

In the subsequent chaos, she had almost forgotten that the man responsible for it all was hiding on the other side of that wall. Her mind still boggled at the insane reasons he had given for putting the entire planet in danger, but his motivation didn't matter. All that mattered was stopping him.

Carter climbed up onto the base of the disabled robot and disappeared through the hole. Dourado followed, picking her way through the rubble and dropping down into the dark hole beyond. There were no overhead lights shining, but there was some light from the glow of a computer screen on the other side of the room, right next to the open door. She didn't see Tanaka, but a prone figure—it had to be Fallon—was stretched out on the floor, partially buried under debris from the collapsed wall. Carter was kneeling beside him, but Dourado hastened to the computer.

Outside, the low rumble of the tracked machines devolved into a tumult of metal crashing and hydraulic systems straining. An ear-splitting shriek filled the tiny room, and a shower of yellow sparks poured in like rain, as one of the robots began cutting through the wall.

Carter grabbed Fallon's shoulders and pulled him from the rubble, dragging him toward the door, but she stopped there. Dourado could see that another one of the robots had moved into position in front of the exit, blocking their escape.

There was only one way they were going to survive this.

She gritted her teeth against the horrible noise, and tried to keep her attention on the task at hand.

The Space Tomorrow access menu appeared on the screen, and she saw the familiar prompt for username and password. She entered information for the admin account Fallon had shown her.

```
User not recognized.
User name:_____
Password:_____
```

She tried again with one of the backdoor accounts she had set up. The results were the same. She tried another, her last. No good.

"*Porra!*" she snarled. "I'm locked out."

Carter bent over Fallon again and started shaking him. "Wake up, damn it!"

Fallon came to, jolting as if startled.

"Password?" Dourado shouted.

Fallon nodded.

"What's the password?" Carter shouted into his face.

"Password," he said. "Cap P. 'At' symbol. Dollar sign. Dollar sign. Lower case 'w'. Zero. Lower case 'r'. Lower case 'd'. Username is M-dot-Fallon."

Dourado stared at him, gobsmacked. "Seriously? Your password is 'password'? Are you an idiot?"

She typed it in.

```
Username: M.Fallon
Password: P@$$w0rd
```

The main intranet menu opened. She navigated through the network, found the robotics subsystem menu, typed in the blanket shutdown code she had used before, and said a prayer.

The tumult ceased.

Lazarus's face, twisted with concern, appeared in the hole a moment later, but when he saw that they were alive and unhurt, he relaxed.

Dourado slumped against the wall, too exhausted to even remain on her feet.

Carter however, wasn't ready to celebrate the win.

She shook Fallon again. "Where's Tanaka?"

"Ow!" Fallon complained, touching a hand to the back of his head, then looking at his fingertips as if checking for blood. "I'm not even sure where *I* am." He glanced around. "Oh. Son of bitch. He sucker punched me."

"He did a lot more than that."

Fallon blinked as if he was having trouble bringing the big picture into focus.

"Tanaka was the hacker," Carter said, speaking as if addressing a child. "He betrayed you."

"Why?" He struggled to his feet, and then jolted forward, throwing open a panel on the large metal cube that dominated the room. He stuck his head in for a moment then just as quickly emerged and slammed the panel shut.

"It's gone."

"Proof of concept," Carter muttered. "This whole thing was a setup so Tanaka could steal the Roswell fragment. All he needs to do now is find another transmitter."

Fallon still looked confused and helpless. "But...why?"

"Why else? He wants to destroy the world."

TWENTY-SIX

Mount Sinai, Egypt

Pierce looked away from the fissure, the light burning inside too bright. Green globs floated across his vision, but through them, he could see the mountain slope rising before him, lit up bright as day. It was not from any source of heavenly or artificial illumination, but from below, from the light radiating out from fissures all across the slope.

The rocky ground nearby erupted in a puff of dust, and a fraction of a second later, the report of a rifle reached Pierce's ears. He ducked, but he knew that staying put was no longer an option. The gunmen—at least ten of them, maybe more—were ascending the mountain, rushing toward them.

"Run!" he shouted.

The unexpected light rising up from the maze of fissures had taken away the cover of darkness, but it also illuminated a path to the top. More shots were fired, the bullets striking all around, some uncomfortably close. But after just a moment or two, the light began to dim, the darkness returning with a vengeance.

"What now?" Gallo whispered.

A few more shots echoed across the slope, then those stopped as well. Flashlight beams lanced through the night, playing up the mountainside, searching for them. The gunmen had spread out and were ascending in a picket line, at least to the extent the broken terrain would allow.

"Back to crawling, I guess." Pierce wished he had a better suggestion, but until inspiration dawned, *keep moving* was the best he had.

"No," Fiona whispered. "Don't move."

Pierce stopped. "What did you see?"

"Those things..."

"What things?" Gallo asked.

"Didn't you see them?"

"I saw," Pierce whispered back. "I think. I don't know what I saw... It looked like... I don't know... Like it was made of pure light."

"They're here. All around us. Do *not* touch them."

Pierce recognized the certainty in her tone. He had heard it before, earlier that day in the passages beneath Arkaim.

"What are they, Fiona?" Gallo pressed.

"The sacred cattle of Helios." Her voice sounded detached. "Not actual cows, but some kind of creatures made of pure energy. I think the Originators made them to store the power they harvested from the sun. Sort of like Energizer golems. Living energy inside a shell made of melted rock. Remember that story Father Justin told us about how the golden calf came out of the fire? I think this is the same thing. They've been here this whole time. Sleeping."

"What woke them up? The earthquake?"

"The earthquake or the Black Knight. Maybe I did it, by bringing the sphere here. Or all those things together. We need to stay away from them. They're dangerous."

Pierce recalled the jolt he had felt when Fiona touched the small tree inside the monastery—the actual Burning Bush of biblical fame, if the monk was to be believed. Had Fiona's touch restored a spark of supernatural life to it, as well?

He glanced back down the hill and saw that the picket line was less than fifty yards away. "Like we needed one more thing to worry about," he muttered.

"If they're similar to golems," Gallo said, "Maybe you can control them?"

There was a brief pause, and when Fiona spoke again, her tone of flat certainty was gone. "I didn't make them, but...I can try."

She lapsed into silence, and Pierce knew better than to disrupt her focus.

The line of flashlights continued moving toward them, slowed somewhat by the terrain, but still advancing.

A shout went up, and then one of the men opened fire.

Pierce ducked his head, covering it with one arm in a futile attempt to protect himself, but the shooter wasn't aiming at him.

Suddenly, the world was filled with light.

TWENTY-SEVEN

It was like staring into the face of the sun. Light filled every pore of Abdul-Ahad's body. Heat like a cleansing fire, burned through him. The holy mountain had opened up, and an army of strange creatures had come forth, summoned by the evildoers after their escape from the monastery.

In that instant, he understood why Israfil had sent them here.

"They are *jinn*," he shouted, letting the others know. If they were still alive. He could not see any of them. He could not see anything at all.

"*Jinn?*" The shout had come from somewhere off to his left, closer to the source of the brilliant eruption. "How do you know?"

God is merciful, he thought to himself. *I am not alone.*

"Can you see?" he shouted.

"Not well," came the reply. "But yes. I was looking away from the flash."

"The creatures? Can you see them?"

"I can see shapes moving on the mountain," the other man said. "Are you certain that they are *jinn?*

Although he did not possess even a fraction of Israfil's wisdom, Abdul-Ahad had spent many years immersing himself in the writings of the Prophet—peace be upon him—and the greater abundance of unwritten traditions. He knew the creatures had to be *jinn*, beings of smokeless fire, rather than *malak*—angels, beings of pure light—because *malak*, unlike both humans and *jinn*, did not have free will. *Jinn* could choose between good or evil. They could also be enslaved, bound in earthen vessels, just as Solomon had once done, binding the creatures in oil lamps, compelling them to guard his Temple. That was what the three enemies were attempting to do—binding the *jinn* in earthly shells, to send them forth to destroy the faithful.

He didn't know how to explain all of this to his brothers, but he did know what had to be done. "Shoot the creatures," he shouted. "Unleash the *jinn*. Let holy fire consume the enemies of God!"

TWENTY-EIGHT

Despite the fact that he was face down and covered up, Pierce was compelled to squeeze his eyes shut against the painful brilliance. The light was like a physical force, buffeting his entire body with incandescent radiant energy. It was, he imagined, like the flash of an atomic bomb. He could feel the exposed skin of his hands grow hot, and then cold. He heard Gallo cry out—in pain or alarm—but her wail was nothing compared to the screams from the gunmen.

The screams faded after a moment, as did the light. Pierce raised his head, but all he could see was a green haze. The still-cool night air was crisp with the smell of ozone. "Gus? Fi?"

"I'm okay," Gallo said. "Can't see a blessed thing, but I think it will pass."

"I'm all right," Fiona said. She paused a beat, then added. "They shot one. That was a bad idea."

"I guess so," Pierce said, blinking and willing his sight to return. There was no pain, and that seemed like a good thing. He had never experienced flash-blindness before, but he had heard stories of the intense, lingering pain of exposure to intense light. Even so, navigating the mountain at night without a flashlight had just gone from being difficult to impossible. It would be at least an hour or more before his eyes readjusted to the darkness. Still, if the light had been bright enough to do that to him, and he had been looking in the opposite direction, the gunmen were surely blinded.

He flipped on his head lamp. The green fog was still there, slowly receding from the periphery of his vision, but through it he could make out Gallo and Fiona, lying flat, shading their eyes. Beyond them, the torn landscape, and at the edge of his headlamp's light, he saw something else.

"Holy shit," he muttered.

It looked nothing like a cow, or any other kind of animal, and yet he could see how an ancient poet, grasping for the words to describe it, might have made such a comparison. A large, bulbous body, was perched atop what might have been legs, and spiraling protrusions that, without too much imagination, could be compared to the long horns of an ox or water buffalo. However, as Fiona had suggested, the creature looked more like a golem—a rough approximation of life— than like an actual living thing.

He tore his eyes away from it and shone the light down the slope. The gunmen were still there, though there were fewer of them. All of them were clutching their eyes, and groping about in the unique pantomime of men recently struck blind. After a few seconds however, the man furthest out swung his rifle in Pierce's general direction.

"Time to go," Pierce shouted.

He grabbed Gallo with one hand, Fiona with the other, and was just starting to move when the shot was fired. The round sailed past them. The man had probably seen nothing more than a bright blur, but that was enough to give him an aim-point. Pierce didn't dare turn his headlamp off. Darkness, and what they might blunder into, was now the greater danger.

As they reached the nearest fissure, the fusillade began in earnest. Puffs of dust erupted all across the mountain. The surviving gunmen were firing blind, trusting in an overwhelming volume of lead to make up for their blindness. Eventually, they would hit someone.

Or something, he thought, and then he made a mental note to come up with a better name for the light creatures. *Anything but* cows.

As they skirted the edge of the fissure, Pierce spotted the creature again, meandering along the far side, eight-feet tall and half again as long. It resembled nothing less than a behemoth made of shifting sand. Pierce could feel its energy, like invisible feathers of static electricity brushing his face.

Too close, he thought, adjusting course to give it a wide berth. But he knew that if a random bullet struck the creature, piercing its shell, they would probably all be vaporized.

As if to underscore that threat, another flash lit up the mountain.

The source of it was behind them, well out of their line of sight, but Pierce felt his entire body glow red for an instant. The light revealed a path through the maze, but as it faded, night blindness returned with a vengeance.

"Can either of you see?"

Fi replied first. "Not much."

Gallo's admission was even more succinct. "Nope."

"Okay. Looks like it's going to be the blind leading the blind." He closed his eyes, trying to remember how the world had looked in that instant of brilliance. Fortunately, the flash had given them another reprieve from the shooting, but how long it would last was anyone's guess. "Single file behind me. Gus, hang on to me. Fi, you hang on to her."

They started forward again, with Pierce counting the steps to the end of the fissure, and then taking a few more just in case, before starting upslope. If he remembered correctly, there was one more fissure ahead, thirty or forty yards—*which is it, Pierce? It matters!*—and then just a very steep climb to the top.

Something brushed against his face, the touch softer than a breath, and he froze. The sensation lingered. His skin began to tingle, like tiny insects crawling across his face.

Gallo felt it, too. "Stop. We're too close to one of those things."

Pierce turned his head back and forth, trying to see around the haze. He knew the creature was somewhere close, no more than ten feet, but try as he might, he couldn't pinpoint its location. "Back up. We'll circle wide, give him lots of room."

"Wait," Fiona said. "Let me try."

She began chanting, her voice so soft that it sounded more like faint musical notes than words. After a few seconds, the tingling stopped. After a few more, she stopped singing. "Okay. Follow me. But keep your eyes shut. I think it's going to get pretty bright."

The chain reversed, with Gallo now pulling Pierce along, as Fiona took the lead. Pierce squeezed his eyes closed, taking Fiona's admonition seriously, but the warning also triggered a memory planted in his head since childhood.

"*Shekinah,*" he whispered. "I know what they are."

"Trying to concentrate here, Uncle George."

Pierce held his tongue and followed along in silence. He climbed with careful, deliberate steps, turning when Gallo squeezed his hand, signaling a change of direction, but his mind was in another place, another time, pondering the nature of the strange light creatures.

"We have to climb," Fiona said. "But whatever you do, don't look back."

Pierce opened his eyes and felt a measure of relief at his ability to see anything at all. There were still a few dark blobs, but he could make out a nearly vertical cliff face. The base of the cliff was strewn with boulders and debris, some pieces worn smooth by centuries of weather, others jagged and sharp, cleaved off from the wall during the recent earthquakes. The fractures formed a natural yet irregular staircase leading up the cliff. High above, a shadowy depression marked the location of a cleft in the rock, perhaps the entrance to the Cave of Moses.

Fiona, still in the lead, scrambled up the staircase and plunged into the cleft. Pierce envied her youthful agility, but then Gallo, who was only a couple of years younger than he was, ascended almost as nimbly. Pierce gritted his teeth, reached down into his reserves, and started up the wall.

Another wave of gunfire erupted in the distance, dashing Pierce's hope that the gunmen were all dead or otherwise incapacitated. It seemed impossible that the three of them had been spotted, and the absence of any nearby impacts suggested the gunmen weren't even trying to hit them.

Then what are they shooting at?

The answer, as unbelievable as it was obvious, gave him the impetus to reach the mouth of the cave an instant before one of the bullets found its mark, releasing a brilliant eruption of cleansing light.

The angle of the cave opening protected the three huddled figures within from full exposure, but the flash revealed the interior of the small cleft, a space large enough to hold them all.

What Pierce saw in that instant made him forget about the gunmen's suicidal actions.

He raised his head, shining his headlamp into the depths of the recess. The LED flashlight was a mere candle flame compared to the brilliance released with the light creatures' destruction, but it was enough.

The walls of the cave were covered in strange symbols.

They weren't Egyptian hieroglyphics, or the later hieratic alphabet, or any other form of writing Pierce recognized. He wasn't even sure it was writing. The symbols might have been intended as decorations. Many of them were illegible, worn down by the passage of time, scrubbed away by the action of wind and sand swirling into the little recess. He doubted it would ever be possible to reconstruct the message. But the symbols were not what had caught his eye. A larger relief had been carved into the rock on the back wall.

From a distance, it appeared to be a representation of the sun, a circle with lines radiating from its underside, but there was something inside the circle, a pair of humanoid figures that looked like kneeling angels, facing each other, heads bowed and wings extended toward one another.

"Oh my God," he whispered. "We got it all wrong. We don't need to find the sun chariot."

He turned to the others, giddy with an excitement he had not felt since he was a child, leaving a movie theater, dreaming of the adventures he would have as an archaeologist.

"We have to find the lost Ark."

TWENTY-NINE

Mount Sinai, Egypt

They couldn't stay. That much was obvious.

Five minutes had passed since the last burst of light, and there had been no more shooting. Pierce was pretty sure the gunmen were either dead—flash-cooked—or blinded to the point of incapacitation. Either way, they were a secondary concern. Priority One was getting out of the cave and off the mountain, while attracting as little attention as possible.

Fiona presented an additional compelling reason for a hasty exit. "I think the cows—"

"Shekinah," Pierce said.

"Whatevs. I think they're attracted to the orb. I mean like a magnetic attraction. I tried to use it to shoo them away, but as long as we're here, they're going to stick around."

"And if we leave?" Gallo asked. "Will they follow us to the ends of the Earth, or just keep wandering around killing anyone who looks at them cross-eyed?"

Fiona returned a helpless shrug.

"If they are what I think they are," Pierce said. "They'll return to a dormant state as soon as we're out of here."

"Shekinah," Gallo murmured. "The glory of God. According to kabbalists, it's the feminine expression of God's divinity. And cows are female."

"Well, yes, but that's not what I mean. Fiona is right. The creatures are some kind of mobile energy storage vessels for the Originators. When they left...or died out...the creatures went into sleep mode, until Moses showed up and found some kind of control device left behind by the Originators. Probably something made out of memory metal like the orb. Maybe it's what inspired the legend of the sun chariot. While Moses held onto it, he could control the shekinahs. Use them to do stuff that must have seemed like the power of God."

"The Plagues," Gallo supplied. "And parting the Red Sea. That's more than a little blasphemous. And it doesn't consider the possibility that maybe the Originators didn't create any of this. Maybe they simply found it first."

"Unlikely."

"How's the saying go? God works in mysterious ways." She smiled, knowing the statement would irk him, and then added. "Is *anything* about all this likely?"

Pierce conceded the point with a subtle nod. "But I'm going to run with my theory until proven wrong. Now, the ninth plague was three days—seventy-two straight hours—of total darkness, which the Egyptians would have seen as a direct attack against Ra, the sun god."

"Three days of darkness. A solar event?"

"I think so. If our assumptions about the Black Knight are correct, he must have used it to redirect sunlight away from that part of the Earth."

"Wouldn't that have caused earthquakes like it did today?" Fiona asked.

"It very well may have. Or worse. Some scholars have theorized that the true cause of the Plagues was a coincidental eruption of the Thera volcano, but what if it's the other way around? What if that solar event triggered the volcano?"

"Which in turn caused the parting of the Red Sea."

Pierce spread his hands. "It all fits. After the Exodus, Moses came back here where he had the Ark made, a golden chest topped with cherubs—"

"We've all seen the movie with you, George," Gallo said with a wry smile. "Many times."

Pierce grinned. After seeing that movie the first time, he had become obsessed with Ark lore, researching all the stories of what it was and what became of it, searching for it, if only in his daydreams. "Well you know the power that was released at the end of the movie to melt Nazi faces? That was a real thing, and they called it *shekinah*. The Ark was so dangerous that it had to be kept in a special tent, the Tabernacle of Meeting. It was made of heavy fabric woven with gold fibers. The lid with the angels was called the Mercy Seat, and when it was in the Tabernacle, it radiated light—shekinah. No one but the high priest was allowed to see the Ark, and even then, only once a year. They had to tie a rope to his foot so that if he died, they could drag his body out. When moving the Ark, they kept it covered at all times, with a blanket made out of the same fabric. No one was ever permitted to touch it. Several centuries later, during the reign of King David, the Ark was being moved by wagon. One of David's men inadvertently touched it and died. Some fringe archaeologists have speculated that it might have been a sort of primitive battery, but I think it was a lot more than that."

Fiona's eyes widened in understanding. "Moses put one of the cows in it."

"No...I mean, yes, he did that, but there's more to it. I think he put the Originator artifact in it. He created the Ark to be the master control device for the entire Originator power system."

Gallo raised an eyebrow. "How did you arrive at that conclusion?"

"Forty years after the Exodus, when Moses's successor Yeshua ben Nun—Joshua—led the Israelite army into Palestine, the priests carried the Ark ahead of the army. When they walked into the

Jordan River, the waters parted, just like at the Red Sea—and maybe just like Fi did at Arkaim—so that the army could ford the river. In the first battle, the power in the Ark leveled the city walls of Jericho. Later, during the battle of Gideon, the Bible says that God hurled stones from heaven to slay the enemy—some kind of gravitational anomaly maybe—and when the enemy forces tried to escape, Joshua commanded the sun to stand still in the sky, which it did for a full twenty-four hours."

"So Joshua did the same thing Fallon did. Another solar event."

"Possibly the same one that inspired the Phaethon legend and Fiona's story of Raven stealing the sun. There's one more solar event mentioned in the Bible. A minor one. During the reign of King Hezekiah, the prophet Isaiah caused the shadow on a sundial to turn backward ten degrees."

Gallo folded her arms across her chest. "So the Ark and the Plagues and everything else... All miracles of the Bible... The foundation of the religious beliefs of half the world's population... It's all hogwash? An alien artifact pretending to be God?"

"Well..." Pierce shrugged.

"Bullshit," Gallo said. "You're a smart guy, but your narrow world-view tends to skew your perspective. You look for explanations without considering that the supernatural might be real. You're willing to believe in the most outlandish theories I've ever heard, unless believing means changing the way you live your life. Everything that you've said fits, but there's no evidence to suggest that the 'Originators' were from another planet, dimension, or time."

"You think the Originators were supernatural?" Fiona asked. "Like angels?"

"Or demons," Gallo said. "We know the Originators were viewed as giants. We know they played with genetics. We know they crossbred with humanity. All of these elements fit with the Biblical story of—"

"The Nephilim," George said.

"The Nephi-what now?" Fiona asked.

"Nephilim," George repeated. "The product of demons mating with human women. They're recorded in the Bible, and other texts around the world, as 'men of renown.' Giants. Like demi-gods, far more advanced than mankind at the time."

"Many scholars who believe the Nephilim story," Gallo started, "also believe the inhabitants of Jericho were Nephilim. Joshua's scouts reported that they were as grasshoppers in the sight of the people who lived there. So if the technology used to destroy the city was the same as Moses used to part the sea and rain down plagues on Egypt, perhaps its origin is more supernatural than alien. The fight between science and religion, and the hostility some people have toward religion—" She cleared her throat while looking at George. "—has never made sense to me. How could a God who created the universe and the scientific laws that allow it to function, not use science to carry out his plans?"

George was quiet for a moment, in part because he was surprised by Gallo's strident point of view, but also because it made sense. While he didn't consider himself hostile to religion, he did tend to categorize it as fiction. But he had seen things that could only be described as miraculous, and Fiona was learning to speak the language of God. At first, he thought the language discounted the stories of Moses and Jesus. They were just guys who spoke the language. But how could a shepherd and a carpenter learn the language of God? And why wouldn't they have used it to improve their lives? Moses wandered the desert for forty years and never set foot in his Promised Land. Jesus was crucified. If they'd had access to the Mother Tongue, or the Ark's power source, why didn't they use those things to change the world?

He smiled at himself.

They *had* changed the world. But not like a human being would have. "I concede the point. The Originators *could* be supernatural. Angels, demons, Nephilim. I can't discount anything, and I don't have all the answers. *But* for the sake of making sense of all this, I'm going to work through it in a way that's easier for me to grasp."

Gallo smiled and turned to Fiona. "This is why men need women willing to challenge their point of view. Makes them more well-rounded."

"Anyway..." George said, trying to suppress his smile. Gallo held the keys to his heart and his mind, and she knew it. "...what I'm getting at is that Moses and the Israelites left with the Ark, but the shekinahs—"

"That's a dumb name," Fiona said.

Pierce smiled. "The important thing is that Joshua triggered the solar event, and he didn't have a transmitter array or any special knowledge—"

"That we know of," Gallo put in.

"That tells me that the Ark is some kind of user-friendly control interface. Maybe Moses taught Joshua a few words in the Mother Tongue, or maybe it responds to psychic intentions. Either way, we can use it the same way. Turn off the Black Knight. Maybe even make it self-destruct, so this can never happen again."

"You really think you can find the Ark?"

"I think we have to. It's the only way to guarantee that Fallon or someone like him doesn't trigger another solar event. Fi, do you think you could make a golem to keep the cows away from us?"

Fiona considered the question for a moment. "Maybe. It doesn't take much to set them off, but I've got an idea. Do you think it's a good idea to leave them here?"

Pierce nodded. "Once we leave, put some distance between them and that sphere, they'll melt back into the ground, just like they did when Moses left three thousand years ago."

"What about the guys with guns?" Gallo asked.

"I think I can deal with them, too," Fiona promised.

"They're probably already gone." Pierce nodded to Fiona. "Do it."

The young woman moved to the mouth of the cave and shone her headlamp down at the piled rocks at the base of the cliff. She murmured the *emet* command, and then, with a loud rumble like another small tremor, the rocks began to move. Thousands of small pieces and a flurry of sand came together like iron filings around a magnet, forming a towering colossal figure that reached as high as the cave opening. Unlike the other golems Pierce had seen her create, this one was not humanoid. Despite its rough composition, he had no trouble distinguishing the shape of a Tyrannosaurus Rex.

Gallo grinned and laid on the sarcasm. "Definitely nothing supernatural about that."

Fiona allowed herself a slight smile, but the crease of her forehead showed her intense concentration. The golem began moving away, shaking the ground with each ponderous step. Fiona followed it with the beam of her headlamp, but after just a few steps, she turned around. "You guys should probably look away."

There was a faint flash of light, nowhere near as brilliant as what they had earlier experienced. Then he heard Fiona cry out.

"Fi?" Pierce whirled around and found her picking herself up off the cavern floor, trembling.

"That doesn't usually happen," she said.

"What? What happened?"

"Feedback. Felt like an electric shock, but I'll be okay." She stood up, shook herself, and managed a wan smile. "Rexie went all to pieces, though. One golem per cow, I guess."

"You're not doing that again," Pierce declared. "We'll just have to make a run for it."

The fact that she didn't protest told him that she was trying to downplay the severity of the jolt.

Pierce peered down at the base of the cliff, and was dismayed to see two of the shekinah creatures milling about nearby. They weren't circling like predators. In fact, they were barely moving at all.

He took a deep breath, and then began the descent, facing the wall as he made his way down the irregular steps the way he might climb down a ladder. Every few steps, he glanced down, making sure that the beasts were keeping their distance. As soon as he was back on the grade, he waved for the others to follow, then returned his attention to the shekinah creatures. There was no indication that they were even aware of his presence. They ignored Gallo's arrival as well, but when Fiona emerged from the cave, the reaction was unmistakable. In unison, the creatures began shuffling toward them. Pierce felt the first tickle of static electricity on his face.

He shone his light away from the creatures and started forward as fast as the loose terrain would allow. A shekinah appeared ahead, trundling toward them on a slow but obvious intercept course. Pierce shifted away from it, but he was stopped after just a few steps by a gaping fissure. The shekinah now blocked their retreat, forcing them to continue along the edge of the fissure, but then another creature came into view in that direction.

Pierce skidded to a stop and searched for another route. The fissure was too wide to leap across, which left only climbing back up the slope, a move that would leave them pinned against the cliff face.

He heard Fiona speak, but it took him a second to realize what she was saying. "*Versatu elid vas re'eish clom, emet.*"

"Fi, no!"

Even as he said it, he felt the ground tremble as a newly formed golem began moving toward the strange creatures. Pierce saw it in the light of his headlamp, a giant T. Rex composed of sand and loose rock, closing on the creature pursuing them. Its massive jaws opened and then came down over the misshapen shekinah.

"Don't look!" Fiona shouted.

Pierce was already turning away, but out of the corner of his eye, he saw the golem envelop the smaller creature. There was a harsh tearing noise, and Pierce could feel electricity cracking all over his body, but the golem's body shielded them all from the worst effects. Some light rays seeped through the cracks between the loosely joined rocks comprising the earthen creation, leaving a few streaks across Pierce's vision. But it wasn't even as bright as a camera flash. As the golem crumbled, Fiona collapsed like an unstrung puppet.

Pierce scooped the fallen girl up in his arms, over her weak protest, and with Gallo beside him, he started back the way they had come. The rubble left from the golem's disintegration made for a precarious crossing, but once past the worst of it, Pierce picked up the pace. His lungs burned from altitude and exertion, and his legs felt like molten lead, but the sight of more shekinahs closing in on them supplied a burst of adrenaline that left him both numb to the pain and energized.

"I can walk,' Fiona mumbled. Pierce ignored her, but then she whispered one more word. *"Emet."*

"Damn it, Fi!"

He felt a rumble rising up through his boot soles as the rubble pile behind them coalesced into another golem, and he had to slow almost to a stop as the construct lumbered past on an intercept course with the shekinahs. Pierce caught only a glimpse of the golem—not a dinosaur this time, but a crude humanoid form—before he heard Fiona's voice again. *"Met."*

The golem crumbled into a heap right in front of the shekinah creatures, blocking their approach, and buying the three of them a few extra seconds to maneuver.

All Pierce could think to say was: "Good thinking."

"I can walk," Fiona said again, and this time, Pierce took her word for it.

THIRTY

With Fiona using the golems to block the creatures instead of destroying them, they reached the monastery walls without triggering any further radiant bursts. The gunmen were also absent, but Pierce remained wary as they made their way around the monastery. The garden area on the opposite side of the complex had been transformed into a triage site, with emergency workers and monks ministering to the wounded.

"I hope Father Justin made it," Fiona said.

Pierce nodded. "Right now, the best thing we can do for him and all the survivors is to get as far away from here as we can."

"How far is that?" Gallo asked.

"We'll just keep moving," Pierce said.

They slipped past the casualty collection point and made their way down the road to the tourist village, also named for Saint Catherine. The hotels were full of visitors who, following both the earthquakes and the rumors of a terrorist attack at the nearby monastery, were waiting to be evacuated by bus to Sharm el-Sheikh. After a few inquiries, Pierce found a local taxi driver willing to make the road trip, for quadruple the normal fare—a very competitive rate given the circumstances, he was assured—and they were soon underway again.

As the hired car raced down the desert roads, Pierce called Dourado and learned of the debacle in Geneva, and the worldwide consequences.

There had indeed been another spate of earthquakes in the western hemisphere. In an ironic reversal, earthquake-prone California had experienced only mild shocks, nothing above magnitude 5.0. But further to the north, the pent-up energy of the Cascadia Subduction Zone, had been released in a massive six-minute-long quake measuring 8.4 on the Richter scale. The entire northwest coast of Oregon and Washington had gone silent. The predictions emerging from scientists and news agencies were ominous. Portland, Seattle, and everything west of Interstate 5 had been devastated by the temblor and the subsequent tsunami. Alaska had been hit with the most destructive temblor since the 1964 Good Friday earthquake that had leveled Anchorage. Hawaii and Japan were bracing for tsunamis that would, in all likelihood, dwarf the disastrous effects of the 2011 Fukushima quake.

That the seismic disturbances had been a long time coming—historically, a 'Big One' hit the region every 300-600 years, and the last one had occurred in 1700—didn't make the news any easier to swallow. Carter was a Seattle native, and Fiona's ancestral home was just a few miles inland on the Oregon Coast. It would be hours, possibly even days, before the true extent of the damage was known. But even the most optimistic predictions were dire.

Yet as terrible as the news was, Pierce knew it was only a shadow of the danger that still loomed on the horizon.

Following the showdown with the renegade robots, the team had regrouped and set up an ad hoc command center at Tomorrowland. Despite his frustration, Pierce knew that the misguided attempt to 'fix' the Black Knight had been the right decision, given the circumstances. At least now they knew who was responsible for the global threat.

Ishiro Tanaka.

Pierce put the phone on speaker mode, as Dourado began relating what she had discovered about the Japanese physicist.

The grandson of a survivor of the Nagasaki atomic bombing, Tanaka had, from an early age, shown a macabre fascination with the destructive forces at work in the universe. Later in life, as a university student, he had become an active and vocal proponent of the Voluntary Human Extinction Movement—VHEMT, pronounced 'Vehement'. They were a group that espoused the belief that humans were a virulent disease and would destroy all life on Earth if they were not themselves made extinct. It was a goal they believed could be accomplished peacefully through anti-natalism—the end of human procreation.

"Vehement wasn't radical enough for him," Dourado explained, "But he became friends with an Indian student named Bandar Pradesh—"

"Bandar Pradesh?" Gallo broke in. "That's not a real Indian name."

"I know, right? Bandar literally means 'port' and Pradesh means 'province.' It's probably an alias or some kind of inside joke. He preferred to go by his hacker name: Shiva. Pradesh or Shiva or whatever you want to call him, took the whole humans-are-a-disease thing one step further. He believed that all life—from microbes to redwood trees to blue whales—was a great big cosmic mistake."

"Huh?"

Carter broke in. "It's the philosophy of pessimism."

"Like Rust, in *True Detective*," Dourado supplied.

"I was thinking more along the lines of Schopenhauer," Carter said. "Death gets us all in the end. Everything we do only leads to suffering, either for ourselves or someone else. Entropy will eventually destroy the universe no matter what we do, and since life is pretty much miserable for most creatures, eradicating life from the universe is a merciful act, sparing future generations from pain and suffering."

"That's dark," Pierce said.

"Geniuses are a little more susceptible to philosophies like that, because they want to understand the big picture and think everything should make sense like a balanced equation. They end up getting scared by what they see."

"Tanaka and Shiva stayed friends," Dourado continued. "And continued to be pessi-bros or whatever. Tanaka worked at HAARP for a while, and then joined Pradesh at a place called Jovian Technologies, but then Shiva disappeared during the Blackout incident in Paris a few years ago."

"I remember that," Fiona said with a groan.

"Tanaka was pretty quiet after that," Dourado continued, "Stopped posting on the Vehement forums and focused on his work."

"Unfortunately," said a new, unfamiliar male voice, "his work was helping me figure out how to turn the Black Knight satellite into a planetary-scale solar reflector."

Marcus Fallon, Pierce thought. *The boy who couldn't resist playing with fire.*

"So that's all he wants? Global annihilation? No negotiation?"

"Seems that way," Dourado answered.

"Do we know where he's going?"

"Not a clue. He could be anywhere. All he needs is an antenna array with a 10 gigahertz transmitter, and he can stop the sun."

"What about the men who attacked the monastery? Were they working with him?"

"Given the timing of the attack, I think that's a safe assumption. Tanaka has been building his doomsday network for a long time, and thanks to the Internet and his Vehement connections, it's worldwide."

Gallo shook her head. "Who knew there were so many people out there rooting for the end of the world?"

"There are a lot of them, and they don't care if they live or die."

"Well, they're all going to be disappointed when we shut down the Black Knight. Permanently."

Dourado let out a cheer and in a gruff voice said, "Today, we are canceling the apocalypse!"

Carter was a little more subdued. "You found the sun chariot?"

"Not exactly." He recounted their misadventure with the shekinah creatures and the revelation in the Cave of Moses. Dourado interrupted only once with the cryptic pronouncement, "So there *is* a cow level."

Pierce assumed it was a pop culture reference. Dourado made a lot of those.

"The Ark of the Covenant," Fallon mused. "It's a real thing?"

For the first time since making the call, it occurred to Pierce that he was being a little too free with information. "That's right," he said.

"And it's an artifact from the same aliens that made the Black Knight?"

Fallon was quick, and well-informed. He also knew more about the meta-material than any of them. *Okay,* Pierce thought. *Time to extend a little trust. I just hope this doesn't come back to bite me in the ass.*

"Tanaka has the Roswell fragment, and I think we know what he plans to do with it. Unfortunately, since we don't know *where* he's going to do it from, finding the Ark and using it to shut down the Black Knight is our best option."

"We don't have much time," Fallon pointed out. "Do you know where it is? In the movie, it was in Egypt. But then they took it to Area 51. Is that where it is?"

"No. Though it pains me to say, that was just a movie. And the premise was flawed. According to the movie, the Pharaoh Shishak—

or Shoshenq—took the Ark when he raided the Temple of Solomon in 980 B.C.E. The raid actually happened, but Shoshenq didn't get the Ark. It's mentioned again in the Bible record during the reign of King Josiah more than three hundred years later."

Carter spoke up again. "The Ark is in Ethiopia. In a chapel in Axum."

Pierce smiled to himself. "That's one of many rumored locations. There are so many different Ark stories, it's no wonder it's never been found. The Ethiopian legend is based on a Bible reference about the Queen of Sheba visiting King Solomon. Two thousand-odd years later, the Christian emperor of Ethiopia built on that story to legitimize his right to rule. According to this new version, Sheba was another name for Ethiopia. Solomon secretly married the Queen and she bore him a son, Menelik, the first emperor and progenitor of the Menelik dynasty, which supposedly endured until 1975. Solomon entrusted the Ark to Menelik, who bore it away secretly to Sheba, where it has been ever since." He shook his head. "It's a pretty fanciful story, concocted for political reasons.

"For my money, the most plausible story is recorded in the Second Book of Maccabees. Shortly before the Babylonians destroyed Jerusalem and carried all the Jews off into exile, the prophet Jeremiah was ordered by God to take the Ark and the Tabernacle and hide them in a cave on Mount Nebo, the place where Moses died. He shut the cave up and never told anyone its location, promising that it would only be revealed when God gathered his people together again and showed them mercy.

"Jeremiah was the son of a *Kohen*, a Levite priest descended from Moses's brother Aaron, and incidentally the derivation of the modern Jewish name Cohen. The Bible account is very explicit about the fact that only a Kohen could safely enter the Holy of Holies in the Tabernacle and approach the Ark. To me, that weighs in favor of Jeremiah being the one to relocate the Ark."

When no one raised an objection, Pierce went on. "Mount Nebo is in modern-day Jordan, but there's some disagreement about whether that identification is accurate. Judging by the fact that nobody's found the Ark in the last twenty-six-hundred years, I'm guessing it's not.

"Cintia, head back to Rome and start digging in the archives. See if you can give us a better search area. We'll head on to Amman and get in position."

"What about me and Erik?" Carter asked.

"Do what you can to help Cintia."

"I'll meet you there," Lazarus said, speaking for the first time. "I should have been there with you."

"From what Cintia's told me," Pierce countered, "It's a good thing you weren't."

"All the same, I'm no use to anyone staying in the rear with the gear."

Pierce weighed the offer a moment. As much as he would have liked to have the big man with him, looking out for them, there really wasn't a need for additional protection. With Tanaka's deception exposed, the security leak that had led the gunmen to them in Sinai was plugged. Besides, Tanaka would almost certainly shift his resources to the matter of finding another transmitter and guarding it. Finding the Ark was going to require actual archaeology—solving an age old mystery and digging in the ground—not the brawling, gun-toting, tomb-raiding of an Indiana Jones.

"I appreciate it," Pierce said, "But I'm hoping we'll have this wrapped up in a few hours. Stay with Felice."

Lazarus didn't press the issue, and it occurred to Pierce that his last statement might have been misinterpreted. He had meant to imply that Carter might be in need of comfort in the wake of the devastating news out of the Northwest, but perhaps the big man had understood it to mean something else.

Stay with Felice so that you'll be together when the end comes.

If he failed to find the Ark, to solve a mystery that had confounded searchers for more than two thousand years, it just might come to that.

"You know, on second thought, if the Ark isn't at Mount Nebo, we're going to be back to square one. We need to cover our bases. Erik, you and Felice head to Ethiopia and check out the church in Axum. If we both strike out, at least we'll have crossed two possibilities off the list."

He tried to sound upbeat when giving them the assignment. It was busy-work, giving them something to do so they wouldn't feel useless. The odds of the Ark being in Ethiopia were about a billion-to-one. However, as he had once pointed out to a certain cheerleader who had given him similar odds of ever going out with him, a billion-to-one meant there was still a chance.

"On it," Lazarus said.

"What about me?" Fallon asked. "What can I do?"

Pierce resisted the impulse to tell Fallon that he had done quite enough. He settled for something only slightly more diplomatic. "We've got this under control, and I'm sure you've got some house cleaning to do. If the world doesn't end, you'll know we succeeded."

THIRTY-ONE

Geneva, Switzerland

A car was waiting for Tanaka at the front entrance to Tomorrowland. He did not recognize the driver, but that was not unexpected. The Children of Durga were many, but scattered far and wide, separated not only by physical geography, but also by culture and faith.

Not all of Durga's children recognized their mother, but they did share a common unifying vision: a belief that the end of the world was not merely imminent, but urgently needed. For some, the end would bring a Rapture of the faithful or entry into a paradisiac afterlife. Others believed that destruction was a necessary part of the phoenix-like cycle of rebirth, and that a cleansed planet would bring about a new and better age. Only a few shared the true vision of

Durga: the enlightened knowledge that life was a bitter joke from a cruel universe.

Tanaka didn't know Durga's true identity. No one did, though Tanaka thought Shiva might have. But while the two of them had shared a bond far deeper than mere friendship, Shiva had only hinted at the depths of his relationship with Durga.

Although born in India, a land immersed in Hindu mythology, Shiva had not chosen his alias for religious reasons. *Shiva is the consort of Durga,* he had explained to Tanaka. *The mahashakti, the form and formless, the root cause of creation, preservation, and annihilation.*

Tanaka had understood that was not meant to be interpreted literally, but it suggested a very intimate relationship between the young man—who had been an orphan and an outcast—and the mysterious leader of their cause. Durga might have been a parental figure, the person who lifted young Shiva up out of poverty and set him on the path. Or perhaps a former lover. Or both. Although Durga was a form of the Goddess in Hinduism, that did not mean the person behind that alias was female.

Shiva was gone now, but the cause remained. Durga remained, and had made direct contact with him in the weeks following Shiva's disappearance.

Aside from Shiva, a true Child of the Goddess, Tanaka had never met another follower in person, but that did not matter. Their unity of purpose found its truest expression in the virtual world, where they could share ideas unburdened by the limitations and animal urges of physical bodies.

However, there was only so much that could be accomplished on Internet forums and chat rooms. Misery and suffering existed in the real world, so the Annihilation, the Great Victory of Durga, the end of death itself, could only be accomplished there. Tanaka would be the instrument of Durga's victory.

Security was also a concern. Compartmentalization and anonymity ensured that only a few knew the full scope and purpose of the plan, and this was of particular concern as the plan came to fruition.

The driver did not know who Tanaka was or that he carried the Roswell meta-material, nor did he know with certainty that the recent earthquakes were the beginning of the end. He might be Christian or Muslim, or something else altogether. All he would have been told was to pick someone up outside the gates of Tomorrowland and to do whatever that person instructed.

And one other thing. He handed Tanaka a throwaway mobile phone.

Tanaka opened the message center and read the only entry there, an anonymous text sent only a few minutes earlier. No words. Just a single question mark.

A message from Durga.

He typed out a reply.

>>>Got it.

A few seconds passed, and then a new message appeared.

>*Second test was a success. Objective achieved.*

Before he could reply, another text arrived.

>*Sent men to Sinai. Contact lost. Success there unlikely.*

Tanaka took the news like a physical blow. He had passed along the information about George Pierce's search for an ancient relic with a possible connection to the Black Knight, but he had not really considered it to be much of a threat to their endeavor. Durga felt differently, and judging by the outcome, the concern appeared warranted.

>>>What does that mean for us?

>*Uncertain. What is status there?*

Tanaka started typing in a response, deleted it, started again and then deleted that, too. When he had slipped away from the transmitter building, Fallon had been unconscious and the three visitors were all in mortal danger. If everything had gone according to plan, all four were now dead, but if he had learned anything from the day's activity, it was that things did not always go according to plan. Proclaiming victory would be premature, but if he equivocated without good reason, the entire endeavor might be derailed. He settled on a compromise that seemed workable.

>>>Unknown. Recommend we keep an eye on things here.

There was a pause, then another text appeared.

>*Agreed. Have your driver stay behind to assess outcome. Continue to prime objective.*

"Stop the car," Tanaka said, as soon as he read the message.
The driver pulled to the side of the road.
"Go back. You're supposed to keep watch at Tomorrowland."
The man glanced over and frowned. "Just me?"
"I have work to do elsewhere."
"And...you're taking my car?"
Tanaka almost laughed aloud. "I'll leave your car at the airport."
The man was not pleased about surrendering his personal vehicle to the cause. It was easy to be a true believer on the Internet. Sacrificing material possessions in the real world was a lot harder.
"Trust me," Tanaka went on. "Very soon, you won't need a car or anything else, ever again."

THIRTY-TWO

Mount Sinai, Egypt

For a long time, Abdul-Ahad did not move. He felt exhausted, completely drained. He could not see a thing. His entire body felt numb, the nerve endings in his skin overloaded. It was as if the pure light unleashed with the destruction of the *jinn* had bleached him to the bone.

But he was still alive.

At first, the realization had filled him with despair. Had he been wrong about attacking the *jinn*? Was that why he had been denied entry into Paradise with the others? But as he lay there, blind, numb, and helpless, he realized why he was still alive.

His ears worked just fine, but for a long time, all he could hear was the soft crunch of *jinn* roaming about on the mountain slope, and much fainter, the cries of alarm rising from the monastery. Then, he heard voices, speaking English.

The agents of the anti-messiah were still alive.

There was nothing he could do to stop them, not in his current condition, and not by himself. But there were other ways to fight.

Israfil must be told, he thought.

God was not finished with him. There was work yet to do.

THIRTY-THREE

Geneva, Switzerland

"The Lost Ark," Marcus Fallon shook his head in disbelief, as the conference call ended. "Well, I guess it isn't any crazier than the idea of using an alien artifact to shut down the sun. Or are the two connected? I can't keep it all straight. Is this all for real?"

Carter stared at him, but it was the pink-haired woman, Dourado, who answered. "If Dr. Pierce says it is, believe it."

She turned away, as if the matter warranted no further consideration and began discussing travel plans with Carter, while the big man, Lazarus, looked on, saying nothing.

Fallon felt like the odd man out, a stranger in his own home. They were done with him. He was of no further use, and they didn't seem to care if he knew it.

He was a little surprised, and not in a good way, at the audacity they had demonstrated thus far, moving into Tomorrowland like a military strike force, destroying his property, commandeering his computers. While it was true that he was partly to blame for the mess, that didn't excuse their rudeness.

We'll just see about that, he thought.

"So what happens next? I mean, once Pierce finds the Ark?"

Carter looked up again. "You heard him. Shut the Black Knight down and make sure this doesn't happen again."

"That's not acceptable."

"Excuse me?"

"The Black Knight is the key to breaking free of the Earth, colonizing other planets. You don't just throw an opportunity like that away."

Carter shook her head. "Maybe you've forgotten already, but the Pacific Coast is underwater. The world is in shambles, and that would be true even without Tanaka trying to send us all to Hell. That's where your opportunity has gotten us."

"Sure, there were mistakes," he said, "but that's no reason to burn all the progress we've made. If the Ark is the key to controlling the Black Knight, then we need to do more research with it."

"You mean *you* need to do more research," Lazarus said, in a low voice that sounded more than a little threatening.

"Yes, as a matter of fact, I've already laid the groundwork. Invested millions. If Tanaka hadn't gone bat-shit crazy, I would already be on my way to working out the kinks. I deserve a piece of this."

Carter continued to regard him with cool indifference. "I guess you could make a legal case for that. Of course, you would have to admit some responsibility for these disasters. And make the case that you could behave responsibly with it." She shook her head. "I know you mean well, Marcus, but you know what will happen if you try to move forward with your research. Someone will turn it into a weapon, just like what Tanaka wants to do."

Not if I turn it into a weapon first, Fallon thought.

And why not? If he controlled the Black Knight, he would own the sun.

He managed a smile of resignation and let the matter drop. Maybe they were done with him, but he wasn't done with them.

THIRTY-FOUR

Mount Nebo, Jordan

"I can't believe they called *this* 'the Promised Land.'" Fiona waved a hand at the panoramic vista spread out before them. From the 2,800-foot-tall ridge overlooking the Jordan River Valley, she could see all the way to Jerusalem, but although there were a few patches of green here and there, and a sparkling blue gem that was the Dead Sea, the landscape was, for the most part, desolate desert.

"It looked very different three thousand years ago," Gallo said. "Remember, this is one of the oldest continuously inhabited regions on Earth."

"Inhabited and contested," Pierce added. "People have been fighting over this real estate through all of recorded history."

"Yeah, it's got kind of a lived-in look," Fiona agreed. She dropped her gaze to the large metal plaque that showed the direction and distance of several important locations, some of which Fiona recogniz-ed—Jerusalem and Bethlehem—and some which sounded familiar. "Qumran?"

"The location where the Dead Sea Scrolls were found," Pierce said.

"Oh." Fiona turned away from the scenic view. Off to her left stood the reconstructed Byzantine church, called the Basilica of Moses, the ruins of which had been discovered in the 1930s. The structure reminded her of the St. Catherine's Monastery, and that made her think about Father Justin, which in turn made her feel like crying. So she turned away from it as well, looking instead to the parking area, which was crowded full of cars and buses. Tourists were snapping selfies with the Holy Land in the background.

Pilgrimage, twenty-first century style.

While the world was still trying to restore some semblance of order following the unprecedented global earthquakes, tourism in the Holy Lands was continuing apace. Instead of canceling their plans and heading home, visitors to the region seemed energized by the possibility that the long-anticipated End Times were about to reach their climax. One such vacationer had explained to Fiona how the Book of Revelation foretold a great earthquake and a time of darkness upon the Earth, just before the End.

Fiona found the prophecy more than a little disquieting. It was probably just a coincidence, but what if it wasn't? She had tapped into some kind of universal knowledge under Arkaim. Maybe all those prophets in the Bible had tuned into the same thing? Maybe whatever was about to happen with the Black Knight was so profound that it sent ripples back through time? Or maybe someone—God, or the Originators, or whoever—had known what might happen, and sent those visions and prophecies as a warning?

Thinking about it made her head hurt, especially since she was already feeling tired and a little cranky after traveling too many miles and getting too little sleep. Twenty-four hours earlier she had been in Russia, preparing for an excursion into the tunnel labyrinth beneath Arkaim. Twelve hours prior—give or take—she had been huddled with Pierce and Gallo in a cave on the side of a mountain in Egypt. Now, she was about to go searching for another cave on another mountain, this time in Jordan.

To the north, opposite the church, stood a tall, creepy-looking cross-shaped sculpture. "What's that?"

"It's a reimagining of the *Nehushtan*," Gallo told her. "The Brazen Serpent that God had instructed Moses to set up to heal anyone bitten by one of the fiery serpents that God had sent to punish them."

"So God sent the serpents, then told them how to be saved from the serpents."

"Christians believe the incident was meant to prefigure looking to crucified Christ for salvation. You'll notice the cross-shaped design of that piece. It's a modern piece, of course. Not the actual Serpent Moses made."

"What happened to the real one?" Fiona asked.

"According to the Bible, it was destroyed a few centuries later. The people had started worshipping it, so King Hezekiah had it destroyed."

"Is that the spot where Moses put it?"

Pierce jumped in. "Remember, the Israelites were a nomadic people, so there was no fixed location for it. This mountain has special significance though, because it's the place where Moses died. God wouldn't permit him to enter the Promised Land, but he did get to see it from here. So this place is a symbolic boundary between the Holy Land and the wilderness, divine grace and exile. That's what makes this the most logical spot for the Ark to be hidden."

Pierce had clearly put some thought into the matter.

Fiona nodded at the sculpture. "It kind of reminds me of a Caduceus. The symbol for medicine."

"Technically, the symbol of medicine is the Rod of Asclepius, the Greek god of healing. A staff with one snake. The Caduceus has two snakes and is the symbol of Hermes, the messenger of the gods.

The two are commonly confused, but it is interesting how the archetype of the serpent as both a healing figure and a symbol of wisdom is mirrored across different belief systems." Pierce nodded at the sculpture. "That definitely has elements of both.

"You'll appreciate this, Fi. Hermes, or Mercury, was also considered the embodiment of wisdom. In Egyptian mythology, he was equated with Thoth, and the Babylonians called him Nabu."

"Nabu... Nebo?"

Pierce nodded. "And the Egyptian word for 'gold' is Nebu. Gold was a sacred metal to the Egyptians, associated with the glory of the sun god. The name for Hathor literally translated as 'golden goddess.'"

"Hathor, the sun cow lady?"

The trilling of Pierce's satellite-enabled smartphone interrupted him, just as the conversation was getting interesting. He grinned when he saw the name on the caller ID. "Tell me you've got good news, Cintia."

He listened for a moment, then gestured for Fiona and Gallo to join him in their rented car. Once they were all ensconced within, he set the phone face-up on the center console. "Okay, say that again."

Dourado sounded like she was stuck in fast forward. It wasn't too hard to imagine her ensconced in her computer room, mainlining Monster energy drinks. "Are you all sitting down? I hope you're sitting down because... Mind. Blown."

"Let's have it," Pierce said, sounding far more upbeat than he had any right to.

"Okay, I'm sure you already know most of this, Dr. Pierce, but I'll start from the beginning. This is from the second book of Maccabees, chapter two. 'The prophet, in virtue of an oracle, ordered that the tent and the ark should accompany him. He went to the very mountain that Moses climbed to behold God's inheritance. When Jeremiah arrived there, he found a chamber in a cave in which he put the tent, the Ark, and the altar of incense; then he sealed the entrance. Some of those who followed him came up intending to mark the path, but they could not find it. When Jeremiah heard of this, he reproved them: 'The place is to remain unknown until God gathers his people together again and shows them mercy. Then the Lord will disclose these things, and the glory of the Lord and the cloud will be seen, just as they appeared in the time of Moses and of Solomon when he prayed that the place might be greatly sanctified. It is also related how Solomon in his wisdom offered a sacrifice for the dedication and the completion of the temple.'"

"The mention of Solomon is significant," Pierce said, as an aside to Fiona. "Solomon built the Temple as a permanent place to house the Ark, and as a reward, he was blessed with divine wisdom."

"Wisdom," Fiona said. "And Nabu, a.k.a. Nebo, is the Babylonian god of wisdom."

"More proof that we're in the right place," Pierce said. "But we need to narrow it down."

"I'm getting to that," Dourado said, the words almost running together like the buzz of a bee's wings. "The chapter begins by referencing another document. This whole account is a synopsis of that other document, but it doesn't specify the actual source. However, there is a similar account in The Apocalypse of Baruch the Son of Neriah, so that's probably what they were talking about.

"Baruch has a vision in which he sees an angel go into the Holy of Holies to gather up the Ark and all the treasures of the Tabernacle, after he commands the Earth to hide the treasures, so that strangers—the Babylonians—would not be able to take them. After the vision, Baruch is sent to find Jeremiah. He tells him everything he saw and then they spend seven days together fasting."

"Baruch was giving Jeremiah his marching orders," Pierce said.

"He doesn't explicitly say where Jeremiah was to hide the Ark, but he does say this later on: 'You priests take you the keys of the sanctuary, and cast them into the height of heaven, and give them to the Lord.'"

"How does that help?" Fiona asked.

"The keys were symbolic of the authority to enter the Temple," Pierce explained. "There weren't actual locks on the doors. Casting them into the heavens would be sort of like giving the keys to your apartment back to the landlord when you move out. And remember, Jeremiah was a Kohen. He had God's permission to enter the Temple."

"There's more to it," Dourado said. "He was being given direction and distance to the place where the Ark was supposed to be hidden."

"I don't understand," Fiona said.

"I'm not sure I do either," Pierce admitted. "Explain."

"This is from later in the chapter: 'And do thou, O sun withhold the light of your rays. And do thou, O moon, extinguish the multitude of your light. For why should light rise again. Where the light of Zion is darkened?'"

"That sounds like a solar event," Fiona said.

"I know, right?" Dourado agreed. "But it also signifies direction. Sunrise. Due east. Mount Nebo is due east of Jerusalem. This is backed up in the Book of Ezekiel. Chapter eleven makes repeated references to the east gate of the city, and the glory of God—"

"Shekinah," Gallo murmured.

"—leaving the city and going to stand on a mountain to the east of the city. And what mountain is east of Jerusalem?"

"The placement of the Temple in Jerusalem was not random. Everything had symbolic importance. So when Jeremiah throws the keys from the door of the sanctuary, it's symbolizing that he should travel due east, toward the spot where the sun would appear to rise over Mount Nebo on the day of the vernal equinox, a heading of ninety degrees, adjusting for changes due to precession."

"Interesting," Pierce said. "You said direction *and* distance?"

"Everything about the Temple was precisely measured, and those measurements reflect a very precise mathematical code. The same would be true of the place where the Ark was to be stored until the return. When he talks about throwing the keys to the 'heights of the heavens,' it's not just a metaphor. It indicates a specific measurement, based on the height of the Temple itself. Forty cubits."

"Forty cubits," Pierce repeated. "Why does that sound familiar?"

"That same number appears in the Copper Scroll found with the Dead Sea scrolls. In part, it reads: 'In the ruin that is in the valley of Acor, under the steps, with the entrance at the East, a distance of forty cubits, a strongbox of silver and its vessels with a weight of seventeen talents.'"

"Where's Acor?" Fiona asked.

Pierce pointed to the west. "It's supposed to be that way, near the site of Jericho, but nobody's sure. No one has ever found a treasure matching that description."

"A Greek talent was believed to be roughly a hundred pounds," Gallo added. "So seventeen talents would indicate a considerable amount of precious metal, far too much for a single strongbox, I would think. The mention of vessels could refer to the sacred vessels of the Temple."

"It might not have anything to do with the Ark," Pierce said, "but the reference to forty cubits is interesting."

"A cubit was about eighteen inches," Gallo supplied. "The distance from the elbow to the tip of the middle finger."

"Actually, it was a variable measurement," Pierce said. "Anywhere from sixteen to twenty-five inches depending on who you ask."

"Exactly," Dourado said. "But the cubit used for measuring the Temple—the Sacred cubit—was 25.20 inches. The same unit of measurement was used for building the Great Pyramid, which is why they are sometimes called Pyramid cubits. That number, 25.20 is important. It's one percent of 2,520, which is the product of 7 and 360."

"Seven is the number of God and there are 360 days in the lunar calendar," Gallo said, as if speaking to herself.

"And 360 degrees in a circle. It's a recurring numerical value in the Old Testament."

Pierce shook his head. "It's a coincidence. Numerologists are always finding patterns that aren't there. Our system of measurement is an arbitrary value established just a few hundred years ago."

"That's not completely true, George," Gallo countered. "Yes, statute measurements were established by Queen Elizabeth, but they were based on earlier systems of measurement."

"But still arbitrary."

"Not necessarily. In the year 240 BC, the Greek astronomer Eratosthenes calculated the circumference of the Earth by comparing the difference in the length of the shadows cast in two different cities at exactly the same time. He calculated the circumference of the Earth to within 1%. He was able to make that calculation because he knew that a circle could be evenly divided into 360 degrees, each degree measuring 700 stadia."

"That's 252,000," Fiona said. "There's that number again."

Gallo nodded. "The error in measurement was due only to the fact that the Earth isn't a perfect sphere, something he couldn't have known. His method was valid and based on known universal constants. Christopher Columbus used his calculations to plot his circumnavigation, and the only reason he stumbled across America is because he didn't know which version of the stadia Eratosthenes had used. Like I told you earlier, the ancients were much more sophisticated than we give them credit for. The statute measurement system was based on an older system, so it's not unreasonable to think that the statute inch was derived from the Sacred cubit, instead of the other way around."

"That's right," Dourado added. "And the statute measurement system was devised in part by Dr. John Dee, who was a devoted scholar of Jewish mysticism. It's pretty mind-boggling. And I would have been tempted to dismiss it all as rubbish except for one thing, or actually, one man. The guy who figured out this stuff, including the actual length of the Sacred cubit, was none other than Sir Isaac Newton.

"All the discoveries he made—gravity, thermodynamics, the properties of light, calculus—it all came out of his search to unlock the mysteries of the universe. He was convinced that the answer was contained in sacred writings, and in particular, measurements.

Two-thirds of Newton's research, most of which is still unpublished, was devoted to theological mysteries, not scientific, though I'm sure to him it was all part of the same puzzle.

"Newton kept finding a numerical pattern in the dimensions of the Temple and the precise locations of sacred spots. Patterns that were reflected in the universe. In the movement of orbiting bodies and the behavior of light."

"Okay," Pierce said. "We'll assume that Newton knew what he was talking about. You said the height of the Temple was forty Sacred cubits."

"Eighty-four feet. If you head due east, as reckoned by sunrise on the vernal equinox viewed from the Temple Mount, and adjusting for the changes due to precession, the azimuth crosses the highest point on the ridge at a distance of 168,000 feet—80,000 Sacred cubits or 2,000 times the height of the Temple. That location is about three miles east of where you are, but definitely not on Mount Nebo.

"The exact number 80,000 appears in the Bible three times, all in reference to the building of the Temple of Solomon. 'Solomon counted out seventy thousand men to bear burdens, and eighty thousand men who were stone cutters in the mountains, and three thousand and six hundred to oversee them.' Did you catch the magic number in there? Seventy thousand and three thousand six hundred...multiply them together and you get 252,000,000 or 2520 times 100,000. If you travel 70,000 cubits from the Temple Mount, 1,750 times the height of the Temple, you hit a spot downslope, about a mile west of where you are."

Gallo nodded. "So 80,000 cubits is the measurement to the mountain, symbolized by the stone cutters, and 70,000 cubits—represented by the men carrying burdens—is the distance Jeremiah carried the Ark!"

"I'm sending you the coordinates," Dourado said.

"Is there a cave at that spot?" Pierce asked.

"There doesn't appear to be one on the satellite photos, but remember, the entrance was closed and hidden so well that the people with Jeremiah couldn't find it."

"A hidden entrance that only certain people can find and open," Gallo murmured, glancing at Fiona. "Where have we heard that before?"

Pierce nodded, but there was an eager gleam in his eyes. "Jeremiah was a Kohen and a Baal'Shem, a Master of the Word."

"The Mother Tongue," Fiona said.

"It might just be one particular word. In occult traditions, the Temple Key Cintia mentioned earlier refers to the true pronunciation of God's name, which possessed extraordinary power and was lost during the Babylonian exile. It was such a powerful word, or so tradition states, that it was forbidden to speak it. That's why we don't know what the actual name of God is today."

"I thought it was Jehovah, or Yahweh. Something like that."

"Those are approximations," Gallo said. "In the Book of Exodus, when Moses asks God his name, God answers: 'I Am that I Am.' The word 'I Am' written in Hebrew corresponds to YHWH—the tetragrammaton—but that's just the consonants. Written Hebrew doesn't include the vowels in between, so the pronunciation 'Yahweh' is just a guess. Jehovah is a Latinized version of it, the same way Jesus is Latinized from Yeshua."

"Actually, that may not be right either," Pierce said. "The name Yahweh showed up later in history. Some scholars think it might have been borrowed from another culture. The oldest name for the deity worshipped by the Israelites seems to be 'El Shaddai' or simply 'El.'"

Fiona didn't have the same encyclopedic knowledge of the subject as Pierce and Gallo, but she did know languages. "'El' is just the word for 'God.' The same root word as 'Allah.' It's a title, not a name."

"Right. And Shaddai is usually translated as 'almighty.' Though there's a lot of debate about its actual meaning. Some scholars think it meant 'mountain' or 'wilderness.' In fact, it could be the linguistic root for 'Sinai,' a reference to the time the Israelites spent there in the time of Moses. Or vice versa. Shaddai could also mean 'destroyer,' or possibly even 'mother.' The feminine form of the same word is 'shekinah.'"

"Shaddai, Sinai, Shekinah." Fiona said, managing a wry smile. "Great Goddess Almighty."

"George, you're confusing the girl," Gallo said.

"Jewish mystics believe that God has seven different names, all of them considered holy. Whatever the true name was, the one thing we do know is that it's in an extinct language."

"The Mother Tongue," Fiona said again, understanding what was being asked of her. Jeremiah had used the secret name of God as a key to lock up the cave where he had hidden the Ark of the Covenant.

She was the key that would open it again.

THIRTY-FIVE

His whole life had been leading up to this moment. A quarter of a century had passed, and the dream that had begun in a movie theater was about to reach fruition.

George Pierce was about to make the greatest discovery in the history of archaeology.

He looked down at the GPS display on the phone. A red pin marked the coordinates Dourado had uploaded. A blue arrow marked his phone's location. The two were nearly touching.

He pulled the car to the side of the road and shut off the engine. The Mount Nebo overlook was behind them, less than a mile away. Pierce could distinguish the church and the sculpture of the Brazen Serpent silhouetted against the azure sky. In front of them, the slope fell away, descending three thousand feet to the blue waters of the Dead Sea, the lowest point on the Earth's surface, 1,407 feet below sea level. The pinned location was just two hundred feet north of the road, a spot that could not have been less remarkable.

There was nothing there to suggest a cave, but as Dourado had indicated, that was the point.

With Fiona and Gallo in tow, he started out across the arid ground, watching as the arrow tip moved ever closer to the red pin. Closer.

A message flashed across the top of the screen.

You have arrived at your destination.

Pierce took a deep breath, savoring the moment, then turned to Fiona. "Anything?"

She shook her head.

He frowned. "Nothing at all? Did you try it with the sphere?"

Fiona held up the orb and waggled it in front of his face. "Zip. Nada. Nothing. Just like on Mount Sinai."

She compressed the memory metal into a smaller crumple— about the size of a ping pong ball—and shoved it into her pocket.

"Let's try the GPR," Pierce said, discouraged, but not ready to give up.

He shrugged out of the backpack and took out the Ground-shark. The ground penetrating radar would reveal any tunnels or void spaces up to ten feet below the surface. "Keep an eye out," he said. "I'd rather not have to explain what we're doing to any curious passersby."

He was not certain who owned the land on which they now stood. A ground penetrating radar survey was considered only marginally less invasive than actual digging, and if their activities were reported to the authorities the consequences would be severe. Pierce's professional reputation and UN affiliation would make matters worse.

Gallo turned toward the mountain, the likeliest place from which they might be observed. "All clear for now."

Pierce switched on the unit and knelt down, sweeping it back and forth. The display showed a dense subsurface—solid rock just below the thin layer of compacted sediment. He covered the target area and then started working outward, expanding the search area one square yard at a time. As he did, he felt less like Indiana Jones and more like a desperate treasure hunter with a metal detector and a crazy dream.

He should have known better. Numerology was just an elaborate form of pareidolia, seeing patterns where none truly existed.

Sacred cubits and recurring numbers, my a—

Hold on.

He stopped, then went back and swept the last section again, eyes riveted to the image on the screen.

"There's a void here!"

THIRTY-SIX

From his concealed position in the back of a minivan parked atop Mount Nebo, Craig Williams stared through the high-powered scope at the three figures. He settled the crosshairs on the kneeling figure— the man, George Pierce—watching him sweep a handheld device back and forth across the arid hardpan. Williams used the tick marks on the crosshairs to estimate the range to target and the time it would take for a bullet to travel that distance.

Three seconds, he thought.

He shifted the scope onto the older woman.

Older maybe, but I'd tap that.

He had not been told her name, but with her long black hair and olive complexion, she looked kind of like the lady in that last James Bond flick, the French actress.

Sophie...no, Monica. Monica... Something.

He decided to call the dark-haired woman 'the French Chick.' She was mostly standing still, though every few seconds, her head moved slowly from side-to-side, looking around.

Williams moved to the last person, the younger woman—she looked like a kid. Black hair, dark skin... *Mexican maybe?* She wasn't glamorous like the French Chick, but she wasn't fugly, for damn sure.

He centered the crosshairs on the side of her head, his trigger finger curling almost subconsciously.

No wind. Three seconds to target.

His finger curled.

"Bang," he whispered.

With a sigh of pent-up frustration, he moved the crosshairs back onto Pierce, the only member of the group who appeared to be doing anything. Exactly *what* he was doing was a mystery to Williams, but he had been hired to observe, nothing more.

No sniping today.

The scope wasn't even attached to a rifle. The man who had contracted him and the rest of the Alpha Dog team had fronted them the money to buy black market weapons, 'just in case,' but he had made it clear that killing Pierce and the others was not the primary objective.

Williams was a veteran of the Iraq war, where he had been a sniper before being discharged. He took a job with a private military contracting firm called Alpha Dog Solutions, so he could keep doing what he did best: kicking ass and taking names.

Alpha Dog's leadership had made some bad decisions, lost key personnel in botched field ops, and ultimately gone bust, but their misfortune had been Williams's opportunity. He had dusted off the name and rebooted the defunct company. The contracts weren't as exciting as they had been back in the glory days, but the Alpha Dog name still held a certain cachet with potential clients, especially those who didn't know any better.

Actually, this was their first big A-list gig, and Williams did not want to screw it up. If the man said watch, then watch he would.

Pierce was no longer on his knees. Instead, he was standing, gesturing wildly. *Found something, did you?*

The French Chick was smiling—she was too cool to get excited—and the Mexican Girl just looked a little worried. Nevertheless, she took a step forward, positioning herself on the exact spot where Pierce had been kneeling a moment before. Her lips began moving, though she didn't appear to be speaking to anyone.

Then, she took a step forward and vanished.

Williams jerked the scope back and forth, trying to locate her again. He reduced the magnifying power of the scope from 25x to 15x, then to 10x. He could see the other two, standing there, staring at that same spot, but there was no sign of the girl.

Where the hell did she go?

Suddenly, she popped back into view. Part of her, anyway. The girl's head and shoulders protruded from the desert floor, but everything below the center of her chest was concealed.

What is that, a trap door or something? he thought.

She made a 'come on' gesture and then was gone again. After a moment, Pierce and the French Chick stepped forward and also vanished.

Williams scanned the area trying to find the hidden door through which the group had passed but there wasn't one. The trio had stepped into the ground and disappeared. He set the scope down and turned to look at his employer.

"Mr. Fallon, you are not going to believe this."

THIRTY-SEVEN

Axum, Ethiopia

Carter's face was hidden by a *netela*—the traditional head covering worn by many Ethiopian women, but when she turned her head to look at him, Lazarus saw an uncharacteristic anxiety in her eyes. Felice Carter was one of the strongest women—no, that was wrong—one of the strongest *people* he had ever known. She had to be, to bear the burden fate had laid upon her. That strength took the shape of exceptional mental discipline. She wasn't without emotion like Spock from *Star Trek*, but she knew how to keep emotion and fear from short-circuiting rational thought.

"You okay?" he asked.

She looked at him, smiled, and gestured out the window of their taxi. "It's just this place. Ethiopia. This is where it happened."

Lazarus nodded. For all their time together, this was something they had never discussed in detail. He had learned of the event before meeting her for the first time, and there had never been cause to question her further about the particulars of that incident. He knew that Carter had been in Ethiopia as part of an expedition looking for prehistoric genetic material in the Great Rift Valley, where the remains of the oldest primate ancestors of humanity had been discovered. They had spent much of their two years together on the African continent, but their travels had never brought them back to Ethiopia, the place where Carter had been exposed to the paleo-historic retrovirus that had turned her into a living evolutionary kill-switch.

Everyone had their issues, and hers was a doozy. But his was pretty intense, too.

"We're at least three hundred miles from there," he said. He meant it to sound reassuring, but they had traveled thousands of miles from Switzerland to Ethiopia. Three hundred miles didn't seem all that far by comparison.

Axum had been the capital of the ancient Kingdom of Aksum, but now it was a small city of fifty thousand inhabitants, poised on the edge of the ever-encroaching desert. There were as many camels as cars on the main paved road. There was an airport though, about five miles from the center of town. The architecture was simple and traditional, mostly adobe-covered brick buildings. Lazarus saw no evidence of earthquake damage. The inhabitants of the region had been spared that additional hardship.

Carter offered a sad smile. "Same country. Same people. We were here for weeks before it happened. I got to know some of the locals very well. And one of them..." She trailed off, her smile slipping along with a measure of her control.

Lazarus didn't press the issue. "Is that when you learned about the rumor of the Ark being here?"

She shifted, packing the emotions away. "Rumor isn't the right word for it. The Ark is part of Ethiopia's cultural heritage. Every single Ethiopian Orthodox church in the world has a consecrated replica of the Ark. That's a tradition that goes back at least to the fourth century. The traditional belief that the Ark is here goes back even further. The Kingdom of Aksum, which is where this city got its name, converted to Judaism in the time of Solomon."

"You did your homework before you came here, didn't you?"

"I saw a special about it on the Discovery Channel." Carter smiled.

"So do you believe the Ark is here?"

She shrugged. "Until last night, I didn't even think it was a real thing. But George seems to think it's real enough, so maybe it is."

"Do *you* think it's here?" Lazarus asked.

Before she could answer, the taxi stopped in front of a dirt road that cut through a wooded area for at least a hundred yards before ending at an enormous, and almost futuristic-looking domed structure.

Lazarus handed their driver two hundred *birr* notes—about twenty dollars—and thanked the man. *"Betam ahmesugenalew."*

The voice was not his own, but an auto-tuned approximation, the Amharic translation supplied courtesy of Dourado's babelfish translation system. The driver replied in the same language, and a fraction of a second later, Lazarus heard the English translation in his earpiece. "No problem."

They got out and started down the dirt path to The Church of Our Lady Mary of Zion, the Ethiopian Orthodox Tewahedo cathedral said by some to house the Ark of the Covenant. Along the way, they passed several locals, all wearing long white garments and head coverings. The women, like Carter, wore *netela* scarves, and the men were similar in wraps called *kutas*. Directly ahead, lay the front of the domed building, with a façade of large arches, the largest of which framed the wooden double doors leading inside.

Lazarus muted the phone so the babelfish translators wouldn't translate their conversation. "That's a church? It looks more like a moonbase."

"That cathedral was built in the 1950s. Modern architecture was all the rage then, I guess. But there's been a church here almost as long as there have been Christians in Ethiopia."

She said nothing more on the subject, remaining silent as they ascended the steps and passed through the large wooden doors and into the church.

Lazarus was a bit surprised at the interior's brightness. The apse was well-lit thanks to a ring of windows atop the dome and several arched windows with clear and colored glass. The peach-colored walls were adorned with murals and icons, all rendered in bright colors. The blue sky in several of the paintings stood in stark contrast to the red carpet and the orange curtains behind the Eucharist altar. He was still trying to process the explosion of color when Carter pointed to the altar. "There it is."

He focused on the rectangular structure, adorned with a relief that he could not quite make out from the entrance, and a gilt overlay. "That's the Ark?"

"In a manner of speaking. It's a *tabot*, a replica, but it does contain a copy of the Ten Commandments made from the original. So in a way, it is *an* Ark of the Covenant."

"But it won't have what we need to shut down the Black Knight." He kept studying the altar. He repeated the question that she had avoided answering. "Do you think the real Ark is here?"

She sighed. "I don't know. I think Pierce is right that there were powerful political reasons for the Ethiopian rulers to claim that the

Ark was here, but I also think you can't just ignore the fact that millions of Ethiopians believe it, and have for more than two thousand years."

"A lot of people think Elvis is still alive. That doesn't make it true."

A faint grin touched her lips. "It doesn't make it untrue either."

"Point taken." He nodded his head in the direction of the altar. "If every Ethiopian church has one, how are we going to recognize the real deal? How do we tell the real Elvis from the impersonators?"

"The real Ark is covered in gold. I'm guessing they didn't go that extra mile with the copies. And then there's the lid with the angels."

He noticed a priest, a middle-aged man wearing gray vestments, moving in their direction. "Game time," he said. "How do we want to play this?"

"I may not be a believer, but I don't feel comfortable lying to a priest."

"Cards on the table, then." He unmuted the mic on the phone and took a step toward the priest. "Good afternoon. I'm Erik Lazarus, Director of Operations for the Cerberus Group. Who can I talk to about borrowing the Ark of the Covenant?"

THIRTY-EIGHT

Jordan

Walking through not-quite-solid rock was a little like walking through dense fog. Although Pierce had donned his headlamp before, he couldn't see the light, or anything else, until the crossing was complete and he stepped out onto the floor of a rough natural cave. Fiona was already there, her headlamp shining down the unexplored passage.

The passage, a narrow slot in the rock just higher than he was tall, reminded him of the Siloam Tunnel in Jerusalem, a seventeen-hundred-foot long tunnel carved in the days of King Hezekiah to provide water to the city during times of siege. This passage was wider, and of course, bone dry.

His excitement was back with a vengeance, but now that the prize was at last within his grasp, he was mindful of the other lessons he had learned from his fictional hero. "Okay, watch your step in here. There might be traps or..."

"Snakes?" Gallo asked with a wry smile.

"I was going to say other dangers, but yes, snakes or some other kind of guardian creature. We need to be on the lookout for stuff like that. Remember those things in Arkaim? I think long-term exposure to Originator relics can have an effect on evolution."

Fiona glanced down at the sphere in her hand. "Maybe I shouldn't be hanging onto this thing then?"

"I'm sure you're safe," Pierce said. "In fact, I know it."

Gallo raised an eyebrow. "Why do I get the impression there's something you're not telling us?"

"Remember how I told you that only the Kohen—someone from the line of Moses's brother Aaron—could safely approach the Ark? Well I think there's a scientific explanation for that. A genetic trait that makes them immune to the more dangerous effects of Originator technology. Fiona has that trait."

The young woman was surprised at this revelation. "You think I'm a Kohen?"

"Not necessarily descended from the line of Aaron, but you possess the trait. My guess is that it's a dominant genetic factor among cultures that held onto the Mother Tongue the longest. That's why you can use the words. You could teach them to me and I could say them until I was blue in the face, but I would never be able to make a golem.

"And there's something else, too. Remember when you tried to clear a path through the shekinahs? You got a shock from it, but I think that shock would have killed anyone else. The point is, I think that's the reason you had that vision of Raven back at Arkaim. You're the only one who can use the Ark to shut down the Black Knight."

Fiona took this news without comment, and for a fleeting second, Pierce wondered if perhaps he was being a little too cavalier about her abilities. But this close to the prize, there wasn't time for sweet talk. Right now, he needed Fiona the Kohen, the Baal'Shem, the last speaker of the Siletz tribal language.

He shone his lamp down the passage, a straight shot angling toward the mountain as far as the light extended. "Nobody has been here in over two thousand years," he said. "We're walking in the footsteps of Jeremiah the prophet."

Fiona shrugged. "The air's pretty fresh."

She wasn't wrong about that. Pierce knew from experience that strange things happened to the air in tombs and caverns that were shut off from the outside world for long periods of time. Methane could seep through the rock and collect into deadly clouds. Decaying rock could produce radon and other poisonous gases. Fresh air could mean another entrance, and that was not a notion Pierce found at all comforting.

Gallo gave his hand a squeeze. She knew how much this meant to him.

There were no traps or snakes, which was a little disappointing but not surprising. Between the sealed cave entrance and the Ark's own self-defense mechanism, there was little need for additional protection. The only real surprise was the length of the passage.

After walking for ten full minutes, Pierce broke the silence. "I thought the Ark would be near the entrance. The location of the Ark's resting place should have been a function of the same calculation that brought us here. Now, the math is all messed up."

"How far do you think we've come?" Gallo asked.

Pierce shrugged. "Half a mile? Less?"

"How much is that in Sacred cubits?" Fiona remarked.

Gallo snapped her fingers. "Of course. There was a third number in that account. Solomon had 80,000 stonecutters in the mountains, 70,000 bearers. And 3,600 overseers."

"3,600 Sacred cubits," Pierce said, grasping the significance. "The final distance Jeremiah would have to travel once he reached the entrance to the cave."

"That's about 7,500 feet," Fiona said, doing the math in her head. "A mile and a half."

A mile and a half. Pierce felt even more certain that they were on the right track. He started counting his steps and checking his watch to judge their pace. The passage itself was an anomaly, far too straight to be the work of nature, but he saw no obvious sign of tool marks on the walls that might indicate the handiwork of laborers.

Ten more minutes passed and Pierce's eagerness to see the prize at the end of the passage grew to something resembling anxiety. The seconds were stretching out like Silly Putty. He checked his watch, expecting five minutes to have passed, and discovered that only thirty seconds had elapsed since his last check.

"Do you think the Ark is distorting time?" he said. "Like in that movie where time slows down the closer you get to a black hole?"

"It only seems to slow down from an outside point of view," Fiona corrected. "It still feels normal to the person near the black hole."

"There's a name for what you're experiencing," Gallo told him. "It's the watched-pot-never-boils effect."

He knew she was right but that didn't make it any easier.

Then, with no apparent warning, the passage opened up into a larger lobe-shaped chamber, at least two hundred feet across, and just as abruptly, it ended.

"It's a cul-de-sac," Pierce said, a gnawing feeling growing in his stomach. He ran to the far wall, then began skirting along the wall, making his way back to the mouth of the passage. "This can't be right. Look around. Maybe there's a secret door. Or..." He turned to Fiona. "Do you sense anything?"

She shook her head.

"George, look up there." Gallo pointed to the ceiling in the center of the chamber. The beam of light from her headlamp had disappeared into a shadowy recess, a hole about eight feet across, and a good ten feet above their heads. "It's an oculus. Like in the Pantheon. Could that be where we need to go?"

Pierce moved to stand under it and shone his light up into the opening. The oculus, a design feature of domed Roman temples from antiquity, was a hole that allowed both sunlight and rain to fall into the interior. This vertical shaft however was dark and without end, but it did underscore a fact that Pierce had not considered. The long passage had gone under the mountain ridge, which meant they were hundreds of feet underground.

"I don't know," he replied. "Everything we've found suggests that Jeremiah came in through the same passage we did. I'll sweep with the GPR. There has to be another way out of here."

He started to unsling his backpack, but as he did, he realized there was something different about the floor beneath the opening, right where he was standing.

"No," he whispered, dropping to his knees, tracing the carved outline with his fingers. "Oh, no."

Gallo and Fiona were at his side a moment later.

Fiona pointed at the carving. "Is that...?"

"A Templar Cross," Gallo supplied. "I'm afraid it is."

"The Ark isn't here," Pierce said, his voice a whisper. "The Knights Templar took it eight hundred years ago."

THIRTY-NINE

Axum, Ethiopia

"**Abba Paulos tells** me that you are interested in the Ark of the Covenant."

Carter stared at the man the priest had introduced as Abuna Mateos, the Bishop of Axum. Mateos had a high-pitched voice and spoke with a cadence that sounded almost musical. He was older, with tufts of wispy gray hair protruding out from under the cylindrical gold-colored cap, which matched his long vestments. But his clean-shaven face looked almost youthful, making it impossible to guess his age with certainty.

"You speak English?" she said.

Mateos, who had been looking at Lazarus, turned to face her with a perturbed expression. Carter knew that look well: the *why are you speaking to me, woman* look. She had experienced it many times during her years working with relief agencies. To his credit, Mateos hid his displeasure with a smile. "Yes. Also French, Arabic, Hebrew, and of course, Amharic."

Lazarus thumbed a button on his phone, disabling the babelfish. "I'm Erik Lazarus. This is Dr. Felice Carter." She noted the emphasis on the title, an attempt to elevate her status somewhat in his eyes. "And yes, we'd like to talk about the Ark."

Mateos listened, without comment or visible reaction, as they made the connection between the recent earthquakes and solar events with the Ark of the Covenant, and more time trying to establish that they were not kooks or treasure hunters.

After about five minutes of this, the clergyman raised his hands. "Let me understand. You believe that Ark can be used to stop these earthquakes. That is your only interest in it?"

"That's right," Carter said. "I know it sounds crazy—"

"Certainly not. God has power over the heavens and Earth. The question before us is whether it is His will to do so. In the Gospels, the Lord warned us that in the Last Days, there would be earthquakes in many places and great signs in Heaven." His solemn face cracked with a smile. "He also said that we should not be troubled by such things, for the End is not yet come."

He paused a moment, studying their faces, as if trying to decide whether or not to trust them. "Please, come with me. I want to show you something."

He led them outside and around to the south end of the cathedral building. At the end of a sprawling courtyard stood the old cathedral, a more traditional looking structure from the seventeenth century. Silhouetted against the old church, separated from the courtyard by a tall wrought-iron fence, were a pair of smaller cube-shaped chapels, the larger of the two topped with an onion dome and a cross.

Mateos pointed to one of the smaller structures. "That is the Chapel of the Tablets, where the Ark is kept. When I was a young man, the Ark was kept in the sanctuary of the church, concealed behind a curtain, just as in the Tabernacle that Moses built, but after many years, the heat—" He squeezed his fist, "—of the Glory of God kept cracking the stones of the floor. So, this chapel was built, according to the same specifications that Moses used. The floor stones, they never cracked again.

"The Glory of God," he repeated. "It is not for men to see. Only one man, the guardian, a brother of the holy order, who never leaves the chapel, may go before the Ark to offer incense, just as in the days of Moses. I have not seen the Ark. No one but the guardian may see the Ark. Anyone else..." He made a lateral slicing gesture. "Dead. So you see, I cannot help you. The Ark must remain in the Chapel."

"What good is having it, if you can't use it when you need it?" Lazarus said. Carter could tell from his tone that he was holding back his frustration.

"It is a symbol of God's presence," Mateo said, his tone still patient, but with a slight edge. "Not something that we are meant to *use.*"

Carter spoke up. "Abuna, has it occurred to you that perhaps this is the reason the Ark was given to your Church? So that it would be available when this time of need arose?"

Mateo gave her a patronizing smile. "My child, has it occurred to you that God sends these signs, these earthquakes, so that we may demonstrate our faith in Him?" He pressed his hands together as if genuflecting. "I am sorry that you have come all this way, but it is not for nothing. Go, and may God's peace be upon you." He bowed his head and then turned away without another word.

When he was gone, Lazarus sighed. "That went well."

"About as well as expected."

"Convenient how nobody ever gets to see it. They never have to prove it's in there."

"Still, if it was a fake, you'd think someone would have exposed it by now."

Lazarus nodded, staring at the chapel, but he said nothing. She watched him for a few seconds. "What are you thinking?"

"George sent us here to check it out. Rule it out. That's what we have to do."

"We can't just force our way in there and take it." When he didn't respond, she repeated the statement. "We can't do that, Erik."

"If it's a fake, we won't need to take it. I just need a few seconds with it."

"How are you going to tell the difference in a few seconds?"

"Like you said, it's covered in gold. It will be heavy."

"And if it's real, just touching it might..." She trailed off. "Erik, you're not... No. You can't do that."

He reached out and pulled her into an embrace that felt almost as indulgent as Mateo's smile. "Pretty sure I'm the only one who can."

FORTY

Under Mount Nebo, Jordan

Fiona stared down at the cross carved into the cavern floor. It was symmetrical, all four arms the same length, like a Swiss cross or a plus-sign, with flaring serifs at each end. "Knights Templar," she echoed. "Crusaders?"

She knew a little about the Templar Knights, but she also recognized that a lot of her knowledge was suspect. The Templars showed up in a lot places—video games, adventure novels, conspiracy theories—and most of what was said about them was exaggerated, sensationalized, or outright fiction.

Gallo answered first. "A Christian military order, founded in the twelfth century. They called themselves the Poor Fellow Soldiers of Christ and the Temple of Solomon. Poor, because they took a monastic vow of poverty, but that didn't last long. They were founded to provide protection for Christian pilgrims in the Holy Land after the First Crusade, but they became very wealthy and influential in the Church. Some scholars have called them the world's first multinational corporation. Of course, they were also fierce and ruthless fighters."

"There have always been rumors that the Templars found the Ark," Pierce said with a scowl. "Along with the Holy Grail, the True Cross, the bones of Mary Magdalene...you name it, the Templars found it. I guess this is one time that the rumors were right."

"Found it how?" Fiona asked. "They didn't come in the same way we did." She paused a beat, then added. "Did they?"

"It's possible," Pierce admitted. "Maybe one of them spoke the Mother Tongue as well. Or..." He looked up, shining his light into the opening overhead. "They might have dug straight down."

"But how would they have even known where to look? Did they work it out, like we did?"

Pierce gave a snort of disgust. "Not likely. Not unless someone told them the length of a Sacred cubit." He stopped, as if the words had triggered a thought cascade. He looked away, as if searching for the answer in the dimensions of the chamber.

"The Templars were headquartered on the Temple Mount," Gallo said. "Perhaps they found some ancient scroll—the Copper Scroll, maybe—describing the hiding place of the Ark."

Pierce continued to stare at the wall, lost in whatever musings had distracted him. Gallo went on. "When they got here, there were probably all kinds of scrolls and maps that don't exist today. They must have found something that led them here."

"So if they took the Ark, what did they do with it?"

"By the thirteenth century," Gallo said, still in history professor mode, "the tide had turned against the Christian crusaders in the Holy Lands. The Templars relocated their headquarters, and the bulk of their treasure, to Cyprus.

"Like any successful business, they had enemies. King Philip of France owed the Templars a lot of money and resented their influence, which went beyond national boundaries. So in 1307, he conspired with the Church to have the order disbanded and their leadership arrested and charged with crimes against God.

"Their assets were seized and turned over to a rival order, the Hospitallers of Malta." Gallo paused and raised a thoughtful eyebrow. "I doubt very much that they, or the Templars for that matter, would have kept the discovery of something as important as the Ark of the Covenant a secret."

"Don't be so sure," Pierce said, returning his attention to them. "The Ark wasn't just a treasure or a holy relic. It was a weapon, and if word got out that the Templars had it, it would have been the start of an arms race. Everyone in Christendom would have gone to war to possess it. In fact, that may have been part of King Philip's motive for trying to overthrow the Templars.

"There's another rumor that the Templars were warned of the plot, and that, before their arrest, they spirited their greatest treasures away in a hay wagon. After that..." He shrugged. "It depends on which wild theory you believe. A lot of people believe that the Templars went underground, guarding the treasure, and eventually reformed as the Freemasons. There's a lot of Templar symbolism in Masonic rites, so maybe there's some truth to it. And if you follow that thread a little further, it might have been brought to America. Several of the Founding Fathers were Freemasons."

"Where do *you* think it is?"

"An excellent question."

Fiona let out a yelp and whirled in the direction of the new voice, her heart already racing out of control. Pierce and Gallo reacted about the same way, illuminating the face of the newcomer. A young-looking, red-haired Caucasian man stood at the mouth of the tunnel leading back the way they had come. He took a step forward, revealing that he wasn't alone. Two more men followed him out of the passage. Both wore military-style fatigues and carried compact Uzi machine pistols. They held the weapons casually, pointed at the floor, but the very fact of their presence was a tacit threat.

"So tell us, Dr. Pierce," the red-haired man said. "Where do you think the Templars took the Ark?"

FORTY-ONE

Pierce recognized the voice. "Fallon?"

"We meet at last," Fallon said with a chuckle, sounding a little like a cartoon villain. Pierce wondered if that was intentional. He started forward, into the chamber, while the two gunmen remained at the mouth of the passage like a pair of sentries. "I'm sorry, I feel as if I already know you, but we haven't been properly introduced. Yes, I'm Marcus Fallon. And you are Drs. Pierce and Gallo. I've learned so much about you." He paused, looking at Fiona. "I don't know who you are, but you seem very intelligent and in such good company, too."

Fiona glanced at Pierce, as if looking for guidance. Pierce gave an almost imperceptible shake of the head. The less Fallon knew about her, the better. Fiona, got the message. She nodded her head at the two gunmen. "Sorry, guns make me nervous."

Fallon laughed. "Don't worry about my friends. They're just here for logistical support. This is a dangerous place, you know. Terrorists and extremists lurking around every corner. By the way, you have got to tell me about that trick with the entrance. Is that an optical illusion of some kind?"

"Something like that," Pierce tried to make it sound like a joke, but he felt no humor. Fallon had tracked them here. Spied on them. Watched them enter the tunnel. Followed them with a pair of gunslingers to provide back-up. "So, you just happened to be in the neighborhood?"

"Something like that." Fallon advanced into the center of the chamber until he was face to face with Pierce. He looked down at the carved cross. "Templars. I've tangled with them many times." He looked up and grinned. "*Assassin's Creed.*"

"It's a video game," Fiona murmured, noting Pierce's blank look.

"So," Fallon went on, "where did they take it?"

"Why are you here, Fallon? I told you, we'll take care of this. This is what we do."

"Oh, I heard you. You made your intentions crystal clear. Find the Ark, and shut the Black Knight down for good." He shook his head. "Have you stopped to consider the awesome opportunity here? I know, I know, mistakes were made. Tanaka... Don't get me started on him. But to turn our backs on this now is just criminal. We can harness the full power of the sun. Do you even realize what that means? Unlimited clean energy. This is the solution to all our problems."

"Isn't that what they said about atomic energy?" Gallo remarked. Her tone was sarcastic, but Pierce detected the undercurrent of fear.

"She's right," Pierce said. "As great as it all sounds, I just don't think we're ready for that much power."

Fallon did not appear surprised by the objection. "*We* could be you, Dr. Pierce. We—you and I—would control this for the good of all mankind. The Black Knight isn't anyone's property. The sun's energy belongs to everyone. Think of the good we could accomplish."

Pierce heard a note of insincerity in the other man's voice. Fallon wasn't interested in being the savior of the world. He wanted to be the man who owned the sun.

"We'll take it slow, of course," Fallon continued. "Establish protocols to ensure that we don't trigger more tidal earthquakes.

That shouldn't be a problem. Set graduated goals, and once we've demonstrated that we've got it under control, we'll begin developing infrastructure to—"

"Stop!" Pierce's shout reverberated through the confines of the chamber. In a more subdued voice, he continued. "Just stop. This isn't going to happen. The Black Knight isn't some gift from the gods. It's a Pandora's Box. It's a land mine, left behind by an alien species, and if we mess with it, it's going to blow up in our faces. I'm not going to let Tanaka do that on purpose, and I'm sure as hell not going to help you do it by accident."

Fallon smiled. "Good. That's why you're the best person to help me with this. Your caution will keep my enthusiasm in check. But we're getting ahead of ourselves. Right now at least, we don't have the means to do any of this." He paused, maintaining eye contact with Pierce. "First things first. The Ark. Where is it? What did they do with it?"

"We are not working together." Pierce spoke, enunciating each word for emphasis.

"You're sure?" Fallon bobbed his head over one shoulder, to the pair of gunmen lingering near the passage.

"If you're the man I think you are," Pierce said, "you aren't going to use threats of violence to get your way. And if I'm wrong about you...well, then I definitely don't want you getting your hands on that much power."

The other man burst out laughing, the sound harsh as it reverberated in the chamber. After a few seconds, he brought himself under control. "Well played. You're right, of course. I'm not a bully. I despise bullies." He sighed. "But I'm not going to give up, either. It's a race, now, and I'm afraid I need to handicap you a bit."

He gave Pierce a hard stare for several seconds, then turned to Gallo. "You're a very intelligent woman, Dr. Gallo. I heard you talking when we came in. I suspect you know as much about the Templars, if not more, than Dr. Pierce here."

"Fallon, don't." Pierce tried to inject a tone of menace into his voice, but it sounded more like pleading in his own ears.

"Here's what's going to happen. My friends and I are going to leave with Dr. Gallo. Pierce, you and your..." He stared at Fiona for a moment. "Whatever you are. You two are going to stay put a little while, to give me a head start."

"You've made your point," Pierce said.

"Oh, no. That ship has sailed. You two are staying here." He turned to one of this hired gunmen. "When we get back to the entrance, I want you to stay behind for...let's say three hours?" He looked back at Pierce. "Is that enough? Three hours. He's going to watch the entrance, and if either of you pokes your head out, he's going to shoot it off."

He flashed a mock-helpless grin. "That's why I brought them along. I could never do something like that, but believe me, they can and will."

Gallo let out a plaintive wail and shrank into Pierce's arms, hugging him, but when she whispered into his ear, her voice was steady. "George, what should I do?"

"It's going to be okay," he promised, but it sounded empty in his ears. "Just go along with him. Do what he says. We'll be fine. One way or another, we're going to find the Ark and stop Tanaka and his death cult. We can figure the rest of it out later on."

"I hope you know what you're doing," she whispered. "I don't suppose you've got an idea about where to look next."

"Ask the Templars."

"This is very touching," Fallon said, "but it's time to go."

Pierce gave Gallo another reassuring squeeze before releasing her. "Fallon, listen to me. The Ark *is* dangerous. If you *do* find it, don't touch it. Don't try to do anything with it. You'll just get yourself killed."

It seemed like the right thing to say.

The other man regarded him with a cool, skeptical look. "Thanks for the warning. For your sake, I hope you're wrong." He turned to Gallo. "Shall we?"

FORTY-TWO

Gallo's heart raced as she stepped away from Pierce. She was afraid, no doubt about that, but she had been in stickier situations. She wasn't that worried for her own safety. She was worried for Pierce and Fiona. Fallon was ambitious and greedy, but he didn't strike her as a killer. The mercenaries with him however, seemed all too eager to carry out his threat. But she held her head high, willing herself to remain strong, to accept this reversal on her own terms.

They exited the chamber and started down the passage. Fallon walked ahead of Gallo, both of them bracketed by the hired guns. After a few minutes of walking, Fallon looked back over his shoulder. "So, where to next? I know you must have some ideas about this."

Gallo considered Pierce's parting advice. *Ask the Templars.* "Ideas are all I have," she admitted. "What I need are facts, to help me start eliminating the least plausible scenarios."

"Dr. Pierce mentioned the Freemasons. Is that a possibility?"

She resisted the urge to snap at him. "As I said, I need facts. People have been speculating about and looking for Templar treasure for centuries. Nothing has ever been found. If we're going to find something, we have to take a different approach. We don't have time to reinvent the wheel."

He gave her a long, appraising glance before returning his gaze forward again. He said nothing more as they made the twenty minute long trek back to the end of the tunnel, giving Gallo a chance to review her own knowledge about the Templars. Her professional area of expertise encompassed the beginnings of the Holy Roman Empire, and she knew more than the average person about the Crusades in the broader context of history. But what she did not have was a working knowledge of the more radical ideas and fringe theories, and that was where she would find the golden thread that would lead her to the Ark.

Which raised the question of whether she ought to. Maybe it would be smarter to lead Fallon astray, clearing a path for Pierce and Fiona to find the Ark. Pierce had told her to go along with Fallon, but exactly what he meant by that was open to interpretation.

Fallon stopped and she almost ran into him. Ahead, the gunman in the lead had also halted as the ceiling sloped down to block their way. "Dead end, boss."

"It's just an illusion," Fallon said. "Keep going."

The mercenary reached out with one hand, testing the solidity of the stone. Gallo held her breath. Fiona's Mother Tongue incantation could change the matter state of rock without altering its appearance, but how long the effect would last was a big unknown. The man's fingers sank into the sloping barrier as if it was a holographic projection.

As the first man disappeared into the wall, Fallon turned around shining his flashlight down the passage behind them. "It looks like Pierce took my advice to stay put."

"Looks that way," agreed the mercenary.

"Did you bring explosives? C-4 or whatever you call it?"

The other man nodded.

"I don't want Pierce following us," Fallon went on. "As soon as we're outside, I want you to blast the entrance."

Gallo's heart skipped a beat. "No!"

She started toward him, hands raised without any idea of what she intended to do if she actually landed a blow. As it was, she never even got close. The mercenary threw his arms around her, restraining her.

"Once we find the Ark, I'll make sure they're dug out. They'll live, provided you remain cooperative."

"You can't do this," she said, the protest tumbling from her lips.

"Oh, but I can." Fallon leaned in close. "I told you it was a race. Now you have a personal stake in it."

Even as Gallo struggled in her captor's grip, the harsh reality of the situation filtered through her panic. Her protests would accomplish nothing. Fallon wasn't going to change his mind. But she also knew something Fallon didn't know. Fiona could walk through walls—at least some of the time. And that gave her hope.

She sagged in defeat and allowed herself to be ushered through the lightless haze separating the tunnel from the surface. Two more mercenaries were waiting outside, guarding the exit, and as soon as they were all clear, one of the men hurried to carry out Fallon's orders. He produced a large satchel, almost overstuffed with blocks of plastic explosives, and re-entered the concealed passage, disappearing from sight. When he came back out again, he carried a spool of wire, which he played out until it was empty. He then attached a small plastic device that looked a little like a grip exerciser.

"Better duck," he advised. "Fire in the hole."

As soon as Gallo was huddled on the ground, the man squeezed the device three times in rapid succession. On the second squeeze, there was a resounding thump underfoot, and a cloud of dust rose up from the area where they had just been standing.

Fallon turned to her. "It's up to you now, Dr. Gallo. If you ever want to see them again, find the Ark for me."

Gallo nodded, pretending to be mortified. It would take more than a cave-in to keep Pierce and Fiona down.

FORTY-THREE

Pierce waited about five minutes after Fallon's departure to start working on the problem of escape. He had no intention of sitting on his butt for three hours, leaving Gallo in Fallon's clutches, but he also knew better than to test the tech billionaire's resolve. Fallon might not have the stomach to pull the trigger himself, but Pierce knew the mercenaries would follow the standing order.

He studied the cross on the floor and the opening above for a few minutes, and reached a decision. "Fi, are you ready to get out of here?"

"Yeah," Fiona replied. "But you heard what that jerk said."

"I did. He said he was going to have one of his hired goons watch the entrance. But maybe there's another way out of here that he doesn't know about." He pointed to the hole in the ceiling. "Think that goes all the way to the top?"

Fiona shook her head. "Maybe it used to, but I think if it did, someone would have found this place by now."

"Good point. So maybe the Templars covered it over once they were done removing the Ark."

"So how do we get up there?"

"That's the flaw in my plan," Pierce admitted. He sank down onto the floor to consider the problem.

He was still doing that when a hot breeze issued from the passage, spiking the air pressure and forcing him to work his jaw to pop his ears. A moment later, a loud boom, like the report of a cannon, rushed out of the tunnel and shook the ground underfoot.

"What the hell?" Pierce jumped to his feet as the tunnel vomited a cloud of dust over them. He squeezed his eyes shut and tried to hold his breath as the grit filled the air. "Son of a bitch," he coughed. "He blasted the entrance."

Fiona covered her mouth and nose with a sleeve and squinted at Pierce through the haze. "He tried to kill us." Then she lowered her arm and broke into a grin. "He doesn't know what I can do."

Pierce answered with a smile of his own. "No, he doesn't."

They didn't wait for the dust to settle, but started down the passage at a jog. The air cleared as they ran, but a cloud of anger soon replaced it for Pierce. Anger at Fallon. Anger at himself for having misjudged the man. Anger at his inability to save Gallo. He barely noticed the cracks and fissures that now crisscrossed the walls and ceiling, or the piles of rubble that littered the floor of the passage. Then he saw something moving in the gloom.

He skidded to an abrupt halt. Fiona slammed into him from behind.

"Go back!" he shouted, spinning around. He grasped hold of her shoulders, then turned her as well. "Now! Faster!"

She waited until they were moving again to ask him why.

Pierce glanced back, his headlamp revealing dozens of writhing shapes. "Snakes."

'Why did it have to be snakes?'

They resembled diamondback rattlesnakes, minus the rattle. Most were two or three feet long, a couple—the fastest—were even bigger. All had a distinctive tiger-stripe pattern of black and gold scales and arrow-shaped heads, a feature common to the type of venomous snakes known as pit vipers. Pierce recalled the Nehushtan sculpture on the mountain above them. Maybe the story was only figurative, but the 'fiery serpents' mentioned in the Bible—Palestinian vipers—were a very real problem in the region.

The snakes were not moving very fast. In fact, even at a regular walking pace, Pierce and Fiona were already pulling away from the swarm, but unlike most wild animals, including snakes, which preferred to keep humans at a distance and attacked only when approached, these vipers were still coming, and appeared to be pissed off.

"That explosion must have cracked open their warrens and dumped them down here," Pierce said, as they reached the domed chamber at the end of the passage.

"They're between us and the exit," Fiona said.

"Yeah."

"We're stuck down here. In a snake pit."

"Yeah."

"Got any ideas?"

"I'm working on it." Pierce ran to the center of the room and stared up at the opening. "We've got to get up there."

"It's too high."

"I'll boost you up."

Pierce bent over and laced his fingers together to form a step, but Fiona just stared at him. "Who's going to boost you?"

"I'll figure something out." He glanced at the mouth of the tunnel, and his light revealed one of the vipers slithering out into the open. It was not alone. The creatures were still on the warpath. Pierce shook his joined hands. "Go!"

As Fiona stepped on his hands, he lifted her up, shoving her toward the opening. Even with the boost, her fingers just grazed the edge.

"On my shoulders," Pierce grunted, keeping his eyes on the advancing snakes. "Hurry."

Fiona planted one foot on his shoulder and stepped up. She wasn't all that heavy, but her full weight pressing down on his collar bone nearly drove him to his knees. He gritted his teeth against the unexpected pain, and then, just like that, the pressure was gone. He looked up and saw her legs dangling down as she wormed herself up onto a concealed ledge.

There was no time to savor the minor victory. A snake, as long as Fiona was tall, was almost within striking distance. He danced back a few steps, even as more of the vipers slithered out of the passage.

He slid out of his backpack and swung it at the closest snake. Instead of retreating, it struck at the pack, sinking its fangs into the nylon. As the pack continued through the arc of the swing, Pierce could feel the sudden change. The pack was a good ten pounds heavier and shaking. The snake was still attached, its fangs snagged in the fabric. He heaved it away and quickly regretted it.

Now he had nothing with which to fend off the rest of the swarm.

FORTY-FOUR

Fiona kicked her legs and wriggled the rest of the way onto the ledge. From below, it had not been visible, but now she could see that it was the bottom landing of a narrow, spiral staircase that corkscrewed around the shaft.

As soon as she was up, she squirmed around so she could see the chamber below. Pierce was gone, driven away from the center by the advancing vipers. "Uncle George!"

"Fi. You've got to find a way out." Pierce's voice was faint, muffled by distance and the acoustics of the chamber. "Tell Cintia to contact Erik. You've got to find the Ark. And save Gus."

She beat her fists against the stone landing, feeling helpless. There was no loose earth with which to form a golem, and she couldn't think of any other way in which her limited ability with the Mother Tongue might be useful. What she needed was a ladder or some rope.

Stairs, she thought. They had to lead somewhere, and maybe at the top, she would find something...anything...that might help Pierce escape the snake pit.

She scrambled to her feet and started ascending, bounding up three steps at a time until the burning in her legs slowed her to single steps. She kept going, refusing to stop for breath, circling around the stairwell again and again, until she started to feel dizzy. Even then she did not stop until, with no warning whatsoever, the stairs ended at a balcony that almost ringed the vertical shaft.

The surrounding walls were smooth, save for a protruding square of rock, about two feet on each side, framing a carved Templar cross, on the opposite side of the balcony. There seemed to be no reason for it to be there, so Fiona figured it was either the release mechanism for a secret door or a booby trap.

One hardly seemed worse than the other, so she ran to it and slammed both her fists against it.

The balcony lurched beneath her, then knocked her down.

"Damn it," she muttered, and thought, *Booby trap.*

But then the floor stopped moving, and she saw that the stone block with the cross was now a good eight feet higher than it had been, and positioned right above an arched doorway leading out of the shaft.

Without pausing to consider what new perils might await her on the other side, Fiona charged through the door and found herself in another round, vaulted chamber. The walls were adorned with painted frescoes. The scenes were reminiscent of stained glass windows in a cathedral or Byzantine icons, though she didn't give the artwork more than a cursory glance. At the opposite end, there was a block of carved stone, about waist high and twice as long, and behind that, several long tapestries covering the wall—black on top, white on the bottom, with red Templar crosses in the center.

The room was a chapel, a secret underground church that probably dated back to the crusades. It was no doubt built by the men who had discovered, and removed, the Ark of the Covenant.

No ladders, but the tapestries gave her an idea. Each was long enough to reach down to the floor of the snake pit.

She ran down the length of the chamber, circled the altar, and grabbed one of the enormous woven panels. She half-expected it to crumble to dust in her hands, but the dry environment of the sealed chapel had preserved the tapestry well. It tore free of the hooks from which it was suspended, but its unexpected weight bore her to the ground. She struggled to get her arms under it, but the woven fabric was so heavy, she could only lift one end.

The removal of the tapestry revealed another doorway, leading out of the apse and perhaps to another stairwell or secret passage. It probably led all the way to the surface, a hidden entrance somewhere on Mount Nebo, but Fiona paid no attention to the possible exit.

Instead, she pulled the heavy tapestry behind her, heading for the door back to the staircase.

The woven curtain snagged on the rough floor, pulling her off balance once more. The utter futility of what she was trying to do crashed down on her like a wave. If she could not even lift the tapestry, how would she ever be able to hold it in place while Pierce climbed up? Was he even still alive?

She fell to her knees, sobbing.

"Fi!"

Pierce was standing in the doorway, breathing hard but smiling. She shoved the tapestry away, bounded across the intervening distance, and threw her arms around him.

"You made it! How?"

"The stairs came down. I thought you did that."

Fiona realized that she actually had. The mechanism outside the chapel had done more than just reveal the hidden entrance. It had lowered the entire stairwell down eight feet to the floor of the lower chamber. She had saved Pierce without even realizing it.

She looked past him to the stairwell. "Can snakes climb steps?"

Pierce chuckled. "Maybe, but I think we're safe for a little while." He gave her a squeeze, then released her and moved into the chapel, scrutinizing the frescos.

Now that there was time for her to look at them, Fiona realized that she was looking at a visual record of the chamber's discovery. The paintings on the right side showed an artist's rendering of a man in a rough-looking garment with his eyes raised heavenward as if in prayer. Then the same man journeying into the desert at the head of a procession of men carrying large bundles. In the final scene, they were setting up what looked like a circus tent in a cave. The panels on the left side showed the story of how the Templars found the secret chamber.

Pierce stared at the last panel on the left, which depicted the same scene as on the opposite side, but with the addition of Templars kneeling before their swords, which were held in front of them like crosses. "This is where they found the Holy Tabernacle of Meeting."

"It doesn't show what happened next," Fiona said. "Where did they take it?"

Pierce moved back to the first panel, which showed priests and Templar scholars perusing scrolls. "They found something that told them where to look. Maybe the same scrolls we read." He moved to the next panel, which showed Templars, some on horseback, others on foot, carrying what looked like short walking sticks. One of the men was kneeling, with his cane lying on the ground before him, pointing toward the rising sun.

Pierce tapped the picture. "That rod, it's too short to be a walking staff. I think it's a measuring stick. Exactly one Sacred cubit. They calculated the correct length six hundred years before Isaac Newton."

"How?"

Pierce shook his head. "There are several references to measuring the Temple in the Bible—the Revelation, the prophecies of Ezekiel and Zechariah. Maybe there was something left of the old Temple in Jerusalem that they were able to use as a baseline."

He moved to the last panel, which showed the warrior-monks ringing the Tabernacle, praying before their upraised swords. "If they'd had the Tabernacle, they would have been able to measure it and work it out backward..." His voice trailed off, and then he turned to Fiona, his eyes dancing with excitement. "I know where the Ark is."

FORTY-FIVE

Chartres, France

Ask the Templars.

Augustina Gallo had wrestled with Pierce's parting admonition for hours. She had pondered the message as Fallon's men drove them to the airport in Amman, then dissected and parsed the words as Fallon's private jet soared toward France, the only destination she could think to give him. Now, standing here at the north entrance to the Cathedral of Our Lady of Chartres, she hoped she had interpreted the message correctly.

Gallo had convinced Fallon to allow her Internet access aboard his plane, albeit with him looking over her shoulder. She was not an expert on the Templars by any means, which meant that before she could even begin to solve the mystery of what they had done with the Ark, she would first have to figure out who they really were.

There were two Templar histories. The generally accepted version began in 1119, when Hugues de Payens founded the order, and ended in 1307 with the arrest of the last grandmaster Jacques de Molay, the official dissolution of the order, and the seizure of all Templar assets. Despite being set against the backdrop of the Crusades, it was more a tale of shrewd business and political scheming than a war story. The Templars fought valiantly, sometimes brutally, but could not hold the Holy Lands against the forces of Saladin, the Sultan of the Levant. Their success derived, not from prowess in battle, but from an astute manipulation of both economic and religious power. That success attracted enemies far more destructive than Muslim armies.

Then there was the other history of the Templars. Pseudo-history to the doubters, true history to the believers. Some, though not all, held that the story began a century earlier than the official version, with the discovery of holy relics in Scotland. All agreed that it continued right up to the present, with Templar influence transforming secret societies like the Bavarian Illuminati and the Freemasons into powerful political and economic entities, all in pursuit of a New World Order. In this history, the Templars were both heroes and villains, guardians of secret scientific or occult knowledge, and diabolical puppet masters.

Gallo, a professional historian, knew all too well that the official version of history was rarely honest or completely accurate, but she

lived by the same principles as a scientist—extraordinary claims required extraordinary proofs. And while she had seen some extraordinary
claims proved true, she always started from a foundation of solid,
reliable information. Pierce, knowing both her background and her
temperament, would have expected her to start with research, but the
more she read, the harder she found it to separate fact from fancy, real
history from conspiracy theory.

Then it occurred to her what Pierce was trying to tell her.

"Chartres Cathedral," she had announced. "That's where we
need to go."

One of Fallon's hired men, a brutish thug named Williams,
made a rude joke about the name, but Gallo ignored him. "The
Templars were involved in financing its construction. Its location
has long possessed spiritual significance going back to pre-Christian
times. If the Templars brought the Ark back to Europe, that's the
most logical place for them to put it."

"And it's still there?" Fallon asked, barely able to contain his
eagerness.

"There's only one way to know for sure."

That had been enough to get them to the idyllic French town of
Chartres, sixty miles from Paris. The church for which the town was
world famous, was considered the best preserved Gothic cathedral
in the world, having survived World War II almost completely intact.
It had also survived the previous day's earthquakes mostly intact,
though a few areas of the exterior were cordoned off with yellow
caution tape.

Gallo stared up at the ornately carved pillars of the north façade. Like
all Gothic cathedrals and most Catholic churches worldwide, Chartres
utilized a long cruciform design, with a nave divided into several bays,
separated by pillars, and a transept crossing the nave, separating it from
the apse. All of the facades were elaborately decorated, but the north
entrance featured the element that had commanded the attention of
Templar historians and Ark hunters for several decades.

"There," she said, pointing to a pillar that showed what appeared to be a wheeled cart being pulled by robed figures. "That's a representation of the Ark of the Covenant being brought from the Holy Land by the Templars. The inscription beneath it is Latin. *HIC AMITITUR ARCHA CEDERIS.* 'Here things take their course. You are to work through the Ark.'"

Fallon nodded and rubbed his hands together. "Work through the Ark? How do we do that?"

"We have to go inside." She started walking along the exterior, passing the impressive flying buttresses that extended out from the main structure like the skeletal ribs of an enormous leviathan. "There's a labyrinth set into the floor of the nave. That's sort of like a spiritual maze."

"I know what a labyrinth is," Fallon said.

"Well, it's been proposed by some Ark hunters that the Ark is hidden on another dimensional plane, and if you walk the labyrinth through to the end, you will be able to step through into that other dimension."

"Seriously?"

"I don't believe it's the literal truth, but there are rumors of a secret tunnel under the labyrinth. I believe that we're meant to walk it to find the entrance, or the means to unlock it. But I should warn you, a lot of people walk that labyrinth every day, and a lot of them are looking for the Ark. It won't be easy."

"For your sake, Dr. Gallo, and for your friends, I hope it's easier than you think."

She stopped, turned to him, and fixed him with a lethal stare. "I'm well aware of what's at stake. You don't need to keep reminding me."

Fallon grunted and motioned for her to keep moving.

They came around to the west entrance and made their way inside. It was early evening, just after dusk, but the cathedral was busy with visitors. As at Mount Nebo, many people had turned to their faith to help them cope with the global earthquake crisis and the uncertainty of what might come next. Given the circumstances, it was probably an appropriate reaction.

She went inside and approached the font, dipped her fingers in, and crossed herself. Fallon stared at the basin for a moment, then did the same, looking almost embarrassed.

"You're Catholic?"

"I'm Irish. What do you think?" He grimaced. "It's been a while, though. I don't really...you know...believe any of it."

She raised an eyebrow, feigning indignation, then nodded in the direction of Williams and the other security contractors. "What about you guys?"

The men exchanged awkward glances but did not answer.

"Maybe they should stay here," she told Fallon. "This is holy ground, after all."

Fallon turned to his men. "We don't need you in here. I don't think Dr. Gallo will try anything, but just in case, keep an eye on the exits."

The mercenaries seemed relieved, as if being in the church building made them uncomfortable. They headed back outside. Gallo started up the nave with Fallon right behind her. As they walked, she studied the carved relief images adorning the bay pillars and the majestic stained glass windows. "Too bad we didn't get here before sunset. It would have been nice to see these windows lit up with natural light."

"We're not here for sightseeing."

"No, but if my theory is correct, the windows hold the secret of finding the Ark."

That got Fallon's attention. "How?"

"Each window depicts a scene from the Bible." She pointed to one window on the north side of the nave. "That's Noah and his sons building the first Ark."

"The one from the Flood."

"Exactly." She pointed down at the dark pattern on the lighter-colored floor tiles, tracing it with a finger through the first few turns, as the path wandered back and forth across the nave. The labyrinth was contained in a circle, at least forty feet in diameter. "When we walk the labyrinth, we'll be looking at the windows and the reliefs in a very specific order. I think that the scenes will form a code, like a combination lock, that will open the secret crypt under the cathedral."

Fallon's earlier eagerness returned in full force. "That's awesome. How did you figure it out?"

She shrugged. "You should take video of your walkthrough. That way we don't have to keep walking it over and over again until we figure it out."

Fallon liked this idea even better. He took out his mobile phone and held it up as he followed Gallo down the well-trod path.

The labyrinth was not a maze, with pathway junctions and dead ends, but a single path that never crossed itself. It wound around and around in an elaborate pattern within the circle, until reaching the center. Walking a labyrinth was a spiritual journey, a physical meditation. Some even considered it a transformative experience, like a baptism. Gallo had a similar hope for her labyrinth walk.

The path started off straight, heading toward the center, but then just before the halfway point, it turned left and began a clockwise curl. After only a quarter rotation, it doubled back in the first of many hairpin turns, returning almost to the original line. It turned left again and continued toward the center. Just before reaching the center, it turned left again, skirting the ultimate goal without actually reaching it.

Gallo and Fallon were not the only ones walking the labyrinth, and while the pattern did not allow for actual collisions, the narrow path meant they were brushing past other devotees, some further along, others just beginning. She studied the expressions on the faces of the faithful, noted the quivering of their lips as they prayed silently, and wondered how they would react when she and Fallon reached the center. Then, she focused her attention on the path ahead, barely noticing the beautiful windows above, and kept her breathing slow and steady.

Ask the Templars, Pierce had said. At first, Gallo had assumed that he was telling her to look into the accepted history of the Templars and their actions during the Crusades, or perhaps that she was to focus on the final chapter in their tale—the fragmentation of the order, and what happened afterward. But as she read about the trial and the persecution of Jacques de Molay and the other senior Templars, of the relentless torture of the Inquisition, and the false confessions designed to mislead their enemies with wild stories of treasure ships and bizarre pagan rituals, another thought occurred to her.

Ask the Templars.

She had a pretty good idea how they would have answered.

By design, the end of the labyrinth walk came with little warning. The path brought her to a spot adjacent to where she had made the first turn, only instead of turning left, she turned right and waked straight into the six-petal flower-shape at the center of the labyrinth. There were a few people already occupying the space, heads bowed and lost in the exultation of completing their symbolic journey. Gallo stepped aside and allowed Fallon, his mobile phone held up and recording every step, to enter the center.

"Now what?" he asked, stepping close and keeping his voice low.

"Now, you see God," she replied, and slammed her right knee up into his crotch.

Fallon curled around the point of impact like a worm on a fishhook, unable to breathe or cry out. As he crumpled to the floor, she plucked the phone from his grasp then knelt beside him as if trying to offer comfort.

She raised her eyes to meet the questioning stares of her fellow travelers. "He will be fine," she said, in passable French. "The spirit is upon him."

The explanation was evidently good enough. No one paid them any further attention.

She bent lower over Fallon's still-writhing form and whispered in his ear. "First, I'm going to call the police and tell them that I've just escaped from a kidnapper. While I wait for them to get here, I'm going to call the authorities in Jordan and have them dig George and Fiona out. If you leave now, and take your hired goons with you, you just might be able to get out of the country before I tell them your name." She patted him on the shoulder. "Better get moving."

Once out of the labyrinth, she ducked into the south transept and looked down at the phone, which was still in video mode. She thumbed the button to stop recording and opened the phone function, but she did not call the police.

After the first ring, Dourado's wary voice sounded in her ear. "Cerberus Group."

"Cintia, it's me."

"Augustina! I mean, Dr. Gallo. Thank God."

Gallo smiled. Dourado was always so very formal. "Listen. I need you to—"

"Let me go first," Dourado said, cutting her off. "I probably know more than you do. Dr. Pierce and Fiona are safe. They got out. They're heading your way. Are you safe?"

Gallo sagged against the wall, the adrenaline of her escape draining away, leaving her feeling weak in the knees. "Safe?"

"Does Fallon still have you?"

She shook her head, momentarily forgetting that she was on the phone. "I got away from him."

"Good. I tracked Fallon's flight to France. Dr. Pierce will be there soon. Do you want to talk to him? I'll patch you through."

Before Gallo could answer the question, she heard Pierce's voice. "Gus? You're safe?"

"I should be asking you."

He laughed. "You didn't really think a hole in the ground would keep us down for long?"

"No. I mean, I hoped you'd find a way out."

"Where are you? Are you safe?"

"I think so." She glanced around, afraid that Fallon had ignored her warning and sent his hired thugs to grab her again, but there was no sign of them. "I'm at Chartres Cathedral."

"Chartres? What made you decide to go there?"

"I figured out what you were trying to tell me." She related her plan to trick Fallon into lowering his guard so that she could escape with his phone.

"You got all that from what I said?" There was a hint of awe in Pierce's voice.

"What did you actually mean?"

He chuckled. "Follow the Templar trail. Find the Ark. But I like your way better. Besides. Now I know where the Ark really is."

"Do tell."

"It's in London. I know I told you to ask the Templars, but that's only the beginning of the story."

FORTY-SIX

Chicago, Illinois

Ishiro Tanaka was a patient man. He had been waiting his whole life for this, for his chance to stop the endless cycle of suffering and death. Now the goal was in sight. He could wait a little longer.

Still, he was not immune to the frustration that came with being stranded.

Twelve hours after leaving Tomorrowland, his plane had touched down at Chicago's O'Hare Airport. International air traffic was still a jumbled mess, but there were flights to be had for the right price, and the Children of Durga no longer had any reason to be thrifty. Twelve more hours and he was still there, stuck in the Windy City, and the prospects of traveling on any time soon were not looking good.

The West Coast was a wreck. Portland and Seattle were still digging out. Anchorage had been leveled. The only aircraft going west of the Rockies were military, carrying relief workers and supplies, and that did not seem likely to change any time soon.

Durga had promised to provide a way for him to continue on to the goal, but as a physicist, Tanaka was all too familiar with the property of inertia. He had lost his momentum, and now it was going to take an extraordinary amount of energy to get moving again.

Another tedious hour ticked by. He sat in his hotel room, a few miles from the airport, watching the news coverage with a mixture of horror and satisfaction. The suffering galled him, but thousands had already been freed from the anguish of the slow death called life, and that was his doing. Soon, very soon, the misery of the survivors would also be at an end.

His phone began vibrating on the night table, signaling an incoming text message from Durga. He snatched it up and read the message. It was not the news he had been hoping for.

>*Pierce alive. Fallon alive.*

Tanaka wasn't sure why Durga was sharing this news with him. There wasn't anything he could do to help now. Before he could articulate a question, the phone buzzed again.

>*Went to Jordan, then France. Believe Pierce is still looking for a way to stop you.*

"And you're telling me this why?" he muttered, but then he tapped in a more thoughtful reply.

>>>*If he's still looking, it means he didn't find anything at Sinai. He's desperate. Grasping at straws.*

>*Straws can break backs. Is there a risk?*

Was there?

He recalled the conversation in the Geneva safehouse a day earlier, when Pierce's people had trusted him with their plan to find some ancient relic made from the same meta-material as the Roswell fragment and the Black Knight.

A sun chariot from some Greek fairy tale?

It had sounded ludicrous to him at the time, but the same could also be said about the Black Knight satellite and the ancient alien explorers who had probably left it behind.

>>>*We can't take any chances. You have to stop him. Go all in.*

Durga did not respond for several minutes, and Tanaka thought perhaps the conversation was over. Then another text arrived, with an accompanying location link for a U.S. Air National Guard facility in Peoria, Illinois, a three-hour drive from Chicago. The message read:

>*Found you a seat on a supply flight leaving at 1800. Will get you close. The rest is up to you.*

He was still processing this information when another text came through.

>*Final message. You will not hear from me again. The victory of Durga begins.*

FORTY-SEVEN

Axum, Ethiopia

Lazarus returned to the grounds of Our Lady Mary of Zion before dusk, but he did not approach the cathedral. Instead, he took a stroll around the outer perimeter. He wore a red and yellow *dashiki* suit, with matching *sokoto* drawstring trousers and a black brimless *kufi* cap. He wasn't sure if the ensemble, which had been purchased at a tourist gift shop, would make him stand out or blend in. Ethiopia was an ethnically diverse country, and his Persian complexion was just dark enough that he could pass for an Abyssinian—someone of Habesha ancestry. Ultimately, he didn't care if he was noticed or pegged as a visitor, so long as they paid more attention to the outlandish outfit than they did to the man wearing it.

As the sun dropped behind the cathedral, he did a quick 360 degree check and then slipped into a wooded area near the southeastern corner of the structure's foundation. One corner of the Chapel of the Tablets extended out beyond the fence separating the church from the outside world, just forty yards away.

Once concealed, he slipped out of the dashiki, which covered his jeans and a black hoodie, and then crouched down to wait for darkness. He waited a full hour, barely moving at all, then another, watching people come and go, or simply passing by on the street. Some carried candles and oil lamps, others bore smoky torches. After three motionless hours, he checked his watch and rose to his feet, although he did not step out from his hiding place. Stiffness wasn't a problem thanks to his regenerative capabilities, but he stretched anyway, cracking his knuckles and then his cervical vertebrae, in anticipation of the go-signal.

It came just thirty seconds later, a harsh explosion. Sounding more like the report of a mortar or RPG launch than something mundane like a car backfiring or a big firecracker. It was in fact the latter, a firecracker about the size of an M-80, with a makeshift time delay fuse and a slight aftermarket modification to increase the volume of the detonation. Carter had dropped the lit firecracker a block away eight minutes previously. If she was following the plan, she was already long gone.

A few lights came on inside the church complex and a few brave souls ventured out to satisfy their curiosity about the noise. Lazarus also spotted a policeman emerging from a concealed watch-post, just outside the church grounds, to investigate the disturbance. When nothing more happened, everyone seemed to lose interest. The lights went out, and the police officer returned to his guard post.

Lazarus waited another twenty seconds, then made his move.

He stole along the edge of the wall, crossing the forty yards to the corner of the Chapel of the Tablets in four seconds. He vaulted up and over the fence like a parkour master, dropped to the ground on the far side, and pressed himself against the rough brick exterior of the Chapel. He paused there only a moment, just long enough to make sure that he had not been noticed, then kept going. The door was on the north wall, just a few steps away.

It opened with no resistance.

Lazarus moved inside with the same decisive swiftness he had once used when conducting military raids. He doubted very much that the lone monk assigned to the lifetime position of guardian would be lurking in the corner with an AK-47, but that didn't mean the venture was risk free. If he was spotted and the alarm was sounded, getting out of Ethiopia would be tricky. If it happened before he was able to verify that the Ark inside the chapel was a fake, it would all be for naught.

He moved inside and closed the door behind him. The interior was dark and still. He waited a few seconds, listening, breathing, tasting the air for any sign of trouble, before clicking on a small disposable flashlight. He kept the light covered with one hand, allowing a sliver of illumination to slip through his fingers. It was enough for him to navigate the interior and make out a few details.

The chapel's layout was simple, a large open room surrounding a tall square enclosure in the middle. The walls of the enclosure were adorned with brightly painted panels, depicting scenes from the Bible and the story of how the Ark came to Axum. Lazarus could not fathom why the builders of the chapel would decorate a room that only a few men would ever be permitted to see.

Three sides of the enclosure had shuttered windows. The fourth wall had a door, screened off behind a partition of colored glass. Lazarus ducked around the partition and approached the door with the same assertiveness he had shown entering the building.

The closed door reminded him of Schroedinger's Cat, the old thought experiment used to explain competing alternate realities in quantum physics. While the door was closed, there were two potential realities occupying the same space on the other side. In one reality, the enclosure contained the highly sought-after Ark of the Covenant, the actual relic from the Bible, imbued with supernatural powers. In another reality, the enclosure contained a forgery. Yet, it was not a case of one or the other. While the door remained closed, the actual truth known only to the guardian monk, the two realities existed simultaneously. The Ark was there for those who believed it was, and it was not for those who did not believe.

Once he entered the enclosure, one of those realities would cease to exist.

Lazarus did not hesitate. He was certain about which reality would survive, but not so certain that he did not harbor a small sliver of doubt. He and Carter were only here because of that sliver, that remote possibility that could not be completely dismissed.

What if that reality survived? What if he found the actual, real Ark?

Sneaking into the Chapel of the Tablets was one thing. Trying to sneak out, while carrying a holy relic that probably weighed hundreds of pounds, not to mention possessing the power to strike anyone touching it dead, would be another matter.

Still, if that happened, at least the question of the Ark's final disposition would be resolved. They could work out the rest of the details later.

He opened the door and saw it. A chest, covered in shiny yellow metal that gleamed as it caught the flashlight's reflection. It looked like pictures he had seen, right down to the angels covering the lid with their outstretched wings.

But that did not mean it was the real Ark. There was only one way to determine which reality would survive. As with Schroedinger's Cat, he would have to open the box. If it was the true Ark, he would probably be struck dead, and given its supernatural properties, there was no guarantee that his regenerative abilities would bring him back. The wrath of God could be tricky that way.

Without hesitating, he stepped into the enclosure, reached out both hands, and took hold of the covering angels.

Nothing. No electric shock. No release of divine retribution.

He lifted the lid, and immediately knew that the metal covering the carved angels was not gold, but something lighter and harder. Polished brass in all likelihood.

One reality blinked out of existence. The Ethiopian Ark of the Covenant was not the real deal.

Time to go.

He set the lid back in place and clicked off his light. The open layout of the chapel would be easy to navigate in the dark. No sense risking discovery now, with the mission almost complete.

He exited the enclosure, circled around to the front door, opened it...and froze in his tracks.

Abuna Mateos stood just outside, flanked on either side by old men in priestly vestments. They all held burning candles, which cast just enough light upon their faces to reveal a hint of disappointment, but not a trace of surprise.

None of the men were armed, at least not that Lazarus could see, and they did not appear poised to attack or to attempt subduing him until the authorities could be summoned. They just stood there, blocking his escape route.

Lazarus considered pushing past them and bolting for the wall, but that wouldn't get him out of the country. Before he could make up his mind, Mateos spoke.

"Are you satisfied, now that you have seen for yourself?"

Lazarus sensed he was being cryptic. Did Mateos know that the Ark in the chapel was a forgery? Did any of the men standing before him? And if they did not, what right did he have to burst the bubbles of their faith? "You could say that," he answered, equally vague.

"I knew that you would come."

"Was I that obvious?"

Mateos smiled. "I saw it in a vision. The Lord told me to expect you."

Lazarus had no response to that. "I'm finished here," he said, keeping his tone firm but diplomatic. "I won't tell anyone what I saw in there."

He hoped the subtext was clear to the older man. *Try to stop me, and I'll tell the world.*

Mateos, however, just shook his head. "I'm afraid it's not that simple."

FORTY-EIGHT

Chartres, France

The pain subsided to a dull ache after about half an hour, but Fallon's dark rage showed no sign of abating.

That bitch, he fumed.

Even more powerful than the pain and anger was the fear. He had abducted Gallo. Taken her across international borders. Buried Pierce and his young protégé alive. In the heat of the moment, he had not even stopped to think about the potential consequences of these actions, but now he was terrified.

How am I going to get out of this?

The answer disturbed him.

Kill her. Kill them all.

He couldn't think of another way to avoid rotting in a jail cell.

But first, a strategic withdrawal. He had limped from the nave of Chartres Cathedral and found Williams waiting outside. If Gallo had left, she had done so unnoticed. Fallon couldn't take the chance that her threat to call the police was a bluff, but he left Williams and the Alpha Dog mercenaries with instructions to keep watching, and headed for the airport, just in case.

Before getting out of the car to board the plane, he called Williams on a borrowed mobile phone. "Any sign of her?"

The mere act of talking sent a fresh wave of pain through his groin.

"Negative," Williams replied. "Maybe she slipped our net. But no sign of the police, either. I think she was yanking your chain about that. They don't want cops involved any more 'n you do."

The mercenary was probably right about that.

"We can go in," the man went on. "Sweep the place for her."

He considered the offer, trying to ignore the pulsating ache between his legs. If they tried to grab Gallo in public it would only make matters worse, and they would be no closer to finding the Ark of the Covenant. The move against Pierce in Jordan had been premature, but his original plan was still sound. Let Gallo and Pierce find the Ark, and then take it away from them.

But if he was going to pull it off, he would need more than just a quartet of hired military rejects.

"No," he told Williams. "Let's hold off on that. Come back to the airport. I've got a better idea."

FORTY-NINE

London, England

The revelation had come to Pierce in the Templar chapel, deep beneath Mount Nebo. Pierce had contacted Dourado, and she had started tracking Fallon even before his plane left the Amman airport. When Gallo had escaped from Fallon at Chartres Cathedral, the Cerberus jet was already in French airspace. Less than an hour later, the three of them were together again, exhausted but no worse for wear.

The clock was still ticking, but now Pierce knew where they needed to go. He had explained his epiphany during the short hop across the English Channel.

"The Templars came to Jerusalem looking for the Ark. They had the same scrolls and scriptures that led us to Jeremiah's secret hiding place. What they didn't have, at least not until they set up shop on the Temple Mount, was a standard of measurement. The true length of the Sacred cubit.

"The fresco we found showed the Templars using a measuring stick. Historically, the length of the cubit was always understood to be the approximate distance from a man's elbow to fingertip. Roughly eighteen inches. And that's the figure they would have been most familiar with. It's a more or less constant ratio of one cubit to average height—not quite one-fourth. Back then, the average height for a man was about five and half feet, but with better nutrition, the average is now almost six feet. As we know, the Sacred cubit is just over twenty-five inches. Based on the one-fourth rule, that could suggest the Sacred cubit was derived from a race of people with an average height of about one hundred inches—over eight feet."

"Giants," Gallo said. "Like Goliath and the Rephaim."

"I know about Goliath," said Dourado, who was listening in on speaker phone. "But who or what are the Rephaim?"

"Everyone knows the story of David and Goliath. Depending on how you interpret the cubit, Goliath was at least nine feet tall, but he wasn't just an outlier. Goliath belonged to a tribe known as the Rephaim, who were known for being giants." Gallo turned to Fiona. "That name translates to: 'the people whose speech sounds like buzzing.'"

Fiona caught on. "They knew the Mother Tongue."

Gallo gave a knowing nod. "It's possible. They were descended from an earlier tribe called the Anakim—sons of Anak. The Hebrews encountered them on the edge of the Promised Land. The ancient Greek word Anax, from which Anak is probably derived, is used to indicate royalty but also divine power. Both the Rephaim and the Anakim are associated with ancient ancestors living in the *sheol*, the Hebrew word for the pit or underworld. And here we come full circle, the Rephaim were descendants of the Nephilim."

"And the Sacred cubit was *their* measurement," Pierce said. "There was zero chance of the Templars figuring that out. To find the precise location where Jeremiah concealed the Ark, they would have needed to know the exact length of the Sacred cubit, and that's a calculation they were able to make from something they found on the Temple Mount."

"That makes sense," Gallo said, "but how does it tell us where the Ark went after they found it?"

Pierce answered with a question. "How do *we* know the length of the Sacred cubit?"

"Cintia told us," Fiona said.

"And I learned about it from the writings of Sir Isaac Newton," Dourado put in.

"So, how did Newton figure it out?"

As Fiona and Gallo exchanged a look, Dourado answered. "According to the paper he wrote, it was by researching ancient writings."

"That's one possible answer," Pierce said, grinning. "But how did he arrive at the correct figure, when all those earlier scholars couldn't get it right? And remember, there was no uniform standard of measurement until the reign of Queen Elizabeth, no way to communicate what those distances meant."

Gallo grasped what he was trying to say. "You think Isaac Newton got his measurements from the Ark?"

"It's the perfect standard of measurement. The Bible gives the exact dimensions of the Ark in cubits. Newton's calculation was the basis for his theories on light, and probably everything else, too. He invented calculus just so he could understand the significance of the Sacred cubit, and that opened his eyes to the laws of gravity and motion. The Sacred cubit was the key to unlocking all of that because it came from the Originators..." He smiled at Gallo. "...aka, the Nephilim, a technologically advanced alie—err, species."

"'If I have seen further than others,'" Gallo murmured, reciting one of Newton's most enduring quotes. "'It is by standing upon the shoulders of giants.' He wasn't just talking about intellectual giants, was he?"

She blew out her breath with a low whistle. "Well, it's not the craziest thing I've heard today. Connect the dots for me. How do we get from the Templars to Sir Isaac Newton?"

"I don't have it all worked out," Pierce admitted. "Cintia, maybe you can fact-check me on some of this. But here's what I think happened: The Templars found the Ark and held on to it for a couple of centuries, believing that they would one day be able to rebuild Solomon's Temple in Jerusalem. When they learned of King Philip's plot against them, the Ark was the one secret they had to keep, so they confessed to the wildest crimes imaginable and spun tales of treasure ships, all to hide the one thing that was more important to them than their reputation or even their lives. They went underground, just like all the conspiracy theories say, creating secret societies that would protect the Ark and preserve the wisdom and knowledge of the Templars through the ages."

"Kind of like us?" Fiona mused.

"Except they were holding off until all those old prophecies about the Jews returning to Mount Zion and rebuilding the Temple came true. They hid their secrets in rituals and stories. Only the highest level initiates would ever know the whole truth."

"You're talking about the Freemasons," Gallo said. "Was Newton a Mason?"

"Let me check," Dourado said. "Okay, it looks like the first lodge in London opened in 1717, ten years before Newton died... Oh."

"Oh?" Pierce prompted.

"I'm sending you a picture. It's the seal of the London Grand Lodge."

The phone buzzed as the image came via text message. Pierce tapped on the screen to open the file.

"Is that...?" Gallo started.

"I think so." Pierce zoomed in on the feature of the seal that he suspected had caught everyone's attention.

"That's the Ark!" Fiona said.

"It makes sense," Pierce explained. "The Masons see themselves as the spiritual heirs to Hiram, the architect of Solomon's temple, where the Ark of the Covenant was kept. The Ark and anything related to the Temple is of paramount importance, symbolically at least."

"Maybe the chicken came before the egg," Fiona suggested. "Maybe they got interested in this stuff because Isaac Newton asked them to protect the Ark."

"It's not that crazy," Pierce admitted. "And a lot of Masons consider Newton to be an influence, if not a member. What we do know for certain is that Newton was an early member and president of the Royal Society."

"More secret brotherhoods," Fiona said, rolling her eyes.

"The Royal Society isn't a secret," Pierce said. "It's the world's oldest and most esteemed scientific organization."

"The Royal Society was founded in 1660," Dourado said, summarizing the result of another Internet search. "But it traces back to an earlier group of scientists who called themselves 'the Invisible College.' The idea for the Invisible College came from a reference to 'Salomon's House' in the book *New Atlantis*, by Sir Francis Bacon. It was an early blueprint for a research institute."

"Once again, life imitates art," Gallo said. "And who better to take as a namesake than King Solomon, the wisest man ever to have lived?"

"Solomon's House might also refer to the Temple," Pierce added.

"You might be right about that," Dourado said. "Bacon was known to be a student of Templar lore. He was also involved in creating the King James Version of the Bible, and he consulted with Dr. John Dee on the creation of the statute measurement system."

"Isn't he also the guy that wrote the Voynich Manuscript?" Fiona asked.

"You're thinking of Roger Bacon," Pierce said. "No relation."

She grinned. "Other than crispy deliciousness."

Pierce shook his head in a display of dismay, and then turned to Gallo. "There's your connection. The Templars relocated the Ark to London. France wasn't safe for them anymore. The Templars already had a strong presence in England, and King Edward sheltered them from the worst of the persecution. England and France were constantly at war, and Edward wasn't about to do Philip any favors. What better place to hide a secret Templar revival?

"Eventually, Edward was forced to comply with the wishes of the Church, and all Templar holdings were given to the Hospitallers, but they had plenty of time to cover their tracks. And when Henry VIII broke with Rome, he kicked the Hospitallers out as well. Which brings us to Sir Francis Bacon, the Royal Society, and to Isaac Newton.

"Newton was as much a man of faith as he was a man of science, but his discoveries were part of the Scientific Revolution, the Enlightenment, and the beginning of the end for universal acceptance of a divine origin for the Universe. I would guess that, as intellectual philosophies gained greater acceptance, the idea of holding onto religious relics like the Ark would have seemed a bit quaint. That probably contributed to the creation of the Masonic brotherhood, a way for men of faith and science to square the circle. Some of the Founding Fathers were both Masons and Deists—hybrid theistic rationalists. Just having the Ark would be an anchor for their spiritual beliefs."

"Dots connected," Gallo said. "Which just leaves one question. Where's the Ark today? You said you knew where it was."

"What's the first rule of real estate?" Pierce asked. "Location, location, location. The Temple Mount was chosen for a specific reason, an alignment of geomagnetic forces that even Solomon probably didn't understand, but was somehow connected to the Originator power grid. The cave where Jeremiah hid the Ark was calculated using the Sacred cubit and the location of the Temple. I would be willing to bet that the Templars used a similar calculation when deciding where to hide the Ark in London. A sacred place they would have identified right from the beginning: Temple Church."

"Of course," Dourado exclaimed. "It was in *The DaVinci Code*! I can't believe I forgot that."

Pierce winced at the reference but refrained from commenting.

Temple Church was, as its name indicated, a Church built by the Templars. The site, chosen by the first Templar Grandmaster, Hugues de Payens, was already sacred ground, albeit in a pagan tradition, having once been the location of a Roman temple in the ancient city of Londinium. The church itself was round, rather than cruciform, an architectural signature of Templar churches, just like the chapel Pierce and Fiona had discovered beneath Mount Nebo. The Templars had outgrown Temple Church, and built a city in Hertfordshire to the north of London, but Temple Church continued to serve an important role in Templar operations as the English royal treasury.

Even on a good day, getting to Temple Church was a bit of a challenge, requiring a local's knowledge of the narrow pedestrian throughways and back streets. At midnight on the day following the biggest disaster to hit the city since the Ragnarok Event, it was an ordeal comparable to escaping the subterranean world beneath Arkaim. Although London had suffered only minor earthquake damage, the subsequent nine-foot-high tsunami wave had flooded low-lying areas near the river as far inland as Battersea Bridge. The affected area included the Temple district, where Temple Church was located. The church itself was high and dry, but everything south of the Strand was barricaded off to vehicle traffic, and despite Dourado's best efforts to find them a route, it took forty minutes of wandering to find an approach.

"Reminds me of Castel Sant'Angelo," Fiona remarked, as they crouched in the shadows, checking to make sure the coast was clear.

"You're not the first to notice that," Pierce said. Indeed, the rugged church bore more than a passing resemblance to the papal fortress and one-time prison structure that concealed the entrance to the Cerberus Group's underground headquarters. "It's the round design. Most churches are cross-shaped, but Templar churches were always round, like the Church of the Holy Sepulchre in Jerusalem."

They remained in hiding for a few more minutes before making the final push to the entrance on the south side of the church. The locked door posed no great challenge to Fiona, who was almost as adept at picking locks as she was at creating golems, and they slipped into the deserted nave.

Pierce swept the surrounding area with his light. The round nave to their left contained the stone burial effigies for which the church had become famous. To the right was the more traditionally Gothic choir and chancel.

"Now what?" Fiona whispered.

Pierce had hoped that the proximity of the Ark would trigger some kind of reaction to which Fiona would be attuned, but that wasn't happening. He felt guilty asking her, yet again, if she sensed anything. Scanning with ground penetrating radar was also out of the question. He had no intention of going back to the snake pit underneath Mount Nebo to retrieve the lost Groundshark unit.

"We're going to have to do this the old-fashioned way," Pierce said. "Look everywhere."

"For what?" said Gallo.

"A secret door. The entrance to an underground crypt."

"There isn't a crypt," Dourado said, her voice audible only through the synced Bluetooth devices they were all using.

"This church used to be the Royal Treasury. There has to be more than meets the eye here."

Gallo cast a dubious eye into the nave. "I'm sure we're not the first visitors to come in here rapping on the walls hoping to find some hidden Templar secret."

"Well, we're just going to have to look in the one place they didn't. Cintia, try to dig up whatever information you can on this place. Maybe there's some old blueprints or something in the history-ical record that might steer us in the right direction. The older, the better."

"On it."

As the three of them fanned out, moving to different corners of the church looking for some irregularity that might hint at the location of a hidden passage, Dourado began recounting details from the historical record. Most of the early information focused more on the Templars and the disposition of the property once they were gone, but after the Great Fire of 1666, history began paying attention to the building itself.

"The fire was put out, right outside Temple Church," Dourado said. "What's kind of unusual is that, even though the Church wasn't damaged in the fire and even though he had thirty other churches to rebuild, the architect, Sir Christopher Wren, decided to refurbish Temple Church anyway."

"Christopher Wren," Pierce said. "He was also a President of the Royal Society."

"Yes, about twenty years before Sir Isaac Newton. He was close friends with Edmund Halley, and it was a discussion they had that prompted Newton to develop his calculations to explain orbital mech-anics. And like Newton, Wren is often linked to the Freemasons, though it's hard to say if he was actually a member of the brotherhood."

"What kind of changes did Wren make?"

"Mostly to the interior. The altar backpiece is his design."

Pierce turned and shone his light toward the far end of the chancel, illuminating a series of carved wooden panels—the official term for it was a *reredo*—which displayed the Ten Commandments and the Lord's prayer.

"Wren's modifications were controversial," Dourado continued, "and in 1841, most of them were undone in an attempt to make the church look more authentic. During the Blitz, a firebomb destroyed the roof and the organ, so they had to renovate again after the war. Wren's altar was taken out of mothballs and reinstalled."

"So, anything Wren might have done back in the seventeenth century," Gallo said, "would have been exposed during the Victorian renovation or the restoration after the War."

"Unless the architects were in on it." Pierce moved back into the nave. He played his light on the stone figures arranged on the floor and positioned behind ankle-high iron rails. "Cintia, what was that you said about the crypt?"

"That there isn't one. When they repaired the damage from the German bombing, they found no evidence of burials or a crypt under the Church. That's how we know the stone knights in the nave are just effigies and not actual tomb markers."

"What else do we know about these effigies?"

"There are nine effigies and what appears to be a stone casket cover in the spot where a tenth effigy would have gone. Five of them are attributed to actual people, the other four are unknown. The effigies were damaged by the bombing, but there are casts of them taken from before the war in the Victoria and Albert Museum."

Pierce noted that all but two of the carved figures had their legs crossed, which was a common burial tradition for Crusader knights. "Which ones belonged to Templars?"

"None of them. At least, not the five that have been identified. They were supporters of the order but they never took the vows."

Pierce examined each effigy in turn, taking note of their layout. Eight of the effigies were located within the inner circle of pillars supporting the ceiling vault, four on each side, arranged in a two-by-two formation. The heads were pointing west, feet positioned toward east, in the direction of the choir, with just enough space between each to create a cross. Further out, on either side, were the last two markers, including the one that lacked an effigy.

He returned to the center, turning slowly, looking for the pattern. "Why does this look familiar?"

Then he saw it and barked a laugh. Fiona came around to stand beside him. "What are you seeing?"

"We're standing in a circle," he said, raising his arms and turning around. "A circle. Keep that image in your head."

He moved outside the inner circle, to the back of the nave and stood looking across the four effigies to the north, with one arm raised, pointing east. "Now. Imagine a straight line passing right through there." After allowing a moment for this to sink in, he moved a few steps to the right and did the same over the effigies to the south.

A circle overlaying parallel lines.

The sigil of Hercules.

"The Herculean Society," Gallo murmured.

"Coincidence?" Fiona asked.

George shrugged. "Could be."

But even as she said it, a loud scraping sound filled the nave, reverberating between the ceiling arches like a sustained musical note. Pierce turned toward the source of the noise and saw the tenth marker, the one without a knight, sinking into the floor.

FIFTY

Pierce glanced at Fiona. She shook her head. Something had triggered the secret trap door, but it wasn't anything she had done. She crept past the effigies and shone her light into the narrow opening. Only part of the casket cover was still visible. After dropping a few feet, it had slid to the side, revealing a narrow flight of stone steps, facing west as they descended into nothingness.

"Somebody knows we're here," Gallo said. "So, do we go down the rabbit hole?"

"The Ark is down there," Pierce replied. "I don't think we have a choice."

He took a tentative step into the revealed passage, then another. When his head dipped below the level of the floor, Gallo gestured for Fiona to go next.

The opening was narrow, forcing her to turn sideways to get her shoulders through. The air rising up from below was cool and damp, and a musty smell filled her nostrils. The floor at the bottom of the steps glistened with moisture, but the passage beyond was not flooded. Pierce was already moving down the tunnel, and she hastened to catch up to him.

The passage followed a straight line for about a hundred yards before ending at a simple wooden door, slightly ajar. Soft light filtered through the opening, and a sweet smell, like pipe tobacco, cut the dank mildew of the tunnel.

Pierce paused there until Fiona and Gallo caught up, and then he pushed the door open wide.

What lay beyond bore only a slight resemblance to the round nave of Temple Church, and it did not look at all like a thirteenth century burial crypt. The area into which they stepped was round—an open semi-circle—and approximately the same width, with pillars supporting groin vaults overhead. The similarities ended there. Instead of a rustic church building with worn and damaged stone carvings and appoint-ments, the chamber here was smooth and refined, with exquisitely worked marble and panels of polished wood. The floor was a chessboard pattern of polished white and black tiles. The walls were adorned with royal blue curtains, pulled back to reveal portraits, and relics on shelves and in display cases. The back of the door through which they had entered matched the décor, so that when closed, it would be almost indistinguishable. Beyond the door, the chamber stretched out into an enormous hall like the ballroom of a Renaissance-era palace. The far end of the hall, about fifty feet from where they stood, was draped in a dark curtain that stretched all the way across the room, though Fiona could see a narrow gap on either end. The most striking difference of all however, and the only reason she could discern any of the similarities and differences, was the fact that this room was illumin-ated with artificial light. Each of the elegant support columns sported an understated wall sconce of brushed brass and frosted glass.

"This is a Masonic lodge," Pierce said. "The checkerboard floor is a Masonic symbol for the duality of nature. Opposing forces. Light and dark. Good and evil."

"Not a big surprise," Gallo said. "We suspected their involvement, after all."

"They opened the door for us," Fiona whispered, even though it wasn't necessary to do so. "Is there a connection between the Masons and the Herculean Society?"

"None that I'm aware of," Pierce said.

"Then it's high time you were brought up to date."

The unfamiliar voice—male, older, with a British accent—echoed in the hall. The rhythmic tapping of footsteps filled the space, and then the man who had spoken stepped into view.

Older, in his seventies, with a mane of swept-back white hair, he stood tall and took long strides, quickly crossing the distance to join them. Aside from his dignified black suit, he was attired with a short, blue and white apron, emblazoned with the distinctive square and compass sigil of the Masonic brotherhood. He strode right up to Pierce and offered his hand.

"How do you do?" he said, his expression serious but friendly. "I am Clive Chillingsworth."

Pierce introduced the others, utilizing formal titles and surnames only—Fiona was introduced as 'Miss Sigler'—then he added, "We're with the Cerberus Group, an independent research organization."

"Is that a fact?" Chillingsworth replied, raising an eyebrow.

Fiona, sensing their shared wariness, pushed ahead. "You opened the passage, didn't you? Were you expecting us?"

The man swung his gaze toward her. "In a manner of speaking. Forgive me, it's difficult to know where to begin."

"Once upon a time..." Fiona prompted.

"Fi," Pierce admonished, but then added. "She's right though. We followed some pretty obscure clues to get here, and now you're telling us that we were expected? What did you mean by that?"

Chillingsworth waved a hand, gesturing to their surroundings. "The Grand Lodge of London was dedicated three hundred years ago, and for that entire time, we have been the keepers of ancient and secret wisdom. I know how trite that must sound, but it happens to be the truth. Come, allow me to show you."

He turned and started back down the checkerboard floor. Pierce followed, but before they had crossed even half the length of the hall, he let out a gasp. "That's it. That's the Tabernacle."

Fiona now saw that the curtain was a long piece of fabric, woven of bright red, purple and blue threads, embroidered with shimmering gold angles, draped over a concealed structure, at least twenty feet high and just as wide.

"This is the real thing, isn't it?" Pierce went on. "The actual Tabernacle created by Moses during the Exodus. The Templars found it under Mount Nebo and brought it back. When the Order was dissolved, they brought it to England and hid it in a crypt below Temple Church. That's what happened, isn't it?"

Chillingsworth looked back at him. "So it is said in our traditions," he confirmed. "The crypt was kept sealed for over two hundred years until King Henry VIII broke with Rome and secretly restored the Templars. A century later, the Royal Society, under the direction of Grand Architect, Sir Christopher Wren, commenced a study of the relics brought back from Jerusalem. He also oversaw the creation of this hall, both as a way to honor the Holy items of the Covenant and to facilitate further investigations. Sir Christopher, and later Sir Isaac Newton, recognized that there was a code hidden in the Sacred Measurements of the Tabernacle, a code that could be used to calculate the End of Days."

Fiona was nodding along with him, right up until that last declaration. "End of Days?" she echoed.

"It was a matter of great concern back then," Chillingsworth said. "I suppose it still is today, but men like Sir Isaac were fascinated with the problem of calculating when the world would end based on chronology and Bible prophecies. Sir Isaac himself predicted the prophecies regarding the End Times would be fulfilled no sooner than AD 2060, which I'm sure must have seemed very reassuring in 1704." He sighed. "We all thought we'd have another fifty years or so, but I suppose even Sir Isaac is allowed a mistake now and then."

Pierce stiffened. "You think the world is ending now?"

Chillingsworth stopped and turned to face Pierce. "Isn't that why you're here? The signs are appearing. An earthquake that shakes the whole world, the sun standing still in the sky. And now...you lot. We were told to look for you when the fulfillment began."

"Okay, you keep saying that. Explain. Are you talking about another prophecy?"

"In a manner of speaking," The man now appeared ill-at-ease. "I gather you have some knowledge of our organization. Our reputation for secrecy, rituals, and such."

Pierce nodded. "I also know that a lot of what people say about you is rubbish. Most of your so-called secret rites are common knowledge."

"Most," Chillingsworth agreed. "But there are certain...shall we say...'nuances?' Aspects of our rites and traditions that are not public knowledge. Matters known and understood only by Master Masons like myself, who have achieved the highest degree of knowledge. One such tradition, which it is said goes back to the time of the Templar Knights, compels us to offer assistance to anyone who invokes the Great Seal. When we saw the other signs fulfilled, we began our vigil, which is why I happened to be here at the Lodge tonight. Of course, you surprised us by coming in through the back door, as it were. We stopped using the Temple Church entrance after it was mentioned in that book—"

"I'm sorry," Pierce interrupted. "What's this Great Seal you're talking about?"

"It's the Ark," Fiona said. "Remember, the Ark of the Covenant is on their coat of arms?"

"That's not precisely right," Chillingsworth said, as he reached into his inside jacket pocket and produced a fountain pen and a business card embossed with the same design Dourado had showed them earlier.

"Invoking the Great Seal refers to demonstrating knowledge of the position of the cherubim within the circle of God's glory." He drew a circle connecting the points of the rays, and then drew vertical lines through the bodies of the paired angels.

"That's the Sign of Hercules," Fiona said, unconsciously rubbing the tattoo of the same symbol on the back of her hand.

The older man faced her. "We maintain video surveillance in the Temple Church sanctuary, just in case. When we saw you describe that pattern of the Great Seal, we knew that the time to fulfill our obligation had arrived." He lowered his head slightly and gave a knowing smile. "I'll be honest with you, most of us thought it was just a myth. But, here you are."

Pierce leaned close to Gallo, though Fiona had no difficulty hearing his whisper. "Alexander must have played a part in organizing the London Grand Lodge. He created, or at the very least, co-opted the Freemasons to keep the Ark of the Covenant safe and secret."

Gallo appeared unconvinced. "Why didn't he just move it to one of the Society locations? Like the Citadel?"

The Citadel was the original headquarters of the Herculean Society, located in a hidden cave beneath the Rock of Gibraltar.

"I'm sure he had his reasons," Pierce said. He turned to Chillingsworth. "As you said, here we are."

There was an uncomfortable silence, as if Chillingsworth was waiting for Pierce to take the initiative. When that did not happen, he motioned for them to continue following him. As he approached the hanging, he resumed speaking. "The outer courtyard pillars and panels are still in storage. There wasn't room to set everything up here. The brazen altar is in another hall. Sir Isaac indicated in his writings that the Tabernacle and all its utensils and relics would need to be restored to the Temple Mount when the time of God's glory arrived."

"Why there?" Fiona inquired.

Pierce was ready with the answer. "Jerusalem has long been associated with geomagnetic currents known as 'Ley lines.' There's a reason Solomon chose to build the Temple where he did. It's a power spot, just like Mount Sinai. I'm guessing the other relics are important, too. Maybe they're part of the control mechanism, or a safety measure so we don't get fried by the shekinah light."

"Well that explains it," Fiona exclaimed. "The Nazis didn't have the Tabernacle. That's why their faces melted."

Pierce tapped a finger to the tip of his nose and pointed at Fiona. "Now you're getting it."

Gallo groaned. "Don't encourage him, dear."

Pierce turned back to Chillingsworth. "I'd like to see those writings, if you have them. I think Newton might have understood how we're supposed to use the Ark to shut down the Black Knight."

"Of course. All our resources are at your disposal." Chillingsworth stopped at the curtain, and, with a theatrical flourish, drew it back to reveal the interior of the sacred tent.

The lights in the hall could not penetrate the thick fabric, but in the beam of Pierce's light, Fiona could make out a rectangular space, twice as deep as it was wide. There was an ornate table to one side, a large six-armed menorah, and directly ahead, up against another heavy curtain, was a small altar. All the objects reflected the flashlight with a deep yellow glow like nothing Fiona had ever seen before. She knew, intuitively, that the metal had to be gold.

"This part of the Tabernacle was called 'the Holy Place,'" Pierce said. "It's where the priests would offer the sacrifices and burn incense every day. The Ark would be in the next chamber, the Most Holy Place, or the Holy of Holies, behind the Altar of Incense. Only the High Priest—the *Kohen Gadol*—could enter into the presence of the Ark. He had to wear a special garment called an *ephod,* woven with gold threads. Some modern scholars have speculated that the vestments acted like a Faraday suit, insulating the priest from the energy of the Ark.

"There was also a special breastplate called the *hoshen*, studded with gems and crystals, which might have acted as a sort of interface or control device, and the *mitznefeta*, a turban with a gold crown inscribed with the true name of God. But I think the Urim and Thummim are the most important components of the ensemble."

"What are those?" Fiona asked.

"No one's really sure. They're only mentioned a few times in scripture and never described, but according to the Bible, they're one of the three ways that God revealed his will to humans—the other two being dreams and prophets. The linguistic roots suggested literal translations of 'Lights and Perfections,' or 'Revelation and Truth,' or simply 'Innocent and Guilty.'

"It's believed that they were a sort of oracular device, a Divine form of casting lots to determine the guilt or innocence of an accused person. Two stones: one white, one black. Put them both in a bag, ask God a question. 'Is so-and-so a secret sinner?' Take out a white stone and they're innocent. A black stone, and—"

"They get stoned," Fiona finished.

"But even that is just supposition. Members of the Latter Day Saints church believed that the Urim and Thummim were sacred crystals, which their founder, Joseph Smith, bound together like eyeglasses, enabling him to read and interpret the Golden Plates that contained the Book of Mormon."

"An instant translator," Fiona remarked. "Just like Cintia's babelfish."

"Only better, because these could read the secret language of God."

Fiona's eyes widened a little at that possibility.

"I'm eager to see them. All that was known about them was that they were to be placed in the small pockets sewn into the *hoshen*." Pierce turned to Chillingsworth. "Do you have the High Priest's garments? We might not need them if my suspicions about Fiona being a Baal'Shem are correct, but why take chances."

A frown creased Chillingsworth's forehead. "No priestly vestments were found when the crypt was opened." His expression indicated that there was more he wished to share, but instead of putting it into words, he stepped through the opening and walked the full length of the Holy Place.

Pierce opened his mouth, perhaps to warn the man of the dangers of approaching the Ark unprotected, but before he could utter a single word, their host pulled back the curtain that separated Holy from Most Holy, revealing the cube-shaped enclosure.

And nothing else.

"Where's the Ark?" Pierce said. Fiona could hear the fear in his voice.

"I'm afraid there's been a misunderstanding, Dr. Pierce. The Ark of the Covenant is not, nor has it ever been, in our care. If the Knights of the Temple found it, they did not bring it here."

FIFTY-ONE

Lake Tana, Ethiopia

Lazarus and Carter left Axum in the back of an old five-ton truck, accompanied by Abuna Mateos and half-a-dozen men armed with AK-47s and machetes, but they were not prisoners or hostages on their way to an execution.

"They are here to protect us," Mateos told them as they climbed aboard. "The roads are not safe after dark. And we cannot afford to wait for sunrise."

Lazarus did not need to ask how the clergyman knew this. The bishop had explained everything early in the night, outside the Chapel of the Tablets.

"The Lord came to me in a vision," he had said. "He told me that you would come for the Ark, and that I was to help you return it to Mount Zion."

"That's not the real Ark," Lazarus had countered. "But you already knew that."

"The vessel you saw *is* a holy, consecrated *tabot*. So, as far as the Church is concerned, it is an Ark of the Covenant. But you are correct. It is not the Ark the Israelites bore through the wilderness, and which Solomon safeguarded in his Temple."

"Well, that's the Ark I need, so if you'll just step aside, I'll be on my way."

"I will take you to it," Mateos had said in a solemn voice.

The true Ark, he had revealed, had indeed been kept in the Chapel of the Tablets until 1991, when political unrest, civil war, and ultimately revolution, threatened the long-standing arrangement between Church and State. Fearing that a new government might attempt to seize the Ark, removing the symbol by which the centuries-old Imperial dynasty had ruled by divine right, the keepers of the Ark had fashioned and consecrated a replica. They had then removed the real Ark to one of its earlier resting places, the monastery of Mitsele Fasiladas on the isle of Tana Qirqos, just off the eastern shore of Lake Tana, about 250 miles to the southwest of Axum.

Lazarus took the bishop at his word. The man had no reason to deceive him with an offer of assistance. Lazarus had been caught red-handed, after all. The clergyman's sincerity however did not automatically mean that his Church was in possession of the true Ark.

Carter shared his apprehension, but they both knew that the only way to resolve the mystery was with a visit to the remote island monastery.

They rode through the night, reaching the lakeside city of Bahir Dar just after sunrise. Mateos sent their armed escort back to

Axum, and then hired a boat to take them twenty miles north to Tana Qirqos.

Lake Tana was most famous for being the source of the Blue Nile, which joined with the White Nile in Khartoum to become the world's longest river. But for Ethiopians it held great spiritual and historical significance. Many of the islands dotting the shallow but expansive lake were home to monasteries, and each monastery was linked to an ancient tradition or miracle. Tana Qirqos, their destination, not only figured into the story of the Ark of the Covenant, but also the history of Christianity.

"Saint Frumentius, who brought Christianity to the ancient Kingdom of Aksum, is buried on Tana Qirqos," Mateos told them, as the boat chugged along. "And there is an altar containing a stone upon which the Virgin Mary rested during her journey back from Egypt."

"Is that really true?" Carter asked.

"There are many such stories in all faiths," Abuna Mateos admitted. "Whether they are true does not diminish their symbolic value. The Lord taught in parables when he walked on the Earth. These places serve to remind us that the foundation of our faith reaches back many thousands of years."

Carter's lips curled into a mischievous smile. "In 1974, about two hundred miles west of here, anthropologists discovered the most complete skeleton ever of a female *Australopithecus afarensis*, who lived 3.2 million years ago. That's my foundation."

"Felice," Lazarus murmured. "Play nice."

Mateos laughed. "We are as proud of Dinkinesh—I believe you call her 'Lucy'—as we are of our spiritual traditions. One need not preclude the other."

"I can appreciate symbolic value," Carter countered. "But I'm a scientist. Facts are the only thing that matter to me."

"And yet you seek the Ark of the Covenant, a powerful religious symbol. And you look for it here, where all we have are our stories, which you do not believe. Curious."

"What we seek," she clarified, "is a powerful device once used by Moses and Joshua to trigger earthquakes and stop the sun in the sky. And we came here because millions of Ethiopians are convinced that you've got that device. The man we work for made a pretty convincing case for why it can't be in Ethiopia. So whether I believe or not is irrelevant. Do you have the Ark? Are those stories true?"

Mateos sagged into one of the chairs bolted to the deck. "The story you know and that all my countrymen believe, the story recorded in the *Kebra Nagast*, the Glory of Kings, which we have told for hundreds of years, is almost certainly false. It is a story created by men to justify their right to rule over other men. I know this. All learned men know this. The Kingdom of Sheba was not in Ethiopia, and neither Solomon nor the Priests of the Holy Temple would have permitted anyone to remove the Ark. However, I also know that the one true Ark is here, and has been for more than two thousand years.

"This is what I believe happened: In the days of Zedekiah, the last king of Judah, God sent the prophet Jeremiah to deliver a message of judgment. The king, angered by the prophecy, ordered Jeremiah to be cast into a cistern, where he would surely have died. But the king's servant—his *abdemelech*—was a godly man. He rescued Jeremiah from the cistern. To repay his faith, God promised the *abdemelech* that he would be spared when the judgement came. Scripture says little else about that godly servant, except that he was an Ethiopian."

"Pierce thinks Jeremiah hid the Ark," Lazarus said. "But he could have had help from that Ethiopian."

"I believe that is how the Ark came to be in my country, but it is only an idea I have. Perhaps there is another explanation, I do not know. I know only that the true Ark is there, at Tana Qirqos. You will see."

Despite the man's evident conviction, Lazarus remained skeptical. From what he could tell, the entire story of the Ark in Ethiopia was like one great big shell game. First the Ark was in the Chapel of the Tablets, but no one was allowed to see it. Then that Ark turned out to be bogus, but the real one was somewhere else. He couldn't help but wonder if the Ark at Tana Qirqos would prove to be just one more deception.

In the early light, the island looked like a fortress rising from the surface of the lake. A solid mass of basalt, it looked at least four hundred yards long and a hundred feet high, surrounded by reedy shallows. The wall itself was sheer, impossible to climb, but the boat's skipper seemed to know where to take them. They circled around the island and put ashore near the base of the wall. Mateos led them along a barely visible trail that reached a section of the island that could not be accessed by boat. There, they found a small compound of stone structures that looked like ancient ruins. In one small round building—little more than a hut—they met a group of wizened monks who smelled of roasted meat and incense. The monks regarded Carter with undisguised disdain—Mateos had explained that women were not permitted to enter the monastery—but they said nothing, deferring to the senior clergyman, who explained their purpose. The exchange happened so quickly, Lazarus did not even have time to contact Dourado and have her activate the babelfish system.

It occurred to him then that they had not checked in with Cerberus HQ since the previous afternoon, shortly after arriving in Axum. Dourado had not called, which probably meant that Pierce wasn't having any better luck than they were.

One of the monks led them up a steep trail that rose to the top of the fortress-like rock, overgrown with scrubby brush and cactuses. The surface of the lake was more than a mile above sea level, but the two Ethiopians, despite their advanced age, moved up the path like a pair of mountain goats. Once atop the rock formation, the trail brought them to another structure, more modern than the monastery, but just as run down. The structure covered a natural rock formation, carved into an altar that looked like a tower of stone cubes.

Their guide muttered something in his native language, which Mateos translated. "This is the altar where sacrifices were made when the Ark was kept here many thousands of years ago."

The monk stared at Lazarus for a moment and then beckoned him forward. Using gestures and pantomime, the monk explained that they needed to move the altar out of the way. Lazarus was a bit surprised at the request, since it appeared to be a solid mass, connected to the underlying rock, but as he braced his shoulder against it and started pushing, he saw a well-concealed seam.

The stone was heavy but not impossibly so, and after a couple of minutes of rocking and shoving, a small square opening was revealed. The monk pointed to the hole and said something that needed no translation.

In there.

Lazarus glanced at Carter, reading the doubt in her expression. Mateos must have sensed their shared skepticism. "The Ark was brought into this crypt through another entrance, which has been sealed to prevent it from being stolen."

The explanation was plausible enough, but then so were all the other excuses Mateos and his Church had employed over the years to prevent anyone from verifying their claims about the Ark. Mateos seemed sincere enough, but if he intended treachery, there was no better place to disappear them than a hidden crypt on a remote island that no one even knew they were visiting.

Lazarus stuck his head through the opening and surveyed it in the beam of his flashlight. The floor was about five feet down and sloped away to form a descending passage that led away into the darkness. Satisfied that it was at least passable, he reversed position and lowered himself feet first into the passage. It was a tight fit, and his shoulders scraped against the stone walls as he pushed deeper into the hewn-out shaft. Carter came next, slipping through with considerably more ease.

The passage sloped, and after about thirty feet, it opened into a larger chamber. Before he reached it, Lazarus sensed a change in the air. Fingers of static electricity brushed his skin like the touch of butterfly wings. A whiff of ozone stung his nostrils, and the air hummed with a sound like an electrical transformer. As he emerged from the passage, his light fell upon on an object shrouded in heavy blankets, with long poles protruding out from beneath the coverings. It was bigger than he expected. The shape under the blankets was longer and taller than the replica he had seen in the Chapel of the Tablets in Axum, almost six feet long, and more than four feet high. Although the relic itself was not visible, the poles returned a metallic reflection—hammered gold.

The hum grew louder as he approached the shrouded object. It was the source of the disturbance.

The old monk's voice rang out in the chamber, and Mateos translated. "Go no closer."

Lazarus looked back and saw the others—Carter, the bishop, and the monk—standing by the wall near the mouth of the passage. Carter's eyes were wide with disbelief.

"It must remain covered," Mateos continued. "Except in the presence of the ordained High Priest, wearing the Crown of God and carrying the Urim and the Thummim in the Breastpiece of Judgement. No one else may see it, lest the glory of God consume them."

"Glory of God," Carter echoed. "Pierce called it shekinah."

"Yes. When it is uncovered, the Ark creates shekinah. Only the High Priest can command it."

It could have been another convenient excuse, another part of the endless shell game designed to con believers into taking it on faith.

It could have been.

But it wasn't.

Lazarus didn't need to see it to know that they had found the true Ark of the Covenant.

FIFTY-TWO

Gakona, Alaska

The Jeep slowed to a complete stop in the southwest-bound lane. There was little danger of a collision with another vehicle. There were no other cars on the highway. Technically, there wasn't even a highway anymore. The earthquake had obliterated several stretches of the remote Tok Cut-off section of the Glenn Highway, leaving it impassable to anything not built for off-road travel. Fortunately, there were plenty of vehicles like that in the 49th State, and more than a few intrepid and opportunistic souls willing to embrace the challenge for the right price.

Ishiro Tanaka handed over a roll of bills, the balance of the amount he and the Jeep's owner had agreed upon before leaving Fairbanks almost six hours earlier, and climbed out. Anchorage would have been closer, but at last report, there wasn't much left of Alaska's largest city.

"You sure about this, buddy?" the driver asked. "It's going to be a while before anyone else comes out this way. You'll be on your own."

"I'm sure," Tanaka said. "I used to work here. I know what to expect."

The driver shrugged. "It's your funeral."

The thought brought a smile to Tanaka's lips.

The Jeep pulled away and executed a tight 180-degree turn, lining up to head back the way they'd come, but before departing, the driver stopped again. "Hey, buddy! Here."

He pitched something in Tanaka's direction, a tall cylinder that looked a little like a small, home-sized fire extinguisher. "For what you paid me, it's the least I can do."

Tanaka recognized what it was even before he caught it out of the air. A canister of Counter Assault bear repellent spray, similar to self-defense pepper spray, but designed for driving off grizzly bears and other deadly wild animals—a must-have when venturing into the Alaskan wilderness. Tanaka wasn't planning to do any cross-country hiking, but he touched the top of the can to his forehead in a friendly salute. "Thanks."

"You watch yourself out here," the man added, and then drove off.

Tanaka stuffed the canister into the pocket of his coat but waited until the Jeep rounded a corner before starting up the adjacent road. A large blue sign with white block letters was mounted on posts at the roadside.

. IONOSPHERIC RESEARCH OBSERVATORY

At the top of the sign, in smaller letters, was the name that formed the acronym most commonly associated with the facility.

HIGH FREQUENCY ACTIVE AURORAL RESEARCH PROGRAM

Directly ahead at the top of a low rise, about two hundred yards from the highway, was an enormous, windowless white building. Between him and it was an eight-foot high chain link fence, tipped with another foot of barbed wire.

One last obstacle to overcome, he thought.

He approached the gate—locked, as expected—and gripped the links. He had never been much of an athlete, never had reason to even attempt climbing a fence, but how hard could it be?

His toes refused to find purchase in the tight diamond-shaped holes between the links, and his arms were too weak to lift his body without help. He tried again, to no better effect, and then hammered his fists against the gate in impotent rage.

For want of a nail, the kingdom was lost, he thought. *I should have brought bolt cutters.*

He gripped the links again, but looked away, toward the trees that surrounded the fenced property. Failure was not an option. He had to get inside.

"Help you with something?"

The disembodied male voice startled Tanaka. He took a deep breath to compose himself, then located the speaker box mounted to the side of the gate.

That's new, Tanaka thought, but then he recalled that the last time he had been here, the gate had been manned by soldiers armed with M16 rifles.

"Sorry," he said. "I thought everyone was gone."

"Well, you thought wrong. This is a restricted facility. I'm afraid I can't let you in."

Tanaka had assumed that the University would evacuate their personnel from the site, but someone had stayed behind as a caretaker. He took another calming breath, then continued in his best professional manner. "I'm afraid we've gotten off on the wrong foot here. My name is Dr. Ishiro Tanaka. I worked here a few years ago. I've been contracted by the government to assess the extent of the damage."

"The University owns the facility now." The man said it like a challenge.

"I'm aware of that, but I'm sure you're aware of the government's ongoing stake in this operation." He paused a beat. "Listen, why don't you give the head office in Fairbanks a call. They'll verify everything."

Phone lines and high-speed networks were down statewide, and satellite phones were unreliable so close to the Arctic circle. Even if the man managed to get through to somebody in authority, there would be no way to confirm or refute Tanaka's claim. He doubted the man would even make the attempt.

There was silence for several seconds, then the voice spoke again. "I'll be down in a second."

Tanaka allowed himself a relieved sigh, as he leaned back against a fence post. A few minutes later, the crunch of tires on pavement and the faint whine of an electric motor heralded the approach of a golf-cart, similar to the robot shuttles Marcus Fallon had used at Tomorrowland, except this one was not autonomous.

A twenty-something man with long hair, wearing blue jeans and a flannel shirt sat behind the steering wheel. He drove the cart down the hill and stopped just a few steps from the gate.

The man regarded him warily for a moment but then dismounted and approached the gate, key ring in hand. "Sorry to keep you waiting, Dr. Tanaka. If I had known you were coming..."

Tanaka waved off the apology. "If it's all the same, I'd like to get started right away. Was there much damage here?"

"A few broken dishes in the cupboards, but nothing serious." The man unlocked the gate and swung it open to admit him. "With the generators, we probably could have stayed online, but the project manager made the call to get everyone back to civilization."

Tanaka stepped through. "Everyone but you, I take it?"

"That's right."

"Good," Tanaka said, and then added. "I'm sorry."

The confused look on the man's face disappeared as Tanaka brought the canister of bear spray up and squeezed the handle.

Contrary to popular belief, bear spray was not more potent than similar products designed for self-defense against human attackers. In fact, the concentration of capsicum—the hot pepper oil used as a blistering agent—in pepper spray could be as high as 30%. By contrast, government regulations required bear spray to contain no more than 2%. The purpose of bear spray was not to harm a bear or other animal, but to discourage it from a distance, which it did with a greater volume of spray under higher pressure, more than doubling the effective range.

At point-blank range, though, a blast of bear spray in the face guaranteed that a generous amount of the mild acid went into the victim's eyes.

The man jerked away, hunching over, covering his face and swearing. A moment later, the curses became a shriek of pain as the capsicum began reacting with his mucous membranes. But those were silenced when Tanaka brought the mostly full canister down on the back of the man's head. The blow dropped the man to his knees, dazing him.

As blunt weapons went, the bear spray canister was a poor choice, but as with its contents, any deficiency in potency could be offset with volume.

Tanaka brought the metal container down again. The stunned caretaker threw up a hand, blindly trying to deflect the assault, but another blow flattened him. Tanaka did not relent however. He dropped to his knees and hit the man again.

And again.

And again.

The canister had become slick with gore and threatened to twist out of his grip every time he slammed it down. He squeezed it so tightly that the pressurized container dimpled under his fingertips, but he kept slamming it down, until the man's head was an unrecognizable mass of ravaged tissue and bone. Then, he fell back on his haunches, turned his head, and vomited.

He had just killed a man.

He knew, on an intuitive level, how absurd it was to feel remorse over a single death. His actions in Geneva had killed thousands... hundreds of thousands...perhaps even millions. And soon, he would bring about the death of every living thing on Earth. Bludgeoning the caretaker had been different only in that it was more immediate.

More...visceral.

But the end result was the same. A few moments of pain, and then an end to suffering forever.

He checked his watch and was surprised to see that it was almost nine p.m. At this latitude, and so near the summer solstice, the nights were short and started very late. That had been one of the hardest things for him to adjust to during the eighteen months he had spent here, back in the early days of the project. The cold and the long nights of winter hadn't bothered him much at all, but eighteen-plus hours of daylight was enough to drive the soberest soul crazy.

That thought brought another smile. In a few hours, the length of time it would take him to retrofit the Ionic Research Instrument—the IRI—to accommodate the Roswell fragment, the distinction between night and day would become meaningless.

He would divert all the sun's light away from the Earth. There would be only night, and in a matter of weeks, a frozen wasteland with no one left to care.

There would be suffering, yes, but in the grand scheme of the cosmos, it would be brief.

He coughed, spat to clear the taste of bile from his mouth, got to his feet, and dragged the corpse off the road and into the trees, where it would not be seen in the unlikely event that someone happened by. Then, he got in the cart and started up the hill.

No more obstacles.

No distance left to travel.

It would all be over soon.

REVELATION

FIFTY-THREE

London, England

As relieved as he was to know that the Ark was within reach, Pierce couldn't help feeling a little disappointed. The Ark had been found, but not by him.

After the somewhat disappointing discovery in the secret Masonic hall under Temple Church, he and the others had retired to a hotel room. Showers and soft beds provided some much-needed physical refreshment, but the mystery of what had become of the Ark weighed on Pierce's mind, keeping him awake well into the wee hours of the morning. He had barely drifted off to sleep when Dourado had called to deliver the news.

"They found it! Dr. Carter and Mr. Lazarus found the Ark in Ethiopia!"

His first impulse had been to question the bold claim. How did they know it wasn't a replica? But during the subsequent conference call, Carter answered all questions and removed all doubts.

Ethiopia.

Pierce shook his head. He had been right to question the story recorded in the Ethiopian *Kebra Nagast,* but wrong to dismiss the many centuries worth of tradition that supported the broader claim that the Ark was there.

Nothing to do about it now. The ship had sailed. The Ark had been found, and his chance to be Indiana Jones had slipped through his fingers. Now it was time to get down to the business of saving the world.

After a quick breakfast, they met with Clive Chillingsworth at the London Masonic Hall, this time entering by the front door in Great Queen Street, just half a mile from Temple Church. The original plan had been to scour the secret archives relating to the Templars' discovery of the Tabernacle and root out a clue that would reveal the Ark's true location. With that matter resolved, he turned his attention to the subject of how best to use the Ark to shut down the Black Knight.

"Sir Isaac foresaw this," Chillingsworth said, after overcoming his initial shock at the revelation of the Ark's discovery. "Or perhaps it would be more accurate to say that he recognized the truth that others foresaw many centuries before."

"You think this is the End of Days foretold in the Bible?" Gallo asked, without a hint of irony.

"It would be irresponsible to ignore the many parallels," Chillingsworth said. "Earthquakes. Signs in the heavens. And the Ark...we mustn't forget that. The prophecies indicate the Ark will be found and returned to Jerusalem just before the End of Days. Sir Isaac believed that as well."

"You also said he predicted the End no sooner than 2060," Pierce countered.

"Maybe what he meant to say is that we can buy ourselves another forty years if we get this right," Fiona suggested.

Chillingsworth nodded. "It may be that the prophecies were not pronouncements of doom, but instructions about how to avert this catastrophe."

"Instructions," Pierce murmured. "Hidden in ancient prophecies."

He glanced over at Fiona, recalling her vision of Raven stealing the sun and moon. He didn't believe in prophecies. Maybe the Originators were time travelers, or existed outside of the limitations of space-time...which he had to admit, smacked of the supernatural.

"So it's not enough to have the Ark?" Fiona went on. "Now we have to get it to Jerusalem?"

"Specifically, the Temple Mount. Based on Sir Isaac's calculations, that is where it should reach peak efficiency. And I'm afraid the Ark alone isn't enough. It must be contained within a structure designed to amplify...or perhaps contain its power."

"The Tabernacle," Pierce said.

Chillingsworth inclined his head in a nod.

Pierce let out a sigh. "So all we have to do is get the Ark and the Tabernacle into Jerusalem under the noses of the Israelis, and then set them up on the doorstep of the Dome of the Rock. Easy."

He did not need to explain the reason for his frustration.

The Temple Mount was sacred to all three great monotheistic religions. In addition to being the location of Solomon's Temple, it was also believed to be the site where Abraham went to offer up his son Isaac as a sacrifice, an act that God prevented. But the incident nonetheless sealed a divine covenant with the descendants of Abraham—Jews and Arabs alike. It was also believed to be the place where Muhammad ascended into heaven, an event that was commemorated with the construction of the Dome of the Rock and the Al-Aqsa mosque. After the Kabbah in Mecca, they were the oldest and most revered Islamic structures in existence. Although the site was under their authority, the Israeli government had honored the long-standing Muslim presence, but many in all three faiths believed that one day, a new Jewish Temple would be built on the spot, an action that would serve as the catalyst for the final great battle.

Some people were actually looking forward to it.

Erecting the Tabernacle on the Temple Mount and placing the Ark of the Covenant inside would, if it became public knowledge, ignite the thousand-year-old powder keg of religious animosity in the Holy Land. Merely the rumor that the true Ark had been found might be enough of a spark to light that fuse.

Saving the world from the Black Knight might very well plunge it into a different kind of darkness.

Maybe Chillingsworth is wrong, Pierce thought. *Maybe those prophecies are a warning. Maybe taking the Ark to Jerusalem is what causes the destruction we're trying to prevent.*

Yet, if they didn't act, Tanaka would figure out a way to use the Black Knight to destroy the planet.

"We have to find a way to do this without anyone knowing," Pierce said. "Absolute secrecy."

Chillingsworth offered a cryptic smile. "I told you last night, all our resources are at your disposal."

"You've got a way to get the Tabernacle into Jerusalem without attracting attention?"

"I can do better than that. If you can get the Ark from Ethiopia to Israel, we'll take care of the rest." He smiled. "Remember, we've been preparing for this for three centuries."

FIFTY-FOUR

Tel Aviv, Israel

The customs official stopped his cart in front of the open loading door, dismounted, and made his way up the ramp into the belly of the cargo plane, clipboard in hand. The plane, its passengers, and its cargo had been accorded special cultural travel privileges, under the auspices of the World Heritage Commission. They were protected by international law. The official was acting outside his jurisdiction.

Lazarus knew all too well that petty bureaucrats and over-zealous law enforcement agents could throw up any number of roadblocks if they felt they were being marginalized, no matter the actual legal status. And

since their actual legal status was a house of cards built on a foundation of half-truths and forged documents, it was best not to antagonize the man.

He stepped forward to welcome him aboard.

The inspector cast a judgmental eye at Lazarus, looked past him to Carter, who still wore her *netela* scarf, and then scrutinized Abuna Mateos and Abba Tesfa Mariam. He glanced down at his clipboard. "I see that you are transporting a religious relic of some kind," he said in English.

Lazarus nodded and gestured to a large parcel behind him. It was bigger than a restaurant-sized refrigerator, resting on a pallet, secured to the deck with heavy-duty, nylon cargo netting.

"What is it?" the man asked, with a hint of suspicion.

"A replica of the Ark of the Covenant. For the Orthodox Church in Jerusalem."

The man raised an eyebrow. "Really? The Ark? It's a lot bigger than I would have expected."

Lazarus returned a helpless shrug.

The inspector moved closer, peering through the gaps in the webbing. As he poked a probing finger through, Lazarus held his breath, dreading the moment when a jolt of electricity would strike the man dead.

"What is that? Straw?"

"Papyrus reeds," Carter said, speaking for the first time. "Cheapest packing material available."

That was partially true. There was no shortage of papyrus on Tana Qirqos. The reeds were so ubiquitous that the locals bundled them together into small boats and cruised around Lake Tana, like stand-up paddle boarders from another century. But the woven reeds on the cargo served another very important purpose.

Protection.

Not for the Ark, but from it.

While Lazarus and Carter had been busy working out travel arrangements with Pierce, Abba Tesfa had returned to the secret crypt, donned the protective priestly vestments, offered incense, and prayed. Then they packed the Ark with several layers of heavy wool blankets and a shroud of woven papyrus reeds.

Once Abuna Mateos explained the situation to them, the monks of Mitsele Fasiladas monastery were eager to help with the Ark's removal and transport.

"They understand what is happening," the bishop had told Lazarus and Carter. "They know that you intend to return the Ark to Jerusalem, just as the Bible foretold."

"Thank God for prophecies," Carter muttered.

Mateos just smiled.

Once the Ark was packed, the monks opened the alternate entrance to the hidden chamber, sealed behind a wall in the monastery complex, and brought the Ark out. They had carried the wrapped bundle with the same gold-layered poles that the Levite priests had once used during the time of Moses.

"Are blankets and straw going to be enough to keep us safe from that thing?" Lazarus had asked.

Carter had answered first. "Wool is an excellent insulator. It should be enough to shield us from any electromagnetic radiation."

"We have done this before," Mateo had assured them.

Getting out of Ethiopia with the Ark posed no great hardship. Security was lax, and the bishop's reputation carried a lot of weight. The cover story—that the Ark was just a sacred replica—was more than plausible enough to get them on the plane.

The real challenge was logistical. It had taken two hours to procure a boat large enough to transport the wrapped Ark to shore, two more to get it to the nearest airport large enough to accommodate the cargo plane Dourado had chartered and sent to meet them, followed by a four-hour flight to Ben Gurion Airport in Tel Aviv.

Now, the customs inspector turned away, satisfied with his unauthorized inspection. "Welcome to Israel. Enjoy your stay."

As he drove off, a white moving truck pulled forward onto the tarmac, backing up so the rear loading door was facing the cargo ramp.

A few moments later, a grinning George Pierce stepped onto the ramp. "I have to say, I'm jealous as hell."

"I have to say, it was amazing. I had a fedora and a whip, and—" Lazarus began.

"Is that a joke?" Peirce said with a chuckle. "You joke now? Maybe the Ark really does have supernatural powers."

"If it makes you feel any better," Carter said, coming down the ramp to join them, "it wasn't where we thought it was going to be either."

"The important thing is that we've got it," Pierce said.

While Carter introduced Pierce to Mateos and the monk, Lazarus opened the truck, which was equipped with a hydraulic lift gate. He used a pallet jack to transfer the Ark off the plane. Once the truck was loaded, Mateos and Tesfa climbed in the back with the precious cargo, while Carter and Lazarus squeezed into the cab with Pierce. A few turns took them away from the airport and onto Highway 1, the main route connecting Tel Aviv to Jerusalem. It was late afternoon, and traffic was heavy but moving.

"Augustina and Fi are on site," Pierce said, as they settled in for the drive. "The Tabernacle is already set up."

"That was quick," Lazarus remarked.

"Chillingsworth contacted a bunch of guys from the local Masonic lodge. They were eager to help. It took us three hours to take the thing down and load the truck in London. They got it back up in half an hour."

"Do they know the whole story?" Carter asked.

Pierce shook his head. "As far as they know, it's an elaborate repro-duction that will be part of their annual consecration ceremony."

Lazarus smiled to himself. They had used a similar deception, which like any good lie, was so much easier to swallow than the truth. If they had told the customs inspector that they were carrying the real Ark of the Covenant, the man would probably have flagged them as religious kooks.

As they continued along, Pierce peppered them with questions about their discovery on Tana Qirqos, dissecting at length the story Mateos had told them to explain how the Ark came to be in Ethiopia, and offering alternatives.

"There's another theory that the Templars might have sent the Ark to Ethiopia for safe-keeping," he told them. "Which, knowing what we now do, makes a lot of sense. They might have found the Ark under Mount Nebo, along with the Tabernacle, and then decided to split them up to prevent anyone from prematurely trying to fulfill the prophecy."

Lazarus shrugged. "You should talk to Mateos."

Pierce chuckled. "I'll do that. I'm looking forward to it, actually."

"You do realize we're going to have to give it back?" Carter said.

Pierce's smile went flat. "That's something else we'll have to talk about."

"George, there's nothing to talk about. This isn't some forgotten relic that we discovered in a lost city. It's theirs, and it has been for a long time. They chose to share this with us. The least we can do is respect their claim to it."

"Like I said, we'll have to..." Pierce's voice trailed off as the sky went dark.

The change was so abrupt that brake lights began flashing on as other drivers reacted to something they had never before experienced.

Lazarus knew how quickly storm clouds could darken the sky, and it was nearly sundown...but this was something different. The sun had not slipped below the horizon, nor was there a cloud in the sky. He looked over at Pierce, whose grim expression confirmed what he knew.

"It's happening."

FIFTY-FIVE

Jerusalem, Israel

Abdul-Ahad felt blessed. Despite his failure on Mount Sinai, Israfil had given him a second chance, entrusting him with a new, and even more important mission.

It almost made the pain bearable.

His eyes felt like they were full of sand, and nothing he could do would alleviate the sensation. At least he could still see.

It had taken him a long time to crawl down off the slopes of Mount Sinai, and despite his best efforts, he had been discovered. Fortunately, the emergency responders had mistaken him for one of the many victims of the attack. Instead of being arrested, he had been treated for his injuries. His eyesight had returned after an hour. He then slipped away into the nearby tourist village where he sent a text message to Israfil, reporting his failure. His unseen guide had praised his devotion and promised that his sacrifice would be remembered by God.

That had seemed like the end of it. He had made the decision to lie low, waiting for a chance to slip away from the active terrorism investigation. After a few hours, pain had blossomed in his eyes, as his inflamed corneas began exerting pressure against the surrounding nerves. The mere idea of trying to catch a ride back to Suez or returning to his home in Saudi Arabia, was too onerous to contemplate.

But then Israfil had sent another message, offering him a chance for redemption.

Pierce, the agent of the anti-messiah, was on his way to defile the holy city, Jerusalem. He could not be allowed to carry out his mission.

Israfil had recruited more fighters, sending some to retrieve Abdul-Ahad from Sinai, and others to keep an eye on Pierce. After hours of wallowing in despair, Abdul-Ahad was grateful to be given the chance to serve again.

Even with expertly forged travel papers supplied by Israfil, traveling in Israel was risky. But as they arrived in Jerusalem, they learned that Pierce had come to them. He was at the edge of the Old City's Muslim Quarter, in the multi-tiered park-like environs of the Damascus Gate. The name of the district reflected a historic tradition rather than an actual cultural division, but the area surrounding Haram esh-Sharif—the Noble Sanctuary, or as the Jews and the Christians termed it, the Temple Mount—was occupied predominately by Muslims. The young Arabs and Palestinians working with Abdul-Ahad, guided by the faceless Israfil, could effortlessly blend in, disappearing among their fellow believers.

It was Pierce and his group who stuck out.

Pierce had arrived earlier, along with the two women and dozens of workmen, all of whom had descended the steps to a cave entrance in the Old Wall. They had transferred crate after crate of cargo from a moving truck. Israfil had advised them to keep watch from their post on a nearby rooftop and wait for a sign. After a couple of hours, most of the workmen departed. Pierce left in the truck, traveling alone. It was frustrating to have the target so close, literally within sight, but as always, Israfil's wisdom was beyond question.

The sign had come, and what a sign it was.

It had come just before sunset. The man assigned to shadow Pierce had just reported that the subject of his surveillance had made a pickup at the airport and was on his way back. Abdul-Ahad had wondered if this was the reason Israfil had cautioned them to wait.

That was when the sky had gone dark with the abruptness of a sandstorm blotting out the sun. Only there was no storm. No weather at all. The sun simply disappeared from the sky, plunging the world into night.

A few seconds later, Israfil sent another message.

>*Eliminate the agents of Masih ad-Dajjal. This is my final message.*
You will not hear from me again. Yawm al-Qiyāmah begins.

Abdul-Ahad's heart soared. He passed the message along to the others and readied his weapon. "When Pierce gets here," he told the others, "we'll follow him into the cave and kill them all."

They had no guns. Only Jews were permitted to buy and possess firearms in Israel, and acquiring them on the black market would have taken more time than they had. But swords and knives were easier to come by and were just as deadly. Pierce and his people did not appear to be armed.

Around them, the world was falling into madness. The air was filled with the noise of sirens and alarms, and occasional gunfire. Israfil had not been wrong. *Yawm ad-Din*, the Day of Judgment, preceding *Yawm al-Qiyāmah*, the Day of Resurrection, had arrived. In his mind's eye, he could see the fighting all across the city—maybe all over the world—as the faithful took up arms to battle the armies of the anti-messiah.

The long promised battle for Jerusalem was beginning.

From the midst of the tumult, the moving truck arrived, its tires shrieking on the pavement, as it skidded to a stop in front of the cave entrance.

Abdul-Ahad gripped the hilt of his long knife with one hand, and raised the other, cautioning his men to hold off a few moments longer. It would take all of three minutes for them to leave their position, but once Pierce was in that cave, he would be trapped. There were no other exits. They could afford to wait a little longer.

The doors on both sides of the truck opened. Pierce was not alone.

More agents of Masih ad-Dajjal.

Two other people—a large man with dark skin and a black woman—got out of the cab with Pierce. The big man would be trouble, but the others would die quickly. Two more black men—definitely

Africans—wearing the garb of Orthodox or perhaps Coptic Christian priests, got out of the back. Both were old and decrepit and would put up little, if any, fight. Abdul-Ahad had no reservations about killing Christian priests, either.

Pierce and the others unloaded a bulky parcel from the truck. Distributing its weight between them like pallbearers at a funeral, they headed into the cave.

A minute passed, and Abdul-Ahad was just about to give the order to move out when two more vehicles—a sedan and another large moving truck—pulled up in front of the cave entrance.

"Who is this?" Abdul-Ahad whispered, keeping his hand up to forestall the attack. Had Pierce foreseen danger and brought reinforcements?

Men began emerging from the vehicles—Westerners. Probably Americans. Four of them looked like they might be soldiers, and as if to confirm that supposition, they produced Uzi machine-pistols and held them at the ready. It was almost as if they were aware that Abdul-Ahad and his men were preparing to attack. They fanned out, taking up positions around the truck, while the fifth man opened the rear loading door and went inside.

Abdul-Ahad's stinging eyes went wide in astonishment at what he beheld next.

FIFTY-SIX

Despite being the guardian of the Ark, there was no way the aged Abba Tesfa was going to be able to bear one-fourth of the Ark's weight. Abuna Mateos was no spring chicken either, but he was carrying a cloth-wrapped bundle containing the special priestly garments that Tesfa would need to wear to safely unwrap the Ark once it was inside the Tabernacle. That left just three of them to bear the still-wrapped relic on long wooden poles, just as the Levite priests had done in the time of Moses. Pierce took the front left corner, Carter took the right, and Lazarus carried the rest from the back. The two men of God were behind them, though Carter couldn't see anything around the Ark's bulk.

The going was tricky. Even before they reached the cave entrance, they had to descend uneven steps, which was no simple feat given the size of the burden they carried. But the urgency of the situation gave Carter an adrenaline boost.

Somewhere in the world, Ishiro Tanaka had just used the Roswell Fragment to activate the Black Knight satellite, turning the sun's light away from the Earth. He had plunged the whole planet into darkness, and this time there was no one around to pull the plug on it.

No one outside their select group knew what was happening. The scientists being interviewed on radio news channels they had listened to during the drive had no explanation for it. Those who believed in holy writings and divine prophecy, and who were already on edge after the previous incidents, didn't need technical details. As far as they were concerned, the End of Days had arrived.

In the time it had taken them to complete the trip into the Old City, pandemonium had set in. There had not been talk of more earthquakes but there were widespread reports of ethnic and religious violence, vandalism, and looting. Even more disturbing were unconfirmed stories of mass suicide. *If it wasn't already happening,* Carter thought, *the media was doing a great job of planting the idea in the heads of listeners.*

She knew it would take days, perhaps even weeks without the sun for the Earth to become uninhabitable, but every hour—every minute—that passed with the world in the grip of End Times hysteria would do irreversible damage.

As Lazarus got the Ark unloaded, Pierce ran into what looked like a small city park. It was situated beneath the towering limestone foundation of the ancient city walls. He unlocked and removed the green metal gate blocking a cave opening, widening the entrance enough for them to get through with their burden. Once they were inside, he called for another halt, so he could replace the barrier. It was a wise precaution given the growing unrest outside. Then they resumed their descent.

Carter took note of the tri-lingual signs and placards near the entrance: Hebrew, Arabic, and English. They were moving too fast for her to read them, but two phrases stood out: *King Solomon's Quarries*, and *Zedekiah's Cave*.

"I know that name," she said, as they began their descent into the subterranean world. "Zedekiah. He was the king when Jeremiah moved the Ark, wasn't he?"

She wasn't that curious, but talking about something other than their immediate plight helped keep her mind off the enormous burdens—both physical and symbolic—that they now carried.

"That's right," Pierce confirmed. "His rebellion against the Babylonians was what led to the destruction of Jerusalem and the first Temple. According to legend, when he tried to escape the siege, he hid in this cave. The Babylonians found him and executed his sons in front of him, then bored out his eyes, so their deaths were the last things he would ever see."

Carter shuddered. "Why is it always the eyes?"

"At the farthest point in the cave, there's a wall with trickling seepage. They call it 'Zedekiah's Tears.' It's all just folklore though. Most of this cave is man-made, quarried out by Herod the Great to build his Temple in the second century B.C."

"Herod? Not Solomon?"

"There's no archaeological evidence to support the claims that Solomon used stone from here, but don't tell our Masonic friends that. This is one of their most revered sites. According to their tradition, this is where the construction of Solomon's Temple began. They have an annual ceremony here and participate in the upkeep of the site. Which is how we were able to get the place shut down for the day so we could set up.

"Although," he added, "that story about Solomon is probably just a ruse to hide the cave's real purpose."

"Which is?"

"This. What we're doing. The place we're going. Freemason's Hall is less than two hundred yards from the site of the Temple foundation stone. That's within the margin of error for Newton's calculations about where to situate the Tabernacle and the Ark. When Chillingsworth told me they've been preparing for this day for three hundred years, I had no idea just what that entailed."

The interior of the cave was spacious, and the light-colored limestone walls reflected and diffused the artificial lighting, making some parts of the underground quarry seem as bright as day. The irony of that was not lost on Carter.

"Almost there," Pierce said.

Carter was glad to hear it. Her arms were burning from the constant exertion. The deeper they went, the rougher and more cramped the cave seemed, though by comparison to the crypt on Tana Qirqos, even the tightest spots felt as wide open as the Grand Canyon. After about two hundred yards, the slope of the floor diminished until it was almost flat. The cavern opened into a large chamber carved out of the limestone. There were a few arched openings leading even further into the subterranean realm, but Carter knew they wouldn't be going much further. Dominating the hall was an enormous tent-like structure she knew had to be the Tabernacle. Walking toward them, holding what appeared to be a grapefruit-sized ball of metal, was Fiona. Gallo was right behind her.

"I knew you were coming." Fiona held the orb up, as if it explained everything. "I felt it. I could almost *see* it."

"Good." Pierce called for a halt and a set-down. The exertion was getting to him as well. "Tanaka has activated the Black Knight," he continued. "The whole planet has gone dark."

"And people are flipping out," Carter added.

"Can you can shut it off?"

Fiona answered without a trace of hesitation. "Yes."

Mateos and Tesfa began an urgent but brief exchange in Amharic, the latter pointing at Fiona and the sphere in her hands. The bishop turned to Pierce. "Excuse me, but are you saying that this child intends to stand before the Mercy Seat? In the presence of the Almighty?"

Pierce's forehead creased in dismay. "Fiona is a Kohen and a Baal'Shem," he said. "You know those words, right? She shares the same genetic heritage as the Levite priests. And she can speak the language of creation."

"None but the guardian may see the uncovered Ark."

Carter interposed between the increasingly frustrated Pierce and Mateos. "Abuna, you need to trust us. We respect your traditions and understand the risk, but Fiona has extraordinary abilities."

The bishop conveyed the message to the older monk, and they shared another exchange in their common language, but Carter could sense Tesfa's increasing obstinacy.

"We don't have time for this," Pierce growled.

Mateos turned to them again. "When the Ark is placed into the Holy of Holies, Abba Tesfa alone will enter to uncover it. He will make an offering of incense and pray to God to allow this."

"Sounds like a plan," Pierce relented. "But let's get to it. Every minute we waste, the world goes a little crazier."

Lazarus broke his customary silence, not to weigh in on the matter, but to shush them all. It the sudden quiet, Carter had no difficulty making out the source of his concern. A rhythmic crunching noise, like a squad of marching soldiers, issuing from the passage behind them.

Pierce muttered an oath. "Damn it. Someone must have followed us in here."

"A lot of someones," Lazarus said, his tone grim. "You guys take care of things here. I'll deal with them."

Before he could move however, the noise stopped. A few seconds later a lone figure emerged from the passage.

"Fallon," Pierce snarled.

The tech-billionaire paused there. In his right hand, was a semi-automatic pistol, though judging by the way he held it, he wasn't sure why he had it.

"Check you out," Fiona said, her sarcasm almost—but not quite—hiding a quaver of alarm. "Looking all gangsta."

Fallon ignored her, surveying the chamber like a mountaineer gazing down from the summit. "So that's it. The Ark of the Covenant." He shook his head in mock admiration. "Thanks for doing the heavy lifting, Pierce, but I'll take it from here."

"Like hell you will."

Fallon stared back for a moment, then glanced over at Gallo, his face twisting in an unspoken promise of menace. He turned his attention back to Pierce. "The Black Knight is a resource with unimaginable potential. We could harness all the energy of the sun. Think of what that means. Unlimited energy. We could conquer every problem. End hunger and poverty forever. Colonize the solar system. We can't let this opportunity slip away."

"You know what's happening out there," Pierce said. "We have to end this now. Forever."

"I can't let you do that."

"Just try and stop us," Pierce said, nodding to Lazarus who returned the nod and started forward.

Fallon paled and retreated a step, stabbing the gun in Lazarus's direction. His smile returned. "I didn't come alone, you know." He looked over his shoulder. "Little help?"

Four men with military buzz cuts and tan fatigues emerged from the passage. They were also armed, but unlike Fallon, they carried Uzi machine pistols, which they leveled at the advancing Lazarus.

The big man cracked his knuckles and continued forward.

"Erik!" Carter called out. "Don't. There's another way."

She drew in a deep breath and leaned close to Pierce. "He might be invincible, but we aren't. Get the others out of here.

Hide in one of those other tunnels. The fewer people out here, the better."

Pierce opened his mouth to ask the obvious question, but then closed it just as quickly. He knew what she was preparing to do.

She turned away from him and took another deep breath. Her ability—it felt more like a curse—was not some superpower that she could exercise with precision, the way that Fiona manipulated soil and rock with the Mother Tongue. It was more like a feral animal kept locked in a cage only by the power of her will. Mostly, the beast stayed quiet, but in dire circumstances—like having four Uzis pointed her way—it woke up and started shaking the door. Control meant not using it, keeping the cage door shut through an effort of will. Letting go was a lot easier, but it meant surrendering to something unpredictable.

It also meant taking, if not the lives of her enemies, their very souls.

Fallon could not possibly have understood what she was about to do, but he seemed to sense the abrupt power shift in the chamber. His eyes went wide with fear, and he turned back into the passage. "Advance," he shouted. "Secure."

The noise that they had heard earlier sounded again, much louder now, and as the marching figures materialized to either side of Fallon and began streaming down into the large hall, Carter's heart sank. This was a threat against which she was powerless.

Robots.

FIFTY-SEVEN

The four human mercenaries backed up against the wall, making way for the eight humanoid automatons that filed down into the chamber. Each one was large as Lazarus, and from the neck down, they reminded Pierce of the T-800 machines from *The Terminator* movie series. Though, they were stripped of anything remotely Arnie-like, and they sported four articulated arms instead of two. The biggest difference was above the shoulders, where the human-like skull had been replaced by what looked like a gimbal-mounted spherical camera inside a protective cage.

"Like 'em?" Fallon crowed, his earlier arrogance returning with a vengeance. "A little project I've been working on. My own variation on the ATLAS robot developed for DARPA. Improved, of course. They're utility bots, designed for working rescue, not combat. But I'd recommend keeping your distance all the same."

Lazarus seemed to take that as a challenge, and charged the line. Pierce had seen YouTube videos of DARPA robots getting knocked down. He expected to see the humanoid machines scattered like bowling pins on impact, but the outcome was more like something from an NFL scrimmage. As the big man drew close, the robots turned toward him in unison, lowering and repositioning like football linemen preparing for the snap. One of them was staggered back a few steps by the collision, but it stayed on its feet. After a moment, it started pushing back.

Lazarus pivoted, trying to use the machine's weight and momentum against it, but its processors and internal gyroscopes reacted faster than even his battle-hardened reflexes, matching him move for move as the others closed in around him like soldier ants.

He tried to break contact, but the robot's metal fingers, stronger and more unyielding than flesh and bone, had closed on his arms like manacles. Instead of wasting energy in a futile attempt to break free, Lazarus widened his stance and shifted his weight onto one foot, then twisted his body hard, whipping the robot sideways and slamming it into the pair that was closing in from his left.

Once again however, the net result fell well short of a spectacular victory. The heavy self-balancing machines were merely jostled, and after staggering back a few steps, they recovered. While that was happening, the others closed in from all angles. Anchored as he was to the first machine, there was no retreat. Three more robots moved in, and despite his best efforts to kick them away, they managed to grab hold of his legs and yank him off his feet. The others regrouped and began moving toward the Ark.

"George!" Gallo's shout was both a warning and a question: *What should we do?*

Pierce had no answer. They were outnumbered and overmatched. Even one of the automatons would have been a challenge for Lazarus, and Fallon had brought eight, in addition to the hired guns.

It was a fight they couldn't win. Like it or not, Fallon had already checkmated them. The Ark was his.

The realization triggered the unlikeliest of memories, and Pierce turned to the others. "Fall back. Find somewhere to hide. Whatever you do, don't look back."

Gallo stared back. "You're going to do something crazy, aren't you?"

Pierce didn't answer, but turned to the Ark and started tearing away the woven papyrus wrapping as the four robots closed in, multiple arms extended, metal fingers open like claws.

Fifty feet away, Lazarus let out a tortured roar. The robots surrounding him had each seized ahold of one of his extremities, lifting him off the ground, stretching him out between them, as if they intended to pull him apart. Pierce could see the strain on the big man's face as he fought against them. The robots' metal feet scraped across the floor, unable to get enough traction to dismember him, but that wasn't going to stop them from trying. Every inch Lazarus gained, he lost almost as quickly.

With another howl, Lazarus pulled his arms in hard enough to slam two of the robots into each other.

The clang of metal striking metal and the crunch of breaking bones echoed throughout the cavern, but the robots did not let go. Lazarus slumped in their grasp, unmoving, unconscious.

Or worse.

Pierce knew he would never be able to endure the same level of punishment as Lazarus, so as the other robots closed in on him, he wormed his fingers into the papyrus mesh, curling them like hooks, and pulled with all his might.

The woven shroud tore down the middle like a dried corn husk. Pierce back-pedaled, ducking away from the grasping arms, but he did not let go of his double-handful of the reedy material. As he pulled it free, the ragged edges snagged the layered blankets underneath, pulling them loose as well, partially uncovering the golden prize they concealed.

The robots did not pursue him, but instead took up defensive positions at each corner of the relic, their quadruple-arms raised and ready to fend off any attack, defending it just as Fallon had ordered. Pierce however, had no intention of getting closer. For the first time since laying eyes on the still mostly hidden object, he knew with absolute certainty that he was in the presence of the true Ark of the Covenant.

The change was barely perceptible, but it was there. A faint hum, almost too low to be heard. A tingling against his skin like static electricity, growing more intense with each passing second. Pierce had a pretty good idea of what would happen next. He flung the tattered papyrus fragments aside and scrambled after Gallo, who was trying to shepherd the others toward the relative safety of the Tabernacle and shouting for them to look away from the Ark. Fiona and the two priests were on the move, but Carter hesitated, concerned about Lazarus.

"Felice!" Pierce shouted. "Cover your eyes."

Just as he reached her, almost tackling her to the ground, there was a bright flash behind them and a loud, harsh pop. The air filled with the crisp tang of ozone and a fouler, fishy smell of burnt insulation. The tingling sensation had abated with the lightning-like discharge, so despite his own warning to Carter, Pierce risked a backward glance.

The four robots surrounding the Ark lay face down, unmoving under a haze of blue smoke.

For a few seconds though, that appeared to be the limit of the effect. Lazarus was still caught in the grip of the remaining automatons. Fallon and his mercenaries were blinking and rubbing their eyes like they had just looked into a camera flash, but they were not out of the fight.

Then things got really interesting.

Without waiting to explain, Pierce dragged Carter along with him, fast-walking to catch up with the others as the entire cavern began to fill with light. In the time it took them to reach the shelter of the far side of the Tabernacle, the reflection off the limestone walls was so bright that the shadow cast by the great tent was indistinguishable.

Then, just as quickly, the brilliance faded.

Carter tried to pull away, but Pierce held her back. "You don't want to go out there."

"But Erik—"

"He'll be okay. We won't."

"What's happening?"

"It is the Glory of God," Mateos said in a grave voice.

Pierce had figured that out already. "Shekinah."

"You should not have uncovered it."

"Seemed like a good idea at the time," Pierce muttered.

The older monk said something in his native tongue, and the bishop nodded to him. "Abba Tesfa says that the shekinah will create for itself a body from the very dust."

"Just like the holy cows on Mount Sinai," Fiona put in.

"It is very dangerous to approach the shekinah," Mateos continued. "Abba Tesfa can command it to return to the Ark, but to do so, he must be wearing the priestly garments. And the Ark must be covered, or more will be created."

Gallo called out. "It's happening again!"

In the space of just a few seconds, the light level in the cavern increased again, building to a climax and then diminishing, as if a switch had been thrown.

The old monk began speaking again, his tone on the verge of panic.

"It should not be happening so quickly," Mateos translated. "Something is not right."

"It's the Black Knight," Fiona said. "Now that Tanaka turned it on, it's drawing more power."

Pierce heard the certainty in her voice, the same assuredness that had guided them out of Arkaim.

The light cycled again, the whole process taking less than thirty seconds.

"Stay here," he said, as the peak brightness signaled the end, or rather the beginning of the next cycle. He ignored the questions of the others and darted out into the open.

The first thing he saw was Fallon huddled with his men against the wall, shielding their eyes. Then he saw the four robots holding a still unmoving Lazarus. They had gone statue still, as if awaiting new orders.

Then he saw the shekinah creatures.

There were three of them, horse-sized constructs that looked like living boulders with legs and horns. They were similar in some respects to Fiona's golems, but as they moved, meandering in circles around the partially concealed Ark, brilliance shone through miniscule cracks in their solid shells, revealing the living light within.

Fiona's words from Mount Sinai came back to him. *The Originators made them to store the energy they harvested from the sun... Living energy inside a shell made of melted rock.*

Now he understood. The Ark had been built to contain the Originator power collection machine, to which the Black Knight and the pieces of memory metal were all connected. When the Black Knight was dormant, the energy trickled into the Ark, but now the process had been kicked into high gear.

Pierce did a quick calculation. Three cycles so far, each creating a new shekinah creature, all in less than two minutes. In ten minutes, the cavern would be full of the creatures, each one a walking bomb.

The light from the Ark was getting brighter again.

"Fallon!" Pierce shouted. The other man's head came up and turned in his direction. "Get over here. And stay away from those things."

After a moment's hesitation, Fallon rallied his men and began moving along the wall toward Pierce, even as the brilliance spiked toward maximum intensity. Pierce looked away to avoid being blinded. In the instant that he did, he saw tiny charcoal gray particles, like fibers of ash, blowing across the cavern floor. They bonded together in fibrous chains, like dust motes transforming into cobwebs, as they were drawn closer to the Ark.

This was how the shekinahs formed their bodies. Pierce recalled reading about a recently discovered phenomenon known as teslaphoresis, in which a strong electrical field caused carbon nanotubes to assemble into wires and even more complicated structures, like pieces of a jigsaw puzzle coming together on command. The Originators had evidently taken the process a step further, drawing carbon from dust particles on the cavern floor, maybe even pulling them out of the air, atom by atom, to form the shells that contained the living energy of the shekinah.

The light peaked and then subsided, revealing a fourth creature standing before the ark.

He ran out to intercept Fallon and the mercenaries. The latter, taking note of his approach, shifted their guns toward him, but he ignored them, focusing on the billionaire. "Tell your robots to stand down."

Fallon gaped at him for a moment, processing the request, then turned toward the four remaining automatons. He cupped a hand over his mouth and shouted: "Secure and remove!"

In unison, the four robots let go of Lazarus, dropping him in a heap on the cavern floor, and then began moving toward the Ark.

"No," Pierce protested. "Get them away from—"

A bright flash and the harsh pop of an electrical current ionizing the air around the humanoid machines drowned out his warning. Their circuits fried by the discharge, the four robots fell over like broken toy soldiers.

Pierce shook his head in frustration then turned to Fallon again. "Stay the hell away from that thing! You'll get us all killed."

Then, ignoring his own advice, he sprinted across the chamber, maneuvering around one of the slow-moving shekinah creatures, to reach the supine form of Lazarus. The big man's face was twisted into a rictus of pain—not from his injuries but from the expedited healing process. Pierce knew all too well how vulnerable Lazarus was at this instant, not physically but psychologically. Lazarus's mental discipline did not make him immune to the agony that accompanied rapid cellular regeneration. But it enabled him to keep the madness that accompanied it at bay. If that discipline slipped...

A few steps away, the light around the Ark was reaching another peak.

"Erik. We've got to get you out of here. Can you walk?"

Lazarus's eyes flew open and locked onto Pierce. For a fleeting instant, Pierce feared his friend had crossed the threshold. But instead of tearing Pierce's head off, Lazarus sprang to his feet. There was a hint of wildness in his expression as he looked around, taking in his surroundings, catching up. Then he nodded.

Pierce turned and led the way back to the Tabernacle at a run, reaching it just a few seconds after Fallon and his men. The mercenaries were holding their weapons up tentatively, as if uncertain whether they were supposed to be guarding the others. When Carter ran to Lazarus and threw her arms around him, the men bristled, as if she was about to attack them.

"Put those things away," Pierce snapped, directing most of his ire at Fallon. "Tell your goons to stay out of the way, and we just might all walk out of here."

322 ROBINSON and ELLIS

Without waiting for a reply, he moved past to join the others and addressed Mateos. "Tell the Abba to get suited up. We need him to keep the shekinahs from killing us all, long enough to get the Ark into the Most Holy."

Mateos relayed this to Tesfa, who nodded and reached for the bundle containing the ancient priestly garments. Even with an efficiency borne of practice, it took a couple of minutes for Tesfa to get outfitted, during which time the shekinah glory cycled three more times. But despite the urgency of the situation, Pierce marveled as he beheld ancient holy artifacts that only a handful of living people had ever seen.

After the tunic-like *ephod* and the gem-encrusted *hoshen* breast plate were donned, Mateos settled the turban onto the monk's head. Pierce glimpsed the writing on the golden crown but didn't recognize the script—it definitely was not Hebrew.

Fiona recognized it though. "That's the Mother Tongue," she whispered. "I can't tell what it says though."

Despite her unique abilities, Fiona was by no means literate in the forgotten language of God. She had memorized certain phrases, and had used her knowledge of the Siletz tribal language to estimate others, but the script was indecipherable. There were hardly any existing samples of it, which meant that even figuring out its alphabet was a virtual impossibility.

"It's the true name of God," Pierce whispered back.

With the addition of the headgear, Mateos was left holding only a small cloth bag, tied shut with a length of red string. Pierce guessed that it held the two most mysterious artifacts associated with the High Priest of ancient Israel.

"Urim and Thummim," he whispered, and he watched as Mateos opened the pouch and shook the contents into his palm, curious to see what they would really look like.

The first item was a smooth sphere of polished transparent crystal, about two inches in diameter.

Tesfa took it and slipped it behind the priestly breastplate.

Was that the Urim or the Thummin? Pierce wondered. *Revelation or Truth?*

Mateos gave the pouch a shake and something else rolled out, another sphere the same size as the first, but it was not a crystal or a stone. The object nestled in Mateos's cupped palm was an orb of memory metal.

Of course, Pierce thought, resisting the impulse to smack his forehead.

Tesfa placed the second orb under the breastplate and signaled his readiness.

Pierce turned to the others. "Gus, get Fi into the Tabernacle and wait for us. Erik, you and Felice go with her. Fallon..." He fixed his stare on the other man. "If you care about making this right, we could use a hand."

Fallon stared back in surprise, either at Pierce's assertiveness or at the request itself. He narrowed his eyes. "We'll help you get that thing in the tent, but we're going to use it to control the Black Knight, not shut it down." Without waiting for an answer, he turned to the mercenaries. "You heard him. Let's go save the world."

The men looked at each other and then back at Fallon. Even Pierce could see their hesitancy.

"This is why I prefer robots," Fallon growled. "You do realize that if we don't get out of here, you don't get paid?"

"We don't have time for this," Pierce said, and turned back to the Ethiopian clergymen. "We have to do this, now."

Tesfa was already moving, not waiting for a translation. Mateo followed him, and so did Pierce.

Lazarus stepped forward as well. "You need me out there," he said. Pierce nodded.

They encountered a shekinah as soon as they rounded the corner of the Tabernacle. Pierce was about to shout a warning, but Tesfa spoke first, raising his hand and chanting in what Pierce assumed was his native tongue. The words, Pierce knew, probably didn't matter. Only the intention of the speaker, in tandem with the Originator artifacts he carried in his priestly garments.

The shambling thing stopped, turned and began moving away.

Pierce breathed a small sigh of relief, but there were at least a half-dozen more of the creatures on the floor of the auditorium chamber, all gravitating toward the group. And judging by the light level, there was about to be one more.

"Don't look at it," Pierce warned. "Keep your eyes shut!"

He covered his face with his hands, but despite these precautions, he could still see a bright swell of illumination accompanying the creation of yet another shekinah. Tesfa's chant however, was keeping the living-light beasts at bay, parting them like Moses parted the Red Sea, clearing a path to the Ark. He lowered his hand and saw that they were almost there.

"When we get there," he shouted, not looking back, "use the poles. Whatever you do, don't touch the Ark itself."

"Pierce!" Lazarus's shout broke through his tunnel-vision focus on the Ark. The big man was pointing to the mouth of the passage leading back to the surface. "Who the hell are those guys?"

Pierce's vision was so bleached by exposure to the intense light that he could barely make out the human shapes gathered there, but then a collective shout issued from the darkness. Pierce did not speak the language, but it was a phrase he recognized all too well. The battle cry of Islamic armies since the time of the Prophet Muhammed.

"*Allahu akbar!*"

Then, a swarm of dark shapes broke from the shadows and charged into the chamber.

FIFTY-EIGHT

Even before reaching the large hall deep within the cave, Abdul-Ahad knew that Pierce and the other agents of Masih ad-Dajjal were attempting to raise an army of *jinn*, just as they had done on the slopes of Jabal Musa in Egypt. The intense light radiating up from the depths, which triggered sympathetic pains in his still-burning eyes, was unmistakable.

"The *jinn* will be bound in earthen vessels," he told the others as they descended toward the source of that brilliance. "Destroy the vessels, and the *jinn* will be freed to consume the wicked for the glory of God."

"Will we die?" asked one of the young fighters.

Abdul-Ahad was ready with an answer. "We will be taken into the bosom of the Prophet, peace be upon him."

When they reached the large chamber, crouching at the entrance to survey what would be their last battlefield, he saw the *jinn*, just as he knew he would, but he saw something else, too.

"*At-tabut*," he whispered. The Chest of Assurance, which God gave to the Prophet Musa, *peace be upon him.* It was written, in the Holy Quran: 'The Chest will come to you in which is assurance from your Lord. Indeed in that is a sign for you, if you are believers.'

Except the Chest was in the hands of the unbelievers.

He raised his knife high, shouted the traditional war cry and charged.

The men with Uzis reacted fastest. They raised their weapons and started shooting. The ululating of Abdul-Ahad's fellow fighters was drowned out by the harsh report of automatic weapons fire and the screams of the injured, but even that was a glorious sound—more faithful martyrs on their way to Paradise.

Some of the unbelievers scattered. Pierce and the big man covered the old priests with their bodies, hustling them away from the fight, as if they were the focus of the attack.

Let them, Abdul-Ahad thought. *The rocks will not hide them from the glory of God. Taste the punishment of the Blazing—*

Something, like an invisible fist, slammed into his chest, spinning him off his feet. As he crashed onto the stone, he felt a tingling at the point of impact, then heat, then fire.

I've been shot.

The notion unexpectedly terrified him. This was not how it was supposed to be. Where was the ecstasy? The euphoria of martyrdom?

Fool, he thought, gritting his teeth against the pain. *There is no reward for failure.*

He struggled to roll over. Around him, the battle seemed to be growing more feverish, the air filled with shouts and screams. The harsh buzz-saw reports of the Uzis drowned out the screams, and the light, growing brighter and brighter again with the glory of God, filled the space.

The shooting told him that at least some of his men were still alive, still in the fight, but for how much longer?

He got to his hands and knees. His left arm collapsed, the pain bringing tears to his stinging eyes. He planted his right hand flat on the floor of the cave and pulled himself forward, toward the Chest.

The brilliance swelled around him, enfolding him with but a taste of the glory that awaited him in Paradise. He squeezed his eyes shut, unable to endure it, raising his head again only when the vision faded.

A *jinn* stood before the Chest, as if sent to block his way, but Abdul-Ahad knew it was something else. This was the sign, promised by God.

He clawed the stone, pulling himself closer. The creature seemed impossibly far away, but after a moment, it began to move toward him.

Even though the earthen vessel contained its glory, with each step closer, he could feel its power coursing through his body. Another step and it was within his reach, offering itself to him like a sacrifice.

Yes, he thought, raising his blade. *God be praised.*

FIFTY-NINE

The blast tore through the Tabernacle like a hurricane. Fiona had been crouched low behind the golden table, where she had taken shelter with Gallo and Carter when the shooting started. They had no clue what was happening outside, who was shooting at whom, but they knew it couldn't be good. Then, with no warning, she was buried under a heavy, shapeless mass of fabric.

Yet, through the mental haze induced by the concussion, she knew what had happened.

Someone, maybe with a stray bullet, had destroyed one of the shekinah creatures. Light, even the cool light contained in the body of the shekinahs, was composed of high-energy particles, and in the confines of the underground chamber, the sudden release of so much densely packed energy was like a bomb going off...in a room full of bombs.

The weight of the collapsed tent made it almost impossible to breathe, which in turn triggered a panic-fueled feedback loop. Frantic, she tore at the fabric, trying to squirm out from under it, but it was too heavy and she was too disoriented, with no sense of which direction to go. If it had been a landslide or a cave-in, she would have created a golem to dig her out, but...

But what?

If you sing to the river...

She had sung to the river, and to the pool under Arkaim, and it had listened to her. If she had learned anything in the years since being awakened to her ability, it was that intention was just as important—maybe more important—than the actual words.

And then there was the Ark.

The Israelite war-leader Yeshua ben Nun, who by all accounts was neither a priest nor a Baal'Shem, had unleashed the power of the Ark on his enemies, and even activated the Black Knight—something he surely didn't even know about—to make the sun stand still in the sky.

Perfect knowledge of the Mother Tongue didn't matter. All that mattered was focused intention. The mere act of speaking the words was enough to make things happen. The Ark responded to intention like a psychic amplifier.

It was practically within reach. She could feel it, resonating in the memory metal orb she carried in her pocket.

"Evaporate," she whispered.

The heavy fabric of the Tabernacle rose into the air, as light as gossamer, and then broke apart like smoke in a stiff breeze.

Her eyes roved the chamber, surveying the damage, yet she did not merely see.

She *knew*.

She saw Carter and Gallo, who had been trapped under the collapsed Tabernacle with her. They were already stirring. She knew they would be fine. Pierce and Lazarus and the two Ethiopians weren't moving, but she knew they were all still alive. Fallon, too. All were stunned but not injured. They had all sought cover when the shooting began, putting enough distance between themselves and the shekinah creatures to survive the multiple detonations.

She did not see the four mercenaries, and knew they were all gone, vaporized by the flash, along with the unknown attackers.

The shekinahs were gone, too, but that wouldn't last. As long as the Black Knight was active, it would continue collecting energy from the sun, transmitting it to the Ark, to create more and more of the creatures until the cavern filled up with them.

Another blast was inevitable.

The first explosion had nearly brought down the entire cavern. Jagged cracks ran up the walls and crisscrossed the floor. The air was thick with dust, and piles of rubble showed where the ceiling was starting to give way.

The next detonation would entomb them all.

There's not going to be a next one, she thought. *It's time to shut this thing down.*

"Bring back the sun," she said, speaking in a clear voice. "Turn off the Black Knight."

Nothing changed. The light continued to shine, growing brighter and brighter with each passing second, and she knew it had not worked. The Black Knight was still absorbing some of the sun's power, transferring it to the Ark, while diverting the rest of it away into the cold of space.

What did I do wrong?

She tried again, imagining a gigantic mirror, spread out like a planet-sized umbrella above the Earth, and then visualized it disappearing and returning everything to normal, but even as she repeated the command, she knew that this second attempt had also failed.

Maybe I need to get closer. She started toward the Ark.

The coverings were gone, blown away along with everything else, revealing the ancient relic in all its glory. It looked a lot like the various representations she had seen, except for the size—it was much larger than in the movies, because the prop makers hadn't known about the length of the Sacred Cubit. The cherubs on the lid, the Mercy Seat, were different. Multi-winged, multi-headed, and multi-eyed, they were mythological creatures instead of the traditional depiction of men with wings.

It occurred to Fiona that she was one of only a handful of people, living or dead, to have ever seen it.

Even fewer had done what she was about to do now.

Gallo's voice reached out through the gloom from behind her. "Fi, don't touch it."

But she did.

Visions of the past slammed through her. Moses, an ancient warrior king, the cow-batteries, and the true origins of the Black Knight, the Ark, and the orbs, and how they all worked together. Fiona stumbled backward, the memory dump hitting her like a physical blow, but she managed to stay on her feet. "It's real," she whispered to herself.

"Fi!" Gallo cried out again. "Talk to me."

"I'm okay," she said, turning, searching the chamber again.

There you are.

She hurried across the rubble strewn floor to the spot where Pierce and Lazarus lay. The latter was already stirring, shaking off the effects of the shekinah detonation faster than the others. He stared up at her. "Fiona? Are you okay?"

There was no time to explain. She pushed past him and knelt beside the crumped form of the Abba Tesfa. He was unconscious, but what Fiona needed did not require rousing him. She slipped the turban off his head, and then reached under the breastplate, rooting around until she found the two objects concealed beneath.

Urim and Thummin, Pierce had called them. *Revelation and Truth.*

She knew intuitively which was which. The memory metal was Urim—Revelation.

She already had the piece of memory metal from Arkaim though. What she needed was the other one, the clear crystal sphere.

The Thummim.

Truth.

The oracular Eye of the blind seer Tiresias, which the castaway king—remembered in legend as Odysseus—had brought back from the Underworld and given to Moses on the slopes of Mount Sinai. Odysseus had washed up there after his ship was destroyed, not by literal sea monsters named Scylla and Charybdis, but by the tsunami wave generated after the sudden explosive eruption of Thera in the Mediterranean. He had landed on the island of Helios, an occurrence she now understood wasn't simply chance. She would use the Eye now to find the hidden word that would unseal the Ark.

The true name of God.

She held the crystal up to her own eye and looked down at the golden plate affixed to the front of the priestly turban.

The transparent sphere flipped and distorted the image, causing the strange script to wriggle and squirm. She tried to hold the crystal steady but the word kept shifting form, morphing into different words, which despite being written in a forgotten language, she was able to read.

Wilderness...
Mountain...
Lightning...
Destroyer...
Creator...
Womb...
Almighty!

I am *the sun and the moon...the lightning and the river and the wilderness.*

The name was all those things, and many more.

The letters became fixed, a single word written in the Mother Tongue, but nevertheless revealed to her. She turned to the Ark again, formed the image in her mind, and spoke the word.

The energy reverses, flowing back to the damaged collector, which orbits high above the world, and then it seeks out the damaged, malfunctioning fragment.

Six thousand miles away, the Roswell fragment ceases to exist, along with the antenna array, most of the HAARP facility, and a troubled man named Ishiro Tanaka.

And daylight returns to the world.

SIXTY

The explosion had rung Pierce's bell a little, and even though he had looked away and covered his eyes when the shooting started, he now saw everything through a murky green haze. Nevertheless, he could tell that something had changed. The persistent electrical hum... The light, rising and falling... The shekinahs...

Gone.

All of it.

"It's over," he whispered. He blinked in a futile attempt to bring the world into focus, and saw Fiona. "You did it."

He thought he saw a weak smile on her face. "Yeah."

Then he noticed the Ark—or rather, the lack of an Ark.

It was missing.

His eyes widened.

Did we destroy the Ark of the Covenant?

"No!" Fallon scrambled to his feet and rushed toward her.

"Fallon!" Pierce's shout went unheeded.

The billionaire's reaction caught even Lazarus off guard. Fiona retreated a step, but Fallon wasn't interested in her.

He dropped to his knees where the Ark had been.

"No," Fallon repeated, dragging his fingers over the floor, as though trying to find some trace of the artifact's essence. "No. No."

He rounded on Fiona. "What did you do?"

Lazarus sprang to his feet and started toward them, and Pierce wasn't far behind. Fiona, however, stood her ground.

"I hit the self-destruct button. The Black Knight is toast."

"No!" Fallon raged again, and before Lazarus or Pierce could reach them, he drew the unfired pistol from his belt and thrust the muzzle into Fiona's face. "Bring it back."

"It's not coming back," she said, holding up her hands, displaying the memory metal ball from Arkaim and the crystal sphere from Tesfa's breast plate. She squeezed them in her fists, and the relics crumbled like pieces of Styrofoam. "Ever."

"No." Fallon said again, grinding his teeth together. His finger tightened on the trigger.

Fiona's lips moved again, but before she could say anything, a section of the cavern ceiling, loosened by the explosion, broke free and came down right on top of Fallon, squashing him like an open hand slapping a fly on a tabletop.

Pierce skidded to a stop a few steps away and stared across the top of the rubble pile at the girl. Fiona had not moved an inch. The falling rocks had come within a hair's breadth of hitting her, but she had not even flinched.

Lazarus knelt and checked Fallon for a pulse. "Still alive."

It was almost as if she had known what was about to happen, and that she would be safe. And the falling rocks had looked a lot like a giant hand.

She nodded to him. "Now it's over."

DISCOVERY

EPILOGUE

Cerberus Headquarters, Rome, Italy

George Pierce stared at the Ark of the Covenant for a long time. Then, with a wistful sigh, he thumbed the button to put the tablet computer in stand-by mode. The picture, which he had taken on his cell before things went to hell, was all that remained of the Ark.

Gallo patted his arm. "Maybe you'll find it again," she said.

What he had noticed and Fallon had missed before being knocked unconscious, was that the Ark hadn't been destroyed. It had vanished. For all they knew it could be in another dimension, resting in that same spot, or somewhere else on the planet. Fiona had given a brief account of her final vision, that had revealed how to use the Ark. She debunked Pierce's Originators theory. While they had existed, it was still unclear where they had come from. Theories now included an advanced human civilization, like Atlanteans, or even the Nephilim, the race of giants first mentioned in the Bible—a book Piece was no longer so quick to dismiss—and appearing in the myths of most ancient cultures around the world. The only thing he knew for sure was that they would never understand how the Ark worked.

But Pierce felt certain it was out there, waiting to be discovered again. He smiled at the thought. The Ark was one mystery he was glad couldn't be solved. Like Alexander the Great, who wept when he saw that there were no more worlds left to conquer, claiming and understanding the Ark would have dulled the spell history held over him. Though he would have preferred a few more solid answers. Perhaps a vision of his own. He wasn't sure Fiona had seen what she thought she saw, or perhaps she had not fully understood it. The idea of God was somehow still stranger to him than aliens, but most of the team had accepted Fiona's story and the Ark's origin at face value.

His smile widened at the realization that, if true, the vision meant the Cerberus Group had been prophesized about, and perhaps even ordained by a supreme being.

Don't drink the Kool-Aid, he told himself. *Not yet, at least.*

Two days after coming closer to the apocalypse than anyone realized, the world was already moving on. A few—those given to a belief in secret conspiracies—had been quick to point out the coincidence of the timing of the solar event and a mysterious fire that had destroyed the HAARP array in Alaska. But most had been eager to accept the general scientific consensus that the event had been caused by an as-yet-unidentified electromagnetic anomaly. It was an undetected cosmic ray storm or a highly-charged iron dust cloud passing through the solar system, which had eclipsed the sun over Western Europe and the Atlantic ocean. The explanation had the ring of truth, and most people had other, more immediate concerns, like burying the victims and cleaning up the damage from the earthquakes. In a month or two, it would be old news, the fickle public already distracted by some new tragedy or scandal.

A ping from his tablet signaled the arrival of another text message. "Cintia's found something."

Gallo walked with him, hand-in-hand, to Dourado's office. Fiona was already there, standing behind the computer expert. She looked up as they entered. "Cintia found him."

"Found who?"

Fiona stepped aside, revealing a photo that required no further explanation.

With a shaking hand, Pierce dug his phone from his pocket. He scrolled through his contacts, tapped a four-letter name, and held the phone to his ear, biting his lip.

Then he said, "Jack, it's George. We need to meet."

ABOUT THE AUTHORS

Jeremy Robinson is the international bestselling author of sixty novels and novellas, including *Apocalypse Machine*, *Island 731*, and *SecondWorld*, as well as the Jack Sigler thriller series and *Project Nemesis*, the highest selling, original (non-licensed) kaiju novel of all time. He's known for mixing elements of science, history and mythology, which has earned him the #1 spot in Science Fiction and Action-Adventure, and secured him as the top creature feature author.

Many of Jeremy's novels have been adapted into comic books, optioned for film and TV, and translated into thirteen languages. He lives in New Hampshire with his wife and three children. Visit him at www.bewareofmonsters.com.

ABOUT THE AUTHORS

Sean Ellis has authored and co-authored more than two dozen action-adventure novels, including the Nick Kismet adventures, the Jack Sigler/Chess Team series with Jeremy Robinson, and the Jade Ihara adventures with David Wood. He served with the Army National Guard in Afghanistan, and has a Bachelor of Science degree in Natural Resources Policy from Oregon State University. Sean is also a member of the International Thriller Writers organization. He currently resides in Arizona, where he divides his time between writing, adventure sports, and trying to figure out how to save the world.

Visit him on the web at: seanellisauthor.com

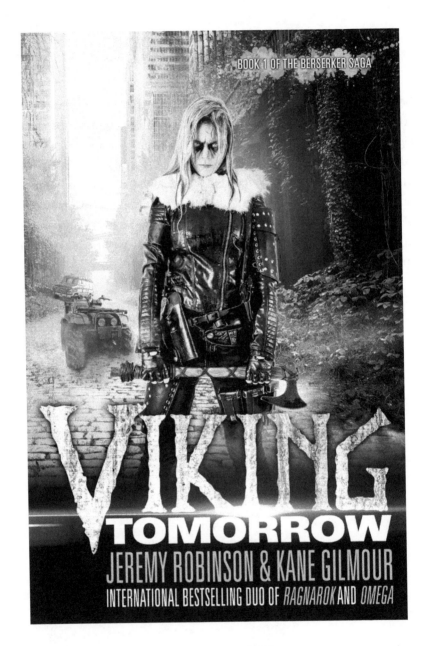

BOOK 1 OF THE BERSERKER SAGA

VIKING
TOMORROW
JEREMY ROBINSON & KANE GILMOUR
INTERNATIONAL BESTSELLING DUO OF *RAGNAROK* AND *OMEGA*

COMING SOON

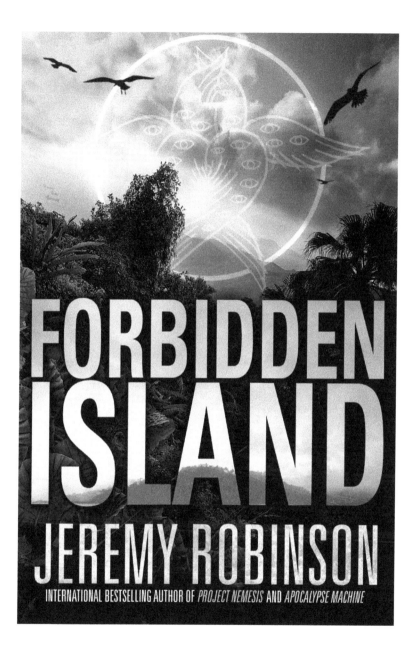

COMING SOON

CPSIA information can be obtained
at www.ICGtesting.com
Printed in the USA
BVHW04s1140130518
516111BV00001B/71/P